Advance praise for *The*

"*The Summer of Keeping Secrets* is a _____
moving forward—and what it really r_____ ___or
and heart, Jill Lynn explores the powe_____ ___e of
love, and the price we pay for things left unsaid. An unforgettable read from
a standout voice in romance."

—Kristy Woodson Harvey, *New York Times* bestselling author
of *The Summer of Songbirds*

"Jill Lynn is a masterful storyteller, taking us on a journey to the past while
keeping us firmly rooted in the present. [She] puts her foot on the gas and
doesn't let go until all of the secrets come tumbling out of the closet. Haunting
and heartwarming, this novel is a page-turner."

—Belle Calhoune, *Publishers Weekly* bestselling author

"*The Summer of Keeping Secrets* will both tug at your heart and make it beat
faster. The story is rich with emotion and poignant moments, but the twists and
turns and unexpected surprises along the way made it impossible to put down.
Highly recommended!"

—Kathryn Springer, *USA TODAY* bestselling author of *The Gathering Table*

"Jill Lynn does an exceptional job of weaving together mystery and romance
with bits of humor and the complicated dynamics of family. I couldn't turn the
pages fast enough!" —Linda Goodnight, *New York Times* bestselling author

"Compelling and relatable, this multigenerational family drama is rife with
complexity, tension, and age-old secrets that refuse to remain hidden. Lynn's
layered characterization and gorgeous prose make *The Summer of Keeping
Secrets* an unforgettable read."

—Nicole Deese, Christy Award–winning author

"In *The Summer of Keeping Secrets*, Jill Lynn writes poignantly of the messiness
of brokenness, which every family faces and has to choose how to navigate.
We each must decide what to remember versus what to forget—all the while
learning to forgive. Lynn's skillful pacing and flair with dialogue also kept me
engaged with this powerful story."

—Beth K. Vogt, Christy Award–winning author

"In *The Summer of Keeping Secrets*...Lynn highlights the challenges that
face adult children who must learn that parents they've idealized aren't perfect,
and mothers who have to figure out how to love hard while also letting go.
I didn't want this book to end!"

—Lee Tobin McClain, *New York Times* bestselling author

Also by Jill Lynn

Love Inspired

Colorado Grooms

For additional books by Jill Lynn, visit her website, www.jill-lynn.com.

The Summer of Keeping Secrets

JILL LYNN

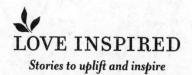

LOVE INSPIRED

Stories to uplift and inspire

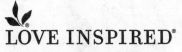

LOVE INSPIRED®

Stories to uplift and inspire

Recycling programs for this product may not exist in your area.

ISBN-13: 978-1-335-54958-7

The Summer of Keeping Secrets

Copyright © 2024 by Jill Buteyn

Love Inspired
22 Adelaide St. West, 41st Floor
Toronto, Ontario M5H 4E3, Canada
www.LoveInspired.com

Printed in U.S.A.

For Aunt Char—you were the brightest of lights in this world. Miss you still.

And for Grandma Lydia—you embodied joy and humor and sass and yet endured much. Save me a seat in your heaven kitchen with polka music playing, fresh cream puffs and drawers full of Milky Ways. XO

Chapter One

Marin Henderson looked forward to her upcoming extended stay in Dillon, Colorado, as much as she would an IRS audit, her annual pap, or consuming those disgusting chocolate-covered cherries with the sugary, syrupy liquid inside.

Except…that wasn't *completely* true. She was a house—a woman—divided. One portion of her loved this town and the alpine environment that could switch from rain, snow, hail or a strange white substance that resembled Dippin' Dots to periwinkle-blue skies and sparkling, high-altitude sunshine in a nanosecond. She loved the weather in the summer—currently a perfect seventy-one degrees. She loved the views of the Rocky Mountains, which, despite it being the first week in June, still wore leftover layers of snow on their peaks like shimmering crowns. Marin even loved the house itself that she'd grown up in—older, simple, well cared for. The kind of place people concentrated on the inhabitants and not the type of countertop or the age and color of the appliances. So many good memories filled those walls.

What Marin didn't love was that the last season she'd stayed at her parents' house for an extensive amount of time had been one of the worst periods in her life.

And considering that in the last four years she'd lost her mother, then her husband, then her father...that was saying a lot.

Marin had quite unwillingly become a poster child for grief.

Her Bluetooth-connected phone rang obnoxiously loud in her car, and Marin clicked to answer.

"Hey, Etts."

"Home, home on the range, where Marin and Lovetta used to play. Where seldom would roam a stupid cell phone, and they stayed outside all day." Lovetta's soprano boomed into Marin's vehicle at rock concert levels, and she notched the volume down two clicks.

"That was a good one."

"Thank you!" Her younger sister by two years broke into song lyrics—made up or otherwise—whenever possible. The habit had started when she participated in musicals in high school and continued long past. "Are we there yet?"

"Almost." Marin turned onto the inclined road that led to their parents' home and the place they'd lived out an idyllic childhood, until that fateful summer—at least for her—squelched those carefree years into a soupy, tasteless pulp.

Ever since the month-long span she'd spent here in her twenties, Dillon created an uneasiness in Marin that crawled along her spine and wrapped talons around her windpipe.

Those weeks had changed and warped things, and the lid never fit the bowl right again after that. This town wasn't as innocent for her as an adult as it had been as a child.

And this visit made her tense in a way previous ones hadn't, because Marin was once again staying for a substantial length of time.

Over the years when she and Ralph had visited her parents, they'd laid low. Baking with Mom. Fishing the Snake River

Inlet with Dad. And once her parents' health had begun to decline, her trips had become focused on their care and the subsequent logistics.

When Marin was in Dillon she treaded carefully, as if someone she knew—or someone who recognized her—might be
lurking around every corner. She constantly feared that a nosy
pot-stirrer would bring up the past and pummel her with questions she didn't have answers to.

"How was the drive?"

"Uneventful, thankfully."

"I'm glad. You could use some *uneventful* in your life."

"Right?" Her arthritic fingers gripped the wheel with tension that would wreak havoc on her later. The familiar street
stretched before her, curving, etching into the side of the hill
until it brought her to the row of houses perched atop the rocky
ledge that lined the cobalt Snake River Inlet and the indigo
Dillon Reservoir. Though *rock* was too quaint a word to represent the boulders jutting from and forming the land. Most of
the houses on the street were semi-mansions—contemporary
boxes or remodels that gave the illusion of rustic with all the
conveniences of modern.

The home Marin and Lovetta's parents had occupied during
their fifty-eight-year marriage—and that Dad had then lived
in until his passing six months ago—was by far the smallest on
High Meadow Drive.

Three bedrooms. Two bathrooms. One oversize, overflowing, storage-slash-laundry room that the family affectionately
referred to as The Armpit.

For someone else, the value of the home would be based on
the location. For Marin, her sister, Lovetta, and for Marin's
children, the value of the home was in the people who'd occupied it.

Marin and Lovetta had discussed their desire that the future
purchaser of the house improve on the bones and structure

rather than demolishing it to build something newer and supposedly better, but they didn't plan to demand anything of the
sort. They had to find a way to be unemotional about selling
their childhood home, because the modest amount of money left
in their parents' estate had dwindled swiftly over the last year.

Dad's request to live out the end of his life at home after his
stroke had incurred major medical expenses. That, coupled with
the cost of living in Summit County, had quickly drained any
reserves he'd had.

Marin and Lovetta had no regrets over conceding to his
wishes. They'd just wanted their father to be as happy as possible
without their mother, and the house had been family to him.

But the lack of funds created additional stress.

Because of Ralph's life insurance policy, Marin could technically float the carrying costs until the house sold and then
replenish what she'd spent before splitting the profits with
Lovetta. But her sister had been adamant that everything remain even between them—especially since she wasn't able to
be here to assist with the purge. If money was needed, she'd
demanded that they both pool their savings to cover costs.

Marin wasn't sure Lovetta understood how much pressure
that added, because the last thing she planned to do was accept
money from her chronically ill sister.

Which meant they'd just have to clean out and sell the house
quickly.

"I don't want to be melodramatic, but are you going to survive this, Mar? I know there's a slew of memories in Dillon
that you'd prefer to avoid."

A vast understatement.

Marin had turned erasing the events of that summer into an
art form. Like a page torn out of a history book, there was no
point in discussing or rehashing something that didn't exist.

"Of course." Marin was quick to assure her sister. Less quick
to believe herself. "I'll be fine. It's going to go great, especially

with the kids' help. We're just going to put our heads down and focus on the work." Marin was oversimplifying things. In truth, if she and her adult children survived their time together in the home that held some of her best and worst memories, didn't get on each other's nerves *and* managed to ready the place to sell, that would be quite the achievement.

Now look who was being melodramatic.

Marin reached the driveway and detached two-car garage, which was located on the west side of the house. She parked in front of the wooden double door, knowing full well there would be no space for her to park in the garage—not with her dad's things still filling it.

"Just pulled in."

"It hurts that I'm not there to say goodbye."

"I know. I promise I'll send you lots of pictures and save whatever you want to keep." After she was diagnosed with MS ten years ago, Lovetta had switched from traveling with friends to hoarding her paid time off in case of a medical appointment or a flare-up. She worked as a Discharge Planner at Vanderbilt University Medical Center, and she was careful not to do anything to jeopardize her career and the fabulous benefits it provided.

"Keep me updated when you can."

"I will."

Lovetta sniffled. "I'm so sorry I'm not there to—"

"No apologies, remember?"

"Fine!" The snort-laugh Lovetta had always despised but never been able to change filled the car, and she blew her nose. "No one is sorry, then. Even though I am."

Marin's head shook, mouth curving. "Talk soon."

Engine off, Marin exited the vehicle like a person who'd just fallen down a flight of stairs—gingerly, painfully, her RA reacting to the lack of movement in her twelve-hour drive from Scottsdale.

Purse and house key in hand, Marin walked the stone path to the front door. Evergreens grew impossibly out of rocks where no dirt was visible, their refreshing scent reminding her of crisp summer nights.

A lump—or more specifically a body—sprawled along the wooden planks of the small front porch. Panic caused the tendons cradling Marin's throat to constrict and then release as recognition of the unexpected figure registered. It was only Slade, though why her daughter was conked out on Gran and Grandad's porch, Marin couldn't begin to understand. Slade had been planning to arrive around the same time as her brother at the end of the week.

A quiet snore sounded as Marin moved up the steps.

Her daughter's pale, skinny legs poured out of jean shorts and ended in white boots with thick black soles, and her current hair color was a shade of blond that was almost silvery white.

Marin had recently stopped dying her hair chestnut and embraced the gray that had been overtaking her scalp for the last decade. Her daughter, it seemed, was in a hurry to age. Except on Slade, the almost silver-blond color was somehow young and stylish.

Marin bent enough that she could shift Slade's hair from her cheek and yet not so far that her knees would give out or get stuck.

"Hi, Love." Slade was named after Lovetta, but even though she adored her aunt, the summer before sixth grade, she'd announced that she was going to go by her middle name, *Slade*— which also happened to be her favorite grandparents' last name.

Marin agreed that *Slade* fit her better than *Lovetta*. Still, she didn't regret that the two women she loved most in the world shared that connection—even though Slade often considered Marin's love to be overbearing and intrusive.

She was working on it! Marin could admit her faults.

Icy blue eyes, which were somehow jaded and vulnerable all at once, opened. Blinked. "Hi, Mom."

"What are you doing here, Love?" Marin stood. "I thought you weren't arriving until Saturday. Same day as Reed."

Slade scrambled up from the porch floor. They hugged. Marin wouldn't classify it as stilted, more…halfway present. Just like Slade herself. Her daughter was always bouncing from one scenario to the next, never focused, horrendous at keeping a job let alone managing a career.

"My job ended early."

"Ended? I hope you didn't quit for this. I was very clear that no one was to jeopardize their livelihood in order to help with Gran and Grandad's house."

"I didn't jeopardize anything to be here," Slade assured her, her expression the mixture of hurt and defiance that she'd worn for most of her teenage years.

Marin had coached herself on the drive today, regarding the upcoming time with her two children. *I will not say anything to upset anyone. I'll keep my mouth shut when it comes to the lives of my adult children, both of whom insisted on helping me with this massive project like the wonderful children they are.*

And yet Marin had started out, somehow, on the wrong foot. But then, she hadn't expected to find Slade at the house. She'd anticipated having the next four days to get organized, shore up old wounds and fears, tuck them away.

Why are you really here, Love? What's going on?

Marin was confident that voicing the question out loud would be a mistake. Slade would take offense at Marin's concern—which she would consider nosiness. Things would digress. Quickly.

Surprisingly, Slade's cheeks creased with amusement, and she squeezed Marin's arms gently, like a mom admonishing a toddler. "It should be a good thing I'm here early to help, Mom. Roll with it. No need to dissect it."

Right. No dissecting. Reed would never show up without

communicating his arrival, but Marin wasn't sure why she was surprised that Slade had. Reed had taken a week off work and planned to be at the house nine days—leave he'd requested ahead of time. But then, that was Reed. Marin's eldest and only son had always been the exact opposite of his sister. Poised. Planned. Purposeful. Full of career goals. Driven. Strategic. She could go on and on.

"So, what happened with your job?" Despite that this probe was also likely off-limits, Marin couldn't set aside that she was a mother who was deeply concerned about her daughter. Was Slade okay? Had something happened? Should she be home interviewing for new jobs instead of here assisting Marin?

"Nothing, really. Let's just focus on the house, okay?"

"Okay," Marin replied, hoping the sometimes painfully deep love she felt for Slade would transfer through the one-word response.

If anyone could understand not wanting to talk about a subject, it was Marin.

At least they'd unearthed something the two of them could agree on.

Chapter Two

Slade Henderson had made a rookie mistake. By arriving early, she'd given away too much.

Shouldn't a mother's intuition regarding her daughter have an expiration date? Say…around the time that child left home?

Slade was thirty years old and hadn't lived with her mom since she'd left for college at eighteen, and yet, her mother *knew*. She always did.

Intent on unloading Mom's vehicle, Slade strode to the car and rounded to the passenger side. Her mother followed, opening the back door across from her.

"The job…" Slade propped her arms against the sun-heated car roof. "It wasn't my fault." At least…not this time. She'd *had* to leave. There hadn't been another choice.

Clearly, Slade was doing a fantastic job of following her *let's just focus on the house* dictate from moments before. But she couldn't resist defending herself against Mom's unspoken judgments.

"It's in my job description to worry about you, Love. I just want you to be okay."

"I'm okay." Or she would be…eventually. Slade always landed on her feet. She would find a way to overcome this latest hurdle, even though it had scarred her beyond anything else she'd ever experienced.

Six months ago, Slade took a job in a law office.

When they'd joked during her interview that they simply needed a body to fill the position and that they could train her despite her lack of office experience, Slade hadn't realized they meant the *body* part literally.

The position had been the first of its kind for her—file, type emails, smile when someone walked in the door, salaried, benefits, potential. Based on her experience there, Slade would also say it was her last.

"I'm sure you'll figure it out. You always do. And I'm here if you need me." Mom's smile had been missing since Dad died, but she reached for it now, attempting to plaster it into place. Slade knew that this, at least, wasn't about her. Mom wore her grief like a sorority sister wore house colors. She and Dad had done most everything together. Slade hadn't realized how unusual that was until one of her friends had mentioned it in middle school. After that, she'd been more aware of their relationship—more embarrassed by it, more covertly impressed.

Mom's grief was pure—like a rare flower that had lived long and well and had bloomed beautifully. Slade's grief came from a darker, more desperate place. She missed her person, her protector, the one who'd believed in her when very few in the world did. Gran and Grandad had been that for her too, and now all three were gone. Living in a world without them was like inhaling forest fire smoke daily and yet, somehow, expecting her body to keep functioning, her lungs to keep filtering.

"Thank you." Slade attempted to appreciate her mother's encouragement…even though it felt as if it had been served with a side of skepticism. They would never survive the house purge if they started out irritated with each other.

"Of course." Mom lifted a box from the back seat of the beige, nondescript vehicle that she'd surely taken in for a checkup before making the twelve-hour drive. She was like Reed in that way. So careful, so calculated. Like life might break if they grabbed on with both hands. The box slipped, and Mom caught it, but her wince was blatant.

Slade hurried around the vehicle and took it from her. "I'm sure the drive was tough on you. Why don't you go inside and open up the house? I'll manage this in a few trips."

Mom's rheumatoid arthritis wreaked havoc on her joints, which was why Reed and Slade had insisted on helping with the house. Since she worked in an elementary school office, Mom had considered attempting the purge over spring break, but both Slade and Reed had encouraged her to wait because a week would never have been enough time. Not when Gran had been a wannabe hoarder…unable to throw anything away or part with old clothing or home items, despite their age or lack of value, storing enough surplus food to survive an apocalypse in The Armpit.

Mom reached for another bag, and Slade gently nudged her to the side. "Seriously. This is something I can handle for you. Please let me."

Her mother's eyes closed, then opened, the navy color shimmering just a hint. "Thanks. I don't know why I'm fighting you."

"It just comes naturally to us." The retort slipped out before Slade could dissect whether or not it would offend.

Thankfully, Mom laughed. "Why is that, huh? I'll just take my lunch cooler so I can unpack it. It's light, I promise. And I'll prop the door open for you."

Slade adjusted her grip and added a couple small bags to her load. By the time she entered the house, Mom was tugging curtains aside, sending dandruff-like flakes floating through the swatch of evening sun. Expansive windows filled the wall that overlooked the deck and the rippling Snake River Inlet as it flowed into Lake Dillon. From the water below, the deck hung partially suspended over the cliff's edge. From above, one could easily experience vertigo when taking in the steep descent.

Gran and Grandad had been ahead of their time in the openness of the house. The kitchen didn't have an island, just a long original farmhouse table with mismatched chairs separating it from the living room. Rustic beams traversed the vaulted ceiling covering the two spaces. The edge of the table at the spot where Grandad had always sat to read the paper, drink coffee or partake in a cookie break with the kids was more worn than the other areas—the wood lighter, the finish rubbed off. Slade set the items she'd carried inside on the dark walnut tabletop and ran her hand along the sacred, blemished stretch, emotion a hot, tight ball in her chest.

Of all the places in the world, this house would always be her safe haven. Always represent home for her. Even if her job hadn't imploded, she would likely still have been tempted to take a leave of absence for the whole house project anyway. To soak up every minute of this last stay.

For as much of her childhood as Slade could remember, she and Reed had spent a month here each summer with their grandparents, sans parents—hiking, biking, traipsing around town, eating Gran's cooking and the constant supply of baked goods streaming from her oven. It would be emotional to let this place go, and Slade didn't do emotion well. But then, what did she do well? Slade wouldn't be posing that question to her mother.

The location of the house plus the views would sell Gran and Grandad's place in a heartbeat.

All Slade, Mom and Reed had to do was remove every piece of nostalgia from it and then walk away.

That last bit might sever a piece of Slade's still-beating heart right off.

"By the way, how did you get here?" Mom moved into the kitchen and began unloading her small lunch cooler into the fridge. "Did you drive? I didn't see a car out front."

"I flew."

Unlike her mother's beige dream machine, Slade's obnoxious yellow vehicle hadn't experienced regular checkups. Every so often, it would make a clunking noise, which Slade religiously ignored. Her car surviving the trek from Florida to Colorado would have been as likely as Reed agreeing to perform karaoke. She'd left the hunk of junk in her apartment parking lot and the keys with a trusted neighbor, in case it needed to be moved or used.

Slade had found the last-minute tickets yesterday, and the airline had allowed her to change her itinerary. It would have been outrageous to pass up an opportunity to get to Dillon early, especially now that she didn't have anything keeping her in Gulfport.

She made two more trips to the car and back inside, also snagging her travel backpack from where she'd stashed it on the front porch.

Slade deposited her mother's rolling suitcase inside Gran and Grandad's bedroom on the first floor, where she would stay, and returned to the kitchen to find her mom stepping through the sliding glass door from the deck into the living room.

"Let's leave the door cracked open for a bit to air out the house." Mom wrung out a dishcloth that had been soaking in the sink and began wiping the counters, a faint citrus smell reminiscent of Gran permeating the air.

"Thought you were going to take it easy?" Slade added the box of supplies she was carrying to the items she'd already deposited on the table.

"I need to give the place at least a wipe down or we'll be sneezing with every step."

"How come you packed all of this?" Slade nodded toward the container filled with garbage bags, paper towels and those cardboard file boxes that fit together like puzzles. "There are plenty of places to get supplies around here."

"Because I had a lot at home. I don't go through things as quickly with just me around." *Without Dad.* The unsaid addition filled the air between them with a crackling, palpable wave of grief. "Is there anything else to grab from the car?"

"Nope. I got it all."

"Thanks for doing that, Love." Her expression softened beyond her earlier attempt into something real. Grateful.

"Of course."

"It's a good thing you're here."

Was it, though? When Mom had woken her on the porch, Slade had been almost certain her mother thought the exact opposite. After a long day of travel—an early flight and a layover, plus the drive from the airport—Slade had just wanted to close her eyes. She'd opened them to find her mom's expression one of surprise, distress, and some other reaction Slade couldn't decipher.

"But wait—I understand that you flew into Denver, but how did you get *here*?" Dillon was almost two hours from the Denver airport, which sat out in a field like the world should come to it instead of it accommodating the world.

"I hitched."

Mom's hand froze under the stream of water where she'd been rinsing the dishcloth. "Did you just say you *hitchhiked*?" She enunciated the word as if she were accusing Slade of murder, drug use or a hit-and-run.

"Yep. With some random guy in a rundown vehicle with a trunk full of ammunition."

Her mother's sigh was reminiscent of Slade's childhood.

"Have a little confidence in me, Mama-Mar." The name Slade had used to tease her mom when she was a teen—a play on an overprotective mama bear—slipped out. "I used a ride-sharing app."

"What's that?"

"It's an app people use to share rides."

"That part I understood," she responded dryly. "Are you telling me you got into a car with someone you didn't know?" Mom flipped off the water and wrung out the dishcloth with agitated squeezes that had to translate like needles jabbing into her knuckles, though at the moment, she didn't seem to be aware of her arthritis.

Just her daughter's apparently outrageous choices.

"Technically, I guess." But Slade wasn't naive. She'd vetted the woman offering the ride. Keely Teoh. Turned out she and Keely had more in common than a small attempt to save planet Earth from emissions. Keely lived in Silverthorne—only a few minutes from Dillon—and the two of them had discussed the possibility of getting together while Slade was in town.

"Why didn't you just tell me you were flying in early? I could have picked you up at the airport."

It had been more relaxing getting to know Keely on the drive than it would have been enduring Mom's attempt to hide her irritation at the lack of notice regarding Slade's switch in schedule.

But how could Slade admit that?

"If you would have swung out to DIA, we wouldn't even be at the house yet. It would have added a hefty chunk of time."

Mom inclined her head as if conceding half a point to Slade. Her burdened exhale leaked out. "I'm thankful you're alive."

Slade rounded the table and snagged a glass from the original flat-front chestnut cabinet next to the sink, sentimental over the fact that everything remained in the same place as it had been when she was a kid. But then, items probably hadn't changed locations since Mom and Aunt Lovetta grew up here.

"I made sure she wasn't a murderer first." She ran the tap water until it was cold and then filled her glass. "Give me some credit."

"And how, exactly, did you do that?"

"I asked her."

Slade's retort was met with a shaking head and begrudging amusement. "Lovetta Slade."

"I've handled things myself for a lot of years, remember?" And failed profusely at times. After Slade dropped out of college, she'd been determined to make it on her own, to not move back home. And she had. She'd filtered through numerous occupations—some she'd loved, others she would never do again. Slade had always managed to survive, though it looked nothing like the plan her mother would have crafted for her. "I promise I'm not completely inept."

At least, not when it came to orchestrating a ride. But when it came to settling down, sticking to one career or not having trouble adhere to her like a tick on a dog... Slade definitely couldn't claim the same.

Chapter Three

"I've been here less than an hour and I already messed up." Marin vented to her sister the second she was back in her car—just thirty minutes after her arrival at the house.

She'd quickly realized that with Slade present, they didn't have food for a late dinner. Marin had planned to eat the left-overs from her lunch and other snacks she'd packed, make her bed and conk out. Perhaps read a little in order to decompress before she fell asleep. Slade had claimed that she wasn't hungry. That she'd be perfectly content with some of the snacks or a granola bar she'd thrown in her bag. But the mama bear in Marin that Slade had referred to in her teasing way—the one who couldn't subdue the curiosity and concern over what was really going on with her daughter's job and her sudden appearance in Dillon—needed to at least feed her cub.

Marin may have failed as a mother in more ways than she could count, but she'd always been the one to have food on hand when the kids stopped by with their friends. She liked to cook. Or at least, liked it when people enjoyed her cooking. Ralph had been her biggest fan in that department. He'd always been perfectly willing to be a guinea pig for any new recipe she was trying.

"I doubt that's true." Lovetta's tone held a reassuring amount of disbelief. "Did she say why she's there?"

When Slade had been unloading the car and Marin had been inside opening up the house, she'd quickly texted her sister about Slade's unexpected arrival.

"Not really." She filled Lovetta in on the sparse details Slade had given.

"Wow. It's all so Slade-like that I'm not sure how we didn't see this coming!"

Marin appreciated the *we*. It was good to be on the same team as someone. She and Lovetta had always been close, but since Ralph's passing, they communicated in some way, shape or form at least every other day, if not every day.

Lovetta was content with the fact that she'd never married or had children, though she sometimes bemoaned that the world wasn't as comfortable with her choices as she was.

"So, what happened with you two?"

"She offered to run to the grocery store."

"What a terrible, rotten child. How could she? You just did not raise those two right. Insisting on helping with the house. Offering to grocery shop."

Despite the guilt Lovetta's teasing heaped on her, Marin laughed. "Right? I'm such a shrew. Why couldn't I just let her go? I'm exhausted and she knows it, which makes the fact that I demanded to be the one to run the errand all the worse."

"You refused because she's Slade, and she would have come back with Velveeta and Wonder Bread."

"And candy. And chips. And nothing resembling a meal."

"Exactly." Lovetta's response held tenderness and amusement. "I'm sure you're doing fine, Mar. Better than you give yourself credit for. Especially with how unexpected it was to find Slade at the house."

Marin wasn't nearly as confident of that. "I appreciate your cheerleading."

"Anytime. It's the least I can do since I'm not there to help."

Marin turned in to the Dillon Ridge Marketplace and then into the City Market lot. Somehow the drive had gone by without her noticing what she was doing, how she'd gotten here, if she'd run over any small children along the way.

"Keep me updated on what happens next. Feel like I'm watching your life unfold as a soap opera."

"A soap opera? Really? I think in order to qualify as that, there would need to be some unrequited love or some kissing or—"

"*Please* do some kissing while you're there." Lovetta burst into lyrics about kissing someone that, based on the twang she added, must be a country song. "I bet I know exactly who would be will—"

"I'm at the store. Gotta run!" Marin disconnected to the sound of her sister's cackle-snort-cackle, a smile sprouting despite the subject Lovetta had just ventured toward.

She checked the time on her phone while heading for the automatic doors. It was quarter after six. If Marin hurried, she could be back at the house, groceries unpacked, food on the table by seven fifteen. For that to happen, she'd need to not run into anyone she knew. But since the grocery store was a large, modern chain, Marin should be able to accomplish that. It would be filled with tourists or people who lived elsewhere in Colorado and owned condos for skiing or visiting on long summer weekends.

Inside the store, she rounded up some vegetables and fruit. Granola and yogurt for breakfast. Quick, easy and requiring no prep. She added sandwich items for lunches. It would be the simplest thing to throw together, and it would work even if she and

Slade weren't hungry at the same time. She put chips—baked—and some other snack items she guessed Slade might enjoy into the cart. Then she tossed in some soup along with a few other basic supplies.

"I really am hard on her. Maybe she's changed. I could have at least let her come along." Slade had visited in Arizona numerous times when Ralph was sick, but she'd usually sat with him while Marin prepared meals or bustled around the house. It had been a good break, though. Slade and Ralph had always shared a special bond. And he'd had the same connection to Reed. Ralph had been father-of-the-year material. The kind of dad who never missed one of his kids' games. The kind who'd sat on the floor for hours to play with them when they were little. From the moment Marin had first met Ralph during the second week of classes at University of Colorado Boulder, she'd instinctively sensed the good in him.

"I'm sorry. Were you talking to me?" The young woman across the aisle from Marin paused.

"Oh no. Sorry." Marin's cheeks heated, no doubt turning hot-flash scarlet. "I was talking to myself. Bad habit."

"I do the same!" She motioned to the two toddlers strapped into the cart, legs dangling through the metal squares under the handle. "It just looks like I'm talking to them." Eyes crinkling with warmth, she continued down the aisle, turning and disappearing from Marin's vision at the endcap.

"If I'd let Slade do the grocery run, then at least I wouldn't be the old lady mumbling to myself in public." The irony that she'd once again spoken aloud wasn't lost on her.

Marin added some flavored sparkling water and sweet tea to the cart, along with some soda for Slade. Her slow adjustment to her daughter's early arrival really had nothing to do with Slade and everything to do with herself and her issues. *I'm taking out my awkwardness over being in this town for an extended period on Slade, and it has to stop. I just need to be okay with being in Dillon again. No one cares that I'm here. No one will even notice.*

At least this time, her running commentary was in her head and not on her lips.

Gloriously, Marin checked out without running into any familiar or prying faces. She rolled the cart into the lot and popped the trunk of her car.

"It's been thirty-four years and this area has probably quadrupled in size. Of course no one knows me. Everyone has moved on." Wasn't it time she did too?

A furtive glance to her left and right confirmed that Marin's one-sided convo hadn't been overheard. The habit of talking to herself had begun after Ralph's passing. The house had been so quiet, so utterly empty. Marin had started engaging in running commentaries while gardening, cooking, getting ready in the morning. She'd talked to Ralph—or at least the memory of him—to ease the silence and the pain. It had helped to hear someone's voice even if it was just her own.

Eventually, the one-sided conversations had switched from monologues directed at a nonexistent Ralph to processing her internal thoughts out loud.

Hopefully, Marin wouldn't launch into a tirade in the presence of her children, causing them to question her mental capabilities.

The sun dipped toward the Rocky Mountains and scattered a swatch of diamonds over the lake as Marin drove back to her parents' house. A breeze had been blowing when she first arrived, but now it was calm. Pontoon, sail and fishing boats dotted the smooth, inky surface, along with a few kayakers. Three years ago, the reservoir recreation committee had secured support for allowing wading in Dillon Reservoir—which locals often referred to as Lake Dillon—while continuing the practice of not permitting outright swimming because of the frigid water temperatures. The nature of the lake was serene compared to the bodies of water that allowed skiing and wake boarding.

Summer in the mountains had always been Marin's favorite. She inched her window open and let the scent of evergreens drift inside, along with the quickly cooling night air.

The excursion and the drive settled something in her, and Marin pulled in front of the garage more relaxed than she'd been all day. She was here. Slade was here. They would get more work done, and Marin would have numerous chances to be patient and loving to her daughter over the course of the next week or weeks...however long Slade planned to stay.

She got out of the car just as a pickup rumbled up the street. The truck slowed, then came to a stop at the end of the driveway. Marin's heart gave a kick of anxiety.

Seriously, Marin, you need to get ahold of yourself. It was probably just a neighbor checking on things, making sure she was legitimately supposed to be at the house.

Marin waved to assure them all was well, though with the sun glinting off the windows of the other vehicle, she couldn't tell if they saw her or responded.

The truck reversed and then pulled into the driveway behind her car.

So much for groceries unpacked and dinner ready by seven fifteen.

The driver's door opened, work boots appearing beneath it as a man removed himself from the vehicle.

And then Marin was face-to-face with Garrett Turner.

She'd expected to run into him at some point while she was in town. Had prepared herself for this scenario—or so she'd believed. But just being near him caused her body to react without her permission. Goose bumps cascaded down her arms and her pulse jumped rope double Dutch–style—a game she and Lovetta had perfected as kids in this very driveway.

"Mar." Garrett's head inclined in greeting. His deep, gravelly voice along with the familiar shortening of her name leveled Marin right back to sixteen…and twenty-six.

Unlike Ralph, who'd slowly gone bald over the years, Garrett had a full head of hair. With time, the color had turned an attractive salt-and-pepper. He sported a neatly trimmed beard, sage green eyes that had always reminded her of sea glass, and somehow, a very similar physique to his younger years—stocky, thick shoulders, trim waist. He wore a T-shirt beneath an open flannel with jeans he'd probably owned for ten-plus years and would never consider replacing until they formed a tear.

"Saw a vehicle and wanted to make sure everything was okay over here." Garrett stayed next to his truck, like they were on opposing sides of a boxing ring. "I've been keeping an eye on the place since… I'm sorry about your dad. He was one of a kind."

"He was." Marin cleared rusty emotion from her vocal cords. "Thank you. And thanks for checking on the house. Are you heading to your parents'?"

"Heading home, actually. My mom and dad moved to be near my sister and their grandkids in Utah a couple years ago—they wanted one level living and could afford more there—and I bought their house. Couldn't resist the views."

Her thyroid inexplicably formed an instant nodule, clogging her throat. "So, you live down the street?"

He gave a crisp nod.

Garrett's family had moved to Dillon and the neighborhood when they were both freshmen in high school. His dad had been in construction, and they'd built a house on the other end of the loop that formed the street. The Turners, much like her family, had been blue-collar, full-time residents, and their home—also like her family's—wasn't monstrously huge.

The similarities had bonded Marin and Garrett, and their fast-growing friendship had swiftly morphed into more.

Back then, the easy access to each other was like unwrapping an unexpected gift.

Now the close proximity was as stifling as an airplane bathroom or a barely functioning elevator.

"That's great that you could keep their place." The lie tasted like vinegar mixed with sand.

They stared at each other for far too long, neither speaking. Was he expecting her to invite him in? Take up where things had ended? She had no plans for that. Especially with her daughter in the house. The past was staying firmly in the past this month. That was one admonition Marin hadn't had to remind herself of while on the drive, because it had been the same for the past three-plus decades.

"Your parents told me when Ralph passed. I can't even imagine how hard it's been. I know how much you loved him."

Marin refused to read into that last comment, instead taking it at face value. "Thank you."

"I sure miss seeing your dad puttering around the house. Can't tell you how many times I found him on a ladder that had seen better days. Under the car, changing oil. Perched on top of something unstable, cleaning windows."

A smile warmed Marin's lips. "He was awful about things like that. Is it peculiar to say I miss that part of him? Because it drove me nuts while he was alive. I was always afraid I was going to get a phone call about him falling off a ladder or breaking something. And yet I never did. At least…not that kind of call."

Dad's decline in the last year of his life—after his stroke—had been slow and steady. Eventually, pneumonia had been too much for him to conquer. Marin and Lovetta had gotten to be with him before he passed. Slade too. Reed hadn't made it in time to say goodbye, but then, Reed was logical and centered. He knew his grandfather loved him and vice versa. Not being able to orchestrate a last-minute farewell hadn't rocked him the way it would have Slade, who wore her emotions like a new mom wore a path in the carpet.

"I suppose grief has a way of turning something you once considered bad into good."

"I suppose." Hadn't it done that with Ralph? The things that had bugged Marin when he was alive *were* some of the strangest things that she longed to experience one more time.

"You have a lot of people to miss these days."

"Yes."

"Hope you're…doing the best you can."

She liked the way he'd put that. Not *doing okay*. Or *moving on*. Or any of the many irritating things people said.

She *was* doing her best.

"I am. Thanks. The kids are coming to help me clean out the house. Slade is already here, even though I wasn't expecting her until Saturday."

"Adult children. It's a whole new ballgame."

Despite herself, despite her desire to not even be conversing with Garrett right now, Marin laughed.

"Ain't that the truth. How are the boys?"

Garrett's wife had exited their marriage and the lives of her sons when they'd been pre-teens. Marin had heard about her departure and the subsequent aftermath from her parents over the years because they'd always had a fondness for Garrett. They didn't understand how Poppy could do that to her husband or her children. Marin couldn't either.

Garrett had handled things—at least from the outside—like the strong, steady current of the Blue River. He'd kept going. He probably understood the phrase *doing the best I can* better than most.

"The boys are great. Happy and settled for the most part."

"Glad to hear it." Continuing the conversation was the polite thing to do. But Slade had offered to help Marin carry in the groceries when she returned. Which meant at any moment, she'd hear them through the open windows and come spilling onto the deck that wrapped partially around the side of the house and was connected to the driveway by two steps.

Any moment now Marin's past would collide with her present.

Garrett, through no fault of his own, represented a devastatingly difficult time in her life. The last thing Marin wanted was to introduce him to Slade.

"I should go." Garrett gripped the edge of his still-open driver's door.

Relief flooded her system. "Thanks for checking on Mom and Dad over the years. They always appreciated you." Marin had long ago relinquished any upset over the fact that her parents had kept their relationship with Garrett. That he'd been like a son to them. Her parents had been extremely good to Ralph too. They'd had enough love to spread around.

Garrett's eyes spoke volumes that his mouth didn't. "Of course. You know they were like bonus parents to me."

She'd known. And that had only made things harder.

Chapter Four

While Mom had escaped to the grocery store—refusing to let Slade go and swiftly turning her *it's a good thing you're here* comment null and void—Slade had done a quick wipe down of the bathrooms, located full-size sheets, made Mom and Reed's beds, and texted her brother to let him know she'd arrived early since they'd originally planned for their flights to land in Denver on Saturday around the same time. The twin-size sheets for the bed in the room Slade considered hers, she had yet to find.

She finished checking the closet and moved on to the low, curved-bottom, six-drawer walnut dresser that had occupied the room as long as the 1970s sea green carpet.

The top two drawers on both sides were spilling with random items and no sheets. The bottom left had clothing in it, and the bottom right was so weighed down it didn't budge when she tugged. Slade dropped to the floor and shimmied the drawer open, finding it overflowing with papers. A stack of yellowed newspaper clippings drew her attention, and she lifted them out.

The first handful were recipes, followed by some write-ups

about Gran and Grandad's church, then a few highlights of local businesses and community events.

Slade was about to dump the pile back into the drawer to be dealt with later when a dislodged headline from halfway through the stack caught her attention.

Did that say *body*?

She pulled the aged clipping loose and read the short paragraph.

Body Found on the Shore of Dillon Reservoir near Snake River Inlet

July 12, 1990

> Police are investigating the cause of death and identity of a man who was discovered on the rocks below High Meadow Drive. Preliminary findings concur his injuries were consistent with a fall, but police are asking anyone with information to call their tip line.

There was a photo of shoreline surrounded by police tape accompanying the article, and based on the landmarks Slade recognized, he was found directly below her grandparents' property. Which meant he'd been at their house when he fell.

If he'd even fallen. The article stated the police were investigating his death. What had they found? And who was the man?

Slade sorted through the clippings for another article regarding the incident, but there was nothing else in the stack.

Really, Gran? You saved everything but not the follow-up details regarding this?

How had Slade and Reed spent so many summers here as kids and never heard about a man dying below their grandparents' property? It felt like a wildly important occurrence that someone had taken a pink eraser to, leaving only a few illegible smudge lines—this article—as proof.

Faint conversation floated through the open window in Reed's room, which flanked the driveway. Was Mom talking to herself again or was someone else here? She'd engaged in the habit after Dad had passed away, and neither Slade nor Reed felt it necessary to acknowledge the coping mechanism.

They all navigated grief in their own ways.

The cadence of Mom's voice reached Slade again, and she grabbed the article and descended the stairs, heading for the door off the kitchen that led to the driveway.

Surely Mom knew about this guy who'd died. Surely there was an explanation as to what had happened on her grandparents' property. *And* a reason that this had been kept a secret for all of Slade's existence.

She pushed open the screen door and stepped onto the driveway just as a man was about to slide behind the wheel of an older but well-kept truck. The T-shirt under his flannel boasted a Stoneridge Construction label. Was this a contractor Mom had contacted regarding the house?

At Slade's arrival, he paused midmovement, seemingly unsure whether he should climb into his vehicle or retreat and greet her.

His gaze met her mother's and held, in some kind of strange, questioning dance.

Mom's hand slipped up to her cheek, pressed against the corner of her eye, then motioned to the man. "Slade, this is Garrett Turner. You might remember his parents from down the street. He lives there now. He's been keeping an eye on the house since Grandad passed, and he often checked on Gran and Grandad over the years. Garrett, this is my daughter, Slade."

Slade recalled her grandparents mentioning someone named Garrett a few times. Including a story about how he'd delivered groceries to them in the middle of a particularly bad snowstorm that had lasted for days.

"Good to see you, Mr. Turner. Thanks for watching out for my grandparents."

"It was my pleasure. Stu and Thelma were easy to assist, if or when they ever let that happen. I gained more from the relationship than I ever gave."

Sounded exactly right. Slade's grandparents had been the kind of people who loved big, who would give their whole paycheck to someone in need. They'd certainly lavished Slade and Reed with affection. Instead of judging Slade's many hair colors over the years, they'd been entertained by them. Gran had even learned to text just so she could communicate with her grandkids, often sending them messages that were half-written or meant for someone else or accidentally voice recorded when she was talking to Grandad. Slade had backed up those messages so she could always have them. She'd had to ask Reed for help on how to make that technological feat happen, but she'd managed it.

"I should get going. Good to see you both. Hope the clean out goes well. If you need anything or I can be of assistance with the house, you know where to find me." He got into his truck and backed out of the driveway, then idled down the street.

Slade watched the vehicle rumble away as Mom buried her head in the trunk, as focused on retrieving the groceries as an environmentalist would be about saving the elephants or protecting bees.

"Have you known Garrett a long time, Mom?"

"Oh. Well. Yes." Mom popped up so quickly Slade winced over her near miss with the trunk lid. "If a person considers forty-five years a long time. We both lived on this street after his family moved to town." Mom had three grocery bags in each hand. So much for Slade assisting her. "You know how small towns are, Love. Everyone knows everyone."

Slade was 97 percent sure Mom was downplaying her connection to Garrett.

The man had said the right things. He'd come across as a helpful, concerned neighbor. No doubt he'd been good to her grandparents. But Slade couldn't shake the sense that she'd walked into a wall of tension when she'd stepped out the door.

She might be a mess regarding most things in life, but her instincts were usually spot-on.

"And Gran and Grandad—they liked Garrett, right?"

"Of course. Was there anyone your grandparents didn't like?"

True. Maybe finding the article had her head spinning too far, too fast, too suspiciously.

"Mom, what is this?" Slade held up the newspaper clipping, causing her mother to place the bags she'd just gathered back into the trunk. She held out a palm, and Slade handed over the article.

As she scanned it, her mother's face turned ashen, and her lips pinched into a rigid line.

She passed the clipping back to Slade quickly. "It's an old article. You know Gran saved everything. That's why we're here." Mom's voice reached for casual but hovered somewhere closer to agitated. "Where did you find that?"

"In the dresser in my room. I was looking for sheets." Slade waited for her mother to expand or explain the article. Instead, she turned back to the trunk. What was so important about these groceries? "So, did you know about this?"

A long breath escaped as Mom swung slowly back to face Slade. She rested a hand against the side of the vehicle, her knuckles fading from peach to murky gray.

"Of course. Everyone in Dillon knows about it. Or at least knew about it when it happened."

"So, what's the story?"

"The police labeled his death an accident."

"The article said the incident was still being investigated. So, he just…fell? He must have been on Gran and Grandad's lot for him to end up where he did. Did they know this person?"

"No, they didn't."

"Then, why was he here?"

"I'm not sure." Her body seemed to sway slightly toward the car.

"Why didn't we know about this?"

"It was a long time ago. I would have never thought to mention it. It didn't have anything to do with Gran and Grandad."

"How could it not? He died below their house."

"Not everything in life has an explanation."

"I still don't understand how Reed and I never heard about this." At least, Slade assumed her brother was as out of the loop as she was.

Mom's shoulders rose with her palms. "There isn't anything to the story. It was laid to rest. You weren't born at the time. And you were children when you stayed here in the summers— who would bring up a dead body to you two? It's just an old newspaper clipping." Slade's phone vibrated, and when she took it out to check the screen, Mom grabbed the bags she'd recently released and beelined for the house.

"It's Reed," Slade announced as she hustled by.

"Oh, good! Tell him the birds are eating from the feeder." Mom managed to wrench open the screen door with loaded hands, and it slapped shut behind her.

Weird.

Slade answered. "Mom says to tell you the birds are eating from the feeder."

"What does that information have to do with me?"

"No idea. Why are you being one of those terrible people who respond to a text with a phone call?"

"Why can *you* never stick to a plan?" Her brother's gruff but affectionate admonition caused Slade to smile. She and Reed couldn't be more different. He was the coloring within the lines to her abstract art. But for some reason Slade had yet to understand, they got along really well.

"Me being here early is a good thing. The house is chock full of stuff. Even with all three of us, it's going to take more time than we planned."

"It's that bad, huh?"

"I don't think Gran got rid of anything before she died, and I don't think Grandad got rid of anything after." They'd stayed here while orchestrating Grandad's funeral, but everything had been a blur and shrouded by grief. Slade hadn't analyzed what it would take to clean out the house at that point or the sheer number of items that filled each cabinet, shelf, closet and room.

"Speaking of. I just found the strangest thing in the dresser in my room." Slade walked toward the end of the driveway so that her mother wouldn't be able to hear her through the open kitchen window. "Have you ever heard about someone dying on Gran and Grandad's property?"

A beat of silence followed her question. "What do you mean?"

"Listen to this article." She read the short piece to him. "The man was found below the house. Isn't it odd that we wouldn't have heard of this before?"

"Yes and no."

Such a Reed answer.

"If this never came up in all the time we spent here with Gran and Grandad as kids, they had to have decided to keep it from us."

"*They* as in Gran and Grandad?"

"Or Mom and Dad. I don't know."

"Why *would* they bring up something like this to us? It happened before we were born." Was someone holding up Mom's cue cards for Reed? Their responses were practically verbatim. "Would you tell your kids about a dead body found below the property they lived at for a month each summer? That's got nightmare city written all over it. Of course no one told us."

Leave it to Reed to boil it all down with logic. "I wouldn't hide it. Certainly not when they were adults."

"Maybe they weren't *hiding* it. Maybe it just never came up. What did Mom say when you asked her about it?"

"How do you know I asked her about it?"

He snorted.

So, she was curious. Besides Reed, who wouldn't be?

"She said it was nothing. That the police labeled his death an accident."

"Well, there's your answer. How is it that you've been there two minutes and you've already dug up trouble?"

"I didn't *dig it up*. It was right there in my dresser drawer." It wasn't Slade's fault that problems seemed to seek her out. "I didn't go looking for it." Though she had gone looking for follow-up details. As any person besides her somehow perfectly controlled, perfectly logical brother would do.

"So, about the house…" Reed's no-nonsense tone indicated he was done with the newspaper-clipping conversation. "If it's as bad as you're telling me, then I'll come early too."

"Wait—what?" Slade might be the type to change her schedule on a whim, but her brother was not. It was one of the things she appreciated about him. He was as dependable as she was fickle. Of course, she was also far more fun than him, but that was a given. "But you have to work. You can't take that much time off, can you?" For once Slade understood her mother's concern that they not jeopardize their careers for this. Reed was a successful computer programmer, which meant he did something with code and web applications and other things that were clear as cryptocurrency to her.

"I'll work remote if I need to. If I get up at five—six, Chicago time—I'll still have plenty of afternoon and evening left to help. If you're there ahead of schedule, then I'm coming too. I can't have you inching into my favorite-child space."

"*That's* not going to happen. Mom wouldn't even let me manage the grocery store run for her. I'd say your spot isn't going anywhere." Slade turned back toward the house, her steps laden with surprise at the conversation she was having with her usually predictable brother. "It would be great to have you here, but take a minute and think it through. We're going to start first thing in the morning. Maybe it will go better than expected."

"What is up with everyone making decisions for me lately? Believe it or not, I can analyze a situation, deduce a plan, and follow through with it."

"I have no doubt you can do exactly whatever it is you just said." Slade also had no doubt that Reed was acting very strange.

"I'll text you my updated flight details. If one of you can pick me up, that would be great."

"Of course one of us will pick you up, but I doubt Lindsey is going to be cool with you—"

"Lindsey will be fine. She'll understand that my family needs me."

Need was a strong take on the conversation they'd just had. It almost felt as if Reed wanted to adjust his plans.

And that didn't sound like him at all. What in the whole wide world was going on? Slade had stepped into a parallel universe and the only person who was making any sense…was her.

Chapter Five

"I think we can just pull onto the shoulder to wait for him."
Slade spoke around a mouthful of Sour Patch Kids candy, and
Marin barely resisted climbing out the driver's window of her car
to escape the smacking noise and to avoid complaining about it.

When her daughter had suggested road trip snacks for the
drive to DIA, Marin should have suspected what she actually
meant: candy.

"People are supposed to use the cell phone lot," Marin supplied, her delivery more clipped than she meant it to be. "I've
just heard DIA is particular about that." She sent her daughter
an apologetic smile across the space separating them.

"No problem. Cell phone lot works great." Slade employed the
calm tone that moms use when dealing with a snarky teenager.

When had their roles reversed?

Slade's phone vibrated in the cup holder, and she checked the
screen. "Oh! Reed says he's already at baggage claim. I missed
a text saying he'd landed early."

Even though communicating with Reed and helping navigate was the whole reason they'd both done the airport run instead of one of them staying at the house to work.

Marin clamped her teeth together to keep the retort from slipping out.

What was wrong with her?

She really was the teenage version of herself.

Irritable. Angry over nothing and everything. And of course she knew why but didn't want to deal with it.

Also a teen specialty.

Reed had switched his flight to midday Thursday, sending Marin's radar regarding him pinging into the red zone. Changing plans for Reed was as unusual as a steady paycheck was for his sister. Marin had told herself for the last two days that he was only doing it because of Slade, that he didn't want to miss out. But she knew those weren't viable reasons for him. Reed was not easily swayed. This switch in schedule didn't make sense, and Marin couldn't shake the premonition that something was wrong.

Which, if she included Slade's elusiveness regarding what had happened with her job, meant that she now had two children she wouldn't be able to figure out.

And one likely trying to figure *her* out.

Ever since Slade had found that newspaper clipping, Marin had been—just as Vince Dunn had once been—on the edge of a cliff. In the last two days, she'd fluctuated between hope that Slade would let any curiosity over the details of the article go and fear that she'd do the exact opposite of that. So far, she hadn't mentioned it again. But Marin couldn't imagine Slade relinquishing her interest that easily.

Marin certainly didn't plan to broach the subject again. Not when she'd spent the last thirty-four years doing her best to forget that summer ever happened.

Her daughter had no idea how many Jenga pieces fit together

surrounding that time...or how easily she could dislodge them all by picking at one.

Marin had purposefully not shared Vince's name with Slade on the off chance that it would deter her from immediately searching for information about his death.

She had no idea if her attempt to keep the past in the past had worked.

"He says suitcases are coming out now, so I bet we'll be able to just swing through and get him without having to park."

"Perfect." Marin slowed her speed to allow more time for Reed to gather his luggage and get to the exit. "I'm sorry I've been short-tempered this morning. I had a dream about Dad and it just kind of...threw me. Not that it's an excuse."

The dream had been the cherry on top of her worries about the kids and the house purge and the article. In it, Marin had been cooking dinner and Ralph had been sitting across the island from her. Just like they'd done more times than she could count during their marriage. Such a simple, everyday scenario, but it had felt so wonderful...and so real. Marin preferred to cook herself, but she'd appreciated Ralph's company and conversation while she did. He'd called their cooking-talking-listening sessions *yappy hour.*

How she *missed* that. Missed him. It sounded cliché, but he'd been her best friend. Her partner in everything. They'd spent the last decades of their marriage making up for the first few years, when they hadn't attempted to understand or love each other well at all.

Marin often thought it was the first terrible years that had created the following amazing ones. They'd fought for each other, and it had been so worth it.

After Ralph passed, Marin had begun referring to the really debilitating days as perfect-storm-grief days. The type where the grief hit from all sides at once, and she couldn't get her head above the swirling, choppy water. She'd learned since losing her mom four years ago, Ralph two years ago and Dad six months ago, that she just had to ride them out. Put the grief on like some oversize fur coat and hunker down for the duration. Attempting to avoid—at least for her—only prolonged the downward spiral.

"It's a perfect excuse," Slade countered, her words soft with emotion. "Dreams about Dad always mess me up too. Don't be so hard on yourself, Mama-Mar."

Marin glanced at her lovely grown daughter, who was being so generous with her despite her cantankerous mood this morning. "Thanks, Love."

Instead of concentrating on the pain, Marin should be celebrating what she and Slade had accomplished over the last two days. They'd worked on purging the garage, posting tools that were worth selling and boxing up plenty for the local thrift store while also filling at least a quarter of the small dumpster Marin had ordered. *And* Slade hadn't brought up the article again.

Win, win, win.

The only disappointment was that their progress in the laden space felt miniscule.

Dad had always been a fix-it man, and the garage declared that. Marin knew that neighbors would often ask him for help. It used to concern her, because it continued years past when she considered it safe for him to assist. Dad's favorite rebuttal to her had been, *What is the point of living if you're not living?* Apparently, living for him meant copious amounts of tools, nails and screws in every size imaginable, and bins of random auto parts that Marin couldn't even identify. Ralph had not been a fix-it man. He'd been the type to hire things out. He'd taken their cars to the dealer for everything, and they'd traded them in before age made it too difficult to maintain them.

The familiar, comforting smell of the garage reminded Marin so strongly of her father that she'd been overcome with emotion numerous times. Slade had also been swept by grief at varying points.

While sorting, they'd exchanged Grandad stories, listened to music Slade played that Marin had expected not to like—yes, she heard herself—but ended up enjoying, and given each other the space to take breaks.

Marin felt so inept at times when it came to Slade and their relationship—what to say, what not to say, knowing half the time she inadvertently offended or irritated her daughter—so it had been nice to see that beneath the tumultuous moments, they were capable of harmony.

Now, if only Slade would level with Marin about what had happened with her job. Because despite her many mistakes in navigating relationships with her adult children, Marin did at least know that pursuing that line of questioning again sans permission was off-limits.

"You see the arrivals lane, right?"

Marin hadn't been paying attention. She adjusted to the correct lane quickly. "Thanks."

See? It *was* a good thing they'd both come.

Their pace switched to a crawl as they approached the arrivals level and traffic increased. Vehicles lined the shoulder as Slade had suggested they do. Marin pulled over just before the door Reed had texted them he'd be at. He rolled his suitcase their way, flashing a grin and a quick wave. Reed wore what looked to be designer jeans, ankle boots and a short-sleeved, button-down shirt. Her son had grown from that gangly boy—all limbs and acne and serious contemplations—into such a successful man.

Slade opened her window. "Re-Re!"

Reed gave a quiet laugh, shook his head. Marin popped the trunk, and he moved to the rear of the vehicle, adding his suitcase before sliding into the backseat.

As usual, he was clean-shaven. His chestnut hair was medium length on the top, shorter on the sides, and his face appeared slimmer, more angular than it had at Grandad's funeral.

"Hi, hon." It was so good to see him! Both of her children, together—*with her!*—for an extended period of time. Marin's friends were hugely jealous of this coup of hers. Time with adult children was a commodity none of them experienced as often as they'd like. Not with busy schedules and long distances separating them.

Many of Marin's friends were already grandparents who made huge efforts to see their grandkids as much as possible. Marin wanted grandkids like she wanted to discover an additional savings account while sorting her parents' things, but she *would not* be bugging Reed about his and Lindsey's timeline. Even though she was extremely tempted to do so.

"Hi." Reed squeezed both of their shoulders as she drove away from the curb and met Marin's smile in the rearview mirror head-on—as if determined to show her that nothing was wrong. That nothing but Slade arriving ahead of schedule and the magnitude of the house purge had merited him doing the same. "Thanks for the ride."

"Of course." At least Reed had given her the opportunity to pick him up. Unlike his sister. *Might need to let that go, Mar.* Lovetta had already chastised her for holding on to something so trite. "How was the flight?"

"Normal. Bumpy."

Denver always was. "How's Lindsey? Is she okay with you coming early? Is she going to try to join us for a bit? Not that it's much of a vacation, but we'd love to see her."

Reed settled back against his seat, the picture of relaxation, his vision cast out the window to where the Rocky Mountains filled the western horizon.

"She's fine. She can't come because of work. But she…isn't upset that I'm here."

"She's always been sweet like that."

Reed made a low, dismissive sound in his throat.

Slade twisted in her seat and slapped Reed on the knee. "I

can't believe you're here! It's so weird and unlike you. Isn't it weird and unlike him, Mom?"

Marin checked the mirror once again, like it might give her some insight into her son's soul or reasoning or *something*. The reflection did nothing of the sort.

"Changing plans might not be his usual MO but wanting to help definitely is."

"Favorite child in the car!" Laughter peeled from Slade. "You always defend him. Always see the best in him."

"I see the best in both of you. I don't have a favorite, Lovetta Slade, and you know it." This was the issue with children! They made things up and then believed them like they were written in stone. Marin loved each of her kids an astronomical amount. But with Slade, she always felt as if she was navigating a remote road without a map. She imagined that was why she so often said the wrong thing to her daughter. With Reed, she felt as if she had a constantly updating navigation system to guide her. He was just more cut-and-dried. You got what you got with him. Which meant she should probably stop doubting his early arrival, thinking it had nefarious origins, and just accept it for the gift it was. *Both* of her children's early arrivals.

"Oh, Mom. I know you love us both." Slade patted Marin's knee just like she had Reed's, then flipped to face the backseat again. "So, brother, what's new? Tell us everything."

Despite Slade's many attempts to glean updates from Reed about the latest happenings in his life on the car ride from the airport back to Dillon, her brother told them nothing—or at least nothing of interest. He'd morphed into the teenage version of himself. The one who gave stilted answers and who had spent a chunk of his high school years hibernating in his room. Not that he'd had the chance to do that at Gran and Grandad's house since they'd just arrived and sat down for a late lunch, but Slade wouldn't be surprised if he did escape from the table the moment he was given the opportunity.

She had almost climbed into the backseat on the ride to slap him—gently of course—and find out if her brother was somewhere inside this robot they'd picked up at DIA.

"Mom, what's the plan with the house?" Reed asked. "Do you have a schedule or a list or a spreadsheet?"

"So, you are capable of conversing." Slade's snarky comment was met with a confused head tilt from her brother. The mannerism had always reminded her of a dog—endearing, earnest, wondering if they were getting a treat or if they'd done something wrong.

"I've been talking." Reed addressed Slade, the spoon in his hand resting against the vintage stoneware bowl in front of him. "It's just hard to get in a word edgewise with you around." The retort was tempered by crinkled cedar eyes that matched their father's. Reed had also inherited Dad's quiet but gentle nature. Quick to laugh or smile. As dependable as the foundations adhering the house to the cliff beneath it.

"I have a spreadsheet," Mom answered.

"I hope this geekiness doesn't infect me while we're all together." Slade ate a spoonful of the Italian-style chicken noodle soup that Mom had tossed into the slow cooker before they'd left for the airport. Slade would have just microwaved it, considering it was premade, but Mom had insisted the smell would permeate the house while they were gone and welcome them when they returned.

Mom was right. Especially with the brooding, chilly weather outside.

"I think we should just wing it." Slade offered her unwanted opinion, humor tugging on her mouth. "No planning. Just sort as we feel led." Mom and Reed's faces displayed alarm, and Slade chuckled. "You two make it too easy."

Slade's middle warmed when Mom laughed outright. Especially since she'd been weighed down by grief this morning.

Any time Mom or Reed stopped planning long enough to remember they were alive, Slade counted that as a victory.

"I read a few blogs with advice of how to go about cleaning out the house, so I tried to incorporate that into the plan." Mom shrugged, as if to say *I am who I am.*

Of course Mom had done research beforehand. Slade would expect no less.

"We started with the garage as suggested," Mom continued. "Because then it would be empty, and we could move furniture out there." Her nose wrinkled with frustration that Slade seconded. "That plan, so far, has been a little depressing."

"That's exactly the word I would use to describe it!" Slade was beginning to think they should have started with a smaller, simpler space. But using the garage as a staging area for what would eventually go to the used-furniture store did make sense.

"By the way, you two, be sure to tag what you want to keep as we're sorting."

"All right." And yet Reed didn't sound convinced. "I can't imagine there will be much."

Slade would take it all if she could, but she had nowhere to put anything and, really, no life to return to. What was she going to do about work? *No use worrying about that right now. Not like I can do anything about it at the moment.* Not without being home, and that was the last place she currently wanted to be.

Human resources hadn't even contacted her yet to discuss what had happened. She'd only gotten an automated form email from them confirming they'd received her communication. That was it. There'd been no outrage. No phone call to check on her. No admittance of guilt. If anything, Jude was probably spinning tales about her, and she wasn't even there to defend herself.

They'll do their job. Just hang tight. Slade had to believe that.

"We should celebrate that we're all together tonight," she suggested. "Order a—"

"Shouldn't we get to work on the house?" Reed responded. "I mean, that is why we're all here."

"You didn't let me finish. If we work on the garage again this afternoon, then maybe tonight we could haul boxes into the living room and sort papers and photos while we watch a movie and order pizza. Create a makeshift fun night out of it." Was Slade the only one who needed a little reward in the midst of work? What had she gotten herself into with these two?

"That's a good idea, Love. I like it." Mom reached across the table and squeezed Slade's hand.

Well. That was nice. Maybe Slade had been too hard on Mom in the car when she'd teased her about having a favorite child. But it was difficult not to let those quips slip out when Slade knew with certainty that her mother didn't believe in her the way Dad or her grandparents had. Even Aunt Lovetta was better at accepting Slade for who she was and not pushing her to be someone else.

"I can cut up the leftover veggies in the fridge too, so we have something healthy to go with the pizza."

Mom beamed. "That sounds perfect."

"Of course. Cooking isn't just on you while we're here. We can take turns and keep doing easy meals like sandwiches. You don't need the added pressure of taking care of us on top of this." Slade motioned to the house as thunder boomed.

It had been raining steadily since they'd sat down to the late lunch, but the weather was intensifying now. Slade had always loved a thunderstorm at this house. Something about it standing tall and strong on the cliff made it feel defiant, as if weather could never level it.

"That's helpful. I guess I just assume when we're all together that meal prep falls to me."

"When we were kids, sure. But we're adults now."

Reed scoffed.

Slade laughed. "Well, at least Reed is an adult. And I'm like a teenager who can warm things up in the microwave."

Mom's laugh was punctuated by a plunking sound. Much like her car, Slade ignored it.

"Mom, what did you mean about the birds eating out of the feeder when Reed called earlier this week?"

Drip.

"Yes." Reed paused with his spoon suspended above his bowl. "What was that about?"

"You used to love watching the birds at Grandad's feeders when you were little. When we got here, the bin of bird seed was sitting by the sliding glass door, so I filled the feeders." *Drip.* "It made me think of you because asking to fill them was one of the first things you'd do when you came to visit. Grandad must have let them go nearly empty before your arrival so you could have that job."

Reed's smile was nostalgic. "Sounds like something he would do."

Drip.

Reed stood and walked to the northwest corner of the room. He looked up, searching. Moisture must have smacked him in the forehead because he swiped and stepped away.

"It seems we have a leak."

"Maybe it's superficial," Slade offered.

The drip answered by doubling in speed.

Slade bowed her head to hide the surge of stress that sound created. Mom didn't need her added worry. The woman already had enough going on in the grief and house-purging departments.

Mom retrieved a bucket from beneath the sink and placed it under the continuing trickle of moisture, then returned to her seat and spooned another bite of soup.

Reed joined them at the table, shooting Slade a what-is-happening look. They both watched their mother for signs of panic, but either she was in shock or she was unruffled in the midst of this new development, because she didn't so much as cringe or furrow her brow.

Mom finally glanced up. "What?"

"You okay?" Concern laced Reed's question. "We'll help you figure this out. I'm sure there's a fix."

"I'm okay, honey. I've been through worse, haven't I?"

True.

"Panicking isn't going to help. In the morning, I'll find a roofer who can figure out what's going on. The blogs said to expect the unexpected. I'd say this falls into that category."

Slade finished the last of her soup and deposited her spoon into the empty bowl with a clatter.

"That, at least, the blogs were right about."

Chapter Six

It was refreshingly pleasant to be in a house with people again. Especially people who didn't despise the sound of him breathing, his supposedly heavy footsteps or any of the other completely random complaints Lindsey had lobbed at him like accusation bombs in the last five months.

Not that Reed was innocent. Plenty of stupid had flown out of his mouth too.

Once the fighting had begun, there wasn't an area of annoyance the two of them hadn't unhooked the grenade pin on.

Slade's suggestion that they watch a movie and sort this evening, after a stint purging the garage, had been a godsend. Reed had appreciated the film taking away any need for deep conversation. He'd expected some questions today from Mom and Slade, but he hadn't anticipated it would be so hard to come up with answers that weren't lies and yet didn't divulge anything he wasn't ready to reveal.

Tonight, Reed had scanned and uploaded documents to online storage while Slade and Mom had created Toss, Shred,

Keep and Scan piles. Even with their grandparents being deceased, they had to be careful not to let someone get their hands on their personal information.

Before coming, Reed had researched a company that specialized in digitizing and organizing family photos. He'd been planning to suggest the option to Mom, a little afraid the task would otherwise fall to him, but with the discovery of the roof leak, he'd stayed quiet. That upsetting development had to be weighing on her, though she hadn't mentioned it again.

With Grandad's passing, Mom had been thrown right back into the same role she'd had when Dad passed—organizer, problem solver, executor of the will. She had to be tired. Reed was, and he wasn't going through anything nearly as tragic as the death of a spouse followed by a parent.

Though a lot of people did consider divorce like a death.

Reed might not be at the threshold of divorce just yet, but it was hard for him not to fear it was coming.

Separation had a way of shining a megawatt flashlight on a person's worst insecurities. Was Lindsey dating other people and not telling him? It had only been a few weeks, but still. They hadn't set any ground rules. They'd just retreated to their respective corners in order to quell the constant bickering.

When Reed had heard about Slade's early arrival, he'd jumped at the chance to leave behind his stark studio apartment with nothing on the walls, a mattress on the floor and one lonely chair in front of the television. Because money had become an issue in their marriage, when Lindsey booted him out, Reed found something as affordable as possible—the basement apartment at the house of a friend who traveled consistently. JP had only been at his place four days out of the last nearly three weeks that Reed had lived there, and the apartment included a separate entrance from the house, so it wasn't a roommate situation…and yet Reed felt as if he'd backtracked ten years in success and life.

He hoped that escaping to Colorado might piece back together the shattered parts of him or at least give him a break from the constant stress he felt back in Naperville. And since he could work from anywhere, he didn't have to request extra time off. Having something to fill his afternoons and evenings—even if it was the daunting task of purging his grandparents' home—certainly sounded better than the lonely existence he'd been wallowing in back in Illinois.

For the first time in his life, Reed was drifting, listless, without a plan. Maybe he'd come up with one in Colorado, but if he didn't, what then?

Slade popped into his room and flopped onto the bed like the ten-year-old version of herself would have done. She was staying across the hall, just like when they were kids, and she'd already taken over the upstairs bathroom counter with all of her toiletries. Which had made Reed think of how grateful he would be to share a bathroom with his wife and all of her lotions and potions for everything from her face to her feet again.

Apparently, his brain was stuck in a circular pattern where all roads led back to Lindsey.

"Please come in. No need to knock." Reed slid a crocheted-covered hanger into his shirt.

"Who hangs up T-shirts?"

"I do."

She tucked a pillow behind her and scooted against the headboard. "You going to tell me now why you're actually here?"

Reed had been dreading this moment. He knew that Mom wouldn't push too hard. She tried to respect her children's privacy. She did her best to be supportive and not nosy, which Reed appreciated and recognized—not that Slade gave her credit for that. But where Mom would back off, give space, Slade was the opposite. She'd barge into his life like she'd just barged into his room. Slade would see right through him, and she wasn't afraid to push.

"I'm here to unload this house. You were right. It's a bigger job than we thought. So how is it that you can take so much time off work?"

Her lips pressed into a thin line. "My job ended."

The shirt he'd been hanging flopped to the floor. "Ended?" He retrieved it.

"Now you sound like Mom."

"Because I'm concerned about you?"

"Mom again."

Reed shook his head and finished hanging the last shirt. He returned to his suitcase and took out his running shoes, placing them under the dresser since there was no room in the closet. He'd had to shove things to the side so that he could fit in his shirts. Yet another line item on the sort-and-purge spreadsheet.

"What happened with the job? I thought you'd started something new."

Slade snorted. "An office job—at a prestigious law firm! With benefits! Because I'm an adult now, and I should start acting like one."

"I never said that."

"Benefits, among other things, are overrated. Trust me when I say that the job was done. I couldn't stay."

He analyzed her. Read the truth there. "You okay?"

Slade blinked rapidly, tears surfacing. "Yeah. Thanks for believing me."

"Not sure what I'm believing, since you're being elusive, but I'm always on your team."

The tense lines on her face softened. The moisture dissipated. Reed didn't press for more details because he wanted that same favor in return.

His phone buzzed from its perch on the dresser, and Reed silenced it.

"Was that Lindsey? Why didn't you answer? I can leave so you can talk to her."

Slade must have caught a glimpse of the phone screen before he declined the call. Lindsey's contact picture was a selfie of the two of them on their last vacation. Reed hadn't been able to make himself change it after moving out. That, somehow, would have felt too final.

"I'll call her back in a bit." Or maybe he wouldn't. She was the one who'd kicked him out. Who'd told him to go. Why should he be at her beck and call?

It was the hurt talking, he knew. But Reed had never done this before. He and Linds had always been so simple together. They'd made sense. They shared the same drive. Or so he'd thought. Now he understood her working so much at the end had been about so much more.

In the last handful of months, they'd done nothing but argue, shout, repeat. They couldn't agree on anything. Reed was still shocked it had all unfolded as quickly as it had. One day they'd been in love, planning for a future, and then shortly after Grandad's funeral, he'd found the credit card bill. In a snap, their mode of operation had changed to accusations, nitpicking, distrust.

"What have you been up to the past few months? I feel like I've barely talked to you, and you certainly didn't spill any updates on the drive today. Or tonight."

Since things had gone haywire with Lindsey, Reed had purposefully kept his communication with Slade to texts or very short conversations because he'd known that she would sense something was off with him.

"I've been working a lot." Reed had buried himself in his job hoping it would act as an antiseptic to the pain and as a way to feel like he was chipping away at the credit card debt... even though he was salaried. But if he was working, he wasn't spending. Which meant extra allotted to the card balance. He could only hope that Lindsey was determined to do the same, though it certainly wasn't a question he'd asked her lately.

Reed opened each dresser drawer in search of an empty one.

Unsurprisingly, they were all full. He pulled the top drawer out of the dresser completely and set it on the bedspread by Slade's legs, which were clothed in colorful leggings she'd partnered with a fitted T-shirt.

"Would it be wrong to dump this drawer right into the trash? There can't be anything of value in here."

"I know. But Mom wants to sort. She's concerned we're going to miss something if we don't."

"Like a rat or a mouse? Or an ancient receipt?" Reed opened the second drawer and unceremoniously chucked the first drawer's contents into it. He had to shove everything around to make it fit, and even then, he barely got the drawer to slide back into its slot. "I might be regretting my early arrival." After reinstalling the now-empty first drawer, he retrieved his pants from his suitcase and placed them inside.

"Speaking of being elusive." The pillow Slade tossed at him bounced off his back.

He moved his running shorts next. "Is it really that strange for me to come early when you said the project is massive?"

Slade's eyebrows reached for her blond-white-silver hairline. "Yep."

Was there any way around this conversation with his sister? Probably not. But Reed might be able to buy some time.

"I'm not ready to talk about anything yet." Reed managed to wedge his empty suitcase into the overwhelmingly full closet. He wouldn't be the least bit surprised if the contents came crashing down in the middle of the night, startling him.

He turned and met Slade's inquisitive, concerned gaze head-on. She was so much stronger and wiser than people gave her credit for. Than she even gave herself credit for.

"I can understand that. But I'm here if you need me."

The panic that had squeezed Reed's throat shut when he'd imagined having to unload every bit of his shame and misery right now subsided.

"Same." He was as there for Slade as she was for him. And he trusted her. He just wasn't sure he trusted himself to be able to dive into what was really going on...or to deal with the fact that he'd very possibly failed at the one thing Dad had given him the best possible example of.

"What are you thinking about this?" Slade held up a yellowed scrap of newspaper that she must have brought into the room with her.

Reed took the article and scanned the short piece she'd read to him over the phone. "I haven't thought about it." Except... that wasn't 100 percent true. He had wondered how something of this magnitude had evaded their knowledge all these years. But then logic had resurfaced. It had happened before they were born. And the summers they'd stayed here, they'd been mere children. Of course no one had mentioned it to them. And it *was* 100 percent true that Reed had too many legitimate problems occupying his mind and energy. Some old article about a body found thirty-four years ago was not at the top of his concern list.

"Do you think Mom told me everything when I asked her about it?"

"I do. What would there be to hide? You think Gran or Grandad had something to do with this?" Reed poked the article, causing a crease.

Slade took it back from him and smoothed it against the bedspread. "Of course not."

"Or *Mom*? She would have been in her twenties. She was already married to Dad at that point and didn't live in Dillon anymore. She probably didn't know more than what the paper said. And Aunt Lovetta didn't move back here after college, so she wouldn't have been around either."

"I'm not saying anyone in the family was *involved*, but I do find it strange that Mom wasn't more curious or concerned about this happening basically on her parents' property."

"I'm sure she was at the time, but if nothing came of an investigation, then there must not be more to it. Should probably just let it go. Mom likely hasn't thought about it in decades."

"I can see that you're going to be of no help."

"Please tell me you're not going to go all Nancy Drew about this." Reed's tank only had fumes remaining, and he needed those to get him through each day. He didn't have the capacity for his sister's cynicism and unquenchable curiosity regarding a past death that had no connection to their present.

"I just want to know what happened. It's odd that you don't."

Slade's phone buzzed repeatedly.

"You going to get that?"

"Nope." She took it from her pocket and ignored the call. "Phone calls are never good news. They can text if they need me."

"That's actually not the craziest thing you've ever said."

"What is?"

"I'm going to need a spreadsheet."

Chapter Seven

Marin had assumed that if she began making phone calls about the leaking roof first thing in the morning, she'd quickly have answers or at least an appointment scheduled for someone to come out within a few days. It was a roof after all—rather important!

Instead, she'd left four voicemails, and the three calls that were answered had been disheartening. Apparently a hailstorm had blown through in May that had caused major damage. Everyone was backed up because of the massive needs in the area.

She could be added to a waitlist, though. Five months for one company, fourteen weeks for the other, and the third hadn't even given her an estimate of how long it would take just to come out and assess. None were viable options.

There were, no doubt, a few companies in town who were storm chasers, but how could Marin trust them? She had no idea what was going on with the roof and could easily be taken for a ride.

Which left her no choice in the matter but to reach out to Garrett. A massive sigh followed, instantly replaced by chagrin and guilt. The man didn't deserve her angst. Not after all he'd done for her. Certainly not after what she'd done to him.

"What other option do I have?" Marin spoke out loud, thankful the kids were elsewhere and not overhearing her one-sided conversation. Reed had set up a workstation in his room—commandeering a small flat-screen television as an additional computer screen—and Slade was purging the closet in her bedroom.

The last thing Marin wanted to do was solicit assistance from Garrett, but if anyone knew how to figure out the roof in a timely manner, it would be him. After high school, Garrett began working for his father's construction firm and quickly went up the ranks, eventually running it alongside his dad and taking over when he retired.

According to Marin's parents, Garrett had grown the business astronomically.

If her parents' estate had excess funds remaining, then Marin could wait for one of the other companies to fix the roof. But dwindling reserves and Lovetta's demand that they equally contribute toward the carrying costs on the house if their parents' money ran out made that option impossible.

Marin refused to let her sister dip into her modest savings, which were a cushion in case she required additional time off work due to her illness. They also provided the option to participate in alternative medical treatments that insurance didn't cover.

All roads led Marin back to the man who had the skills to fix the leaky roof and who had already offered his assistance if needed.

Was there a time in her life Marin could get through a crisis *without* relying on Garrett?

In the kitchen drawer, Marin found the small notebook where

her parents had kept phone numbers. The whole house felt like someone had pressed Pause on her parents' lives, and at any moment, they might return. More than once, Marin had glanced onto the deck expecting to see her father sitting in one of the Adirondack chairs. It was equal parts painful and endearing to be here.

Marin craved putting off the phone call to Garrett as much as she craved Ralph being present during the upcoming retirement years they'd planned to enjoy together, but she metaphorically pulled on her big-girl britches and dialed the number listed for his business.

Surely the man wouldn't answer his work line. Surely he had someone else for that.

And if he does, they aren't going to do me any favors. Not like Garrett would.

As the phone rang, Marin paced between the dining table and the couch. The lake was a brilliant turquoise today, the smooth surface giving the illusion that yesterday's inclement weather had been a figment of their imaginations.

The warped wood floor beneath the bucket, though—evidence that this wasn't the first time the roof had dripped rainwater tears—was a jolt back to reality.

"This is Garrett."

The man could do no right by her. First she didn't want him to answer, then she did. And now that he'd fielded the call himself, she was irritated. Marin felt as unsettled as she had during the tumultuous, hormonal, menopause years.

"Hello? Can I help you?"

"Garrett, it's Marin."

A beat of silence expanded. "Did you run into an issue with the house?"

Was she that obvious? "Yes, actually. I wasn't expecting you to answer. I thought I'd have to go through your office to get to you."

"This is my cell."

"My parents had it listed as… Did they just bug you on this whenever they needed anything?"

"Nothing they did ever qualified as bugging me."

Of course not. How very Garrett. No wonder they'd loved him so much.

"I know you said to reach out if we needed anything." Marin wasn't sure why she was stalling. Garrett had a business. She would hire that business. This didn't have to feel so personal, if not for the fact that she was basically asking him for a favor. Asking him to slip them in before or alongside another customer or job, no doubt.

"And I meant it. What's the deal, Mar? You sound weird."

She barely resisted responding with a very junior high *you sound weirder* in response. "The roof started leaking yesterday afternoon."

"How much? Like a steady stream or a drip?"

"Drip. But a consistent one. I called around for a roofer or someone to come check it out, but everyone's booked."

"Offensive. I offered to help you with anything needed on the house, didn't I?"

Chagrined, Marin stopped pacing, her eyelids shuttering. "You did. I just…" What was there to say? That she didn't want him around her or her children? Garrett had done nothing wrong. He'd done everything right, but he'd still been the one to suffer.

"Well, since I'm your last resort, that tells me how desperate you are."

"It has nothing to do with you. It's just that the kids—"

"Mar, I'm messing with you."

Oh. Her breath rushed out.

"I'm booked today, but I'll swing by on my way home tonight."

Of course he would rescue them. And Marin absolutely could

not be bitter about it since that's exactly what she was asking him to do!

"Thank you. I really appreciate you helping us out."

"Don't thank me yet." His tone brokered amusement. "You haven't seen the bill. And we have no idea what's going on with your parents' roof."

"So, after you give me the lowdown, I can wax praises?"

"After I diagnose and fix, you can send all the accolades my way."

Despite the stress created by the setback with the roof, Marin laughed.

Diagnose and fix. Garrett made it sound so easy. But then, maybe it would be. For him.

Marin might be able to share his optimism if she could be assured that this was the only hiccup with the house purge they'd experience along the way. But she knew better.

Life—and anything involving Garrett—never went according to plan.

Chapter Eight

Slade was on the deck, her body folded in half and resembling limber kitchen tongs, her nose at shin level.

Reed muscled open the ornery and outdated sliding glass door and stepped outside. "Do you ever just get stuck like that?" The cool evening temperature was a refreshing change compared to the heat and humidity back in Naperville.

"Nope." Slade popped her earbuds out, sliding them into a small side pocket on her leggings. She lifted her arms toward the sky and then glided back into the previous position. "You should do this with me. Nothing soothes the body like yoga. We're all going to need something to fight off stress while we're here." Her head gave an agitated shake, counteracting the tension relief she'd claimed to be experiencing. "I can't believe the garage took so long. I don't think Mom had that on her spreadsheet for four days."

"Technically, it wasn't four. You guys picked me up yesterday, and that took up a chunk of the day."

Her upside-down mouth quirked. "True. You did delay us."

"And then this morning, you worked on your room while Mom dealt with the roof, and I set up my workstation. At least we got it finished this afternoon." They'd even managed to sell a handful of tools to a guy who'd just moved to the area and get Mom's loaded vehicle to Resaddled—the Summit County thrift store that supported rehabilitating rescued horses—before it closed.

"True." Slade slid her hands under her toes in a position that Reed would call Downward Facing Pain-in-hands-and-feet. "Yoga would rid your body of some of that tension making your shoulders look like they're attached to your ears."

Insulting. Shouldn't Slade be concentrating on her own issues? There was an air of woundedness surrounding his sister that Reed had never witnessed with her before, even in grief.

"I'm going for a run. I'm dealing with it in my own way." He resisted a teenage huff. "And my shoulders take offense at your judgment of them." Reed glanced at his reflection in the sliding glass door. "Glad to know I look like a body builder without the muscles." Maybe he'd finally uncovered the reason Lindsey had kicked him out. He rolled his neck, creating enough clunking and crackling to mimic static on an AM radio station and effectively ruling Slade correct on her assumptions about the strain his body was under.

"Your shoulders should thank me for swooping to their defense. Sure you don't want to join me?" She placed the palms of her hands onto her yoga mat and moved into a stretch that elongated her upper body and extended her legs. "I'll teach you some simple positions."

"Thanks, but no thanks." He tempered the rejection with a grin. Simple for Slade would not be simple for Reed. His body didn't move in the fluid ways his sister's did. He was more of a homemade robot with rusty joints in need of WD-40. But running? That made sense to him. He used to run because it kept him in shape, but ever since the trouble had started between him and Lindsey, he'd been running to subdue some of the angst constantly threading through his system. Angst that was consistently growing, like a trashcan that overflowed day after day and received no maintenance, no relief.

Slade switched poses effortlessly, this time to downward-facing dog—one of the only yoga positions Reed could actually name. Slade had taught yoga on and off over the years. At one point, she'd entertained the idea of starting an online channel, but due to her complete disdain for anything technological, she'd eventually decided against it. To edit her own videos would have been excruciating for her, and to hire someone would have been too pricey when she was starting out.

Slade had held so many jobs that Reed often teased her there wasn't anything she hadn't tried or couldn't do. And he believed that second part. If his sister put her mind to something, she'd figure out a way to at least attempt, if not succeed, at it.

"Mom was acting so weird this afternoon while we finished the garage, wasn't she? Chipper one second, quiet and brooding the next."

"Probably because you were interrogating her."

Slade had attempted to bring up the article again to Mom while they were working. *Who was the man? Why was he on Gran and Grandad's property?*

But Mom's responses had been rote and aligned with the ones she'd given Slade previously.

Either she didn't know anything, or she didn't want to talk about it.

"I just don't understand how she doesn't know any more details. I searched for follow-up articles while cleaning out the closet in my room this morning, but nothing surfaced." Slade stretched her right leg into the air behind her. Reed winced at both the position—which he could never imagine attempting— and the fact that Slade was still contemplating that article and hunting for additional information.

Technically it was his fault that Slade didn't understand his lack of capacity to expend energy on a guy who'd died thirty-four years ago, because Reed hadn't admitted what was going on in his life to her.

But she obviously had a clue something was up with him.

Maybe he should be thankful for that article since it took the spotlight off him.

"I'm sure Mom's just focused on all there is to do with the house. She has to be overwhelmed, especially with the added stress of the roof leaking."

Reed wasn't sure if Slade's exhale was part of her yoga or a huff of annoyance at herself or Mom—or maybe him.

"You're right."

"I'm sorry, what did you just say?"

She laughed and switched to her left leg.

"Earlier Mom said someone was stopping by about the roof tonight," Reed said. "Started with a G, I think."

Slade dropped from the yoga position into a heap on the deck. She moved to sitting and wrapped arms around her propped knees. "Did she say his name was Garrett?"

"Maybe. Not sure. Did you hurt yourself?"

"No, I'm fine. What else did she say?"

"Nothing. Why? Do you know this guy?"

"Not really. If he's who I'm thinking of, I met him the other day. He's a neighbor. He stopped by, offered to help with the house if we needed anything." The skin around her eyes tightened almost imperceptibly. Reed had spent much of his existence deciphering his sister's responses. He would categorize this one as curious with a side of suspicion.

"Wait—so he offered to help with the house and now he *is* helping with the house? How strange."

"I don't appreciate your sarcasm, brother."

"Isn't yoga supposed to make you less cynical?"

"Making someone less cynical is not one of yoga's great claims.

Although…it's not impossible, since it's good for you both phys-ically and mentally." Her arms lifted above her head in a fluid motion. "I mean, look at me. I'm the picture of peaceful, calm energy."

"Except for when your inner detective comes out, which is nothing but analytical and distrusting energy." She laughed and gave an unapologetic shrug. "Which explains why you're suspicious of a neighbor who offered to help actually helping." She inclined her head in begrudging admission. "And also why you're annoyed with Mom."

"Not annoyed exactly…more curious as to why she's being vague."

"About what?"

"Everything! The neighbor. The body."

"Did you ever think that maybe you're reading into things a bit?"

Her cheeks creased with a saucy smile. "Nope. Not once."

Reed laughed. "If you and Mom can't get along, this is going to be a long couple of weeks."

"We've been doing pretty well, actually. Outside of this af-ternoon." When Mom hadn't forked over any additional de-tails about the article, Slade had turned a bit irritable for the remainder of the sorting. "Don't you think we're doing okay?"

"You have been from what I can tell. But questioning her about everything isn't going to help."

"I'm not questioning her about everything."

"Just the body. And the neighbor."

"Right." Slade's expression morphed from amused to ear-nest. "Of course you're not going to understand, Reed. She doesn't question everything about you." Along with Slade's insightfulness, she had a sensitivity that definitely played into her relationship with their mother. She might portray an image to the world that nothing bothered her. That she was a yoga-loving, sunshine-and-flip-flops kind of girl, but Reed knew she'd learned to live without their mother's approval—at least in her mind—because she believed she'd never had it.

"She doesn't—"

"She does. And I'm okay. For the most part." Slade rubbed her thumb over the small butterfly tattoo that decorated the inside of her wrist—the first thing she'd done when she turned eighteen. One on a list of many things that Slade had chosen to do that Mom hadn't understood or agreed with. Around the same age Slade decided to use her middle name, his sister developed an I'm-going-to-take-on-the-world-by-myself-and-no-one-can-tell-me-what-to-do edge. Reed could understand how hard that would be for a parent. That Dad had weathered Slade's stubborn—sometimes offensive—strength better than Mom was understandable.

"Mom doesn't look at you the same way she does me. You're not winning this one." She held up a finger, effectively cutting him off before he could speak. "You can defend all you want, but it's the truth."

Maybe Slade was right. They'd had the same upbringing. Same love. Same parents. And yet they were completely different people who'd taken completely different paths.

Their growing up years had been filled with more than a few arguments, but once they'd become adults, they'd chosen to get along well. Reed was glad to have Slade on his side because he wouldn't want to go up against her.

He had half a mind to warn Mom that Slade was about to do some digging, but he would much rather live in a bubble where he pretended that his sister would let this stuff go and the three of them would simply clean out Gran and Grandad's house, sell it and return to their lives, their relationships better than they'd ever been, their home situations somehow repaired in their absence.

Right. Like that would ever happen. Marriage issues took

work. Reed would never deny that. But when you'd already tried all the fixes and had come up short, what then?

His traps muscles tightened like a thousand pulleys controlled them, once again proving his sister correct.

"I came out here to tell you I was going on a run, not to get into a fight."

"We're not fighting. We're having a discussion."

True. And Reed should know the difference since he'd certainly had his fair share of fights in the last handful of months, and on a scale of one to ten, this conversation registered at a one. Everything with Linds had been in the eight-to-ten range or off the charts. It had been exhausting living like that—with all the battling and anger and shots fired. Turned out living without her was just as hard in a different capacity—a lonely, empty, confusing one.

"Go for your run." Slade shooed him. "I don't want to talk to you anyway. You interrupted my namaste."

Reed laughed as he headed for the deck stairs. At least with Slade he was safe. They might disagree about something, but they had each other's backs.

Evidently they both had things going on in their lives that they weren't ready to talk about. And who knew—maybe Mom did too. Maybe they were all messes converging on this house in the hopes of some sort of healing. As if Gran and Grandad could reach down from heaven and fix it all with a tap or a touch. But even if that was the case—even if they were all dealing with something—Reed would like to believe that they'd all be okay. That somehow they'd make it through their respective storms.

And if not?

He'd add that to the list—better yet spreadsheet—of questions he didn't have answers to.

Chapter Nine

The sound of a truck grabbed Marin's attention as it rumbled toward the house, then downshifted. Since Marin already had on her wooden-soled sandals—she'd reached the age where being on her feet all day either required arch support or warranted a leg cramp in the middle of the night—she stepped outside in time to see Garrett ease into the driveway as if his decade-old Chevrolet was a brand-new, low-profile sports car. Back in high school, Garrett had never been the kind to go flying down the interstate or tearing into the school lot. He'd always stuck to his own pace and operated in a calm, consistent manner. Even staying in town after what had happened with Vince was a testament to his steadiness.

Decreasing evening temperatures kissed Marin's bare arms as she moved to greet Garrett by his driver's door. She'd worn capri-length coral pants today with a sleeveless navy top. Even though Dillon's heat didn't compare to Arizona's, the seventy-four-degree weather coupled with the high-altitude sun had still warmed the house considerably.

Back when her parents' home was built, almost no one installed air conditioning in the mountains, but in the last couple decades, it had become a far more typical convenience.

Marin didn't plan to dive into whether it was Slade's renewed interrogation about Vince this afternoon, the temperature, or Garrett's impending arrival that had her operating as flushed as a tomato on a grill.

When Slade brought up the article again while they were finishing the garage, Marin had endeavored to keep her answers smooth, emotionless, and matching the ones she'd given her daughter previously. Slade had eventually dropped the line of questioning, but a *tick-tick-tick* had taken up residence in Marin's gut, like an impending bomb that would at some point detonate.

Garrett exited his truck and latched the door behind him. Slade was on the far side of the deck doing yoga, and Marin had peeked out and confirmed that she had in earbuds, so in this momentary cocoon, it was just the two of them with no concerns about Slade—or anyone—grasping at threads.

"Hi. I'll show you the leak."

He followed her into the house and toward the end of the kitchen that butted up to the main-level bathroom.

But instead of inspecting the ceiling, his vision stayed on her. "Hi, Garrett. How was your day?"

Marin had gotten right down to business, hadn't she?

"Technically, I did say hi." Though it hadn't exactly been an exuberant greeting. Sometimes, Marin had the tendency to focus so intensely on work—especially when her to-do list was long—that she left her social skills locked in a drawer.

"You did. *Technically.*" He emphasized the word, his mouth easing into a full-fledged grin that was equal parts familiar—past—and foreign—present.

Marin had shared her first kiss with this man. She'd thought, during their sweet, innocent high school years, that she would marry him. In the way teens imagine everything as long-term, everything as larger than life.

Their friendship had been sturdy, though, Marin was confident of that. Otherwise, Garrett would never have been able to support her in the way he had when she came home that summer.

"My day was long, thanks for asking," he continued, his tone playful. "Keep thinking one of these days I'm going to retire or at least cut down in hours, but I can't seem to escape this business."

"That's probably because everyone in town thinks they can call you and you'll show up at the drop of a hat." Her lips curved to match his. "Like Thelma and Stu's daughter. Demanding, that one."

Garrett's chuckle was as comforting as her mother's famous strawberry shortcake.

"And how was your day, Marin?"

If only she could truly level with him about her day—her concerns over the house, over Slade's discovery, over her children. But Marin had placed Garrett in that role once before and it had burned them both terribly. She couldn't return to the scene of that crime.

Plus, there were too many secrets—including his—that needed to stay buried about the past. For everyone's sakes.

"Slade and I lost our mojo from earlier in the week. She's not happy with me."

He nodded gravely. "Breathe wrong? Give her advice she didn't ask for, or better yet, not give her advice when you should have somehow known she wanted it?"

Marin laughed. "You should be a comedian for the nuances of adult children."

The corners of his eyes creased, the wrinkles he'd gained over the years somehow adding to his appeal. Garrett radiated calm comfort—with himself, his surroundings, and somehow, even her. Was it possible that he'd actually become an even better version of himself with age? It was the kind of thing a person strived for but so often didn't accomplish. Marin liked to think she'd morphed into a better version of herself too, but considering that she was here with her adult children and yet afraid of all they could find out about her and their father and even Garrett... Maturity did not seem an apt description.

Lovetta had once asked Marin why she didn't just level with the kids about past indiscretions, and Marin had fumbled to answer.

When was the right time to drop a bomb on your children? To ruin the perceptions they'd held their whole lives? Did you pencil that in your planner for when they were six or ten or twenty? Marin had no idea, and while sharing her issues was one thing—scary though that may be—the events of the past didn't just involve her. She wasn't ready to make the choice for someone else about what was known or not known regarding their actions, or lack thereof.

And so, she stayed silent.

Even if Marin were at liberty to speak openly, her children knowing the truth would only cause them pain. Sometimes, there were no winners. Sometimes, one path wasn't better than the other. It was simply another route. Either held potholes. Either could become a crumbling bridge in an instant.

Over the years, Marin buried things so deeply that she almost, *almost* managed to forget. Or at least could pretend to forget. But being here awakened all of it. Once they finished the house and returned to the regularly scheduled programming of their normal lives, Marin would be able to rebury the past and move forward again.

Right?

Garrett's analytical gaze traced the ceiling. "I need to get up there to see what's going on." That teasing glint focused on her. "You coming?"

She laughed. "Absolutely not. I'd probably break a hip."

His responding chuckle warmed her in a much different way than the afternoon heat had. "You'd do nothing of the sort."

They reached the screen door that led toward the driveway just as Slade came in from the deck through the sliding glass door.

Garrett paused to greet her. "Good to see you again, Slade." He gave his trademark head nod—quick, assertive. The equivalent of a cowboy tipping his hat. "I like that you use your grandparents' last name as your first. Feels like a great way to honor them and keep their memories alive."

At the mention of her grandparents, Slade visibly softened. "Thank you. I love going by their name." Her vision bounced to Marin, her mouth curving. "Mom fought for it for my middle name, so she deserves all the credit."

Marin inclined her head in mock acceptance.

"We're headed out to check the roof leak. Your mother is jonesing to get up there and see what's going on."

Slade gave an amused scoff. "Oh really?"

"Nope." Garrett's eyes sparked with mirth. "Not even close to the truth."

"We should get going so we don't hold you up all evening, Garrett." They'd racked up enough Garrett-Slade time by now to qualify as polite, hadn't they? Why continue? Based on Slade's probes after she first met Garrett, Marin would assume her daughter's radar regarding the man was still flashing red.

Throw in the article Slade had found, and the whole scenario was kindling awaiting a match.

Marin moved past Garrett to open the screen door, inhaling his clean, soapy scent. How did he smell the same after all these years? Suddenly, Marin was sixteen and throwing rocks into the lake with him. Seventeen and having him help her sneak into the house later than her curfew. Eighteen and bawling about heading off to college without him.

Garrett probably believed that Marin had met Ralph at school and never spent another moment thinking about him. If so, he was wrong. Breaking up with Garrett had been excruciating. Marin had been torn between two worlds. But when she met Ralph, something inside of her had caught and held on. And in all the years they'd spent together, that same magnetism never ebbed.

How could Marin have explained to Garrett what she hadn't even understood herself at the time?

She'd wounded him deeply. And yet here he was once again.

Garrett exited through the door Marin held open. Slade still had her fingers wrapped around the handle of the sliding glass door.

"Is that thing stuck again?" Marin nodded toward the door, but Slade didn't answer. Her vision tracked Garrett's departure. "Anything on your mind, Love?"

"What? No. It's good. Door's fine." She cracked a reassuring smile. "Sorry. I just finished my yoga, and I'm in that buzzing stage where my whole body feels like it was just on a vacation. My brain's a little checked out right now."

"Wow. I had no idea yoga was so...impressive."

Slade brightened. "It's fantastic." Her hands clasped in front of her. "You should try it with me, Mom! I would adapt poses for you. It would be really good for your RA. It's great for reducing inflammation."

Marin wasn't sure she could add another thing to her plate while in Colorado, even it if would benefit her health.

"I'll think about it." She didn't want to refuse immediately and offend her daughter. Especially since she seemed to do that without even trying.

"Okay. I was thinking I'd make grilled cheese for dinner. Is that too simple?"

"That sounds perfect." Marin could definitely go for comfort food tonight, even if carbs had become her enemy over the years. "Thanks, Love." She stepped outside and found Garrett situating a ladder against the side of the house.

"Do you need me to steady that?"

"No, it should be fine. You head up first and then I'll follow." He deadpanned so well that Marin's mouth popped open. The excuse on her tongue was quickly cut off by Garrett's laughter—much deeper and more boisterous than it had been inside. "You make it too easy, Mar." He climbed up the ladder and onto the roof with the agility of a man half his age.

"Shouldn't you have some kind of safety gear?" she called up.

"I would if I needed to." His answer floated down. "Not my first rodeo."

Right. Garrett had done this before. Marin was the one in uncharted waters. The one nearly drowning in uncertainty. And Garrett was doing the rescuing, per the usual.

Marin paced a small strip of the driveway near the bottom of the ladder while Garrett was on the roof. She stayed close in case he needed assistance—with what, she wasn't sure. Finding the leak? Catching him if he tumbled off the roof? She was as inept in this situation as white shoes during mud season.

Normally, Marin walked every day, but since her arrival in Colorado, her exercise had been lacking. She could feel that deficiency in her joints and stress levels. Walking helped not only her RA but her mind. If she was going to survive this time and remain healthy, she really did have to take care of herself.

Both of her children were doing exactly that—Reed with running, Slade with yoga. Marin was proud they'd developed such good habits, especially with the levels of stress they must experience. The world was much faster paced and more cutthroat than the one she'd lived in as a young adult. Yet even with far fewer pressures, she and Ralph had managed to mess up so much.

"Found rusty nails," Garrett called out.

"Is that good or bad?"

"Means I'm getting close."

A minute later, he climbed down the ladder.

Marin met him at the base. "How bad is it?"

"There were a couple of underdriven nails causing issues. The good news is you need the whole roof replaced."

Marin's jaw dropped. "How, exactly, is that good news?"

"You'll have a brand-new roof when you sell. Insurance will cover it since there's damage from the hailstorm. Everyone else around here is getting theirs replaced. I should have thought to get up there and check it earlier." A car drove past, and both Marin and Garrett waved in greeting. "If I had, then I might have found that patched spot before it started leaking."

"Insurance would be a godsend." It made sense that the roof had storm damage just like everyone else's did. "Wait—did you say patched spot?"

Garrett gave a definitive nod.

"My dad patched it, didn't he?"

"Looks like it. He just missed a couple nails."

The patching sounded exactly like something her father would have been determined to conquer himself. Unfortunately, in his older age, he'd obviously not completed the job with his usual precision. Which had led them here.

"He was always so determined to live just like he'd always lived."

"It served him well, didn't it?"

"Except for the fact that he's not here and the roof is leaking, sure."

"His demise had nothing to do with how he lived."

"You're right." Marin pressed a finger against the corner of her right eye to quell the pesky twitch that had started in Colorado. "I'm not upset with him. He lived a good, long, happy life. I'm just—"

"Overwhelmed by the project at hand. And grieving."

"Exactly." Garrett had a knack for understanding her, that

was for sure. "This is something we should be doing, right? Lovetta and I shouldn't just leave it for the buyer?"

"I'd definitely do it. Especially since insurance should cover it. If you push it off on to the buyer, they're going to gouge you on price."

"But what if someone comes in and tears this place down?"

"There's a lot for sale at the other end of the street. If someone wants to start from scratch, that's where they'll do it. I would imagine someone might remodel the bones of the house, or even add on to the northeast side, but I don't think it will get demolished."

Right. Well, Garrett would know. "So, we fix the roof."

"Yep. It'll be fine. We do this all the time. You just pick out the color and my crew will handle the rest."

Because Garrett would take care of them…and the house. It was in his nature. Probably why he'd gotten himself into trouble thirty-four years ago.

There was no proof that he was involved. Why does your mind always go there?

Because he hadn't been where he'd said he was. How would Marin's mind *not* jump into the deep end?

"How far out are we talking on the roof?" Marin braced herself. If it took months, would they have to wait to put the house on the market until after?

"There's a shingle we can get quickly. Could have them by next week if you're not too picky on color."

Next week? Tears materialized, and Marin blinked quickly to combat them. "I absolutely promise I will not be picky on color. If you told me what you recommended right now, I'd sign on the dotted line without even seeing it."

His stubbled cheeks creased. "That's a terrible idea. I could sell you pink shingles."

"Except you would never do that. Getting shingles that fast is fantastic. How far beyond that would the install be?"

"We could start right away."

Wait. What? "But every other company I called was booked out for months. How are you not?"

"Again, you remind me of the lengths you went to in order to avoid me." His sage green eyes twinkled with teasing. "We are booked out for months."

"But—"

"I'm bumping another house back. Their roof isn't leaking. They'll be fine to wait. Won't even know the difference. Every construction company around here is scrambling. People know the work will get done well with us, so they're content to wait."

"Garrett, you can't do that!"

"Actually, I can. It's one of the perks of owning a business. Along with the many vacations, the light stress load, the low liability."

She cracked a watery smile at his banter. "This is too much." Marin's declaration was heavy with pieces of the past. He'd kept her head above water that summer. He'd been her floatation device and her lifeboat and her medic.

A rush of warmth enveloped the lonely parts of Marin. After Ralph's passing, she'd had to keep going. Had to take care of things. Marin hadn't realized how much she'd missed that feeling of knowing it wasn't all on her until Garrett had provided it for her just now.

"How can I ever repay you for this?" *You've repaid him all these years by keeping quiet.* True. And Marin would continue to do so. The details missing from that night were ones that never needed to come to light as far as she was concerned. Ones she didn't care to know. Ever.

"Dinner." He carried the ladder to his truck and loaded it, then faced her. "I'm not asking for anything romantic. Just thought it would be nice to catch up. I don't know about you, but I could use a friend."

That's what she'd said to him all those years ago. *I could use a friend.* Marin remembered exactly where she'd been standing when Garrett stopped by. She'd been staring out over the deck railing wearing a ratty T-shirt and pajama pants, a cup of coffee having gone cold in her hands. Garrett had asked what he could do, and Marin had whispered those words.

And true to his, that's exactly what he'd been to her. She was the one who'd crossed a line.

"I'll think about it."

Those effervescent eyes of his seemed to dance with a level of mirth and joy that Marin wasn't sure she had the ability to feel anymore. After three of her people passing, she'd settled for functioning, for moving through each day. She'd forgotten the kind of living Garrett embodied was even possible.

He opened the door to his truck and paused to deliver a roguish grin before climbing inside. "I'll take that as a yes."

Chapter Ten

Slade's hands trembled as she scanned the text conversation again. She'd never expected her exit from Duerson, Wilshire and Boerne to affect anyone but herself. Evidently, she'd been sorely mistaken.

She slipped the phone into her legging pocket and entered the kitchen to find her mom pouring coffee into a vintage ivory mug.

Mom held up the pot. "You want?"

"No, thanks." Slade couldn't handle the strong liquid right now. Not when her stomach was churning like Boca Ciega Bay during a hurricane. "Mom, do you mind if I borrow your car this morning? Do you have anywhere you need to be?" Slade slunk to a seat at the table and watched her mother bustle around the space—taking a cutting board out of the drawer, washing a pineapple in the sink.

In contrast, Slade's limbs felt weighted. As if her mother's simple movements were more than she could manage right now.

"I don't mind. My only plans are here." Mom nodded toward the combined kitchen and living room space. Swatches of morning light swept across the wood floor and tumbled over the couch and loveseat.

Slade was tempted to curl onto the vintage furniture and huddle under Gran's quilt, but considering it was a gorgeous, bright, sixty-eight-degree morning, that would raise major suspicions regarding her physical and or mental health.

"Thanks. I'm going to meet Keely for breakfast in Silverthorne." Slade slid her hands into the front pocket of her thin, sea blue, softest-thing-she'd-ever-owned hoodie, which she'd paired with calf-length leggings and flip-flops. It would likely be too warm to wear the sweatshirt all day, so she had a tank top underneath, but after Nora's text, she'd been unable to resist comfort clothing and a layer of protection from the world.

"Who's Keely again?"

"She's the one who gave me a ride here from the airport. We bonded on the drive. I really like her." And Slade had learned, the older she got, how unusual it was to click with someone from the start and not experience any red flags.

"That's right. I'm glad you're getting out of here for a bit. Do you want any fruit before you go?" A round of loud, cheerful bird chatter floated in through the cracked-open sliding glass door, and Mom glanced outside, her lips curving. "They've been doing that since I got up."

Slade barely resisted sticking her head outside and releasing a screech that would send the cheerful little creatures scattering. Behavior which would *definitely* bring her mental capacities into question.

"No thanks on the fruit." She wasn't even sure she would be able to eat breakfast. Slade's last-minute invitation to Keely this morning had been purely out of the need to distract herself. An attempt to shove aside the text conversation she'd engaged in with Nora when she first woke, which had derailed so quickly.

At first Nora had just been checking in.

Hey! Missed you at work this week. Assuming you're on vacation and not sick? Hope you're okay.

It had taken Slade a few minutes to formulate a response.

Not sick. I actually left the firm due to some issues. Sorry I didn't let anyone know. It happened really fast.

Slade had gotten friendly with a few women at work, Nora being one of them. And while they didn't hang outside the office, they often ate lunch together or stopped to chat at each other's desks. Slade had contemplated letting that group of women know she'd quit, but she hadn't known how to formulate that announcement without diving into the why behind it.

And she'd been nowhere near ready for that conversation.

Oh no! What kind of issues?

Slade had stared at the screen, unsure of how to answer. Eventually, Nora had handled it for her.

Issues that had something to do with Jude Wilshire? Because he's been acting really strange since you've been gone.

Slade's thudding heart had crawled into her throat.

Yes. How's he been acting?

Like he's everyone's best friend and the world's most caring boss.

So, either he knew she'd communicated with HR, or he was just preemptively shining up his reputation in order to disprove their interaction had ever happened if she were to say something.

He DISGUSTS me.

In her anger, Slade had let the tidbit slip without intending to. Nora could be trusted, but Slade had already made so many mistakes that she didn't want to add to that list by revealing something she shouldn't to one of her coworkers.

Since her arrival in Colorado, Slade had done some research online regarding Jude's advances. She'd signed up for a free advice booklet from a law firm in Florida that handled workplace issues like hers. It detailed what to do and what not to do in a situation like she'd encountered. Amazingly, painfully, she could check the box next to every wrong move.

If Jude had fired her, she would have recourse. But in quitting, Slade had greatly jeopardized any chance of that.

She should have stayed working and forced an investigation regarding Jude.

She should have done so many things differently.

And yet, that office was the last place on earth she ever wanted to step foot in again.

You and me both. Nora had responded. You do know you're not the only one who's had to deal with his advances, right? Because I'm assuming that's what happened.

Slade could kick herself for being so naive. For not realizing Jude's tentacles stretched beyond her. She'd just been reeling. Finding a way to survive.

I had no idea. I'm so sorry, Nora. Why don't you leave? Can you work somewhere else?

I'm a single mom. I have two babies to raise. I can't give up the money or the benefits, and nothing I find is as good as this job— outside of Jude.

Of course Nora couldn't just quit like Slade had. Nor should she have to.

All the women go scattering when he visits our end of the building. We're all sick of him. He's a predator.

All.

And Slade had left the others to fend for themselves. Single moms like Nora. Women who had fought for their positions and refused to give them up as easily as she had.

Did you file a report with HR? Nora had asked.

Yes! Slade had tried to do the right thing. She'd forked over every detail, even though writing that account of what had happened was like experiencing it all over again.

Did you hear back from them?

Not yet.

You do realize that Jude is besties with Brockton, right?

Brockton...the head of human resources?

That's the one.

Slade's stomach had started functioning like it was a rusty engine someone had added salt water to instead of oil, and her whole body had erupted in a massive bout of tension. The kind she'd noticed Reed wearing like a second layer of skin since his arrival.

This was all Jude Wilshire's fault. He was the one who'd committed the offense. And even two thousand miles away, even though she was innocent in all of it, Slade was still dealing with the effects of that.

She wanted human resources to contact her and do their job.

She wanted Jude to be held accountable for his actions.

She wanted to move on and leave it all behind.

And yet none of those things were happening.

Slade went to the cupboard and filled a glass with water from the sink. She chugged it in one long drag, then refilled it and returned to her seat at the table.

"I promise I won't be gone long and then I'll get straight back to work."

Mom's smile sprouted behind her coffee mug as she paused from cutting pineapple to sip the liquid. "I'm not your keeper, Love. It's okay to have breakfast with a friend. The house is going to be a long haul. We're all going to need breaks and space along the way." Mom moved to the table with her coffee and sat in the chair across from Slade. "There's no pressure to be here every second of the day. You two are already doing and giving so much more than I ever expected. I don't want you to feel that you have to stay until the house is finished either. You have a life to live." *And a job to find.* Slade filled in the thought since Mom thankfully didn't. "This project isn't on you."

"It's not just on you either. I want to stay and see this through. If you're okay with that." Yes, Slade had a life to rebuild in Florida, but she couldn't fathom not being here for as long as it took to clean out the house.

Besides, putting off returning to Gulfport was sounding better and better...especially after those heartbreaking texts.

"I'll gladly accept your help for as long as you want to be here. Just make sure you're taking care of yourself, okay?"

Slade swallowed the snort begging to escape and managed a nod. That's what she'd been trying to do back in Florida, but clearly, she'd majorly mishandled the situation.

"Keys are in my purse, which is on the dresser in my room. I was thinking I'd tackle part of the kitchen today. Not the items we use daily, of course, but some of the baking supplies. Things like that."

Pain slashed across Slade's abdomen. "Gran's baking supplies... I wish I could keep them. But the fact that I don't bake makes that counterintuitive." Grief for both her grandparents and even her dad seemed to lurk around every corner in this house. And yet, Slade adored her time here. "I used to love helping her bake. She always let me assist and never got upset when I made a mess."

Mom cringed. "I'm guessing *I* did get upset at home when you made a mess. Sorry about that. If I could go back and change my response in those situations, I would."

"You were fine. I did tend to create the aftermath of a tornado when I—" Slade used air quotes "—helped out."

"Even if it's just for nostalgia's sake, you could pick out a few things." Mom moved to refill her coffee. "Maybe her cake decorating kit or the cookie cutters—"

"The cookie cutters! I loved those as a kid. They have to be vintage."

"What isn't vintage in this house? Including me." Her mother's quick burst of laughter was reminiscent of Aunt Lovetta's, minus the snort that often accompanied her aunt's.

"You're not that old, Mom. Nobody's putting you out to pasture yet. You have plenty of good years left." When the house was done and Mom returned to her life in Arizona, she would find her way. She'd travel with friends or visit her future grandkids. She'd flourish, because despite how often Slade and her mom clashed, she could say without hesitation that her mom was a fighter. A survivor.

Slade would like to attribute those same descriptions to herself, but Nora's revelations were making her feel like the opposite—a runner, avoider.

"Some days I'm not so sure. It's so strange not to have Dad around during these years. I wonder how we would have been with each other when we finally reached retirement. Some couples drive each other up a wall."

"You would have gotten along well. You two were best friends.

I always appreciated that about your relationship. Not that I ever said it. And I'm sorry he's not here to enjoy retirement with you."

Mom grew teary. "Thanks, Love. I wish I'd been better at telling you how proud I was of you when you were growing up. You've always been so strong, and you always figure things out, even when life throws unexpected stuff your way."

Slade swallowed around the golf ball that materialized in her throat. If her mom only knew.

"Actually, you did tell me that a fair amount." Granted, it had been delivered in a you-could-do-even-better way half the time, but then, maybe Slade had read too much into Mom's tone over the years and not enough into the words themselves. Slade hated how she and Mom tiptoed around each other. And yet, she understood it. They were just so different. For Reed, it had to be like watching two pieces of china slide around on a car dash. Were they going to crash into each other and shatter or would they somehow survive the ride unscathed?

Slade's phone buzzed, and she checked the screen with more than a little trepidation.

It was only Keely. **On the way. See you soon.**

"I better go." Slade popped up. "Thanks for letting me use the car. Text me a grocery list, and I'll grab some supplies before I head back." She paused at the end of the table. "Unless you'd rather shop yourself…"

"That would be really helpful. Thank you for offering. Again. I'm sorry I didn't accept the last time."

Slade's exit halted at the bright, shining approval radiating from her mom. It felt almost painful. Like something sparkling and valuable at the bottom of the lake that was too deep to dive for. Because Slade couldn't help but wonder… If her mother knew the whole of what was going on in her world right now, what would she think of her daughter then?

Chapter Eleven

The packed Buffalo Café hummed with Saturday morning energy as Slade weaved her way toward Keely, who was already seated in a corner booth. A couple attempted to corral their young toddler into a high chair while a group of older women in the center of the open restaurant leaned closer to each other, probably to hear better over the child's cries.

Slade slid in across from her friend. "It's packed in here."

"It's a local favorite." Keely's teeth flashed white against her lovely, bronzed skin. She had her hair up in a casual top knot, and she wore round, tortoise glasses. Unlike Slade, she was dressed for the warm weather in an Army green, sleeveless T-shirt dress.

When Slade had first seen Keely's photo during their pre-rideshare chat, she'd thought the twenty-eight-year-old resembled a young Lucy Liu. Though in personality, Keely was far more brilliant engineer than famous movie star.

They focused on the menu until they both knew what they wanted. Slade still wasn't sure she could stomach much, but she decided on a Denver omelet because it contained veggies, and she could use more of those in her diet. If she didn't finish it, she'd take part of it home.

The waitress that stopped at their table had gray hair pulled back into a low ponytail. Tendrils escaped the sides, framing her face, and pink readers rested against the black polo shirt she wore with matching jeans. The dark color contrasted with her peach skin, which held sunspots and other signs of age, and along her right arm, a ten-inch, faded scar.

"We match." She pointed to the streak of white in her hair that was similar to Slade's. "Except I've had this since I was in high school, and I assume you have not."

"You're right. Mine is man-made."

"I'm Della-Sue." She untucked a bright pink serving pad from the pocket of her half apron. "What can I get you ladies to drink? And then I'll come back to get your meals." Her greeting was punctuated throughout with slight pauses, and the words weren't fully articulated. Della-Sue's speech had its own unique cadence.

Slade ordered a peppermint tea, thinking it might soothe her stomach, and Keely coffee.

"Be back in a minute."

Keely filled Slade in on what was new with her, and Della-Sue returned shortly to deliver their drinks.

She flashed an inquisitive smile at Slade. "Do I...? Do we know each other? I'm sorry if we've met before." She slipped her readers on and made the motion of knocking knuckles against her skull. "This thing doesn't always work like I'd like it to. Motorcycle accident a few decades back."

That sounded terrible and explained the scar. "I don't think we've met." Though Slade could be wrong. "My mom grew up here and I used to visit in the summers when I was a kid."

"Who's your mom?"

"Marin Henderson—maiden name Slade."

Della-Sue's blue-gray eyes brightened and widened, then glimmered with moisture. "The Slades. I adored your grandparents. I was so sad when Thelma passed. She was really good to me."

"Me too." A rush of emotion surfaced.

"No wonder you look so familiar. You're the spitting image of your mother. We went to high school together. I always thought she was so—" the *S*'s slurred slightly "—beautiful. How is your mom?"

"She's good. We're here cleaning out my grandparents' house."

Della-Sue's apricot lips pressed into a thin line. "That has to be so hard."

"It is. But I'm thankful it's been going well." If not slowly. "The biggest setback is that we found out the roof is leaking. But Mr. Turner—Garrett—is helping with that, so hopefully it won't delay things too long."

"Garrett. Of course." Della-Sue's head bobbed. "Those two were always close."

I knew it! Mom *had* downplayed her connection to Garret. "Did they hang out in high school?" Slade should let Della-Sue get to her other tables, but she couldn't resist a little digging.

"Oh yes. And after." Della-Sue tapped her pen against her notepad. "In their midtwenties."

That didn't make any sense.

The teenager working the host stand sat two tables in quick succession, and Della-Sue's brow furrowed. "I better take your order so I can get caught up." She wrote their requests down and then bustled off.

"Do you think your mom remembers her?" Keely asked.

"I don't know. Although…that *midtwenties* mention was strange. My parents got married straight out of college, and my mom never lived here again after school."

"Maybe she has the timing off."

"Must be."

Keely pushed her glasses up the slope of her nose. "How's the house going?"

"Good but slow. I think we're all realizing we're in this for the long haul. And I can't believe that Reed and I originally planned to arrive today and stay for a week. That would never have been enough. It took us so long just to do the garage." Slade curled her hands around the hot tea mug. "Oh! I have to tell you what I found."

Keely lowered her coffee cup to the table, her attention piqued. "Gold? Buried treasure? Bag of cash? Priceless recipes? Please say it's recipes."

Slade laughed. "I found an old newspaper article that said a man's body had been found on the rocks below my grandparents' property thirty-four years ago."

"A body? Like someone fell or had a heart attack or was murdered or what?"

"My thoughts exactly. I searched online the last few days trying to figure that out, but I couldn't find anything about him. Didn't help that I was missing his name. But then last night, I decided to check for obituaries, and I found a Summit County historical site with a database of local deaths going back decades. There was an obituary that coincided with the date of the article and detailed his death as a tragic accident. Has to be him."

"What's his name? Maybe I've heard of him."

"More coffee?" Della-Sue popped by and at Keely's nod and thanks, began refilling her mug.

"Vincent Dunn."

Brown liquid overflowed Keely's cup. "Oh no!" Della-Sue yanked the pot upright. "Sorry. Let me grab a rag." She hurried off.

Keely gave a slight shrug. "Doesn't sound familiar. But I've only lived here a couple years."

"My mom brushed it off when I asked her about the article. She said the police had ruled his death an accident. But I have so many questions. What was he doing there? Rock climbing? Casing the neighborhood? Attempting to break in? Why was his body found *there*? Was it really just happenstance, like my mom implied?"

"The kitchen is cranking today." Della-Sue delivered Keely's plate, which was steaming and smothered in green chili. She set Slade's down at the slightest angle, and a quarter of the hash browns slid onto the table. "Goodness." Her head shook with agitation. "There I go being clumsy *again*. Sorry about that." She tugged a dishcloth from her apron and swept up the small mess along with the coffee spill. "I'll get you a new side of hash browns." Della-Sue's rhythm this time was choppier, her speech harder to understand. No doubt because the restaurant was overflowing with people, and she was slammed.

"Please don't. I won't even eat everything on my plate," Slade assured her.

"Are you positive?"

"Absolutely."

"Okay, then." Della-Sue straightened her shoulders and gave a nod. "Aren't you a sweetheart—just like your grandmother. I'll be back to check on you both in a few." Numerous patrons greeted Della-Sue with familiarity as she made the rounds in her section.

"So, are you going to look into what happened with this Vincent Dunn more, now that you know his name?" Keely cut into her huevos rancheros, spilling the slightly runny yolk. She took a bite, her eyes rounding in obvious pleasure. "This is so good. I wonder if they would share their green chili recipe with me."

"Maybe Della-Sue will ask the chef for you. And I'm definitely going to look into it more. I'm curious what happened. I don't understand why my family isn't."

"If it were me, I'd be tempted to do a little research. You've got me hooked at this point, so I'm game for helping if you want."

That's what Slade needed to hear—that she wasn't alone in her interest and that wanting to understand Vincent's death didn't make her a cynic or excessively curious or in need of a psych eval—all impressions she'd gleaned from Mom and Reed at varying moments.

She *was* normal. Ish.

"I just might take you up on that. Thank you." Slade raised her tea mug in a cheers gesture and sipped. The peppermint was smooth and refreshing, and her stomach settled from the jumpy irritableness that had plagued it all morning. She took a bite of her omelet, tasting the just-right spices, the tangy ched-dar, the veggies…and the seared broccoli. She hated broccoli. Why had she ordered an omelet with it?

She'd been distracted, to say the least.

But while she might have been wrong about the broccoli, Slade *had* been right: looking into Vincent Dunn would pro-vide the perfect distraction from her work situation. It would give her someplace to bury her head while she waited for things to flesh out back in Florida.

She hadn't thought about the law firm or Jude in at least five minutes.

And this morning, that was a record for her.

It might even be a record since her arrival in Colorado.

Chapter Twelve

Reed had naively assumed that because he was in shape, running at altitude wouldn't be that different from running at home. And that instead of doing the loop his grandparents' house resided on, like yesterday, he could manage the ascent from the neighborhood entrance with only a small amount of additional effort.

He'd been wrong on both counts.

One quarter of the way back up the hill—a word he used lightly, since this mini mountain would be considered a ski slope in the Midwest—Reed heard a vehicle approaching. If it was his sister returning from breakfast with her friend, he would be hard-pressed to resist a ride home.

He moved to the side of the road, grateful for the break, fighting the urge to hunch over and prop palms against his thighs in an attempt to catch his breath.

An elderly couple peered at him like he was a fish out of water as they crawled by in their staid, silver SUV that likely had mileage in the toddler years. They exchanged waves, and once the vehicle passed, Reed forced his feet to move again.

Good thing it wasn't Slade. She would enjoy his floundering far too much.

Reed's lungs clamored for oxygen as he pushed to finish the ascent at a decent but still-able-to-stand-upright pace. When he reached the crest, endorphins flooded his system and he slowed to a jog. This was his favorite part—limbs loose, mind clear, the accomplishment of the run under his belt. He imagined this was how Slade felt after yoga.

At the house across the street from his grandparents', a woman with white hair shuffled to her mailbox, the slippers on her feet creating a *skitch-skitch-skitch* sound against the pavement. She wore a loose, olive green shirt and pants of the same color, which hung on her frame as if they were two sizes too big. It looked like something that might have been in her closet for the last forty years...or something an influencer would don now, labeling it new and inventive.

Reed was certain she'd lived in that house when he'd been a kid, but he couldn't remember her name. She paused next to the mailbox, her vision trained on him as if she too wanted to place him but couldn't.

"Morning." Reed greeted her when he was about ten yards out, leaving a wide swatch so that she wouldn't feel threatened by him in any way. Something about her stance, her gaze, seemed almost confused...as if she couldn't recall why she'd left the house.

Maybe because the mailbox she'd opened was empty.

He was two strides past her when she called out. "Wait!" The command held a slight tremor.

Reed's stride immediately faltered. He didn't want to miss the best part of his run, but how could he ignore her?

Manners were too ingrained in him for that.

He paused and turned back toward her.

"Aren't you the Slades' grandson?"

"I am."

"Are you visiting your grandparents? I haven't seen them lately."

Reed assumed the woman suffered from dementia, with a question like that, but one could never be too sure. He tested the waters. "They've actually...passed on. My mom, sister and I are working on cleaning out their house."

Her forehead furrowed. "They did? Oh yes. Right. I knew that. I'm Ruthie Swink. You used to play with my son, didn't you?"

"Actually, I think it was your grandson." Which had happened once...maybe twice. As Reed recalled, the grandson had only been at Ruthie's sporadically.

"Our house used to have children in it all the time. My daughters had friends over a lot. My son...sometimes. He had one friend who was—" Her expression pinched. "My grandkids came around for a while, but now everyone is busy with their own lives." She delivered the verdict without malice. Though her vision did transfer to the structure of her home and her expression grew nostalgic, almost as if she could peel back the layers of time and revisit those years.

"I'm sure they wish they could visit more often." Reed wasn't sure of that at all, but he had to say something comforting and encouraging, didn't he?

"How long are you in town, dear?"

Good question. Reed had originally planned to be here for nine days, but now that he had his work set up, he could stay however long it took to get the house done. The idea of not returning to his distressing world and stark existence back home held great appeal.

Instead of using full vacation days for next week as originally planned, he was going to work mornings in order to be able to extend his time in Colorado into the following week or even longer if the house purge required it.

Not that his employers would even check on his hours. His bosses were of the strange and foreign mindset that employees should take off what they needed to in terms of vacation or personal days. And then they hired the kind of personnel who didn't take advantage of that system.

Reed tracked his hours every week, partially to prove to himself that he was fulfilling them and partially to be able to prove that to someone else, if needed. He did the same with his vacation days.

Outside Grandad's funeral, he'd taken off next to nothing this year, because he and Lindsey certainly hadn't been going on any vacations together.

So as long as his work got done and his deadlines were met, he was set.

Before he'd formulated an answer for Ruthie, his phone buzzed in the zippered pocket of his running shorts. He tugged it out, the photo on the screen of him and Linds so content and carefree nearly leveling him. He *really* needed to change her contact picture. The desire to have what it represented again was staggeringly painful.

"I'm sorry, Mrs. Swink. I need to take this." He held up the phone and swiped to answer before he missed the call.

"It was good to see you, dear. Tell your grandparents I say hi. And tell those kids to quit messing around at night! I hear things, even though my husband tells me I'm wrong."

"Got it." Reed responded as if her ramblings made sense. "Bye, Mrs. Swink." He held the phone to his ear as she made her way back up the driveway toward the house. "Hey." He spoke to Lindsey. "Sorry about that."

"No problem. Did I interrupt something?"

"Nope. I was just talking to a neighbor."

"Oh." A beat echoed between them. "I didn't realize you'd met anyone over in JP's neighborhood."

"I'm actually in Colorado."

"That's right! I completely spaced about your trip. Wait—I thought you were flying today. How are you already there?"

"I actually ended up coming out a couple days early because Slade did and the project sounded like more than we'd bargained for." Reed hadn't filled Lindsey in on his updated travel plans because the other night, after she'd called him, she'd texted shortly after to say she'd just had a question about the ice maker, but she'd figured it out. No need to return her call. So Reed hadn't. He'd been trying to let her take the lead with communicating, and they hadn't had a conversation since before he switched his schedule. He'd been hoping that by giving her space, she'd realize there was a gaping hole in her life and that she missed him desperately.

So far the only desperate one appeared to be him. His strategy was working as well as expecting the Colorado weather to be consistent. Overnight, two storms had rolled through and then cleared in a matter of minutes. Though it had been enough moisture to cause the roof to drip again. Thankfully, because of Garrett, they at least had a plan in place for that.

"It's so strange not to know where you are," Lindsey said quietly. "Or what you're doing."

Even though this is what you asked for. Reed managed to keep the retort under wraps. Before things had dissolved between them, he'd never been this cynical. Felt like he was borrowing a page from his sister's no-one-is-to-be-trusted-including-his-mother book.

"I feel the same. It's odd not knowing what you're up to or if you're okay." The curiosity over why Lindsey had called was eating at Reed. But then, maybe she didn't have a reason. Maybe she was just checking in.

That would be a huge improvement for them.

When Lindsey still didn't offer up a purpose for her call, the tension in his body began to subside. "So, what's new with you? How are you?"

"Apparently, I'm vicious."

The slight gain in relaxation Reed had just experienced quickly vanished. "How are you vicious, exactly?"

"I just got asked out. And my first evil thought was to call and tell you."

Reed clawed at the stress hive that popped up on the inside of his elbow.

"I'm hearing myself now, though." Her distressed exhale echoed between them. "I'm going to hang up."

"Wait." Reed had begun walking after Ruthie made it back inside her house and now found himself at the end of the loop. He turned back toward his grandparents'. "Who asked you out?"

"No one you know."

"Did you take your ring off?" Reed studied his, a flash of anger at Lindsey and the reason for her phone call tempting him to contemplate sending it over the side of the cliff.

The sun glinted off the thick platinum band they'd taken more time to pick out than he'd thought possible. If it had been up to him, Reed would have grabbed the first ring he saw. But Lindsey was adamant that he find something he loved.

Really, they ended up finding something *she'd* loved. Reed had never admitted to her that this ring was his favorite because she was his favorite and she'd lit up at this particular band.

If Reed chucked the ring, he would only end up swimming in regret, crawling around on the rocks at the base of the cliff searching for it.

There was nothing like a marriage separation to turn a person into a middle schooler all over again—the indecision, the lack of confidence, the mood swings...all while pretending to have it all together.

"I'm still wearing my ring," she answered. "Did you take yours off?" Lindsey's voice held hurt, and despite the illogical-ness of her questioning him when she'd been the one to kick him out, Reed understood the wounding she felt—or would feel—if he had removed it.

"No. I'm still wearing mine too." Reed paused at a bench that was tucked between the lots of two houses. It faced the lake and boasted the neighborhood name on the back, so it must be available for public use.

He followed the short, worn footpath to it, rounded the bench and sank to a seat. "So, what did you say to the person who asked you out?"

"Of course I said no. We are still married."

"Separated." *By your choice.* Reed wasn't sure why he'd filled that in. Maybe he'd said it in the hopes of hearing Lindsey re-spond with something encouraging like—*but not for long!* Or—*it's just a phase, Reed. We'll get through it.*

She didn't reply to his comment at all.

"If you said no, then why are you calling to tell me about it?"

Lindsey didn't answer at first, and this time, Reed was deter-mined to wait her out. A fishing boat puttered along the inlet below the cliff, and two paddleboarders glided in the opposite direction toward open lake water.

"I guess I just..." He could picture her bottom teeth press-ing into her upper lip. "I just wanted to know if you'd care."

Searing hope jolted through him. If she wanted him to care, then that meant *she* still cared. And since Lindsey had been calm and stoic when she asked him to move out, Reed had been questioning that very thing.

"Of course I care, Linds. That has never been the issue."

"So I'm the issue. My problems are—"

"Stop." Reed cut her off and then softened his next delivery. "Let's just not...okay?"

Lindsey went quiet again. "You're right." Her voice gained momentum. "Thanks for stopping me. It's not worth it."

Was she saying that *they* weren't worth it? Or that the fighting wasn't worth it?

The one thing Reed feared more than their arguments was deafening silence. Because that would mean there was no more *them* to fight for.

"Sorry that I stooped to this level of immaturity." Remorse that resonated in Reed weighed down her statement. "I don't even recognize myself anymore."

"Same. What happened to us?" He spoke the thought out loud, not really expecting an answer. Knowing there wasn't a specific one. Reed had a few ideas regarding the various bricks that had crumbled during their derailing. Some which had been disintegrating since long before the two of them had even met.

Lindsey's dad had left her mom, and consequently her, when she was young, and the two women had become incredibly close over the years. Perhaps codependent. More like friends than mother-daughter. Her father had started over with a younger wife after abandoning them, and he'd had children with her. He'd then proceeded to act as if his first family didn't exist.

They hadn't communicated in years, but that didn't mean his choices still didn't affect Lindsey to this day.

And then about eleven months ago, Lindsey's mom had been diagnosed with breast cancer. She'd finished her treatment and was doing well now, but something had broken in Lindsey during her mother's fight. She was constantly worried about her mom. Even about her own health.

It had been a tumultuous road that Reed had tried so hard to help her navigate.

And before that news had sent her spiraling, they'd been trying to get pregnant.

Actually—they'd stopped trying *not* to get pregnant. As if

there was a difference. They'd thought they were so smart, forgoing birth control before they were fully ready.

They'd planned to be casual about it—*we won't worry if we don't get pregnant right away! We're going to give ourselves extra time before we're desperate to have kids, so that we don't undergo the stress we've watched our friends go through!*

They'd been so naive.

Because once hope seeped in, you couldn't put a cover on it and just forget the option existed. After a year had passed and the pregnancy tests continued to be negative, they'd undergone testing themselves.

Nothing is wrong was a double-edged sword.

It meant there was nothing to fix…but also nothing to fix.

They'd tried to follow all of the don't-stress-just-relax adages, but when a clock was constantly *tick-tick-ticking* in your mind, it was like ignoring a waterfall dumping on your head, continuously attempting to drown you.

Stress from each of those veins had slowly filled Reed and Lindsey's world like a steadily rising river during snowmelt.

And then he'd found the hidden, maxed-out credit card bill filled with line after line of online shopping sites for clothing and home décor and kitchenware. Nothing they'd *needed.* Which made her choice to overspend all the more confusing.

Lindsey had responded to his confrontation over the debt with her hackles raised, and Reed had been stunned and wounded by her deceit.

It had taken more than one thing to bring them to this painfully low place. And he imagined it would take far more than one solution to get them out.

"I don't like this version of us." Her statement was void of malice and laden with heartbreak.

"Me either." Reed kept his tone even, nonconfrontational, matching hers. It was the first time in a long while that they'd been able to speak to each other without bitterness. "But I also don't know how to stop the cycle."

Maybe there were too many things to process, too many problems burying them. Because they had tried. They'd been to counseling. Both had attempted to change. Lindsey had apologized for the spending, but Reed had never quite believed she meant it. It had felt like she was checking off an item on her to-do list, but in the hidden vestiges of her heart, he feared that Lindsey was white-hot angry with him. And he wasn't exactly sure why.

It was as if he was the basis for their problems.

And for all Reed knew, she was right.

He had no earthly idea how he'd been given the best example of how to be a husband from his father and had still somehow botched it up so badly.

Reed had observed his parents' relationship over the years. He'd watched Dad apologize when needed. He'd witnessed the way his father had loved their mom with intention. As if he somehow knew the painful cost that losing her would incur, and he'd always put in the work necessary to avoid that outcome.

His whole life, Reed's family had claimed he was just like his dad in so many ways. But little did they know that in this arena, he couldn't have fallen further from the mark.

Chapter Thirteen

Marin had hoped—with all of the angst of a young child wishing for a pony—that Garrett would forget about his request that they have dinner together.

But much like the pony that never materialized in her childhood, that wish had not been granted.

On Saturday evening, he'd been over finalizing roof details—once again helping her when he shouldn't even be working—and before he'd gotten into his truck, he'd paused with his hand on the driver's door and turned to her.

"Monday night?" he'd said, as if she'd know what he was referring to. As if they were smack-dab in the middle of discussing dinner plans and he was confirming details.

Marin had played innocent. "The shingles will be in that fast? That's amazing!"

Garrett's low laugh had sent shivers up her spine, like the dial on one of those strongman carnival games.

"I'm glad to see you've retained your sense of humor over the years."

"Garrett." Marin had lowered her voice. "You know I can't."

"I know nothing of the sort. We're not kids anymore, Mar."

And that was part of the problem. Marin was an adult, and unlike in her twenties, she needed to act like one.

"It's not a good idea."

"Eating," he'd replied, "is always a good idea."

A laugh had escaped. He had her there. Marin did love food.

"It makes no sense for us to go gallivanting around town together like our history doesn't exist."

"Gallivanting, huh?" A quirk had claimed his mouth. "I'm going to have to start keeping a Marin dictionary for all the big words."

She'd laughed, well aware that while Garrett might downplay his intelligence and success, it was there, nonetheless. Another word he'd likely tease her about.

"Being seen in public together might get people talking. Isn't that the last thing you'd want?" Why wasn't he more careful to safeguard himself? Sure, he'd lived in Dillon this whole time and weathered the storm after Vince's death, but Marin didn't understand why he was willing to risk those waters rising again.

"I don't think old tales are going to suddenly level me when they've been swirling this long. But I acknowledge your concern." *He acknowledged her concern.* Insert an eye-roll emoji! Marin wasn't protecting herself—at least not only herself—she was protecting him! Why couldn't he see that? "Maybe you're right." He continued. "Going out doesn't make sense." Marin had released a pent-up exhale of relief. "We'll just switch it to my house, then. I'll grill steaks."

And *that* was how she'd ended up in her car on Monday evening, driving five houses down when she could have easily walked. Marin had taken her car so that her excuse of leaving the house—stopping by Garrett's, errands and walking by the Blue River in Silverthorne—held up.

When Slade had assumed Marin's visit to Garrett's had to do

with the roof, Marin hadn't corrected her. Even though she'd signed the paperwork for the shingles on Saturday.

The idea that she'd omitted pertinent details of her evening agenda to Slade and subsequently Reed didn't sit well with Marin. But what else was she supposed to do? The last thing she needed was Slade unearthing more than she already had.

In an attempt to make her excuse tonight at least partially truthful, Marin had filled the trunk of her car with donations for the thrift store, and after dinner, she would run into town and drop them off. And if she had time, she'd walk too. She'd worn summery, navy wide-leg trousers and a white sleeveless shirt with her wooden soled sandals, and had stowed her walking shoes in the car in case she managed to fit in the latter.

But in order to make all of that happen, her time at Garrett's needed to be cut short.

Marin pulled into the redone stamped-concrete driveway, in awe of the facelift that Garrett's house had undergone since she'd last seen it. Rustic wooden beams flanked the front stone steps, and a beautiful glass door created views straight through the house and out to the shimmering water behind.

Marin knocked lightly, momentarily entertaining the idea that if Garrett didn't hear her, she could slink away with the airtight excuse that she'd shown up and he hadn't answered.

The man appeared through the glass, dressed in jeans and an open flannel over a T-shirt.

"Hi." He propped open the door for her. His hair was slightly damp, and he wore leather slippers. The casual vibe he gave off felt too intimate. Marin barely resisted running, and the saliva necessary for speaking evaporated.

"You going to come in or are we having dinner on the front step?" Garrett's mouth formed that teasing grin that made her whole nervous system screech to a grinding halt. "Dealing with you is a little like coaxing a stray dog to trust me. Want me to grab some scraps to lead you inside?"

"Offensive." Marin tempered the comment with a faulty smile and forced her feet to transport her into the slate-tiled foyer, which opened to an expansive living room on the left and a gorgeous rustic kitchen on the right. It was as if she'd walked into a multimillion-dollar house—mountain lodge in style and modern in convenience.

Actually...that was exactly what she'd stepped into.

"Do you greet all your guests in such a welcoming way?" Cool air threaded along her skin. Unlike her parents' home, Garrett's must have air-conditioning.

"I don't have many guests. Everyone is married and busy."

"I have that issue too. Although my widow's group has been great. It's nice to be around people who get what I'm going through without me having to try to put it into words."

"I'm glad you have them." Garrett led the way, and Marin followed him into the kitchen. He motioned for her to take a seat at one of the four leather stools that lined the butcher block island.

"Can I help?" Doing something would be good for her hands, her nerves, her everything.

"Nope. Have a seat."

Marin slid onto a stool as Garrett padded over to the fridge. He retrieved a bottle of sparkling water, holding it up for her approval like a maître d'.

"Bubbly or flat?"

"Bubbly, please." Marin leaned against the back of the chair, and it gave slightly under the pressure, creating a rocking motion.

He filled a glass and slid it across the island to her.

Garrett was the picture of relaxation as he removed the steaks from the fridge and placed them on a large platter on the island.

Marin distracted herself from the attractive image of a man cooking—especially this one—and focused on the house. The appliances blended behind panels that matched the gray-brown cupboards, and rustic beams complemented the light gray walls and vaulted ceilings. The furniture was quality leather—the kind that made you want to curl up with a cup of tea and read a book or watch snowflakes flutter outside the window while you were tucked inside by a roaring fire.

"Garrett, your home is gorgeous." It was almost unrecognizable from the house Marin recalled from her teen years. "I can't believe all that you've done."

"Thank you. It was fun to do some work for myself for once. The house down the hill never quite felt like home after Poppy left. Looking back, I wish we would have made a change when the boys were younger. I think living there was hard for them after."

"Do they ever hear from her?"

He brushed the steaks with oil. "Sporadically. It took her a bit to reach out to them after taking off. That was what hurt them the most. If she'd just kept in touch, it would have gone a long way. Their relationships with her are strained, but they've worked it out over the years. They have boundaries with her, and they do their best to accept her for who she is. It's not perfect, but it's…manageable, I guess."

"I'm sorry about what happened between you two. I never really got the chance to tell you that."

His tender but resilient eyes met hers from across the island. "Thanks. I got it all settled with myself a long time ago. But I appreciate that."

"What are the boys up to these days? I don't think you said."

He rummaged in an island drawer and removed a large spice jar. "You didn't ask." His mouth curved.

"You're right. Every time you're over at the house I'm trying to get you out of there as fast as possible."

"You don't say," he deadpanned.

"It's not about you. It's about that time. I hope you realize that. The kids don't know that Ralph and I had marriage issues. At first, it was just because they were young and it didn't make sense to discuss something like that with them. Especially since it happened before they were even born. But then as they grew older, and Ralph and I had reached a good place with each other—"

"You didn't want to dive back into that old, hard stuff."

She lifted her palms. "Exactly."

"I'm not judging you for anything, Mar. You handled that time and what came after the best you could. We all did. I don't think it's terrible that you and Ralph didn't go into those details with your kids."

"Thanks." It was nice to hear he didn't consider her evil for not revealing all. She sipped from the glass Garrett had handed her, the water's slight lemon tang popping against her taste buds. "How long did it take for things to die down around here?"

"You mean after you left town and I had to weather the Vince aftermath on my own?" He raised an eyebrow, somehow—despite how serious the situation had been—still teasing her.

Marin winced. "Yeah. That."

Garrett's low laugh caused a rush of awareness to cascade across her skin. *Down, old girl. He's not yours to toy with.* Not this time. Marin had hurt Garrett horrifically twice in their lives. She wasn't about to add a third to the list. Not when she lived in Arizona, and he lived here. Not when she didn't want her kids to know what had transpired between them in the past.

She didn't even want to know what had transpired in the past.

And then there was the rumor mill. She could only imagine the tales they would spin if she were to be linked to Garrett and how quickly those speculations would taint the many amazing years she'd had with Ralph.

"A few years. Every so often it'll get brought up. But honestly, Vince didn't have a great reputation or a group petitioning for justice for him. I've even had people tell me they were grateful a piece of scum like him wasn't around anymore."

"That's a terrible thing to say, no matter how awful the man was."

"I agree. I still feel for Della-Sue. Vince wasn't a prize by any means, but they'd been together a long time when he died. She's never found anyone else. At least not that I know of."

Over the years, Marin had thought of Della-Sue and wondered how she'd fared after Vince's death. Sympathy rose for the woman who had endured much.

"I always felt guilty that Vince—"

"Stop." Garrett's admonition was gentle. "He made his choices. It was nothing you did." He picked up the platter of steaks and the grilling utensils. "Let's go onto the deck. Can you get the door for me?"

"Sure." Since Marin had reconciled with Ralph after Vince's death, and subsequently left town, this was the first time she and Garrett had ever discussed anything regarding it. And hopefully the last.

There were things Marin had done and not said at that time...and things Garrett had said but not done. But despite the loopholes in that fateful night, Marin was content to go on without answers. Forever.

Contrary to the old adage, the truth in this situation would not set anyone free. In fact, it could very well do the opposite.

Marin popped up as fast as her rusty hips would allow, snagged both of their drinks, and met Garrett by the sliding glass door. It opened as smoothly as butter melting on mashed potatoes, unlike the cantankerous one at her parents' home.

Just another item that a new owner would soon be dealing with.

Garrett started the grill and Marin ran her hand over the large, long teak table, which looked as if it could fit twelve with ease.

"Did you build this?"

"Yep. I liked the idea of something that could stand the test of time. Something to fill with grandkids." He scraped the grate of the grill even though it was perfectly clean. "I guess I never answered your earlier question about the boys."

"You didn't. You were too busy goading me."

"Goading, huh? I'll have to add that one to my Marin dictionary." Amusement laced his tone. He put the steaks on the grill, and they sizzled when they came into contact with the hot metal. "The boys are good. Cy works for Stoneridge. He runs his own crew, and we try to stay out of each other's way as much as possible so that we can continue working together."

"Makes perfect sense."

"Thought you'd understand that. How do you like yours done?"

"Medium rare."

"Atta girl. Byron lives in Denver. He's an architect. He works at a firm downtown, and he and his wife live in some fancy loft that would make me feel like I was in a concrete prison. But they love it. They're constantly going to concerts and sporting events and out with their friends and, as far as I can tell, have no plans to settle down with children anytime soon."

"What is wrong with our children that they won't give us grandkids?"

"Right? It's killing me not to tell Byron to hurry up."

"I have to bite my tongue all the time with Reed. I'm not sure what they're waiting for."

"And you don't want to be the type of parent who presses."

"Exactly. But I'm pretty desperate for a grandbaby. I'm surprised you are too."

"Why? 'Cause I'm a man?"

"Well...yeah."

"I loved raising the boys. Going to all their activities. There were some hard years, especially with Poppy taking off like she did, but we muddled through."

They'd both muddled through their respective issues. Maybe a mutually supportive friendship wasn't the worst idea Garrett had ever broached. Marin was certainly enjoying herself more than she'd expected to.

"Can I grab some place settings for us? Will you at least allow that?"

"That would be great. There's a salad in the fridge too, if you have room for it. I hope it's okay I kept things simple."

"Simple is perfect for me." Marin slipped back into the house, making sure to shut the door behind her because of the air-conditioning.

She found silverware inside drawer number three and sturdy navy dishware in the first cupboard she checked. She removed the salad from the fridge, which, while she wouldn't label sparse, certainly wasn't overflowing with leftovers or the evidence of family meals. Marin felt the solidarity of that.

In so many ways, she and Garrett were in the same boat. Close to retirement, no grandkids, alone.

Ouch. That last one smarted a bit.

On her way back outside, Marin snagged a handful of disposable napkins from his dining table and added them to her stack. She stepped onto the deck to find Garrett moving the steaks from the grill to the secondary platter he'd brought out.

They sat across the table from each other, and suddenly everything felt more intimate.

There was that word again.

But somehow, in the span of a few minutes, the energy had changed. Marin couldn't exactly put her finger on why. Maybe because Garrett was no longer grilling, and his full attention was on her.

Or maybe because—no matter how much she'd like to deny it—Garrett had aged well.

She appreciated the lines that hugged his mouth and eyes. They made her feel better about her own. *Life lines*, as she referred to them. They represented babies, heartbreak, healing, hope, love. How sad would it be if her face was void of all that living?

Garrett sliced into his steak, the juices spilling onto the backdrop of the plate, the corners of his lips tugging up.

"What's that smile about?"

"You've stayed longer than I'd pegged you for already."

Marin almost choked on a bite of salad. She finished it carefully and swallowed. "I didn't say I wouldn't stay long." Only to herself.

"But you thought it. It was part of your plan for the evening."

What was the use in hiding it? He obviously had her all figured out. "How do you know me so well?"

"Old habit, I guess. But I also think you're enjoying yourself more than you'd expected to. And now you're wondering how long you can be away without your kids figuring out what you're really up to."

Marin set her fork on her plate. "I told my kids where I was going."

His eyebrows reached for his salt-and-pepper hairline.

"Sort of."

Garrett's chuckle reverberated between them. "It's not like I'm going to call Cyrus later and fill him in on our evening. I just like teasing you because it makes your ears turn pink."

"They don't—" Marin touched her earlobe. Yep. Seared like the steaks. "You're a terrible man, Garrett Turner."

"Tell yourself whatever you need to in order to get through the day, Marin Slade Henderson."

She liked the addition of her maiden name. She'd gone without it for a long time, but Marin still loved the connection to her parents. It was why she'd dug her heels in on that being Slade's middle name. And look how fortuitous that had turned out to be.

"We've come a long way, haven't we?" Garrett intoned. "Lived through more than a few roadblocks."

"And construction zones. And then some."

"I think we did all right with what we were handed, don't you?"

Marin speared a bite of steak with her fork. "Some days, yes. Some days, I'm not sure about anything at all."

Chapter Fourteen

Slade finished her evening yoga, showered, then donned striped cotton pajama pants and a vintage *Chicago* T-shirt that was of the old and soft and irreplaceable variety.

It might only be seven thirty, but who in their right mind would get fully dressed when they weren't planning to leave the house again in the evening?

Slade's social life in Dillon was eerily reminiscent of the one she'd had in Florida. Though she did have a great group of friends there, she was one of the only remaining singles. And while she appreciated the invitations to dinners and nights out, at the faintest sign of becoming a third or fifth or seventh wheel, she bailed and returned home to Netflix, her brightly decorated apartment and her candy stash.

Which made it sound like she was a middle school girl trapped in a thirty-year-old body.

Not that far from the truth.

Slade knocked on Reed's door even though she knew he'd just left for a run. Mom was also gone, stating that she needed to stop by Garrett's, run some errands and that she might walk a favorite paved trail of hers that curved alongside the Blue River in Silverthorne.

When Reed didn't answer—as expected—Slade pushed open the door, finding his room dark and perfectly organized, smelling of soap and deodorant and a faint hint of fabric softener. He'd set up a rectangular folding table as his makeshift workstation while in Dillon, and it held his laptop, the small television screen he'd commandeered, and his wireless mouse and keyboard.

Slade disconnected the laptop from the extra screen and held the computer tight to her chest while exiting the room, her pulse skipping and jumping and generally reacting as if she were committing a crime.

She wasn't!

Slade had asked Reed for permission to use his laptop, because while she was usually the type to act first and beg forgiveness later, Reed was the type to have his technology protected by passwords, biometrics and five-step verification. Because two-step verification would never be enough for tech boy.

The Vincent research Slade had done up to this point had been on her phone. But she needed a break from the small screen, and she hoped that a change in her approach—even just in switching devices—would somehow uncover a trail she'd been missing.

She carried the computer downstairs, the sun-warmed deck kissing the bottoms of her bare feet as she stepped outside and experienced that awestruck hitch she always felt when faced with the gorgeous evening temperatures, the sun heavy in the sky, the peaceful calm that often swept through following an afternoon rain.

Rain that plunked into a bucket inside the house, reminding them all of the roof's inadequacies, but still.

The view from this deck could cure cancer, but it couldn't

seem to quiet the unease Slade was feeling since engaging in that text conversation with Nora on Saturday. In the aftermath of Nora's revelations, Slade tried to convince herself that she'd done her best with a terrifying and terrible situation. But no amount of attempted persuading lessened her guilt.

She couldn't stem the thoughts running in a constant loop in her mind: *I should have known. I shouldn't have abandoned the others to fend for themselves.* The situation with Jude and her previous work equaled a mess, no matter which way Slade twisted the images in her rearview mirror.

Continuing to work with Jude would have killed her...and evidently, leaving was going to do the same.

In the shower just now—when Slade had run fingers through her hair after conditioning—she'd come away with at least twenty strands.

A byproduct of stress, no doubt.

Slade and Nora hadn't communicated since their conversation on Saturday, which Slade considered a relief. She wasn't sure what else to say to her friend and coworker. She wasn't sure how to make something dreadful suddenly not dreadful.

If she had that ability, she would have made that happen a while ago.

At least now she understood why HR had never reached out to her.

Had Brockton shut down her complaint? Deleted it? Declared it untrue?

If Slade hadn't received the automated response from human resources regarding the form she'd filled out, she would have assumed her grievances had never been delivered.

But she did have proof. Thankfully, she still had that confirmation in her inbox...not that she knew what to do with it.

And right there was the reason she had to focus on something else. Had to keep busy with the house, with researching

Vincent's death, with concentrating on anything but the one thing she couldn't fix.

A slight breeze fingered through her still damp hair as she settled into her favorite Adirondack chair, feet tucked beneath her, steel blue mountains and the calm, cobalt water spread before her.

Last night, Slade had spent time scouring the internet for information on Vincent.

She'd assumed that having his name would make it easier to find details about his death, but her theory had been proven untrue. She'd found countless pages that led her to the wrong Vincent Dunn——who knew it was such a common name? And countless pages that promised to reveal all in exchange for her credit card information.

Slade had also assumed that old newspaper articles would be available online.

Wrong again. It seemed she would have to visit the library for those.

Eventually, her lack of success had exhausted her, and she'd fallen asleep.

So far, the only thing Slade had uncovered was how terrible her research skills were.

If the lack of information online were any indication, it would seem that no one had cared overly much about Vincent's death. Maybe it had all been open-and-shut, like Mom had implied. Maybe Slade was barking up an artificial tree that was never going to bear fruit.

She opened the laptop, entered Reed's password and navigated to the internet browser, adding Dillon to her search this time. She found numerous sites about the town but nothing that included Vincent.

Slade broadened her search to include Summit County instead. She paged through the results, clicking through to numerous dead ends. She dove deeper, going into the second, third, fourth pages.

Just as she was about to give up, she caught on Vincent's name in connection to a Summit County High School reunion site.

Slade clicked through and had to scroll to find the mention of him.

There. He was included with a list of deceased classmates. The date of his passing on the reunion page matched the one she'd found in the obituary.

It *had* to be him. But—Slade's mind reeled with confusion—that would mean that Vincent had *not* been a new transplant to Dillon as she'd imagined. He'd lived here for at least his senior year of high school.

She used her phone calculator to do the math. Vincent had graduated two years before Mom, so there was no guarantee they knew each other. But in a town as small as Dillon—where Mom claimed everyone knew everyone—how was it possible they hadn't been acquainted?

They'd walked the same hallways. Maybe even had the same classes.

Why had her mother not revealed Vincent's name or that they'd attended the same school when Slade asked about him?

The connection only served to ignite her curiosity.

The other deceased classmates on the reunion page had notes or mentions under their names. Classmates sharing a memory or discussing what they missed about the person. But the space under Vincent's name was blatantly blank.

Had no one known him that well? Had he simply been shy and quiet? Or maybe there wasn't anything good to say about him, so they'd followed the old adage and not said anything at all.

Why was information about Vincent so sparse?

What Slade needed was to find someone who lived in town at

the time of Vincent's passing, who liked to talk. Who wouldn't mind sharing the story behind his death.

But the only people Slade knew in Dillon were Keely—who obviously didn't know anything—her mom, and now Garrett. If Slade couldn't ask her mom about Vincent, she certainly couldn't ask Garrett.

And it wasn't like she could pop into The Buffalo Café and start asking strangers or head down to the police station and request the report from thirty-four years ago.

Though that second option would *really* simplify things.

Maybe Slade needed to find a bench outside the police station and hope that a handsome, single officer would stroll by, find her attractive, offer to buy her a cup of coffee and happily reveal all that his father—who would have conveniently worked as a detective at the time of Vincent's death—knew about the details surrounding his supposed accident.

Slade shook her head at the very random, amusing and entirely impossible scenario she'd just conjured.

Either the altitude was getting to her or she was running out of ideas.

Already.

Reed found his sister on the deck after his run and subsequent shower. She was sitting in one of the Adirondack chairs that looked out at the lake, her eyes closed and face lifted to the sky, her expression serene, legs tucked under her.

His laptop that she'd asked to borrow was on the outdoor table behind her, lid closed.

She wore pajama pants and a T-shirt, her feet bare. Reed had donned sweats and a T-shirt after his shower, since he wasn't really a pajama guy. Lindsey used to take that as a challenge. Over the years of their marriage, he'd sporadically found obnoxiously designed pajama pants folded neatly and placed on his side of the bed. She'd given him a pair covered in goofy photos of them, a pair that glowed in the dark, a pair plastered with cats. The list went on and on. Reed would, in turn, move them to Lindsey's side of the bed. Inevitably, he'd find her wearing them, the drawstring waist cinched tight, the bottom of the legs flowing past her feet, the size dwarfing her.

Lindsey had been so stunningly attractive in those silly pajama pants. She would strut around the house like she was in a ball gown on a red carpet. Her eyes would flash hints of caramel from the brown depths, and she'd raise one sassy eyebrow. *If you want the pajama pants back, Straight A's,*—a nickname she'd coined for him after finding a stack of his old report cards—*you're going to have to come and get them.*

Reed had grown to *really* love finding pajama pants on his side of the bed…not that he'd ever worn any of them.

"I don't ever want to leave here." Slade spoke as Reed slid onto the Adirondack chair next to her.

"Are you referring to that spot or this house or Dillon? And why do you get the seat with the best, most unobstructed views?"

"Because I'm special." She flashed an unrepentant grin in his direction. "And in answer to your first question—all of the above. Cleaning out this house is like trying to sweep sand outside in an Arizona windstorm, but I still love being here."

Over the weekend, they'd begun purging kitchen items they wouldn't need to use while staying at the house, and then they'd moved on to Grandad's desk and the living room storage. Yet another of Gran's hoarding spots. It felt as if she'd saved every scrap of paper, every receipt, every photo, every church bulletin. Sorting it all in order to make sure they didn't toss something important was time-consuming. But despite the uphill climb on the house, Reed was still grateful for a project to distract him from his imploding marriage, missing his wife and the stark, unknown future.

"We did have a lot of good memories here." The Cliff House—a label Reed used as a child and beyond in regard to his grandparents' home—was one of the few places where he'd been able to set aside his perfectionist tendencies. Grandad had always said that attempting something equaled success and succeeding was a bonus. From fishing and not catching anything to hunting for a particular wildflower but coming up short, he'd always cheered them on for trying something new. And he'd always taught them that the simple things in life like making a pie crust with Gran or changing the oil with him were just as important as the big things, like a first job or a college graduation.

Reed's desire to sit with Grandad right now and envelop himself in the peace the man had always personified was staggering.

But somehow, even without his grandparents being present on the premises, this house radiated with an invisible warmth—like a Wi-Fi signal that covered every square inch. It was almost as if the dwelling itself had a personality, as if the house was part human and had somehow shared in the lives of its inhabitants.

Hope felt more attainable here. Like Reed could reach up to the bright, sapphire sky, grab a handful and take it back with him to Illinois. Spread it like pixie dust over himself and Lindsey. Fix what they—so far—hadn't been able to fix.

Did Slade feel that too? Was that why she didn't want to leave? Reed wasn't about to open that conversational door with his sister. If he did, once Slade learned that he and Lindsey were separated, she'd be concocting some far-fetched plan for them to buy the house from Mom and Aunt Lovetta and live here like single spinster siblings.

"How'd your job search go?" Reed nodded toward the laptop.

"Did I say I was planning to use your computer to job search?"

Hadn't she? "I just assumed since your job ended that you'd be looking for another one while we're here."

"Huh. That would make sense."

Reed laughed. "It would." She'd accuse him of sounding like Mom if she could hear his thoughts, but he was concerned about Slade and her job loss. What was her plan after their time in Dillon? Shouldn't she be executing her next move *now* and not waiting? How could she afford to not work? His sister wasn't exactly the poster child for having three to six months in reserves.

"I guess I've been avoiding that reality. I don't have a reference from my old job, and I doubt another firm will hire me without one, so I'll probably have to do something else."

"Which shouldn't be a problem. You have enough experience to fill five resumes."

Slade's eyes narrowed. "Is that a compliment or a dig?"

"Compliment. It's impressive how many things you've tried. At least you know what you like and don't like."

Her expression became less guarded. "I guess that's true. I did enjoy working at the law firm."

"So why aren't you there anymore?"

"Sometimes, you just can't stay."

Before Reed could unpack that Slade-ism or his fears that it correlated to how Lindsey felt about him, his phone vibrated in his pocket. He checked the notification and experienced the usual gamut of wariness warring with hope when he saw it was a text from his wife.

What would it be this time? Good, bad, or somewhere in between?

They hadn't communicated since that conversation on Saturday morning regarding someone asking Lindsey out. A concept that made Reed's skin heat with anger and jealousy and every other emotion Lindsey had wanted him to feel when she called. They'd ended things in a peaceful place, though. Hopefully, this text would be more of the same.

Reed scanned the message and then tossed the phone across

the deck. It skidded toward the edge, narrowly missing plunging to the depths below.

"Whoa." Slade's head reeled disbelievingly in his direction, her pupils deep, dilated pools of black.

Reed was not, under any circumstances, the kind of person who lost their temper or had a short fuse. Apparently, the full depths of his despair and demise were yet to be discovered.

His sister silently pushed up from her chair and retrieved the phone.

She inspected the screen, running her fingertips across it. "It's not broken. Though you did your best. I think we'll just leave this right here for a sec." Slade placed the phone on the dining table behind them and returned to her chair as calmly as if she'd picked up a scrap of paper blowing in the wind.

She squeezed his arm, the touch warm, comforting, quick. "You going to be okay, Re-Re? I'm worried about you."

Funny. He was worried about Slade too. He just usually wasn't in the same boat as his sister.

After a minute of silence and some pathetic attempts to breathe deeply, Reed extracted himself from the deep-seated Adirondack chair and moved to the outdoor dining table. He picked up the phone like it was a baby rattlesnake and forced himself to open the text and read it again, his grip tightening with each word.

"My wife went to see a divorce lawyer today." Was he still allowed to refer to Lindsey as his wife? What was the correct terminology in this no-man's-land they were in? He dropped back into his seat and placed the phone on the wide arm of the chair between himself and his sister.

"What?" Slade reared back, jaw slack.

"She asked me to move out a few weeks ago."

"You and Linds separated, and you didn't tell me?"

"I didn't tell anyone. I couldn't. Talking about it would make it real, and I needed it not to be."

Slade's lips compressed. "Somehow, I completely understand that."

"I thought we were separating in the hopes of reconciling. That's what Lindsey said at the time. And since what we'd been doing—which was fighting—wasn't working, I thought maybe she was right. Not that she gave me a choice in the matter."

"Where are you living?"

"I'm renting the basement apartment at a friend's house."

"I'm so sorry." Slade blinked back moisture. "This is shocking. You and Linds struggling doesn't make any sense. What am I missing here? Was it always hard? Like, from the start? You guys always seemed so good together. You were couple goals."

"*Were* being the operative word there. And no, it wasn't hard from the start." It had been the opposite, actually.

"When did things change?"

"Just after Grandad's funeral."

"Did she—?"

"Cheat? No. And I didn't either."

Slade snorted. "I would never have considered that second option a possibility."

"I wouldn't have thought any of it possible."

"If it wasn't infidelity, then what happened? Wait—" Slade scooted back from her agitated position on the edge of her seat, her spine creating a thump when it connected with the backrest. "You don't need to answer that. I'm sorry for pushing. You don't need to tell me anything at all."

The tendons cradling Reed's throat tightened, and he had to swallow numerous times before he could speak.

"Thanks, Slove." When Slade first decided to go by her middle name and not her first, Reed, being a typical older brother, had refused to fully participate. He'd combined the two and succeeded in irritating her at the highest levels. He still considered it one of his greatest teen achievements. Like he should have won a prize for the level of annoyance he'd been able to conjure in his sister.

"I still hate that nickname."

He grinned. "I know."

Her head swung from side to side, and despite her obvious desire not to, she laughed. "I wish I had a nickname for you that you hated."

"Re-Re does the job nicely." It had been her attempt to annoy him back. Reed *had* hated it, but he'd been smart enough to act as if it didn't bother him, so Slade hadn't used it all that much. Now it made him laugh when she pulled it out of the archives.

"Good to know!" Her eyes lit up with a spark of victory that quickly faded to concern. "What kills me the most is that you've been going through this alone for months. I should have been there for you. I should have realized something was up and forced it out of you."

"I kept it from you on purpose. I didn't want anyone to know. I thought if Lindsey and I just worked hard enough that we could salvage things. I thought if I applied myself to our issues, I could turn our marriage around. But the more I tried to fix, the more things seemed to implode."

"I can't imagine how frustrating that's been for you. Especially when you're used to being able to solve things." And just like that, Slade had boiled it down to the main crux.

With most problems, Reed made a plan—or worked up a spreadsheet—and tackled the issue by dividing it into manageable chunks and then accomplishing each step. But their marriage troubles hadn't conformed to his normal mode of operation. It was the first time in Reed's life that he wasn't able to solve something or find a work-around.

His marriage with Lindsey was his biggest failure, and he didn't know what to do with that knowledge. Didn't know how to comprehend or accept it.

"We both wanted a baby." Reed's voice cracked. "But that wasn't *the* issue. At least, not the only one. There were a lot of things that happened before and at the same time. And then Linds maxed out a credit card I didn't even know existed."

"Wow. That's just… That's a lot."

He agreed.

"So, her text today…what was that about? I take it you weren't expecting her to see a lawyer?"

"Definitely not. When we separated, my understanding was that we both wanted to reconcile. I tried to view it as retreating to our own corners in the hopes that it would reset us. Allow us to meet in the middle again. The lawyer is a mutual friend of ours, and I'm close with her husband. Lindsey said an acquaintance saw her leaving the office, and she was concerned that rumors would spread like wildfire. She didn't want me to hear it from someone besides her, so she was just letting me know. She didn't want me blindsided." And yet here he was, the human embodiment of blindsided.

There was, at the core of Lindsey's reasoning for relaying the information, a level of integrity that Reed appreciated—or would appreciate if the subject matter was different. But at the moment, he couldn't scrape his way to the surface of anything close to gratefulness for her honesty.

Reed picked up the phone.

"Do you want me to go inside? Give you some space to answer her?"

"No. Please stay." His thumbs flew over the keys. When he returned the phone to the armrest, Slade snagged it quickly.

She set it on her lap, screen down. "I won't look, but I'm just going to hold on to this for a second. Just to keep it from making a full descent, depending on the answer you get."

Valid. "I just told her that I thought the separation was in the hopes of reconciling, not divorce. I'm sure there's some rule book that I'm supposed to be following about what to reveal and what to hold close." Reed had never played dating games well. If he'd liked someone, he'd called or texted. If they didn't respond, he moved on. He'd been honest from the start with Lindsey about that, and she'd been relieved not to have to guess with him—what he was thinking, feeling, planning. Except now they'd entered this weird, uncharted territory where everything felt like a chess move. Like every step could ignite a land mine.

Reed should probably just level with Lindsey and ask her for the straightforward truth—were they over? But that was one inquiry he wasn't sure he could handle the answer to.

Chapter Fifteen

"There is no rule book." At least, that's what Slade hoped, because she'd never been one to follow the beaten path. But Reed... He was all about the paved, cleared road. Not having his attempts to heal things between him and Lindsey succeed had to be eating him like a swarm of mosquitos on fresh baby skin. "And I say that confidently because I have absolutely no expertise in the arena of relationships."

Reed laughed—it was dry and rusty and faint, but surprisingly, he still had the ability.

"There is nothing wrong with telling Lindsey the truth," Slade continued. "With admitting that you don't want your separation to lead to divorce. I have no doubt that your direct, straightforward nature was one of the things she fell for in the first place. It's okay to still be you. Grandad would tell you to be honest with her and yourself, and Dad would have some equally wonderful advice that would certainly help more than I can. I'm sorry I'm not them."

"*I'm* sorry that I'm not them. If I was, I wouldn't be in this predicament in the first place. They both gave me the best examples of how to be a husband. It kills me that I somehow wasn't able to follow in their footsteps."

Slade's jaw dropped. "Are you telling me that you truly believe that you're not like Dad and Grandad?"

"Absolutely."

"That might be the craziest thing you've ever said. We're going to have to disagree on that one." Slade wasn't sure how to go about convincing her brother that he was wrong, wrong, wrong when it came to his viewpoint on that issue.

The phone vibrated in Slade's lap, and she palmed it, holding the screen out toward Reed. "Can I trust you with this thing?"

"I'm not entirely sure."

"If she destroys you in any way right now, I'm crawling through it."

Reed cracked a pained quarter smile. "I appreciate that. Though I'd rather not hurt Lindsey. Or be tortured in return."

"Noted." It was so Reed to care for his wife even when she was causing him pain. It further proved Slade's point that he was a good, good man—just like the two who'd helped to raise and influence him.

Reed took the phone from Slade and scanned the new message. "She says she feels the same and hopes for reconciliation too." He exhaled. "She only went to see her friend—the lawyer—because the friend pushed her. She let herself be convinced that she should hear what next steps would look like if we did head down that road for some reason." Reed shoved the phone toward Slade. "Put that far away from me, would you?"

She rose and deposited it on the table, then returned to her seat. "How do you feel about that answer?"

"You sound like a therapist."

"Just one of my many hats."

He tilted his face toward the sky, eyelids shuttered. "The situation doesn't sound as bad as it first did."

"I agree. And counselors never give you that kind of response. They make you do all the work and come to conclusions by yourself. At least Lindsey didn't seek out the advice."

"Though of course she let herself be convinced to go in." Reed's fingertips dug into his temples. "It is what it is, I guess."

They sat silently as the world continued operating around them, the distant hum of boats and vehicles mingling with Aspen leaves fluttering in the slight breeze.

"Of all the things I thought you might be going through, you and Linds having trouble was not one of them." Where had Slade's instincts been in this situation? If Reed were more himself at the moment, he would no doubt tease her for claiming to have such great intuition and then missing the mark so completely.

"What did you think was going on?"

"Something with your work not going absolutely perfectly. Like you having a 99.9 percent success rate on a project when you were aiming for a hundred. Or you making too much money and not knowing what to do with it. That was a high contender."

Reed's snort ended with a laugh, which was a victory in Slade's opinion.

"What other strange things have you been brewing up?" He glanced her way.

"What do you mean?"

"I assume you've looked more into that article about the body. What have you found out?"

Slade obliged her brother's desire for a subject change. "His name was Vincent Dunn. Have you ever heard of him?"

He shook his head.

"Me either. While you were out running, I figured out that Vincent went to Summit County High School. He graduated two years before Mom."

"So that's what you were up to with the laptop."

"Yep." Though job searching would probably have been the

better choice. "Why do you think Mom didn't mention that they went to the same high school?"

"Attending the same school two years apart doesn't mean they knew each other. Maybe Mom doesn't like to talk about what happened because it was hard on Gran and Grandad. No matter who the guy was, they would have felt bad about his death. That's just who they were."

"True." Reed made it all sound so logical, and yet Slade's internal alarm kept beeping like a smoke detector with a dead battery. "When I had breakfast with Keely on Saturday, our server said she knew Mom in high school."

"That's not headline news. What's your point?"

"Della-Sue said—"

"Who's Della-Sue?"

"The server at The Buffalo Café. She mentioned that Mom and Garrett had been close when they were younger. In high school…and in their twenties."

"That doesn't make sense. Mom didn't live in Dillon after college."

"I assume she had the timing off. But Della-Sue still confirmed that I *was* right—when Mom first introduced me to Garrett, she definitely downplayed their connection and how well she knew him."

"Mom claimed she didn't know Garrett?"

"No…she admitted knowing him."

Reed's expression held a hint of impatience and a heap of exasperation. "What *exactly* did she say?"

"That they grew up on this street together. And that everyone in a town the size of Dillon is acquainted with each other. Which makes the fact that she didn't mention knowing Vincent even more circumspect."

"You didn't exactly uncover a bombshell." Reed raised his palms and then dropped them back to the wide, weathered armrests of his chair. "I know you think Mom is acting weird or off, but she seems normal to me, albeit sad and maybe a bit stressed about the house."

Slade experienced a prick of guilt for overanalyzing their mother's behavior. Mama-Mar *was* grieving. Who acted normal under that kind of burden?

"I need you to stop with the Mom theories." Reed's tone held bite, and his hunched body language broadcasted exhaustion. "I don't think they have merit." He softened his delivery. "And I'm completely overwhelmed by my marriage issues."

It was rare for Reed to be short or impatient with Slade. He was consistently the opposite of those descriptions with her. Encouraging even when a job loss was her fault. Nonjudgmental of her often questionable approach to life and work. A few years ago, he'd even sent her money during a particularly tough stretch. Slade had managed to pay him back, but she'd definitely felt guilty about that wrinkle and subsequent fail on her part.

Her brother had always been the more logical one.

So, Slade should probably listen to him on this and set her conspiracy theories aside.

She could admit that the experience with her old law firm had her on edge and suspicious of pretty much everything.

"Okay. I'll let the Mom stuff go if I get to keep looking into what happened to Vincent Dunn."

He reared back in surprise. "Seriously? You're agreeing?"

"Regarding Mom, yes."

"I don't see why you're so curious about a guy who died thirty-four years ago."

"But why was he *here*?" Slade motioned to the cliff and the water below. Just being on the deck sometimes gave her vertigo. Why would anyone have gotten close enough to the edge of the cliff that they could fall to their death?

"I hate to say this, because it sounds like I don't care about a human being and I do, but...what does it matter? Nothing you find is going to change anything. He'll still be gone."

Slade was quiet for a beat. Reed had leveled with her about his marriage, and she could do the same with him about Jude, but something held her back. Something made her tongue the consistency of lead.

Plus, how could she add anything to the load he was carrying right now?

"I just... I need the distraction, okay?"

Reed scrutinized her like he would a finals study guide. "Okay." And that was it. He didn't push, didn't poke.

Slade teared up.

"If there's anything I can do... You know I'm here for you, right?"

"I know. Thank you." She squeezed his arm, grateful, relieved.

A car engine sounded, and they both turned to check the driveway as Mom pulled in.

"What do you think she would say if she knew about me and Lindsey?"

"That she loves you. She'd be supportive. Especially since it's you we're talking about."

Reed rolled his eyes. "As if she wouldn't be supportive of you? She earned the name Mama-Mar for a reason, didn't she? That protective bear instinct covers both of her children."

Yes, but it had always felt different when applied in Slade's direction. More stifling. More hypercritical.

Mom turned off the engine, and Reed delivered his next statement quietly and quickly—before the car door opened. "I don't want either of you to blame Lindsey."

"I won't because I know how hard that would be on you. But you have to promise you'll stop thinking this is all your fault."

"What if it is?"

"It's not." Slade wasn't naive enough to think Reed wasn't part of the problem. Certainly, he and Lindsey had both contributed to their demise. But she also knew who her brother was at his core, and there wasn't a chance this side of the Mississippi that Reed should be pinning all the blame on himself.

"Isn't this a nice sight?" Mom joined them on the deck, nothing but her purse in tow. Hadn't she been out running errands?

Reed must have witnessed the internal question flash across Slade's features, because he gave a quick head shake—a millisecond reminder that she'd agreed to abandon her suspicions.

He hopped up and slid a chair for their mother next to his. "Are you referring to the view or us?"

"Thank you." Mom sat, and Reed returned to his chair. "Both. But mostly you two. There were so many years I thought you guys would never learn to get along."

"I was like ten years old when we would fight," Slade protested. "Show me a ten-year-old who doesn't argue with their sibling."

"And eleven. And twelve," Mom filled in. "And thirteen. And—"

"I was *not* the only one at fault! Reed wasn't as innocent as you thought he was. Did you know he used to force me to wrestle with him in order to gain control of the remote? I couldn't win, of course. Because I was dainty and precious and pure of heart."

"Ha!" Reed's bark of laughter was a small victory in and of itself. Slade might not be able to help him mend his marriage, but making him laugh counted for something, didn't it?

"And here I thought you were both at fault for your tussles," Mom delivered dryly.

"Slade *definitely* wasn't innocent," Reed supplied. "Did you know she used to hide under my bed and scare me when I walked into my room? And then when I started looking for her there, she switched to other places, so I never knew where she was going to pop out of. It was like that torturous jack-in-the-box baby toy."

Slade had forgotten about that! "I was *such* a mastermind at harassing you. Honestly, I'm so impressed with my younger self." Slade had been creative in discovering ways to torture her older brother, but only because he'd started it.

"You two." Mom's tone was part nostalgic, part entertained. "I'm glad you have each other like I have Lovetta. That's what I'd hoped for you."

"We definitely have each other's backs, so you can lay your fears to rest, Mom." Slade's stomach twisted at all that Reed had revealed to her tonight. If she could take his pain from him and carry it, she would. Mom had no idea just how much her wish had come true.

"I can hardly keep my eyes open. I think I'll head to bed even though it's early." Mom snagged her purse from the deck and stood. "Good night." She paused behind them. "I'm glad you're both here. I really don't know what I would do if you weren't."

"We're happy to be here." Slade spoke for both of them, especially now that she knew why her brother had fled Naperville ahead of schedule. "Night, Mom. Wait—" She swiveled to face her. "Do you need help grabbing things from the car? Didn't you say you were running errands?" Slade ignored Reed's subtle kick to her chair.

"I was removing things from the house, not bringing more in. Although the thrift store was closed when I got there, so that part was a waste." Mom entered through the sliding glass door, and Slade waited until she was out of earshot to pounce.

"She ran errands and came back with nothing? What's that about?"

"She *just said* she was dropping off, not picking up."

"And that took her how long? Didn't she seem almost relaxed to you? Something *is* weird."

Reed snorted. "That would be terrible if she's figured out a way to unwind a little during all of this. Earlier, she'd mentioned walking along the Blue. Maybe she actually did that. Besides, you said you'd drop this line of questioning."

"That was before Mom created more things to question!" Slade's skin heated with a flash of guilt. Reed had admitted he didn't have the capacity for her suspicions. The least she could do was honor that and let them go. Her brother had enough stress going on without her adding to it.

Besides, as she'd already deduced, Reed was likely right anyway, so Slade would be saving herself the torture of sticking her foot in her mouth or causing undue drama.

It would be nice, for once, to avoid that from the start and not have to clean up the mess after.

Now, if only she could go back and do that with Jude.

Chapter Sixteen

"You're in a good mood." Lovetta's face filled Marin's phone screen from its perch on the hutch shelf. A *rat-tat-tat* sounded on the roof, followed by a popping noise. "Especially with all of *that* going on."

"You can hear that?" Marin removed one of their mom's floral Bavarian porcelain dinner plates from the hutch where they'd been stored and wrapped it in packing paper. She couldn't bear to get rid of the set their parents had received for their wedding. She or Lovetta would keep the dishes. Or Marin would store them for Slade to have one day when she had space.

"I'm pretty sure everyone within a mile radius of me and you can hear it." Lovetta was on a bench outside the hospital, taking her lunch break. Greenery filled her background along with the sounds of birds chirping.

"That ruckus is one glorious sound, isn't it? The roof getting done feels so good."

Lovetta erupted in James Brown's "I Feel Good."

Marin shimmied her hips to Lovetta's rendition as she carried her sister with her into the kitchen, filled the teakettle with water and placed it on the burner.

When Lovetta finished the chorus, Marin continued, "I was worried the shingles wouldn't come in or something would hold it up. I can't believe it's actually happening." True to his word, Garrett had bumped them ahead of his next job. The shingles had arrived quickly, and somehow, his crew had started seven days after they'd first discussed the project.

If Marin wasn't here witnessing it, she wouldn't believe it.

"I'm definitely not going to complain about you getting us special treatment," Lovetta said. "We'll take every advantage that man is willing to give us. Does he still have a thing for you? Or does he make a new roof happen in a week for every woman in Dillon? Real talk—is he wearing a shirt or no?" A hum of appreciation came from her throat. "He was never my type, but I won't deny he always looked good. I remember you ogling him on more than one occasion."

"I've never ogled anyone." Except…back in the summer in high school, Garrett would do yard work sans shirt. And there was a slight possibility Marin remembered those first shocks of bone-tingling attraction, that teenage infatuation. "You've been reading too many romance novels and letting your imagination run wild. Things here are very much like the stack of textbooks I have no idea why Mom kept, that I tossed yesterday. Besides," Marin forged ahead before Lovetta could interrupt with more of her teasing insinuations, "Garrett's not even here today." His crew had shown up but not him. A relief, to be truthful. Of course Marin liked and appreciated Garrett, but it was so much easier to breathe and function and not let life spin out of control when he wasn't present.

So, Lovetta was right—Marin *was* in a good mood. Because the roofers had showed…and because Garrett hadn't.

Footsteps sounded on the stairs, and Reed joined her in the kitchen.

"Reed!" Lovetta squealed, morphing into a teenager who'd spotted their favorite rock star. "Hi, honey."

Reed pivoted until he located his aunt's face on the counter, beaming at him through the phone screen. He greeted her, and she peppered him with questions about his work and Lindsey and if he was using all his vacation hours for the house purge.

Marin prepped her tea, giving them space to catch up.

"Thank you so much for helping with the house, honey. I feel terrible that I'm not there. I've been telling everyone at work how generous and selfless my niece and nephew are to help out like this."

"We're happy to assist. Although you may be giving us more credit than we deserve." Reed's quiet laugh was reminiscent of Ralph's. Sometimes, Marin caught his profile and had a moment where he *was* Ralph—in his younger years. Her breath would stall, and she had to force her limbs to function again and her nervous system to jump-start. She had to remind herself that while Ralph had given her Reed, her husband was, indeed, gone.

A loud thump sounded above them, and Lovetta reacted by shifting back from the screen as if the roof might come crashing into her world.

"Sounds like a headache waiting to happen. I'm not jealous of missing this part." Lovetta checked her watch. "I've got to go. It was so good to see you, Reed! Say hi to my namesake for me. Love you all!" She clicked off after their goodbyes, and momentary silence reigned.

Marin and Reed both looked up, and the shuffling and rhythm of the reroofing returned.

Reed opened the fridge and stood in front of it like a woman mid–hot flash.

"Looking for anything in particular?"

He shut the door. "No. Maybe. I don't know." He delivered

a smile that Marin would file under Forced. "Just browsing, I guess."

"Were you able to get anything done this morning with all the pounding?"

"Not really. I thought noise-cancelling headphones would work, but they definitely weren't enough to combat the distraction."

"Should we make an early lunch? I didn't eat breakfast this morning because of meeting with the Realtor." They'd popped into Reed's room quickly in an attempt not to disrupt his work. Marin had been relieved to set the ball in motion regarding listing the house once they'd finished cleaning it out. And she'd gotten the okay to leave the beds, couches and dining table for showings, which made it so much easier for them to continue living in the space while they worked.

"Sure."

"How about eggs on toast?" It was a staple she'd made throughout their childhoods. Simple. Contained protein. Relatively healthy when made with the right bread.

"Sounds good."

At Reed's approval, Marin removed the eggs from the fridge and two frying pans from the drawer under the oven. She grabbed the spray olive oil and some butter from its spot on the counter, along with the loaf of whole wheat bread.

Reed moved to the coffeepot and poured the remaining liquid into a mug. "Where's Slade?"

"She took a carload down to the thrift store and then planned to do yoga in the park with her friend Keely." Marin had encouraged Slade to take a break this morning since she hadn't left the premises since Saturday.

"That's actually good."

"It is?"

Reed sipped his coffee and made a disgruntled face. "I forgot to add cream." He opened the fridge door and added a dollop.

After returning the creamer to the shelf, he swung the door shut again. "I just meant it's great she got out for a bit."

"You make it sound like we're running a work release program."

His mouth quirked. "I didn't mean it like that. You seem happy today, Mom."

And you seem distracted. "I do?"

"You're humming."

"I was?"

He nodded. "Why do you think that is?"

Why was she happy or why was she humming? Either way, strange question. "Have I been tearing around here like an irate bear outside of today? Because Lovetta just said something similar."

Reed laughed. "It's just… I'm glad to see you relaxed. That's all."

"Thanks, hon." Marin internally shrugged and sprayed the pan. *Was* she acting differently? "Like I told Lovetta, I'm relieved that the roof is happening, especially so quickly. I kept thinking something would delay it, so I didn't let myself believe it would actually get done, until the roofers showed up this morning. It's a pretty big weight lifted."

"That makes a lot of sense. Is Garrett here?" Reed moved to her left and began buttering the slices of bread.

"Nope. Just his crew."

"Are you worried at all that he's not?"

"That he's not here?" Where was he going with this line of questioning? And why did Marin suddenly feel like she was on the witness stand? *It's probably innocent. Garrett has been the one in charge of getting the roof scheduled, the shingles ordered. Don't overthink it.* "Not at all. I completely trust that his guys know what they're doing." Marin was careful to keep her expression schooled, her movements fluid as she cracked eggs into the heated pan.

"And that's because you two grew up together?" Reed added the bread to the heated square pan.

She'd definitely become the star witness in what she feared was her own trial. "Well, I don't trust the teenage version of Garrett." Marin paced her response so that it wouldn't come across as rushed or defensive. "I trust the version of him who took over his dad's construction company and made it even more successful. It's not like he's new to this, honey. Garrett knows what he's doing."

"True."

Marin wasn't sure how to respond. Thanks? Glad you agree? She flipped the eggs, and Reed reached into his back pocket.

"I think the vibrations from the roof shifted things around in my closet, because while I was working this morning, there was a small avalanche in there. My fault since I moved stuff around when I got here. I came across these photos when I was picking up the contents of the boxes."

They were three-by-five, the edges holding the slight curve of time and elements. What if they were from that fateful summer? Was *this* why Reed was acting strange?

Marin wiped jittery hands on the kitchen towel and reached out for them. "Let me find my readers." She scanned the countertop and the dining table from her perch by the stove while her pulse mimicked the thumps and clunks on the roof.

"Hold still." Reed plucked the glasses from the top of her head. "Here."

Marin's laugh held hints of panic, so she quickly stifled it. "Thanks." She perused the stack of about ten photos quickly, her relief instant when she realized that while they did feature her and Garrett together, they were from her high school years and not later.

Truth be told, she didn't remember if photo evidence of that summer her corner of the world had imploded even existed. But she could recall so many other minute details from that time. How her dad had been stoic and calm during the swarm of police after Vincent's death. How her mom had made the officers coffee and baked goods. How Garrett hadn't been where he'd said he was.

Marin flipped the slices of bread and turned off the heat on both burners. "This was prom my junior year." She studied the nuances of the photos again—the boys in bow ties and cummerbunds, the girls in pastel dresses with teased hair and an overabundance of shimmering makeup. They could have signaled a satellite dish with their sparkle. "I loved that pink-blush dress so much. Gran spent more on it than I thought she would, though we did find the shoes on clearance. We'll probably come across them while sorting."

Reed's cheeks creased. "I would not doubt it."

"Are there more photos?" Marin handed the stack back to Reed. "I'd love to look through them." For nostalgia's sake and to make sure they didn't hold details that could wreck lives.

"Yeah, I can bring the box down."

"That will be fun to sort through." She hoped. Marin plated the toast and slid the eggs on top. They both moved to the table, the legs of their chairs creating a familiar hum against the wood floor as they sat across from each other.

"Was that Garrett in the photos?" Reed cut into his egg with his fork, sending the slightly runny yoke spilling across the bread. "Was he your date?"

"Yes. He was. A group of us went together." Marin added salt and pepper to her eggs, then slid the condiments toward Reed. Technically, there wasn't anything wrong with her kids knowing about her relationship with Garrett in high school. It was the connection to their twenties that made her lungs empty of oxygen.

Marin felt as if she had so many glass balls up in the air that she'd never be able to catch them all without one shattering.

She was attempting to protect so many people.

Her children.

Ralph.

Garrett.

Herself.

And while in theory, she should be able to level with her kids about the marital issues she and their father had gone through, she also understood that doing so would create so many problems. Including shining a spotlight on the past. The last thing anyone needed was for dark corners to be revealed. Or for someone to take a current look at Garrett's or Marin's faulty alibis.

Reed added salt and pepper to his egg. "Slade said that when she met Garrett, there was some tension between you two. She got the impression you were downplaying your connection to him."

Of course Slade had sniffed that out. Marin's breathing stalled as she waited for his next delivery.

"I told her she was fishing in the wrong creek." The Grandad-ism extracted a rusty smile from her. "But then I found these pictures, which made me question if she was right. So, I thought I'd come straight to the source."

Marin's pulse thrummed so loudly she was afraid that Reed could hear it.

Ever since she'd returned home from Garrett's on Monday evening, Marin had been expecting an interrogation. As if her kids somehow knew where she'd spent the majority of her time that night.

She also felt guilty for her lies of omission. Marin had decided no more. Leaving the past in the past was one thing, but falsifying information in the present was a line she couldn't—wouldn't—cross again.

"Well…" Marin's shoulders raised along with her heart rate. "We did date in high school."

Reed's fork stalled inches above his plate, and his vision jumped to her. "Why didn't you tell us?"

"When should I have done that?" Marin forced herself to take a bite of the meal, but the flavor was lost on her. It could have been cardboard or flour or dog food for all her taste buds knew.

"When you introduced him to us."

"Like, this is Garrett, and he was my boyfriend in high school?"

Reed gave a small laugh, and his eyes held kindness that steadied Marin. They were just a mother and son having a conversation. It didn't have to become bigger than that.

"I guess that would have been a little strange. But you could have mentioned it at some point."

"I suppose it felt awkward to bring it up. I mean, your dad and I were married for thirty-eight years. It didn't seem like pertinent information." Marin swallowed, her mouth as dry as an overbaked biscuit. "Garrett and I were still together when I left for college and met your father. I basically broke up with him to be with Dad." She wasn't sure why she was sharing all of this. Except…if she gave Reed enough details, enough reasons to believe her as to why she hadn't said anything, then maybe he—and Slade—would be able to let things go, to not dig further. "I hurt Garrett badly, but when I met your father, something just clicked. I just *knew* he was my future. That he was the one for me."

That time had been gut-wrenching.

The breakup with Garrett had gone wretchedly—another word he'd likely find amusing outside this context. Garrett hadn't understood how Marin went from tormented over leaving him to falling for someone else in the span of such a short period, and Marin hadn't been able to explain it well. She'd known that Garrett was the kind of soul that, once planted in a small town, would stay until his dying day. The kind that didn't uproot even in the most treacherous storm. And Marin had been ready to explore the world—or at least live someplace besides Dillon. It was the one dark stain in their relationship—the one red flag that she'd ignored. Until Marin went to college and realized that she wasn't alone in wanting to *not* return to the town she'd grown up in. That it was *okay* to want something different.

But that had left her and Garrett in a precarious position. She'd met Ralph, and Marin had used him as the excuse for the breakup with Garrett, but truthfully, it was about more than that. She hadn't done a good job of articulating her hopes and dreams back then, because she hadn't wanted to offend Garrett's desire to stay in Dillon. There was nothing wrong with the path he'd taken. And there was nothing wrong with the path she'd taken.

"I guess you could say it was a sensitive subject at the time and then something I didn't revisit after the fact. I didn't see any reason to mention it." And that was the truth.

The only question was if it would be enough of the truth for her children.

Chapter Seventeen

"How did this guy fall off a cliff—or get pushed or jump or whatever—and we can't find anything about his death?" Keely wrinkled her nose from her spot across the large library table.

"That's the question that's been plaguing me from the start." When Slade's interest was first piqued by Vincent, she thought she'd do a little research and easily find out what had happened to him. But digging into the story had turned into a marathon, not a sprint.

When Keely and Slade had made plans to attend yoga in the park—which sported a gorgeous view overlooking Lake Dillon that, once again, made Slade never want to leave this town—and then visit the library to search for any other articles about Vincent Dunn, they'd both assumed archived copies of *The Summit Daily* would be on microfilm or in some search-able format. But they'd discovered that anything dated before 2002 was kept in hard-copy storage. They'd had to sign the papers out from the circulation desk with the promise that they wouldn't leave the building and then peruse them.

They'd been at it for twenty minutes, and they'd only gotten through one paper each. They had no idea where an article about Vincent might be buried, so they'd decided to be meticulous from the start so they wouldn't wonder if they'd missed anything.

Keely dug into her tote and pulled out what looked to be a freshly baked cinnamon muffin wrapped in cellophane.

"Want any?" she offered.

Slade's mouth curved. "I'm good, thanks. I'm pretty sure you're not supposed to eat in the library."

Keely covertly moved the muffin to her lap, keeping the cellophane beneath it as a makeshift plate/barrier. "Some of us have low blood sugar and need to eat more often. They can't discriminate against me like that. Aren't you starving after yoga?"

"Not really." With all the stress between her job, the house and Reed's disintegrating marriage, Slade's appetite was nearly nonexistent. "Are you ever not starving?"

Her friend grinned. "Not really." Keely brushed some crumbs from the table where she'd first opened the muffin and then leaned forward, her eyes widening. "Oh!"

"Did some get on the paper? I doubt anyone is ever going to know. The last time someone checked these out was probably decades ago."

"No. Listen to this." Keely read aloud. "Body beneath High Meadow Drive has been identified as Vincent Dunn. Police are investigating a person of interest in the case, but they are not releasing more information at this time." Her vision swept from the paper to Slade. "A 'person of interest' doesn't exactly fit with the he-just-fell theory."

"No, it does not." Who had the person of interest been, and what had made the police suspect their involvement? The article created more questions than answers.

Slade had just reached the classifieds section in the paper from the day after Keely's, so she placed it in the dead-end pile.

"One more each?"

Keely nodded, so Slade slid the next day's paper over to her and snagged the following for herself.

They both concentrated on scanning. If they didn't find anything, Slade would have to come back to the library, and it was hard to carve time away from the house purge and the enormity of all that needed to be done there.

Especially for something like this, which fell under the category of frivolous to probably everyone on the planet but her.

Slade's phone vibrated on the table, and she flipped it over to see a text from her mom.

Reed and I are going to start on Gran and Grandad's room. No rush for you to come back. Just wanted you to know.

That was nice of her, to keep Slade updated. And she was probably aware that Slade wouldn't want to miss out on sorting their things. She'd better get back before they tossed something invaluable to her.

"Unfortunately, I think I need to go." Slade set her phone down on the table. "I'll just finish this one quickly." That way, if they returned, they could start with the following paper. Slade's vision flitted across the page, her hope deteriorating with each article. If they didn't find anything, what would they do next? "Wait. I've got something." Her heartbeat skipped as she stumbled upon a barely noticeable mention of Vincent. She read the updated information from the short piece to Keely. "Vincent Dunn's death has officially been ruled a death of undetermined origin, and the investigation has been closed."

"That's it?"

"That's it." Nothing about what had happened to the person of interest in the case. Nothing about anything, really.

"What's a 'death of undetermined origin'?"

Slade looked it up on her phone. "*Undetermined* is used when there isn't evidence to support a specific manner of death." The article went on to list a number of circumstances that would qualify…including falls. "Huh. That sounds a bit like saying 'hey, we're not sure what happened, and no one cares overly much, so let's close this case and move on.'"

"I thought the same thing."

"I wonder if that's the last article."

"It kind of sounds like it. But how do we know for sure?"

"We can't…unless we scour weeks of papers." Which sounded fruitless…and time-consuming. And while Slade was all about the distraction Vincent research provided, she couldn't be away from the house that much.

"Or years of papers. Who knows when a development might have occurred."

"True. So basically, this is mission impossible."

"Guess so. At least we found what we did."

"Something…and nothing." While the person-of-interest lead had obviously been dropped, the fact that at some point, someone had been questioned or considered a possible suspect was startling information. Who had it been? And why had they been cleared? What was their connection to Vincent or her grandparents' property?

Obviously, there was more to the man's death than the open-and-shut case Mom had implied.

Per the usual when it came to Vincent Dunn, the info they'd uncovered this morning had been like finding a clue and turning onto a dead-end road all wrapped into one.

Slade had a collection of random puzzle pieces that didn't fit together, and no box showing the whole picture so that she could make sense of it all.

Keely let out a sigh representing the disappointment Slade also felt. She rolled up the used cellophane from her muffin and tucked it into the pocket of her bag.

Slade lined the three articles—including the original one

she'd found in the dresser drawer—next to each other on the table and pressed the papers flat. She scanned them into her phone—a trick that would make Reed proud...if he knew what she was up to and approved of it.

Which he likely wouldn't.

But he *had* said she could continue pursuing the Vincent trail as long as she left the Mom trail alone.

And Slade had been doing a very good job of that all week, so technically she was obeying orders.

After returning the papers and exchanging goodbyes with Keely, Slade got behind the wheel of Mom's beige dream machine and headed back to her grandparents' home, the lingering headache she'd been fighting all morning resurrecting itself on the drive.

Last night, she'd been unable to sleep. Her mind had been spinning regarding her job—the loss of it, the reason for her exit, what her next plan needed to be. She'd begun to accept that Brockton had buried her complaint and that nothing was going to be done about Jude. She feared that everything would continue just as it had been...everything except her having a place of employment or a paycheck.

Slade had tossed and turned so long that she'd finally grabbed her phone and scrolled through job openings in Gulfport and the adjacent areas, thinking that doing something to change her circumstances would bring relief.

But instead of lifting her spirits, the search had sent her spiraling.

Despite her many previous careers, Slade had no idea what to attempt next. Should she fall back on an old standby? Try something new? Find another law firm without a sleazeball partner?

And then there was that tiny, oh-so-important detail that had kept her from applying anywhere as of yet—references.

Slade could list her employers from before the law firm on an application since she'd left her previous positions on good terms, but that gap in her resume and references would surely show.

And if she admitted that she'd had issues at her old firm and that the workplace environment was unsafe, they might assume that *she* was the problem.

After all, they didn't know her.

The job search had created more stress than relief, so Slade had set her phone aside and practiced Ujjayi breathing until sleep had finally, finally come.

When Slade arrived at the house, numerous trucks lined her grandparents' street, so she parked to the east of the property. She wasn't the least bit sad about avoiding the ruckus that accosted her when she opened her driver's door.

Slade paused at the end of the driveway to observe the construction site. Things seemed to be going in all directions at once—materials barreled onto the roof on a conveyor belt, and old shingles flew over the side and into the large dumpster that replaced the smaller one Mom had previously gotten for the house purge.

"Morning." A raspy male voice sounded behind Slade. She jolted in surprise and then turned in the direction of the greeting. The man closed the passenger door of his truck, which was parked at the west edge of the driveway. "Sorry. Didn't mean to startle you. I was trying to prevent that from happening since I wasn't sure you knew I was behind you."

"I appreciate that, as I definitely did not." Ever since Jude, Slade had been jumpier than usual. Another gift he'd so kindly imparted to her.

"I was just getting something out of my truck." He lifted a stack of papers as evidence and approached her, his easy gait broadcasting relaxed confidence.

He sported a Stoneridge Construction T-shirt, faded jeans, work boots and a clean-shaven, baby face.

He paused in front of her. "You in need of a roof?"

Slade pointed over her shoulder with her thumb. "I'm getting one."

The skin kissing his eyes pinched with empathy. "You must be the granddaughter. I'm Cyrus." He offered his hand, and Slade shook it. When was the last time anyone had greeted her with a handshake? Especially after Covid. His skin was calloused, his grip firm without being bone crushing.

"Slade." She removed her hand from his, her arm swinging back to her side, fingers engaged in a *Pride and Prejudice* hand flex.

"Nice to meet you, Slade of the Slades. I'm sorry about your grandfather. Your grandparents were amazing people."

"Thank you."

"How, exactly, did their last name become your first? I like it by the way. Not that you need my approval."

"It's actually my middle name, but I decided to go by it years ago."

"That just makes me want to know what your first name is."

Slade rarely shared that information with anyone. She'd never felt like Lovetta fit her. The only saving grace was sharing the name with her amazing, funny, delightful aunt. It certainly hadn't been easy to see Lovetta scrawled across her coat hook in first grade when the ones next to hers were labeled Maddie or Kaitlyn or Ava or something equally cute.

"Gertrude? Fifi? Misery? Boo-boo? Blink twice when I'm getting close."

Slade laughed.

Cyrus groaned in amused frustration. "What do I need to do to find out?"

"Earn my trust."

He released a low whistle. A determined grin that was anything but stingy ignited, creasing Cyrus's clean-shaven cheeks. "Noted."

Why did Slade feel as if she'd just thrown down a gauntlet?

"Cy." One of the roofers called for him. "Got a question for ya."

"In a minute," he called, his vision never leaving Slade. "So where do you live when you're not working on your grand-parents' house?"

"Florida." *Although, at the moment, I'd love to not live there.* Maybe Slade should apply for a job with Cyrus and his roof-ing crew.

"How long are you planning to be in town?"

"However long it takes to get the house emptied and ready to sell. Probably another week."

Sympathy furrowed his brow, adding maturity to his counte-nance. "It has to be hard to let go of your grandparents' home."

"It feels a little like losing them all over again."

Cyrus's head bobbed in understanding.

How had they jumped in so deep so quickly?

"Well, if you ever need a break from all of this, let me know." He dug into his back pocket and removed a wallet, plucking a business card from the depths that looked as if it had been stored there for a decade—the corners bent, the print faded. "That's my cell." He nodded at the card, which had somehow switched from his hand to hers. The man was a smooth opera-tor. Aunt Lovetta would start singing that eighties song if she could hear Slade's thoughts right now.

"I'm a big believer in texting at any hour," Cyrus contin-ued. "And I firmly disagree with the three-day rule." His smile amped up to full force. It was a little like trying to stare at the sun. Blue halos sprouted in Slade's vision. "Seriously, though, whatever I can do to be of service—on this job or anything else—don't hesitate to reach out."

Was he providing good customer service or was he asking her out?

"In the interest of full disclosure, I'm twenty-nine." *Interest-ing. Slade would have guessed twenty-three.* "Never been married. No priors. Some mom issues, though I've done my best to work through those. And the freezer in my garage is used for meat on the rare chance that I actually get enough time off of work to go hunting."

"Am I interviewing you for something?"

"A date. Think about it and let me know. We could also classify it as *hanging out.* I'm open to negotiation. Wait. You're not one of those granola girls, are you? The kind that blends grass or only eats things that don't have feelings."

Slade certainly dabbled in the health world when it came to yoga or even massage, which she was also trained in, but when it came to eating, Mom claimed she was thirteen. And on that… Mom was right.

"Not a granola, though I probably should be. No priors. Only two bodies in my freezer, and I've never been anywhere close to being engaged or married."

"We're going to have to save that to unpack another time."

"The bodies?"

"The *never anywhere close* to engaged or married."

"And how is it that you're interested in me? It's not like you know anything about me."

"I believe, if I'm not mistaken, that's what dates are for. To get to know each other."

He had her there. It had been a while since Slade had been on one, and obviously, she was out of practice.

"Plus, I can tell you're one of the good ones, Slade of the Slades."

"And how can you tell that?"

"I get a sense about people."

Slade used to think she was one of the good ones until she'd abandoned everyone who worked at the law firm with her.

"Cy!" The same man who'd called for Cyrus a few minutes earlier gave a shrill whistle. "Seriously, man. Talk to the girl later."

Banter from the crew followed.

Slade didn't need a mirror to confirm that her Scandinavian white-as-printer paper cheeks had turned cotton candy pink.

Cyrus's nutmeg veneer didn't portray a similar reaction, but he flashed a boyish grin that caused his toffee eyes to twinkle and his eyebrows to reach for his chocolate hair.

And Slade had just mentally boiled the man down to a walking dessert.

That could be problematic.

Cyrus backed toward the person who'd shouted for him, his amused, transfixed gaze still on Slade. "Don't lose that card!" he called out, and then he swiveled, leaving her standing at the end of the driveway, mouth slightly agape at their strange, swift encounter, which had happened as fast as a truck losing its brakes on the I-70 descent into Denver.

What a bizarre sequence of events this morning had held. Somehow, Slade had gone from researching a dead body and coming up with next to nothing, to running into a live one that could very well amount to something...if she let it.

And how silly would that be when she didn't live here? Stupid, really, to even consider contacting Cyrus.

Slade should tear up the business card he'd given her right this second.

But for some reason...she didn't.

Chapter Eighteen

Even though she'd been staying in her parents' bedroom while purging the house, Marin hadn't removed anything until she and the kids had started cleaning it out together yesterday.

Perhaps because it felt like a bit of a museum or a time capsule…or perhaps because if she tossed anything, it felt as if her parents would walk in and question why she was getting rid of their possessions.

She'd experienced a similar feeling when she'd gone through Ralph's things about a year after he passed.

The finality of giving away a person's clothes—the very place their lifeblood had flowed, the items that had hugged their skin—was pure torment.

Marin was thankful not to be going through her parents' most personal items alone. Her kids created a buffer for her from the stark grief. Their banter and commentary kept her afloat. She couldn't even fathom how long the house would have taken if they'd only come for a week as planned.

The sound of a saw and other construction noises intensified as she removed two boxes from the shelf in her parents' closet and placed them on the flowered bedspread.

The crew was fixing the water-damaged portion of the ceiling inside the house as well as continuing with the outdoor work.

"Gran's sweater!" Slade sat with the soles of her feet touching in front of her, looking as comfortable and limber as a toddler. She lifted the soft, striped cardigan to her nose and inhaled. "I have *so* many memories of her wearing this. It smells just like her. This is definitely going in my keep pile. Unless…" Her vision shifted to Marin. "Do you want it, Mom?"

"It's all yours."

Reed stood in front of the open closet. "Should I just haul an armload of the hanging clothes out to your car? Do you think the thrift store will take them that way or do we need to fold?"

"I would imagine it's fine to move them on the hangers since they display clothes that way in the shop."

"Wait!" Slade scrambled up from the floor. "I haven't looked through those yet."

Reed gave her the space to do that, sharing an amused glance with Marin behind her back. But his grin was short-lived. He'd been pensive ever since he stepped out of the room earlier this morning to take a phone call.

"Why didn't Grandad give any of Gran's clothes away after she passed?" Slade slid hangers to the left as she sorted.

"Maybe he couldn't deal with the loss of her things on top of the loss of her," Reed supplied. "He always said Gran was his person."

"I loved when he said that." Marin gave Reed's arm a quick squeeze of encouragement. It wasn't like her son to be so morose. "Reed, honey, do you think you might be missing Lindsey? I wonder if she could come out for a few days. Or maybe you should head home."

Slade and Reed's gazes sought each other's like magnets. Tension filled the bedroom.

Marin would step back from the land mine she'd just neared if she had any idea where or what it was.

"Slade and I are not leaving you to handle the rest of the house on your own, Mom." Reed released a long rush of air. "And Lindsey and I... We're not on the best terms right now."

No. Marin's heart crumpled. "Oh, Reed." Her tears were instant. They pooled along her lower lashes, and she swiped them away.

Reed's Adam's apple bobbed before he continued. "I'm sure you have a million questions, but honestly, so do I. It's not something I can boil down to she did that, or I did this. It's... complicated."

"Relationship troubles always are." Marin's eyelids momentarily shuttered, as if that could block out and erase her son's pain.

"I only found out a few days ago." Slade had paused from sorting, one hand gripping the sleeve of a button-down shirt, her expression mimicking the sorrow surely visible on Marin's.

Marin experienced a flash of jealousy that she quickly stifled. Hadn't she just told her children the other night how she wanted them to be there for each other? She couldn't bemoan the fact that they were. Or that she was the last to know.

"Part of why I didn't tell you and Slade was because I knew you'd both hurt for me. For us. And I already hated that agony for me and Lindsey. I didn't want to inflict it on anyone else." Reed held her gaze, instilling determination into his. "I'm doing as well as I can right now, so you don't need to worry about me."

"Always taking care of me, aren't you? You don't have to protect me, honey. If I've learned anything in the last few years, it's that I can handle more than I thought I could." And yet, wasn't that exactly what Marin was doing? Attempting to protect everyone but feeling like the villain because it meant she couldn't reveal all.

She hugged him, holding on extralong. "What can I do to help?"

"Nothing. I just need to…muddle through."

If anyone understood muddling, it was Marin.

After a squeeze of nonverbal encouragement that was probably more for her own comfort than his, Marin stepped back. "I'll try to give you space, but please let me know if there's anything you need. Anything I can do."

"Thank you."

Marin was shocked she was still standing after Reed's revelation. So many questions pinged in her brain. What did he mean by *not on the best of terms*? Were he and Lindsey divorcing? Were they just in a rough patch? What had happened?

Somehow, she managed not to voice any of them. Probably because she very much recognized Reed's need for space. Didn't she give herself all kinds of room and grace and privacy regarding the past? The least she could do was give Reed the same, regarding his present.

His behavior since his arrival made so much more sense now. Her sweet son!

Marin's heart severed for the thousandth time in her life. "Maybe the break will be good for you two." She couldn't help but scrounge for some semblance of hope. "Sometimes, absence really does make the heart grow fonder." It certainly had that summer Marin escaped to her parents. She'd missed Ralph so much. Had wanted, more than anything, for him to fight for her, miss her, pursue her.

It had taken Vincent's death to wake Ralph up. To make him realize that he could have lost Marin for good.

No one knew what Vincent's true intentions were that night, since they'd been thwarted—Garrett would have a heyday with that word—but speculations had run rampant. Especially with those who knew that Vincent had developed an obsession with Marin in the weeks before his death.

"I sure hope so."

The pain evident in Reed's answer leveled Marin. She wanted to hug him again. She wanted to engage in a good cry over what he'd just revealed. She wanted to know the details.

Instead, she let her body collapse to a seated position on the bed next to the boxes she'd gotten down.

Slade stepped back from the closet with four items—one of Grandad's flannel shirts, one of his sweaters, plus a scarf and light jacket of Gran's. She dumped the unfolded clothes into a bag she'd labeled for herself and then returned to the closet.

"I'm not sure how I'm going to get everything you and I want to keep back home in my car, Love."

And then Marin would end up storing Slade's stuff until she had a place with enough room for it. So basically, Slade's keep-sakes were becoming Marin's keepsakes indefinitely.

"I'm feeling your silent judgments coming at me fast and furious, Mama-Mar." Slade didn't turn, her attention still focused on the clothing.

Marin cringed. Oops. "Never mind! We'll figure out the logistics later." The last thing Marin wanted was for Slade or Reed to donate something they would miss. Better to save more than not enough.

"I think the closet multiplied overnight. There's so much shoved in here."

Reed stood behind Slade, arms crossed, semipatiently wait-ing for his sister to finish. "Maybe if you hadn't spent so much time checking on the roofing crew in the last twenty-four hours, we would have gotten through more of it."

"Slade checked on the roofing crew? Why? Was there an issue?"

"No issue. She was out there flirting, distracting the con-tractor."

How had Marin missed this? And which contractor were they talking about?

Slade tossed a disgruntled, amused glance over her shoulder at Reed. "I wasn't flirting. And he was the one who sought me out. I couldn't just be rude."

A harrumph of amusement came from Reed. "There was definite flipping of hair."

"There was not!"

"Are you telling me he didn't ask you out? Because I'm willing to admit when I'm wrong. Unlike you."

Slade gave a squeak of indignation. "I can admit when I'm wrong. But it just happens so rarely."

Reed snorted.

"I was right about Mom and Garrett, wasn't I?"

Marin had begun sorting the smaller of the two boxes, but at Slade's comment, her fingers froze, a pair of Gran's nylons strangled in her grip.

"What did you say about me and Garrett?"

"Just that I knew when you first introduced him to me that you didn't relay the whole story."

Blood rushed through Marin's veins, creating a drumming in her ears.

"I told Slade about the photos I found yesterday and that you and Garrett dated in high school," Reed filled in. "I assumed you didn't care if she knew."

"Oh…right. Of course not." As long as the discoveries stopped there. It made sense that Reed had mentioned their conversation to Slade, and yet Marin felt as if she'd lost another layer of skin and protection.

"My point is simply that I knew there was more to your relationship. And I was right." Slade delivered a haughty look Reed's way. "Even though Reed had assumed I was wrong."

Marin sincerely hoped her daughter's intuition had a limit.

"But in answer to your question—" Slade's voice lowered,

and a smirk played into her delivery "—he did ask me out. But who doesn't?"

Reed gave a bark of laughter, and Marin rose to dump the nylons, socks and scarves from the box into the black trash bag. When she returned to her seat on the bed, the second box shifted and tumbled to the floor, sending notebooks sprawling across the carpet at her feet.

She knelt and began gathering them. "Who asked you out?"

"I don't know how you missed their constant flirting, Mom." Reed assisted her in gathering the notebooks. "The guy spent far more time talking to Slade than he did doing anything with the roof."

"That's not true! He did his job. And I can't help it if he's enthralled with me."

"*Who* is enthralled with you?" Why wouldn't either of them answer her question?

"Cyrus," Slade supplied. "He's the lead on the roof."

Marin knew exactly who he was, and she had not seen that coming. She was thankful her head was bent over the spilled notebooks to prevent Slade from witnessing her shock.

Marin was a little surprised, based on how cynical Slade had been regarding Garrett from the start, that she would be flirting with or entertaining the idea of dating his son.

"Did you guys meet Cyrus when you were kids?"

Both of her children regarded her with blank stares, so she tried again. "When you would stay with Gran and Grandad, did Garrett come by with the boys?"

"What do you mean Garrett with the boys?" Slade held up a winter hat that Grandad used to wear. Despite the warm temperatures, she put it on, causing her blond-white-silver locks to flip out below it. "We never knew Garrett as kids. Did we, Reed?"

"I would say no." Reed finished picking up the notebooks

and set the box back on the bed, farther from the edge than Marin had the first time.

Did her children not realize…? Marin's stomach twisted. "Slade, you do know…?"

"Reed, you can take the clothes on the left. I've already sorted through that." Slade tossed the hat into her keep bag. "Know what?"

"That Cyrus is Garrett's son."

Slade's wide eyes landed on Marin. "Wait—what?"

"Garrett has two sons. Byron is an architect in Denver. And Cyrus works for the construction business his grandfather started and his father continued."

Scarlet splashed across Slade's cheeks. "Why wouldn't he have told me that?"

"Why would he have ever imagined you didn't know?"

Slade rubbed fingertips against her sternum. "I'm just now realizing that he never said his last name. This is all so weird. Especially since you dated his father."

"In high school. I don't think that makes him off-limits for you now, does it?"

"I don't know what to think. Except for *ew*. The idea of us dating when you dated feels like incest."

"That's a bit extreme."

"Seriously, Slove. They were like seventeen. It has nothing to do with now."

And twenty-six. Though Marin wouldn't qualify what had gone on between them that summer as *dating*.

"Are you encouraging me to go out with Cyrus?" Slade asked Reed. "I would have thought you'd be in the logical, you're-not-going-to-be-here-much-longer-why-entertain-the-option camp."

"Based on how much you two talked yesterday and then this morning when he got here—"

"It wasn't that much!"

Reed inclined his head, broadcasting his disagreement. "He's successful. Your age. And I assume he's respectful or you wouldn't give him the time of day." Reed waited for her nod of agreement. "Then, I don't see why a date is a terrible idea. Location is a simple fix."

"Location is a simple fix?" Slade's eyebrows jutted up. She reached over and checked his forehead with the back of her hand. "It doesn't make sense to date someone in Colorado when I'm not staying here."

"Not that it would necessarily turn into anything serious. And even though you'd actually like to stay here, as you declared the other day."

"You want to stay in Dillon, Love?" Marin was surprised… but also not. Her daughter had always felt a special fondness for this town and her grandparents and the summers she'd spent here.

"I mean, sure. In a perfect world. But realistically, I don't see that happening."

Reed rocked back in shock, his mouth bowing with a spark of teasing. "When have you *ever* been realistic?"

Slade threw a shirt at him.

"But how would that work with—"

"I don't know how it would work, Mom." Slade sighed like she was carrying planet Earth on her back. "That's why I'm saying it doesn't make sense."

Why did Marin feel like she'd just pressed her daughter's face into the ground after she'd stumbled?

"There's nothing wrong with not knowing your next plan yet." *I just want you to be okay. That's all I've ever wanted.* Marin abhorred when her desire to protect translated as overbearing or controlling.

Slade focused on her brother. "What is up with you playing matchmaker anyway?"

"I just don't want you to pass up on something good because…" He faltered.

"Because if you and Lindsey are struggling," Slade filled in quietly, "then what hope is left in the world?"

He gave a nod. "I don't want us to mess you up." Of course Reed would be concerned about how his problems affected Slade, even when he was still in the midst of them.

And of course Slade would be affected by his issues because she loved Reed fiercely and had more than once categorized his and Lindsey's relationship as something to aspire to one day.

"You won't." Slade's attempt at a smile went from *don't worry about me!* to someplace far more pensive the moment Reed's attention centered on the closet and the clothes she'd already sorted through.

Quiet filled the room. Reed took a load out to the car as Slade finished going through the last of the hanging items.

Once again, Marin wondered what she was missing. She opened one of the notebooks that she and Reed had just picked up. Her throat constricted when she realized they were her mother's journals.

Gran had kept track of events more than emotions, but before Reed returned and while Slade was distracted with the closet, Marin sifted through the pile, on the hunt for the year Vince died. Her mom would have surely transcribed the details of those days, that week, even the month Marin had stayed with them in Colorado.

Things like which police officers she'd invited in for coffee and cookies. How the detective had checked the house alarm system and found it wasn't turned off or triggered, therefore clearing the three of them as having anything to do with Vince's death.

But Mom wouldn't have known to document that Marin had been skirting the alarm while escaping the house since her teenage years.

Sometimes, decades later, Marin would wake up in the middle of the night, with her pulse thundering, her brain in overdrive, anxiety making her lie awake, and wonder just what she'd covered up by that omission…and what could happen even now if someone shined a light on that dark, viciously stormy night.

When she finished looking through the notebooks and didn't find that year, Marin shuddered in relief.

"You okay, Mom?" Reed had just returned from loading her car.

"I'm good." At least she was now.

"What are those?" Reed nodded toward the stack of notebooks.

"Gran's journals."

Slade let out a squeak of excitement and flew across the room. She flounced onto the bed, causing the stiff mattress to recoil and the box to almost go toppling again.

"I've been wondering when these would show up!" She snagged a notebook from the stack and opened it, running her fingertips over her grandmother's cursive, the pages crinkling as she flipped through them.

"It looks like she made entries each day about what she did, who she saw."

"I remember her telling me that they were more of an accounting of her day than processing anything emotional. She said she kept track of her activities because it made her feel like she'd accomplished something, especially during the stay-at-home mom years when Lovetta and I were young."

Slade hugged the notebook to her chest. "Reading these is like peeking into her world. I love hearing her voice in them, even though she's only relaying her activities. Can I have them?" Her gaze swept from Marin to Reed, who was at the closet, retrieving another armful of hanging clothes. "Or I could try to scan them if everyone wants copies."

Reed faced them, hangers clinking as clothes cascaded over

his arms. "There are so many of them. You wouldn't make it through scanning one of those notebooks."

"I know how to scan one page at a time. And if I had a nice, helpful brother I'm sure I could figure out how to do it faster. But since I don't, you're probably right. It might kill me."

Reed's cheeks creased as he paused in the doorway. "I don't need the journals. They're all yours as far as I'm concerned." He exited with the load of clothes.

"Same for me." Marin couldn't imagine sorting through all the notebooks and deciding what to do with them. Her mother had written the most mundane details. Not exactly thrilling reading material.

And for that, she was eternally grateful.

Chapter Nineteen

After they finished Gran and Grandad's bedroom late in the afternoon, The Cliff House settled into a contemplative silence, its temporary inhabitants retreating to their respective corners to regroup.

Despite their attempts to take breaks and take care of themselves during the house purge, Reed assumed the current mood was caused by fatigue. And even though they were nearing the final stages—they would knock out his bedroom tomorrow and then move on to The Armpit, which would likely take the better part of a week—they were all feeling the emotional weight of saying goodbye to Gran and Grandad's home.

Mom had seemed distracted at the end of sorting. Likely overcome by the emotion of handling her parents' personal things and the weight of what he'd revealed. She'd gone on a walk, doing the loop at the top of the neighborhood.

Slade had been in a funk ever since Mom had revealed that Cyrus was Garrett's son. And then this afternoon, she checked something on her phone, and her mood had darkened in a flash.

She'd been so irritable that Reed was giving her a wide berth. After a quick dinner of sandwiches, she'd holed up in her room.

And Reed himself had been reeling ever since Lindsey had called and flat-out leveled him this morning.

He'd stayed quiet regarding the new developments when discussing his marital problems with his mom and sister because he was tired of dissecting his and Lindsey's issues. He was tired of himself.

Now Reed once again headed to the neighborhood entrance at the bottom of the hill in the hopes that the climb back up would cause him to pass out, giving him a respite from his misery.

Though even the best runner's high in the world wouldn't make a dent in his current torment.

When Lindsey called this morning, she'd relayed that she'd had dinner with her mom the night before. She'd asked about him and the house before delivering the hit that had buckled his knees.

The moment she'd said, "my mom has some advice for us," Reed's internal alarms had begun flashing and screeching.

He loved his mother-in-law, but she was jaded from the demise of her own marriage and the atrocious way her husband had treated her. Chad had left Linds and Gina to start another family as easily as tossing out rotten food. It made sense that Gina had wounds and trust issues. Rightfully so. But transferring her turmoil to Reed and Lindsey's situation—as if they were at all related or similar—had created an anger in Reed he hadn't thought possible.

Gina's advice was that they part ways amicably now—as friends—before things got vicious between them. That they should cut their losses and move on.

All day Reed had fluctuated between confronting Gina and drowning in the panic that with one suggestion from his mother-in-law, his marriage was officially over.

There was no one—outside himself—that Lindsey trusted more than her mother. At least…that's how it used to be. But now Reed didn't even know if he was in the top five of Lindsey's inner circle.

Lindsey had rushed to assure him that she didn't necessarily agree with her mom's advice, but the blow had already been delivered.

Reed had ended the phone call so fast that he wasn't even sure he'd said goodbye.

He'd just known that continuing the conversation would end in chaos and destruction, and he'd been determined to avoid saying something he would regret.

Reed no longer knew what to believe when it came to his wife's wishes and desires. But he did know he couldn't keep living in limbo like this.

The ups and downs, the hopes and disappointments were too much for a body to weather.

A raindrop plunked against the back of Reed's neck as he reached the halfway point of his run. He checked the sky, surprised to find dark clouds had materialized. Hadn't the sun been shining when he left the house?

The rain continued in sporadic droplets as he crested the last turn of switchbacks leading to the loop. He experienced a moment of reprieve when his feet hit level ground, but it was short-lived.

Ruthie Swink stood in the middle of the street, wearing a loose shirt, flowered pajama pants and those tattered slippers from the other day, her expression broadcasting stark confusion.

She spun in a slow circle as if struggling to figure out where she was.

Maybe even who she was.

Reed approached slowly so as not to startle her. "Hi, Mrs. Swink." As he neared, he could see that her hair was disheveled, her pupils wide with fear. His rib cage squeezed with empathy. "Remember me? I'm Reed. The Slades' grandson." He paused a few feet away, standing between her and any vehicles that might enter the street. "I used to play with your grandson." Hopefully, the exaggeration would assist him in earning her trust. The neighborhood didn't encounter a lot of traffic, but he still needed to get her off the road.

She observed him with a wariness that would make Slade proud. "And the other boys too?" Her voice carried a slight tremor.

"Yep. The other boys too." Again, Reed allowed the embellishment. "We should move to the side of the road, Mrs. Swink. It's dangerous to stand here."

"Call me Ruthie. I never liked being called Mrs. Swink. My mother-in-law wasn't a nice person. She would come over and run her finger along our furniture and wrinkle her nose at the supposed dust. I stopped cleaning before she came over just to spite her."

Despite their precarious circumstances, Reed's smile sprouted. So, Ruthie had some spunk in her. Or at least she used to.

"Good for you. Let's move over here, all right?" Reed took two steps and waited for Ruthie to follow, but she did not.

He returned to her side. "Is it all right if I assist you?" Reed wasn't sure what she would do if he touched her, but he had to get her moving. He reached out tentatively, carefully, and tucked her hand through his arm. "Walk with me, okay? It's a little wet out, and I don't want you to slip."

As if eavesdropping, the rain switched from random droplets to a steady drizzle. Ruthie began to shake, and her hair quickly gathered a sheen of moisture.

She would be soaking wet shortly. Reed wished he would have grabbed a sweatshirt for his run so that he could protect her with something, but they were at the mercy of the elements until he got her back to her house.

"Is your husband home, Ruthie?"

"I don't know." Her brow furrowed, but the question must

have provided enough of a distraction that she shuffled her feet along with him as he moved off the road. "I thought he was with me?"

Hopefully, Mr. Swink wasn't panicking about his wife's whereabouts.

"I'll walk with you to your house, and we'll see if he's there."

They made it a couple yards before Ruthie stopped and studied him again. "Do I know you?"

Reed was tempted to run home and grab his mom's car. It would be much easier and safer to transport Ruthie that way. But what if she wandered off in the time it took him to do that?

What if she ended up back in the street and someone driving in the rain didn't see her in time to stop?

"You do know me. I'm the Slades' grandson. I knew your grandson."

This time she didn't show any recognition. Didn't take the bait.

"Tell me about your son while we walk." Last time he'd seen her, Ruthie wanted to talk about her family, so maybe if Reed got her focused on that, she wouldn't realize he was guiding her home. "What was he like?"

"He was a good boy." Their movement started again, just as Reed had hoped. "He ran track in high school. Went to state two times." Reed nodded and listened, steering Ruthie around a small puddle. "He got good grades. He even tried to befriend that one boy, tried to get him on the straight and narrow." Ruthie's footsteps faltered as if her mind had been transported to the past and gotten stuck.

"Who was that?" Reed applied slight pressure to her hand, and they regained their painstakingly slow pace. Convincing Ruthie to keep moving was a little like putting quarters in one of those mini merry-go-rounds. As long as Reed kept her talking, she shuffled forward. But the minute she got distracted, she stopped and stared at him like he was abducting her.

"Vinny."

His pulse gave a hiccup of surprise, but he kept their stride steady. "Vinny who?" Was she referring to Vincent Dunn? If Slade were present, she'd be flipping out at the possibility.

"I can't remember." Agitation weighed down her answer.

"It's okay," Reed quickly assured her, not wanting anything to upset her or stop her from continuing toward the house. "It doesn't matter."

"Vinny died, I think." Her free hand pressed against her cheek. "I can't remember how. It was sad, but he was always in trouble. No one was surprised." Her voice grew stronger. "That was how my son went down the wrong path. Instead of lifting Vinny up, the opposite happened."

A car engine sounded behind them and grew closer. Reed propelled Ruthie into her driveway, relieved when she didn't pause or protest. He wasn't sure if she recognized her house or was just following his lead at this point.

The vehicle pulled into the driveway alongside them and came to a rocky stop.

The driver's door flew open. "Ruthie!" An elderly man— Mr. Swink, Reed presumed—hurried around the hood of the car toward them. "Why are you outside? You were supposed to be resting."

"I was?" Her voice quivered. "I do feel tired all of a sudden."

Reed introduced himself as Mr. Swink stepped to Ruthie's side and took her other arm.

"Thank you for helping her home."

"Of course, Mr. Swink."

"Please call me Kurtis." He stepped toward the house, but Ruthie didn't budge. "Come on, dear. It's raining. We need to get inside."

"This young man is helping me. Doesn't he remind you of Pete?"

"Sure, dear." Mr. Swink seemed to be taking the same agree-with-whatever-Ruthie-said-in-order-to-get-her-moving approach that Reed had adopted earlier. "We can talk about it more inside, okay? He needs to get home now and out of the rain, just like you."

"Should I assist her into the house with you?" Reed offered. "We had a pretty good rhythm going."

"I would greatly appreciate that."

Between the two of them, they managed to propel Ruthie forward.

"Where did you find her?" Mr. Swink's bald head glistened with moisture, and his chambray shirt filled with rain dots that quickly connected.

"I was out for a run and found her a few houses to the east, standing in the middle of the road."

"Oh, Ruthie." Kurtis's voice broke with tender remorse.

Ruthie's teeth began to chatter.

"I'm sorry I couldn't get her home faster with the rain. I think she's pretty chilled."

"I'm just glad you found her when you did, or it could have been so much worse. Usually, I have a caregiver who stays with her while I run errands, but she canceled at the last minute. Ruthie had just gone down for a nap before I left, and I thought I could get back before she woke up." The self-loathing evident in Kurtis's tone was something Reed had come to understand firsthand over the past months. "I should have known better. I should never have risked it." Kurtis patted Ruthie's hand. "I'm so very sorry, my dear." His quiet apology to his wife gutted Reed. Another thing he understood down to his marrow. He wanted to say those words to Lindsey and have them be enough to cover all of the pain, the heartache, the fighting. But he'd tried and it hadn't made a difference.

Nothing seemed to. They were stuck. And Reed wanted, more than anything, to get unstuck.

They'd reached the steps leading into the house. Kurtis hurried ahead to open the door—unlocked due to Ruthie's exit, no doubt—and held it so that Reed could help her inside.

Unlike his grandparents' house, the Swinks' house had been remodeled over the years with hints of dark wood, beiges and greens. A calming space that would hopefully instill that same feeling in Ruthie, now that she was back home.

"Would you mind if I grabbed her walker?" Kurtis asked. "It will be easier to get her down the hall with it."

"Of course not. Happy to assist."

The man hurried down the hallway as Reed continued to support Ruthie.

"Done," Ruthie announced.

"Yes, we're done with the walk. You're safe at home and your husband will help you dry off shortly."

"No." Her head shook vehemently. "D-u-n-n. Dunn. That was Vinny's last name. I always thought it was a rather ominous name when he was a teenager. Turns out, I'd been right."

So, she had been referring to Vincent Dunn. And her son had been friends with him…which meant she might know some of the details surrounding his death. If she was coherent enough to remember that time.

Reed felt as if he'd been forced into a game of hot potato. Was he supposed to lob that information to his sister or hold on and endure fourth-degree burns? It was a repeat of yesterday, when the photos had tumbled out of his closet.

Reed's spirit had sunk when he'd come across the ones of Mom and Garrett, his conscience warring over how to handle the situation. Eventually, he'd settled on going to the source, fairly confident that Mom would tell him there'd been nothing between her and Garrett. That they'd simply gone to the dance with a big group of friends—just like Reed and his high school crew had done on more than one occasion. At which point he would have been able to reveal that inconsequential information to Slade.

That mission had, of course, failed. Reed had instead been forced to admit to Slade that he'd found the photos…and that she'd been correct regarding Mom downplaying her connection to Garrett. Slade had, of course, crowed over being right— especially since Reed had been the one to ask her to let the Mom theories go.

And now Reed was back in a similar dilemma. He would happily hand over the information that Ruthie might know something about Vincent, except he had to protect their frail, elderly neighbor from his nosy, obsessed sister, didn't he?

"Here we go!" Kurtis came down the hallway, pushing the walker. When he reached them, Ruthie sank onto the small seat. "I can't thank you enough—"

"No need, Mr. Swink. I'm just glad I found her when I did."

"Me too. It's hard to see her like this." Moisture pooled in Kurtis's eyes. He cleared his throat. "I miss her, and she's right here."

Sympathy rose up in Reed. "I'm so sorry."

"I'm grateful for all the good years." Kurtis brightened. "We've had more than so many. Thank you, again, for rescuing her." He shook Reed's hand with a firm grip.

After saying goodbye to Ruthie, whose eyelids were drooping as if she might fall asleep on the seat of the walker, Reed stepped outside, closing the front door behind him.

The rain had stopped, and a rainbow skimmed the southern peaks. A sign of hope, and yet, the weight of all Reed was carrying was a noose around his neck.

He tugged his cell phone from the zippered pocket of his running shorts.

Reed was done of the d-o-n-e variety. He wanted a marriage like the Swinks. Witnessing Kurtis's care for his wife in the midst of her decline had ignited something in Reed. He was ready to fight for that kind of marriage and love…but the cycle he and Lindsey were in wasn't progressing them toward that goal. Their current communication style was creating further division, not fostering healing.

They had to do something different. Something *had* to change.

Reed called Lindsey and waited as it rang...and rang.

"Hey," she answered a bit breathlessly, but the greeting still held a tenderness that had been AWOL for too long, causing Reed to immediately second-guess his plan. But that, in and of itself, was the whole problem. They were constantly going back and forth and up and down and round and round.

"Did I interrupt anything?"

"Nope. Just carrying a laundry basket up the stairs." She laughed, and amusement echoed in him.

"So, you were working out."

"Exactly!"

This might be the best conversation they'd had in ages, and Reed was about to break it and them in one fell swoop. His stomach revolted at the thought.

"I wanted to talk to you about something."

A beat of silence ensued. "That doesn't sound good."

"That phone call this morning."

Her exhale filled his ear. "I'm sorry I did that to you. That I keep doing it to you! I keep laying this stuff on you and I know I shouldn't. I am such a mess right now. I'm sorry, Reed."

"I get it. I do. We're both messes right now. But I can't help but wonder..." Reed crossed the street and sank to a crouched position, a hand gripping his stomach like it could calm the storm raging in him. If anyone were to drive past, they would assume he was sick and stop to check on him.

They would be right.

He forced himself to continue. "I can't help but wonder if we should take a break from communicating." He winced at her pained intake. "Just for this last week I'm in Colorado. And then when I get home, we'll get together. We'll see each other and talk face-to-face. It's always easier—for me at least—to discuss things in person. And these phone calls and texts... They're not getting us anywhere, Linds."

He was 90 percent sure she was crying, and he was 100 percent sure that hurting Lindsey was worse than any injury or wound he'd ever encountered.

"I guess that makes sense." Her hollow response gutted Reed. If only they were together right now. Then Reed could at least hug her. They could talk. They could stop this cycle. Except... it wasn't like things had been good when he was back home.

Reed's current approach might be wrong, but he could not continue operating how they had been for one more day.

"I'm not sure I'm even capable of what I'm asking for." His voice cracked. The sound of a vehicle starting caused him to stand from his squatted position. The last thing Reed needed right now was to be interrupted by a helpful neighbor. "Maybe if we give ourselves a little space it will reset something. That conversation this morning broke me, Linds. Living in this chaos is killing me."

Lindsey blew her nose. Reed focused on the evergreens shifting in the slight breeze instead of on the mental image of her crying. If Reed allowed that vision to take root, he'd veto this irrational plan in a heartbeat.

"I shouldn't have... I'm sorry that I keep delivering terrible news to you. I promise I'm not trying to be evil."

"I know you're not. I guess that's why I'm thinking if we give ourselves a little break in communication, then at least we won't say anything else we regret."

"Okay." She sniffled, sounding a smidge calmer.

Her agreement was the lid closing on his coffin. What had he done?

"So, we'll talk when you get back?" she asked. "You'll let me know when you're coming home?"

Home. A double-edged word. Reed wanted his address to be

the same as his wife's. And he had to believe that making a switch in their patterns would get them there. Somehow.

"I will. I'll text you when I know my travel plans." He and Slade had been discussing rebooking their respective tickets for next weekend.

"I love you" was on the tip of Reed's tongue, but he swallowed it. Instinct told him this wasn't the moment to let those words fly.

He would just have to trust that she knew for now.

They said goodbye and disconnected.

Reed's legs buzzed and refused to obey his brain as he engaged in a Ruthie Swink shuffle up the driveway to the house.

Had he done the right thing?

Reed was starting to realize there was no "right" thing. There was only the attempt to change. The attempt to do *something* different. And that, at least, he was doing.

Chapter Twenty

Nothing could divert Slade's focus from the HR email she'd found in her spam folder late this afternoon as they'd been finishing Gran and Grandad's room.

A friend had texted Slade to see if she'd received an automated invitation to an upcoming party she was hosting. Slade had checked her spam and stumbled upon both items. The law firm response had come from a different address than the complaint confirmation email, which explained how it had gotten buried.

The communication she'd been waiting on since she filed the report that fateful Thursday night had been sent last week.

Last week!

After she read it, though, Slade was grateful the email had ended up in spam.

If she could go back and unsee it now, she would.

After a quick dinner, Slade had retreated to her bedroom. She'd attempted to distract herself by searching for information about the person of interest in Vincent's case online, but once again, she'd come up short.

Though her research skills were no doubt sorely lacking to-night.

Even switching to reading Gran's journals wasn't holding her attention.

Slade's phone dinged with a text, and she grabbed it from her nightstand—the only remaining piece of furniture in her room besides her bed. They'd carried the dresser and other odds and ends out to the garage already because Slade hadn't been using them—a fact that had about sent Mom and Reed over their own proverbial cliff.

Was it so strange that she was operating with a stack of clean clothes and a pile of dirty ones on the floor?

Slade didn't think so.

The stark room was both an encouragement—look at what they'd accomplished!—and a knife right through her heart, because it was one step closer to letting go of the house.

Slade clicked on the text.

What are you up to?

It had come from a local number.

She slid Cyrus's business card out from the small drawer in her bedside table where she'd stuck it yesterday.

The number matched his cell. The card also contained his last name.

Slade had definitely missed that connection to Garrett.

How had Cyrus gotten her number? When he'd left at the end of his work today, he'd said goodbye to Slade and then waited, almost as if giving her the chance to stop him or accept a date or make plans of any sort to see each other again.

But despite Reed's surprising encouragement and the fact that Cyrus had been growing on her like a barnacle on a pier pylon, Slade had remained silent and let him walk out of her life.

Maybe because of what Reed had deduced earlier.

Maybe because logistics did matter.

Maybe because she now knew who he was…and that their parents had dated.

And maybe because of a hundred other reasons she couldn't quite put her finger on.

Slade's thumbs hovered over the screen, filtering how to respond. Eventually, she settled on banter—a staple in any of the conversations she'd had with Cyrus so far.

Who dis?

You know exactly who this is.

She laughed. You sound like a creeper!

What are you doing right now? Want to hang out?

Did she? Yes. But Slade was stuck on what her mom had relayed earlier. Why wouldn't Cyrus have mentioned he was Garrett's son? Did the lack of information reveal deception or was it simply an oversight?

She formed a text. I found out today that Garrett is your dad.

You didn't know?

Well. That definitely leaned more toward the oversight theory.

Did you tell me?

I guess not. I just assumed it was common knowledge.

Slade believed him, but it was still all so strange. Especially since Mom had been secretive regarding her relationship with Garrett in high school. That still reeked of suspicion to Slade, even though Reed deemed it normal that Mom hadn't brought up ancient history.

Did you know our parents were a thing in high school?

I think my dad may have mentioned something like that once. Why?

Isn't it weird for us to date—Slade deleted "date" and inserted "hang out"—when they used to be romantically involved?

Just using the phrase "romantically involved" regarding her mother was wigging her out at middle school levels.

Slade's phone vibrated with a call from Cyrus. She answered. "Now I know you're a serial killer. Seriously—who answers a text with a phone call?" Her brother *and* Cyrus, apparently.

"People who want to have actual conversations." She pictured that slow-burn grin of his accompanying his retort. "I'm not following you on the parent thing. What am I missing?"

"You don't think it's strange that our parents dated?"

"No."

"That's it? Just no?"

"Right. I don't see the issue. It's not like they're dating now. Plus, you just classified us in the hanging-out category. So, if we're not dating and they're not dating, I definitely don't see the problem. I wouldn't even if they were *and* we were, but I'm guessing you would."

"That would push things to the top of the bizarre meter, for sure."

"But we don't have to worry about that since it's not happening."

True.

"Now back to my original question. Do you want to get out of there for a bit?"

She really did. Gran and Grandad's house wasn't exactly happening for a Saturday night. Reed was probably asleep on the couch, a documentary playing on the TV, and Mom was probably in bed reading. Hanging with Cyrus was certainly a better option than sitting here dwelling on things that couldn't be fixed.

"Fine. I do. Your persistence has paid off."

"Just the kind of enthusiasm every guy wants to hear." His teasing caused Slade's smile to sprout. "I'll pick you up in twenty minutes."

Slade changed from her pajamas into a vintage Dolly Parton T-shirt along with frayed jeans and her Doc Martens ankle boots, then popped into the bathroom to brush her teeth. Despite—or more likely because of—her teenage habits when it came to candy, she was careful about dental hygiene.

By the time she ran fingers through her hair and added a hint of her favorite lip gloss, her phone buzzed with another text.

I'm here. Want me to come in and declare my intentions to your mom and brother?

Slade laughed. NO. I'll be out in a sec.

She skipped the squeaky middle step on the way down and slipped out the front door without running into either of her family members.

It wasn't like Slade needed to hide that she was going somewhere with Cyrus. They'd certainly all discussed him today while cleaning out Gran and Grandad's room. She just wasn't ready for her brother's told-you-so look...or a just-be-careful one from her mom.

Cyrus leaned across the cab of the truck and popped open her door for her. "I would have come around to let you in, but I didn't want to scare you off since we're just *hanging out*."

Slade slid inside. "Good thinking." The cab of his truck smelled like a combination of crisp, clean soap, mint and hard work.

She buckled up as he drove away from the house. "Where are we going?"

"You'll find out."

"True crime documentaries have been based on less."

His laugh was ever-changing, it seemed. Tonight, it had a quiet, peaceful edge that Slade wanted to curl up in like a soft blanket.

"I told you there were no bodies in my freezer."

"That doesn't mean you didn't bury them."

That creasing mouth and low chuckle answered her again. He exited the neighborhood and headed toward Keystone. The sky was morphing from light to dark, the night peaceful and calm. Cyrus didn't fill the vehicle with small talk, and Slade felt strangely comfortable with that. It was as if he was taking her away from her problems, her world, and somehow—maybe because of that sense he'd claimed to have—he knew just how much she needed the reprieve.

He wore jeans and a button-down, and a baseball cap was perched on the dash of his truck. Slade's usual type when it came to dating was artistic or at least creative in some capacity...and sometimes without a job. Though she was the one who could check that box currently. The man inches from her wasn't anything like anyone she'd ever dated before—not that this little outing qualified as a date.

Cyrus turned into a neighborhood and began winding up, up. Eventually, he pulled into a long driveway. It curved through a stretch of pines and then straightened to display the kind of gorgeous, modern-rustic mountain home that would be featured on the pages of an architectural magazine.

Lights glowed around the property, but the windows were dark.

"If this is your house, I may have to reclassify this as a date."

He parked in front of the three-car garage and killed the engine. "So, you're telling me you're in this for the money?"

"Of course. Did you think I was in it for anything but money?"

"I thought you were in it for the true crime documentary."

Slade laughed.

"It's not my house."

"So, we're just doing some breaking and entering then?"

"Not exactly." He hopped out of the truck, and before Slade could do the same, he was on her side, opening her door.

Her boots made a soft thump on the asphalt drive. "I thought you weren't going to make this date-ish?"

"I've already got you here and you don't have a way home without me, so no need to keep up pretenses."

Instead of heading for the front door, Cyrus strode to the side of the house. After a second of contemplating how much this scenario resembled a crime reenactment, Slade followed.

The terrain on the side of the home was steep, and Cyrus paused a few feet up to offer her a hand.

For some reason, Slade accepted his assistance. She could climb this hill by herself, but the temptation of physical comfort, even if it was just in the form of their hands touching, was too much to resist.

"Are these people home?"

"Nope."

They reached a plateau in the backyard and Cyrus released his grip. Security lights powered on as they moved around the perimeter of the house, illuminating a black spiral staircase that appeared to extend to the roof.

"How do you feel about heights?"

"I guess we're about to find out."

The *cling-cling-cling* of their shoes meeting the iron stairs filled the otherwise quiet night as they wound their way up.

Again, Cyrus stopped at the top and offered her a hand. Again, he disconnected their contact immediately after assisting her onto the observation deck. Again, Slade experienced a surprisingly profound level of disappointment at the physical withdrawal.

Cyrus removed protective coverings from the furniture as Slade spun in a slow circle. The rooftop deck had an L-shaped outdoor couch in one corner, next to a built-in grill, a skinny high-top bar with stools, a glass door entrance to the house and luxurious loungers flanked by metal side tables.

Expansive and intimate and open to the heavens.

She tipped her head back and took in the vast sky littered with stars like endless broken shards of sparkling glass.

"It's stunning." A hum of appreciation came from her throat.

When her vision switched to Cyrus, he was observing her with an expression that said his enjoyment was based on hers.

"You approve?"

"It'll do in a pinch."

"When you're in need of a rooftop deck, this one will suffice."

"I guess." Slade released an exaggerated sigh that ended on a laugh. "Are you sure these people aren't home? Or that a neighbor won't call the police? I keep thinking the po-po are going to show up any minute. Keep expecting red-and-blue lights."

His mouth curved in a delicious half-moon. "They're not home. They have houses everywhere, and they're hardly ever here. I watch it for them while they're gone."

"Like you live in it?"

"No. I keep tabs on houses for a number of customers."

"When you're not installing roofs and running a crew."

"Yep." He moved to one of the chaise loungers and spread out on it, his body elongated, his shirt slipping up to reveal a swatch of toned stomach.

Slade cast her gaze elsewhere as she slid onto the chair next to his and adjusted the back to allow for better viewing of the sky.

It was as if a fake backdrop had been lowered to within their reach and either one of them could grab a handful of stardust and tuck it into their pocket.

Cyrus unzipped a backpack she hadn't noticed him carrying and removed a thermos and some small metal glasses. He filled one and handed it to her before doing the same for himself.

"Is this how the documentary starts?"

His low laugh sounded. "Sun tea with peaches and mint. One of the few good things my mom taught me."

Slade's first refreshing sip exploded on her tongue. "Yum. How is it possible that your mom wasn't amazing if you're such a great person?"

His face creased with humor and then turned serious. "Any credit for who I am goes to my dad."

Me too. Slade had been wary of Garrett since the start, and her mom hiding a relationship with him in high school hadn't helped matters, but if the man had raised Cyrus, that had to count for something, right?

Slade raised her glass. "To our dads."

They toasted, the metal creating a slight *clink*. "How long ago did your dad pass away?"

"About two years. The grief has improved over time, but there are still days that it feels fresh. The worst is when I dream that he's alive, because it's like a nightmare in reverse. So amazing during the dream, but then I wake up and realize it's not true. He's still gone."

A scrape of understanding came from Cyrus's throat.

She shifted toward him. "What about you? What happened with your mom?"

"She took off when I was in middle school. She's a drifter. Never stays in one place for long. Always trying something new. Not great at holding down a job."

Slade swallowed over a sharp pain that materialized. *He isn't describing me.* Just because she didn't have a job at the moment didn't mean she was unreliable. Slade had always worked and always paid her way.

Cyrus continued. "I don't know that she was leaving us so

much as she was leaving conformity. She just never fit the mold of an orthodox mother. Ever since she took off, she's felt more like a flighty aunt than our mom. She floats in and out of our lives whenever she feels like it. It's easier to handle as an adult. I have boundaries with her. But as kids, she messed us up for a while."

"I'm sorry." And she was. No child should have to endure abandonment from a parent. "It sounds like you've done really well with what you were handed." Would someone say the same about her? Slade experienced a prick of guilt at the issues between her and her mother, which now felt superficial. She and Mama-Mar might be stark opposites, who often failed to mesh with each other, but Slade always, *always* was able to depend on her.

"There has been so much good in my life." Cyrus's shoulders lifted in a slight shrug, his gaze sky bound. "Still is. I refuse to complain."

Slade appreciated his outlook. She needed to employ that same approach in her own life. So Jude had attempted the worst with her. He hadn't succeeded. He hadn't won. Yet. Though the latest development with HR made her feel as if he was on his way to victory. And as if she was on her way to someplace even darker than the hole she'd been cowering in since her arrival in Colorado.

Slade tucked her hands behind her head and inhaled the night, the beauty, the company. An owl hooted in the distance. Cyrus's breathing beside her was steady. Calming. She felt as if her respiratory system was mimicking his. Like she was taking her first deep breaths in over two weeks. Her first true inhale since Jude.

"What made you say yes tonight? When I left the job today, I was certain I would never see you again. But then I thought, what can it hurt to try one more time? The worst she can do is refuse."

The worst she can do is refuse. He'd put himself out there—
for her.

Reed was definitely right in his assessment that Cyrus was—
as the man had coined it when he first met Slade—one of the
good ones.

Starting something between them still didn't make sense. But
ever since Cyrus had handed Slade his card and swooped into her
world like the human equivalent of hot chocolate and a weighted
blanket on a snowy day, he felt like the only thing that did.

Chapter Twenty-One

Slade didn't answer Cyrus's question immediately, and in what she was learning was his typical mode of operation, he didn't push.

He dug into the backpack again, retrieving a bag of Sour Patch Kids, which he opened and offered to her. Slade poured a pile into the palm of her hand and returned the pouch to him, but he left them on his chair.

"You're not having any?"

"I'm not a big candy person."

"For me, that would be like saying 'I'm not big on breathing.'" She popped a couple of the treats into her mouth, her taste buds rioting at the burst of painfully good tartness. "If you're not into candy, why do you have it along?"

"I've been doing my research on you."

"I assume that same research led to my phone number?"

"You could assume that."

Was it Mom or Reed who'd revealed her addiction and her number? Based on this morning's conversation, she would guess door number two.

"Did you stop on the way over to grab these, or did you have some stashed in your lair just in case I reached out?"

His eyes crinkled with humor. "I stopped on the way."

"Phew. As to why I accepted when you asked to hang out tonight…" Slade sank farther into her chair, like it could catch her, save her. Dreading answering his inquiry. "I was trying to take my mind off something."

"Happy to be of assistance." Tenderness and compassion radiated from him even though he continued to gaze at the stars and not at her. It was the way he gave her room to process and think and decide that drew Slade to him the most.

She'd never reacted well to demands. It was part of the reason she'd struggled so much with her mom. The more Mom had battened down the hatches, the more Slade had fought to pave her own way.

But that didn't make her reaction right.

"Did I tell you I was working at a law firm?"

"Yep, but that's all you said."

"I left my position there." Whether she trusted him or was just tired of lugging around the burden alone, Slade found the truth spilling. "In my last week, my supervisor had asked me to take on a project of switching some data entry to a new system, and it required overtime. So I was working late." Slade had accepted, spurred on by the extra funds and the chance to prove that she could move up at the company. Despite what Reed and Mom likely thought, she did have ambitions—or at least she had.

Slade could tell that Cyrus was listening intently though he didn't speak. "I was tired, so I went to the break room to make coffee. Jude—one of the partners—must have realized I was working late. I don't know if he stayed because of me or if it was just happenstance."

"The first."

"That's what I thought too."

"I don't want to know what happened next." Cyrus's declaration was part growl. Like he might rip someone to pieces with his claws. The instant defense of her and belief in her were beyond comforting.

The man was Team Slade before he even knew what had happened.

He could have no idea how much that meant to her.

"Jude had given me creeper vibes before that night, but he'd never done anything that I could pinpoint. He was...careful. Calculating. Now that I look back, I think he was testing me. And I failed the test. Or in his mind, I passed it. If I had balked at the slight touches previous to that, he might have backed off. But I thought I was imagining things. It's hard to qualify someone brushing against your leg or picking a hair off your blouse or squeezing your arm as improper. It was all so fast and slight that I convinced myself it was nothing."

The thing that killed Slade the most was that she'd questioned Jude's intentions long before their last interaction. But she'd silenced the blaring alarms and gut feeling because she'd liked the job. Because she'd needed the job.

Cyrus's intense, pained gaze focused on her.

"I've definitely bounced around in my careers—I like to try new things—but I was enjoying the law office. I didn't want to leave the firm or raise a red flag, so I kept my head down and ignored him. Until that night."

If Slade had realized they were the only two still working in the office just a smidge earlier, maybe she could have prevented what had happened next.

A slow-burn fury radiated from Cyrus. His Adam's apple bobbed. "Did he—"

"He didn't get that far." But he'd still done enough. For as long as she lived, Slade would never be able to forget Jude's hands on her—everywhere at once. Never forget the way his body had formed to hers like molten metal. The way her lungs had emptied, and the room had spun. She'd been afraid that she was going to faint and wind up completely defenseless. "When he pressed up against me in the break room, I was so stunned that it took me a few seconds to respond. Once I realized what he was doing and that he expected me to…participate, I snapped."

"Don't tell me there was a knife on the counter behind you."

A flash of unexpected humor surfaced but quickly faded. "No. Thankfully. Because if I had injured him, I would no doubt be the one in trouble. The one accused of assault." Slade hugged herself in an attempt to quiet the shaking echoing through her body. "I kicked, slapped and generally lost my mind. I think I must have surprised him because he let go of me." There might have been a well-placed knee involved too. The details were hazy. Slade only knew her reaction had created a crack—an opening—and she'd grasped it with every red-alert fiber coursing through her. "I ran. My desk was near the front door, and my purse was accessible because I'd just gotten something out of it."

When she'd fallen partway across the parking lot—her body spilling and shattering onto the pavement like a glass jar of ink—her keys had flown numerous feet from her grip. Slade had whipped her face toward the building, expecting to find Jude towering over her.

But for some reason, he hadn't followed her.

When Slade had nightmares about that night, Jude *was* usually standing over her. And sometimes, in the most terrible scenarios, he dragged her back inside the building.

She'd scrambled to her car, trembling so severely that it had taken what had felt like an eternity to get her key into the ignition, though in retrospect it had likely been seconds.

Somehow, she'd managed to drive home. Slade had turned the water in the shower to scalding and stood in the stream as if it could wash away the encounter. *It didn't amount to anything.*

She'd repeated that over and over. *Nothing happened.* She'd re-peated that over and over too, but she hadn't for one moment believed either claim.

It wasn't until the shower that the words Jude had been lob-bing at her as she'd run connected in her brain, from scattered fragments to semicoherent thoughts.

She'd misunderstood his actions and intentions.

He knew people everywhere and everyone was in his pocket.

If she talked he could cause her to lose not only her job but her apartment, her reputation, her everything.

She would never win going up against him.

Slade had filed a complaint with human resources that very night, afraid that if she waited, she'd talk herself out of it. Her hands had been so unsteady that she'd had to type and delete numerous times to get the details down.

So many people suffered rape, and Slade hadn't. She told herself that her trauma was slight, that the encounter had only lasted a few seconds, so it didn't make sense that she felt violated at the deepest levels. But despite her denial and minimizing, something had been stripped from her...and something pain-fully raw had taken its place.

"I filed a report with HR that night. And today I found an email in my spam folder that said they were opening an investi-gation...into him *and* me. He's saying I came on to him and that my accusations are retaliation because he didn't reciprocate."

Fiery eyes and a slacked jaw answered her.

"I also found out from a coworker last week that this isn't new behavior for him. I abandoned so many women—"

"If he's been inappropriate with them, then they need to come forward too, Slade. You can't do this all on your own."

"They can't afford to lose their jobs like I did. They can't afford to quit." Salty tears settled in the grooves at the corners of her lips.

"And you can?" Cyrus reached over—slowly, carefully—and

tugged her hand in his direction. He held on with a tight grip, the warmth and callouses and gesture leveling her.

"Aren't you going to tell me it's going to be okay?" Bitterness that had nothing to do with Cyrus laced her tone.

"I'm not sure if it's going to be okay." Cyrus tucked her arm against his strong, solid chest, and wrapped both of his around it. "Right now, it sounds like the opposite of that. But I do think *you're* going to be okay."

"Are you going to tell me it's not my fault now?"

Cyrus stared at her so intently that Slade felt it in the marrow of her bones. "It's not your fault. And you didn't do anything—*anything*—wrong." He delivered it like there was a period between each word. Like his was the only and final judgment, case closed.

Slade's tears made the stars shimmer, expand, then narrow. "I always thought there was a reason that I hadn't had anything like this happen to me. Like I was stronger or off-limits or something. Like no man would ever come at me like that. I thought I was different. I thought I was exempt from this type of behavior."

"You should be exempt from that type of behavior. Every person should be."

"I've never understood before how someone could talk about abuse and question if they were somehow complicit in it. Somehow at fault in allowing it to happen. But when you experience it, everything shifts, and you start to wonder... Did I send a wrong signal? Did I make it worse somehow? Did I open a door without realizing it? I mean, I did get a new berry-bronze lipstick that week."

Cyrus gave a small, emphatic head shake. "Stop."

"Maybe the skirt I was wearing was too short."

"No."

"What about my personality? Too inviting?"

"Slade."

"The color of my hair—"

"You *know* it was none of that. Tell me you know that."

"I know it here." She tapped a finger against her forehead. "But here…" Her hand hovered over her chest. "Here, it just feels like I somehow unknowingly made it worse. He'd given me the creeps from the start, and I didn't say anything. Didn't do anything."

"What are you supposed to do about the creeps? File a report? Slade, you did not make this happen. You did not make this worse. *He* did all of that. It's on him, not you. That's what he wants you to think and feel. That's how men like him manipulate. Don't go down that road. Don't give him that satisfaction."

They stayed silent as Slade's tears slowed. As Cyrus's thumb traced against her hand in a continual comforting motion.

"Your mom and brother… Are they helping you with this? It's a lot to handle alone, Slade."

"Is it that much, though? Nothing actually happened."

"Plenty actually happened."

"I haven't told them."

His brow pinched. "Why not?"

"Because I'm the screwup."

"You're not—"

"I am. You've known me for two minutes."

"Ouch."

"I didn't mean it like that. It's just…for some reason, you see the good in me. Or the potential at least. And that's never been my role in the family. I'm afraid…" Tears welled again. "I'm afraid they'll think I *was* part of the problem. That I led him on. That I was at least partially at fault for what happened." Slade's jaw clenched. "And I really wasn't this time." At least that's what she wanted to believe.

But if she couldn't believe that about herself…how could she ever convince her family?

Chapter Twenty-Two

"And I thought the garage was overwhelming." Marin stood in the middle of The Armpit and turned in a slow, agonizing circle.

Overflowing shelving lined each of the walls, stretching from floor to ceiling. And when that space had run out, her parents had begun stacking bins and boxes and bags in front of the shelves.

Marin would like to blame her mother for the hoarding, but Dad must have been complicit too, or he would have tossed some of this over the years.

Yesterday, they'd knocked out Reed's bedroom in a day, and Marin had thought they would carry that momentum into The Armpit.

She'd been far too optimistic.

Slade's nose crinkled as she took in the space. "We should call this room The Place Things Go to Die."

"Maybe we don't sort," Marin suggested. "Maybe we just toss it all without looking."

Reed sipped from a brown, eclectic coffee mug that Lovetta

had made in high school ceramics class. "Feel like you might have some regret if we did that, Mom."

He was right, of course. Who knew what they would find in here?

Reed had decided to use full vacation days this week since they planned to knock out The Armpit over the next four to five days, load the trailer that the used furniture store would drop off at the end of the week, and give the house a final once-over.

Despite having cleaned out every room but this one, there were still some small odds and ends to deal with. The purge was both coming to a close and never-ending. And Marin was both nostalgic over saying goodbye to the house—and her children—and ready to wrap things up.

Only that meant leaving the place where she'd been shaped and loved and where her parents would always live on in her mind.

She covertly ran fingertips under her lower lashes.

"So, do we have a plan of attack?" Reed peered into a box and then let the cardboard flap fall closed. "Or are we just diving in?"

"You know my answer to that," Slade quipped.

"A free-for-all, of course." Reed's eyes crinkled as they met Marin's. "What do you think, Mom? Should we Slade-style it?"

Marin laughed. "I don't think a spreadsheet can make this room any less overwhelming."

Reed's phone buzzed, and he tugged it from the pocket of his shorts, checked the screen, declined the call and returned it to his pocket in one fluid motion.

Maybe it had been a spam call...with a contact photo that resembled him and Lindsey on a beach. Marin's heart ached for the two of them. She'd been attempting to be silently supportive—to not ask questions or probe—but it had taken a Herculean effort not to dig deeper into his marital issues.

She'd left the door wide open in case her son wanted to process, but Reed had yet to walk through it.

He motioned to the box he'd just checked the contents of. "Old Christmas decorations in this one. Do you want to sort those, Mom?"

"No, but if you come across any ornaments, let me know. There are a few I'd like to keep."

"Noted." Reed crossed the room to retrieve a garbage bag, which he hung from a piece of shelving for easy access. He then returned to the Christmas decoration box and began removing items that were too threadbare to donate, tossing them into the trash.

Slade plopped onto the floor and started on one of the stacks next to her.

Apparently, they were diving in.

Marin opened a bin and found mismatched sheets and old towels that had been used for rags. She dumped the whole lot into the garbage.

One down and what felt like hundreds to go.

"No ornaments," Reed relayed. "Just garland, tinsel and lights left in this. Thrift?"

"Yep."

He headed outside to Marin's car, which had made so many trips to the local thrift store over the last couple weeks it should be able to navigate the route by itself.

"Gran had such great style." Slade had donned a pair of Gran's heels and a black faux-fur hat with a feather in it.

Marin laughed. What would they do without Slade's comic relief? She'd definitely kept them entertained during sorting, despite whatever was going on with her. On Saturday afternoon while finishing Gran and Grandad's room, she'd been blatantly irritable. And then yesterday, she'd fluctuated between happy and snippy, sometimes by the hour.

Marin both wanted to understand what was causing those swings and was deathly afraid to ask.

She imagined the good moods had something to do with Slade's quickly budding relationship with Cyrus. Marin had heard the rumble of Cyrus's truck picking Slade up the last two evenings along with her muted exits from the house. An escape that Marin herself had perfected when she was younger.

"More for the keep pile?" she asked Slade, determined not to nitpick this time if she answered in the affirmative.

"I don't think I have room for the shoes, and they pinch a bit, but this hat is a definite yes." She tugged a new box from the bottom shelf, even though the one she'd been going through was only partially sorted.

"Don't you want to—"

Slade glanced up.

Finish with the first box before you start a second?

"Never mind!" Marin turned to the stack nearest her and opened the top box, giving herself a mental high five for not engaging with Slade. Somehow, the whole room would get done…even if it exploded into a bigger mess along the way.

"Huh. That's weird." Slade turned on the flashlight on her phone, shining it into the shelving space she'd just removed the box from.

"What's weird?" Marin asked, just as Reed reentered the room. "Don't tell me there's a dead mouse back there. Or a live one." She shuddered.

Slade sat up, her expression contemplative. "No mouse."

"Then, what is it?"

"I don't know yet. Reed, check this out."

He joined her on the floor, and she handed over the phone with the flashlight still beaming.

Reed completed the same inspection as Slade.

"You two are giving me heart palpitations. What do you see?"

He sat back, knees propped, and handed the phone to Slade. "Maybe you should sit down, Mom."

"A chair is the one thing this room doesn't hold. Just tell me. Do we need to hire an exterminator? What's down there?"

"I think there might be termites." He delivered the verdict slowly. "There's some piles of sawdust."

Wonderful. Marin's phone buzzed in the back pocket of her ankle-length pants. She checked the screen, saw it was Garrett.

"Hey," she answered, her voice broadcasting hints of panic with tannins of despair. "We're having a bit of a moment here. Can I call you back?"

"What's going on?"

"Reed thinks we found termites."

A beat of silence followed. "I'll be there in a few minutes." He disconnected before she could argue. But she wouldn't have anyway, because evidently she was the kind of person who would let her first love rescue her over and over again, even though she wouldn't let herself feel for him again.

"Garrett's coming over," she announced. "If it is termites, we're going to need his help fixing the damage. And I'm sure he knows a pest company we could use." Marin inhaled, hoping the kids didn't sense the tremor. "We'll figure it out."

"We will." Reed spoke with confidence. "There's a fix, I'm sure."

A fix that would cost thousands and take time, no doubt. Marin appreciated Reed's calmness right now, but she also had the strangest desire to punch a fist through the wall.

"Let's get this spot cleared out so he can check it when he gets here." Slade and Reed began methodically moving boxes, stacking them on top of the piles on the other side of the room.

One heap began to shift like the leaning tower of Pisa, and Reed shoved the stack tight against the metal shelving to keep it from toppling over.

As the mess increased, Marin's pulse followed suit. Her least favorite part of sorting was the chaos that came during and how the disarray worsened before improving.

Marin let her children unload the shelf since they were in better physical shape than her and not losing their minds right now like she was. Under the guise of doing *something*, she rifled through the box she'd been working on before the possible termite revelation. Though if she were given a pop quiz on the contents, she would come up blank.

Marin had reviewed her parents' funds yesterday and been relieved to find that they were on track to list the house without having to dip into her and Lovetta's savings.

But wouldn't termites greatly delay the sale? And how much would fixing the damage cost?

She absolutely refused to use Lovetta's reserves toward carrying costs. But if Marin didn't honor her sister's wishes, there was a possibility it could create a rift between them. Lovetta had a stubborn, prideful streak that Marin did her best to avoid igniting.

"Hello!" Garrett's greeting came from the direction of the kitchen, which meant he must have let himself in the unlocked screen door.

"We're in the storage room," Marin called out.

Garrett stepped into The Armpit, and Marin's body reacted with a heaving sigh of relief—like an infant being returned to their parent's arms after a night with a babysitter. A response to him that she'd tried desperately to tame while in Colorado but had obviously failed profusely at.

"Morning." That trademark head nod of his greeted them. "I hear you have some visitors."

"Down here." Reed motioned to the spot he and Slade had cleared.

Garrett approached the shelf. "Help me move this thing?"

He and Reed pulled the shelving away from the wall so Garrett could get behind it and inspect.

Excruciating silence reigned, and Marin's eardrums filled with the *whoosh-whoosh-whoosh* of her revved heartbeat.

"This doesn't look like termite damage." Garrett's verdict caused a breath Marin didn't realize she'd been holding to release. "Pests aren't my area of expertise, though."

"So you could be wrong?"

The corners of his lips and his lucent green eyes tipped up, the accompanying teasing glint registering throughout her body like a hydration IV.

"When have I *ever* steered you wrong, Mar?"

Hot-flash level heat overtook Marin's body despite her lack of permission. *Please, please* let her be the only one noticing her response to his tender and—if she remembered how this all worked—flirty delivery.

"I know a guy who deals with pest control. I called him on my way over, and he wasn't far, so he's going to stop by."

"You should print I Know a Guy on a shirt." Because that was Garrett in a nutshell. *I've got you covered. I don't deal with that directly, but I know someone who does.* Basically—*you're not alone in this.* And wasn't that what *everyone* wanted to hear in times of crisis? The man was always, always assisting...at least when it came to Marin and her seemingly endless issues.

Marin's body orbited back to normal temps and a less erratic pulse. "That's amazing. Thank you so much." Waiting was always the hardest part. This way, they'd have an answer and could formulate a plan.

A knock sounded on the front door, and both Garrett and Reed headed that way. Marin was grateful to have her son take the lead on this discussion. She heard the men make introductions, and then they returned to the storage room.

"This is KC." Garrett's thumb looped in the other man's direction, and Marin introduced herself and Slade.

KC wore an embroidered logo shirt and navy uniform pants

with scuffed but clean boots. He was tall and lanky with silver hair. Attractive and yet Marin felt no attraction.

The other man her age in the room though… Marin had tried desperately to deny and shut down her reaction to him while in Colorado, but she was failing miserably.

KC got right down to business, kneeling to study the area behind the shelf.

Garrett and Reed flanked him, leaving Marin unable to observe his expression.

She rested her back against a stack of boxes, and Slade joined her.

Had Marin eaten breakfast today? She didn't think so. She'd had coffee, and then she and the kids had congregated in The Armpit. Maybe the caffeine minus food was the cause of the jitters she felt.

"We'll figure it out, Mom." Slade's arm pressed against Marin's supportively.

"Thanks, Love." They waited in silence for KC's verdict, which came quickly.

"Definitely not termites. It's carpenter ants."

Was that better or worse? "What does that mean?" Marin asked.

"They usually don't cause as much damage as termites—or at least not as quickly. But they do need a food source to survive, whether it be other insects or—"

"Actual food?" Slade groaned. "The box next to where we found them contained rice and cereal."

"You'll want to get rid of anything like that."

"We're getting rid of all of it." Marin swept a hand over the space.

"Good. I can get someone over here to treat them at the end of the week, if that works."

Marin floundered to form a coherent response, fighting to keep her emotional floodgates from breaking open.

"That would be great," Reed filled in. "We appreciate it."

"Happy to help." KC took down Reed's cell number and then left for the job he'd been headed to when Garrett had no doubt called in a favor.

Marin focused on Garrett after KC's departure. "How bad is the damage they've already caused? Will it be major to fix?"

"Won't really know until the wall gets opened up, but..." His eyes sparked with that calming mirth again. "I know a guy who can handle it. You can always leave me a key so my crew can get in here after you all leave."

"We're going to pay you. Obviously. No special treatment."

He raised his palms in defense, amusement creasing his cheeks. "I would never. But don't worry about it causing issues with Lovetta. It won't be that much."

When they'd been discussing roof details at one point, Marin had told him about Lovetta's demand that they share carrying costs if needed and the additional stress that created.

"How would you know the price when you haven't seen the damage yet?"

"I have a Spidey sense about these things."

Marin's laugh was watery, emotional, grateful. She had no doubt it was less Spidey sense and more generosity of spirit.

"We'll keep you on schedule for selling, Mar."

And by *we*, he meant *he*.

Despite the better-than-it-could-have-been news, Marin's system was still teetering at the edge of shock. Still shaky and near tears.

She pressed her fingertips against her twitching eye, but it didn't quell the flutter.

"I just thought the word *quell*," she relayed to Garrett. "Thought you'd appreciate that one."

"I'll add it to the list." His mouth hitched with that grin that had the power to undo her. "Would you two mind if I borrowed your mom for a bit?" His vision swung from Reed to Slade. "Need to discuss a few house things with her."

What kind of house things? Marin had thought everything with the roof had been completed without issue on Saturday.

"Of course. No problem." Reed's response was as steady as he was. "We'll be good, right, Slade? We'll sort what we can and make a pile with any questions for you, Mom."

Slade nodded quickly, her brow creased. "Yep, no worries at all."

No worries? This coming from the girl who'd been wary regarding Garrett from the start?

Marin must be acting stranger than she'd realized for both kids to be shoving her out the door.

They must think her near a breakdown.

Was she? Was this weird, buzzing feeling what one felt like?

Even with the grief she'd plowed through over the last handful of years, she'd managed to hold herself together.

Of course it would be this house in this town that would be her undoing.

Garrett guided her out of The Armpit, through the kitchen and into his truck.

Had she said yes to this outing at some point? Marin couldn't remember agreeing to Garrett's request to steal her away, but she also didn't have enough fight left in her to argue.

She inhaled the simple, clean scent of Garrett that filled the cab of the truck while he rounded the vehicle and slid into the driver's seat.

It was incredibly comforting.

He was incredibly comforting.

His hand froze on the keys dangling in the ignition. "So are you, Mar."

Apparently, she'd said that out loud. What other thoughts had flown out of her mouth in the last few minutes? Maybe that's why both kids had shooed her off, their foreheads furrowed with concern.

"What's going on with the house? What did you call to tell me?"

"Nothing. That was a cover-up. I called you because I wanted to see you, and my patience regarding waiting for you to want to see me had run out." Garrett started the vehicle and backed out of the driveway.

Warmth started in Marin's toes and rushed up, up, up. Wait—did she even have shoes on? She glanced down. Yes. Her wooden-soled sandals, of course. They'd been her trusty sidekick for the duration of the house purge.

"Do you ever get a foot cramp at night?"

Garrett's truck floated lackadaisically down the street a few miles under the speed limit.

Lackadaisical—another for his list.

"Not often. Did you know you can drink pickle juice if you do?"

"I've heard that." Marin borrowed a Lovetta snort-laugh. "We sound so old."

His chuckle ignited. "We are old."

"Where are we going?"

"Food is always a good idea, and I'm sure you could use a reset after this morning's latest discovery. So...breakfast?"

Food *was* always a good idea. "I don't remember the last time I went out for breakfast."

His response was quiet, subdued. "Is that something you used to do with Ralph?"

"No. Ralph didn't love breakfast. But I do."

That smile again. It echoed through every cell in her body. "So do I."

Chapter Twenty-Three

"Are you going to answer that?" Slade paused from sorting a box of pinecones and other nature crafts as she watched her brother decline a call for the second time this morning.

Since Garrett had whisked Mom out of the house, they'd kept working, though they had discussed their concern over Mom's demeanor after the carpenter-ant revelation.

Slade had witnessed her mother weather a lot of hard things, and usually she didn't so much as sway.

Today, she'd been uprooted and tossed around like a lawn chair in a Colorado gust of wind.

Hopefully, whatever house topics Garrett had to talk to Mom about would be good news and not bad. Slade wasn't sure Mama-Mar could handle another blow right now.

"I'm not going to answer." Reed's response held a note of defiance that was abnormal for him. "You're the one who said phone calls were never good news."

He had her there. "Was it Lindsey?"

"Yep."

Slade waited for Reed to go into more detail, but he just continued rifling through a box of boots and coats, tossing some into the trash bag and others into the thrift box.

Slade dumped the crafts into the trash, a pang of guilt igniting. She'd love to keep them since they were Gran's handiwork, but even for her, there was a limit. And she doubted the thrift store would take them.

"On Saturday evening, I told Lindsey that I thought we should stop communicating until I got back to Illinois." Reed's casual delivery of such a huge decision detonated like a bomb, stealing the oxygen from The Armpit.

It took Slade a few beats to wrap her mind around the news he'd just delivered.

"That's quite the revelation. Were you planning to have that conversation with her?"

He sighed. "No."

"But that's…" *not at all like you*. Reed used a spreadsheet to decide on the best kind of toilet paper.

"She called on Saturday morning and told me that her mom thought we should cut ties while things between us were still amicable. And I just… I can't handle the back and forth anymore. Hearing that and knowing how much Lindsey values her mom's opinion about killed me."

"Good for you." Slade delivered the encouragement evenly, despite the anger coursing through her. Reed and Lindsey were struggling enough. They did not need her mother adding kerosene to the fire. "Did Lindsey agree?"

"She did. And yet she keeps calling and texting me even more than before we had that conversation. She says she has to talk to me about something. That it's important."

"Hmm." Sounded suspicious. But then, what didn't to Slade?

"I know what you're thinking because I'm thinking it too. Why can't she just text whatever it is? Why the drama?"

"The thought may have crossed my mind. You set boundaries for a reason. It's okay to follow through with those. It's also understandable if you want to make sure she's all right."

"So, you're saying I can do no wrong."

"Basically."

"That's absolutely no help at all." Reed's voice wavered. "Do you think I'm shooting myself in the foot by not answering or responding?"

Slade hated seeing her confident brother reduced to this level of doubt and vulnerability. He was right to push the pause button on this cyclic pain.

"No. All the gurus say boundaries are a good thing."

"How many gurus do you know?"

"Lots."

He laughed.

"Maybe the space will be just what you and Linds need. Like Mom said, sometimes absence helps."

"I hope so. But we said the same thing when we separated, and that's gone as well as a dog dancing with a pack of coyotes."

Slade's mouth quirked at the Grandad-ism. "All you can do is try, right?"

"True." Reed turned his attention back to the winter items, his lips pursed as if stemming information.

"What else is going on? There's something more eating at you."

"Nothing." He emptied the last items from the box and began breaking it down.

Slade crossed her arms and waited.

"Fine. I'll tell you. But you have to promise beforehand that I get to be in charge of this, okay?" He added the cardboard to the recycling pile. "You can't take it and run. I get to be the gatekeeper."

What was he talking about? "The gatekeeper of what?"

"Promise me first. Then I'll tell you."

"I'll do my best."

"That's not good enough in this situation. I need a firm commitment."

Since Slade wasn't going to get anywhere without agreeing, she caved. "Fine. I accept your terms. Now, what's up?"

"When I was getting Ruthie Swink home—" Reed had told them about finding Ruthie in the middle of the road during his run "—she started telling me about her son and his friend Vinny."

"Our Vincent?"

Reed snorted. "Ours, huh? Yes—Vincent Dunn. She did confirm that's who she was talking about."

"She called him Vinny?" The shortened name definitely implied familiarity. All this time, answers to that night could have been a stone's throw from where Slade slept. "And she's lived on this street since we were kids, which means she likely did before that too. Which means—"

"They were probably here at the time Vincent died. Have you found anything new about him lately?"

"Keely and I looked up newspaper articles at the library on Friday. We found out that for a split second, there'd been a person of interest in the case, but the article didn't mention a name. I also looked through Gran's journals for that particular year, but it wasn't in the box. The lack of information made me feel like I was back to square one. But maybe talking to Ruthie could fill in some blanks."

"She's a frail older woman with dementia, Slade. You can't just barrel over there and bring up the past."

"You already told me I'm not allowed to do anything without your permission."

"True. And that's exactly why I set up boundaries for you like the gurus say to." Reed grinned and then inclined his head in concession. "But I do think maybe we can stop over at some point to check on her. Together, so I can keep tabs on you."

"You make me sound so vicious."

"Not vicious. Curious. There's a difference." His volume dropped. "I hope."

"I'm happy to have you go with me. It's about time you started taking part in this investigation."

Reed groaned and massaged fingertips into his temples. "It's not an investigation. And I'm going to err on the side of protecting our poor elderly neighbor versus aiding your rampant, illogical curiosity."

"Yes, sensei. So?" Slade rubbed her hands together. "Can we go see her now? Mom's gone. It's perfect timing."

"I don't think that's a great idea. You saw Mom. She was shell-shocked, and it didn't even turn out to be termites. We should probably just knock out more of The Armpit."

Slade was losing him. And with Mom out of the house, it really was the best opportunity for them to run over to the Swinks.

"How about this—if Ruthie can't tell us anything, I'll consider dropping the Vincent research."

"You'll *consider* dropping it. That's about as big of a promise as a politician planning to lower taxes."

"Fine. If we go over there and Ruthie can't tell us anything, I will drop the Vincent digging."

Reed froze in the middle of opening a plastic storage tub. "Seriously?"

"Yep. This is it. My last hurrah."

"Just because he was friends with her son doesn't mean she knows anything about his death."

"I understand that." Slade bounced on the balls of her feet, her palms pressed together in a begging motion. "Now can we go? Pretty, pretty please?"

"You do realize that I'm rooting for her not to know anything about that night, right? I'm all for you giving up this inquest."

"I know. And I'll take that as a yes." She gave a little clap of excitement. "I'll snip some wildflowers and toss them in a vase and be ready in five."

Marin hadn't thought through the concept of breakfast—in a public place—until she and Garrett were seated at The Buffalo Café, menus in hand.

The restaurant was about a quarter full—not a huge surprise for a Monday. No one was glancing in their direction with curious or judgmental stares, and yet, Marin's skin crawled.

"I thought we were avoiding being seen in public together?"

Garrett's shoulders lifted along with his mouth while he focused on the menu. "Oops."

"What if someone—"

"You're widowed and I'm divorced." His vision swept up to meet hers. "What does it matter if someone sees us together?"

"It has nothing to do with the present. You know that. How are you so nonchalant about everything that happened in the past?"

His eyes held a glint of steel. "Because I had to learn to be."

And there it was. The real truth. She'd left him behind twice. Once because she'd wanted a different life and Ralph. And then again for Ralph—abandoning Garrett to face the aftermath of Vincent's death alone.

"Morning, what can I get—" The server with a streak of silver hair and pink reading glasses perched on the end of her nose froze at the edge of their table. "Oh." Her breath leaked out, her sternum dipping with the rush of air. "I heard you were in town." She spoke to Marin. "Welcome back."

"Morning, Della-Sue." Garrett greeted her with his hallmark head nod.

"It's good to see you, Della-Sue." According to the slight impediment in her speech, she still suffered from the effects of the terrible motorcycle accident she'd been in shortly after high school. "How have you been?"

"Good. This place keeps me busy." Della-Sue motioned to the restaurant. "I miss your mother so much. She helped me a lot over the years."

Marin's heart gave that hiccup of grief she'd learned might fade but would never fully dissipate. "I'm glad to hear that. I miss her too."

"I met your daughter the other day. She reminds me of you."

Marin chuckled. "I'm sure she would appreciate that."

"How's the house going?"

"Good, but only because of Garrett."

"Of course." Della-Sue's expression almost seemed to pinch before clearing. "That's great of you to help out, Garrett. Let me get your drink orders."

They both ordered coffee, and Della-Sue moved on to another table.

Marin waited until she was out of hearing range. "I was unaware she knew my mother."

"Your mom knew everyone."

A smile sprouted. "That's true." Her mom had always checked on single mothers or low-income families, bringing them a meal or a kind word. She'd headed up the prayer chain at their small church.

She'd been one of a kind.

"I haven't seen Della-Sue in decades."

"She's worked here all those decades. She's a staple. You know how this area is. Ever since her accident, everyone has been protective of her."

"I like that."

"Me too. And wouldn't you know, we were just seen together in public—*and* someone knew us—and neither of us imploded."

Marin laughed. "One point for you." And wasn't that so Garrett? Making things better and easier, one step at a time. "You do realize that I'm not worried about being seen with you. As I said, I'm worried about what it will stir up for you."

"People have been stirring for years. You don't have to protect me, Mar."

And yet, wasn't that what he'd done for her so many times? Was it so strange for her to desire to return the favor?

"How come you get to save me, and I don't get to save you?"

"Who says you're not?"

Marin had to look away from the tenderness radiating from his sea glass eyes. She'd opened the door, and he'd strolled right through it. What had she expected? Ever since she arrived in Colorado, there'd been a tug between them. She'd tried to avoid it and him, but it hadn't dissipated. If anything, it had strengthened like the current of the Blue River during snowmelt season.

"When Ralph and I were separated, I was..." Marin wouldn't say she was suicidal, but she had experienced the desire to no longer be in her body, to avoid the pain. "I wasn't sure how to keep going. Wasn't sure if I wanted to."

Della-Sue delivered their coffees. "Be back in a minute for your order."

She hurried off and Marin continued. "You're the reason I'm sitting here. You're the reason I'm still breathing." Empathy creased his expression. "Did you ever forgive me for leaving...twice?"

If Marin wanted to keep things platonic between them, she should also keep her mouth shut and her questions silenced. But she couldn't resist asking when she'd always wondered.

Garrett's nod this time was less cordial but still definitive.

"Of course. Just because we led different lives doesn't mean we didn't care about each other. I wished you the best, Mar."

He'd watched out for her then and now. But just how far had he gone that summer in order to protect her? It was another question Marin always wondered but never wanted to know the answer to.

Some people might accuse her of hiding under a rock when it came to the truths of that night, and Marin wouldn't deny it. Because if Garrett *had* done something, she would go to her grave protecting him. Knowing what happened the night Vince died wouldn't solve anything...it would only make her complicit and complicate things.

And based on the fact that Marin was sitting across from the man she'd been trying to avoid—along with her feelings regarding him—and couldn't fathom walking out of his life for a third time...she would say things were complicated enough.

Chapter Twenty-Four

"Reed!" Kurtis Swink stood inside his open front door, delight causing his aged skin to groove with deep smile lines—as if finding two troublesome thirty-somethings on his step who were curious as to what his wife knew regarding a night thirty-four years ago was the best thing that had happened to him in years.

A ball of guilt lodged in Reed's trachea. "Mr. Swink, this is my sister, Slade." He spoke over his screeching conscience. "We just wanted to stop by and check on the two of you. See how Mrs. Swink is doing." *And my sister would like to interrogate your wife.*

"So kind!" The man's bushy eyebrows danced. "Please come in. We love company, and people so rarely stop by anymore."

"We brought Mrs. Swink some flowers." Slade held up the small jar she'd found in The Armpit and had artfully filled with wildflowers.

"Ruthie, did you hear that?" He turned toward his wife, who was seated on the sofa, a small book clutched in her lap.

"The Slade grandchildren have stopped by. They brought you some flowers."

Ruthie showed no recognition and gave no answer. The book fell from her grip, and Mr. Swink strode over to retrieve it for her.

Reed and Slade stayed frozen on the front step.

"How did I let you talk me into this?" Reed asked under his breath.

"I'm not sure," Slade answered in the same reduced tone. "I'm even questioning your logic right now."

"But you also don't want to leave."

She gave a small huff. "He's so excited to have company. How can we?"

Mr. Swink hurried back to them. "This is perfect timing!" He radiated pleasure. "I just put water on for tea."

"Tea sounds…" It was seventy-six degrees, and the high-altitude sun was a fireball against Reed's back. He broke into a sweat just contemplating the idea of ingesting a boiling liquid.

"Wonderful," Slade filled in. "That's so kind of you, Mr. Swink. But we really don't want to intrude." At the genuineness in his sister's response, Reed's muscles loosened. Slade might be curious and cynical, but she was also good to the core.

"You're not an intrusion in the least." The teapot began to whistle. "I need to get that." Mr. Swink motioned them inside. "Have a seat, please. I'll be right back." He bustled off toward the kitchen.

They stepped inside, closing the glass door behind them.

Reed was almost certain he'd seen an air-conditioning unit on the side of the house, but there was no sign of that indoors. Even in shorts and a T-shirt from one of the half-marathons he'd run, Reed's overheating gauge reached for the red. And yet, both of the Swinks were wearing cardigans over their shirts, along with full-length pants.

"Mrs. Swink, this is my sister, Slade." Reed and Slade seated themselves on the love seat across from Ruthie. "How are you feeling today?"

"Very well, thank you," she replied primly, showing no recognition of him or the events from Saturday.

Reed had hoped to redeem their visit by encouraging Mrs. Swink somehow, but based on the fact that she didn't remember him, they might only end up upsetting or confusing her.

"Here we go." Mr. Swink returned with a tray overflowing with tea mugs, cream and sugar, and a package of store-bought cookies. He set the tray on the coffee table between them. "Doctor your tea as you like."

Slade added a generous portion of cream to hers, along with two sugar cubes. Reed hadn't even realized that a person could still buy sugar cubes.

"Thank you for all of this." Reed raised the cup and forced a sip of the peppermint tea that just might send him into a menopausal hot flash.

Slade tugged the neck of her sleeveless shirt away from her glistening skin and discreetly placed her tea on the coffee table, as if attempting to escape the added heat of it in her hands.

"How long have you two lived here?" she asked.

Reed's thunderous expression swung to his sister. Was she already digging?

Her quick head shake denied his nonverbal accusation. Her shoulders inched up as if to say "chill, I'm only making conversation."

Ruthie munched on one of the cookies Mr. Swink had brought out, crumbs pooling at the corners of her mouth.

"Fifty-nine years," Mr. Swink answered. "We built this house just before your grandparents built theirs. We were one of the first in the neighborhood."

"So amazing." Slade brightened at the topic. "I love this neighborhood. We have so many good memories from the summers we spent here."

"Do you live here now?" A chunk of cookie fell into Ruthie's lap, and Kurtis discreetly swept it onto his napkin.

Reed's chest squeezed with a strange jealousy. Would he ever get the chance to love Lindsey again from anything more than long distance? Based on the way she'd been blowing up his phone when he'd asked her for space, he was beginning to doubt it.

His mind was stuck in a constant loop—was Lindsey okay? Was he wrong not to respond to her? And why wouldn't she just tell him what was going on in a text if it was something important?

On their short walk over to the Swinks, she'd called him two more times.

Reed's thumb had itched to answer.

Instead, he'd turned the phone off. He would check it after this to make sure work didn't need him, but he wasn't wrong to have asked to communicate in person instead of operating like they had been.

Reed was sticking to his no-contact-until-he-returned-home plan, because nothing had been working before that, and he was so *done* driving around the same cloverleaf on repeat with no freeway entrance in sight.

"We're staying here for a short while this summer," Slade responded to Ruthie.

Kurtis gently squeezed Ruthie's hand. "These are the Slade grandkids, dear. They used to visit in the summers, but now they're cleaning out the Slade house. Thelma and Stu both passed, remember?"

Ruthie nodded, uncertainty and sorrow filling her expression.

Reed was so grateful he'd found her on Saturday before she'd been injured or worse.

"Is there anything we can do to help out?" Slade asked. "Grocery run? Yard work? We could bring a meal over."

Mr. Swink cracked a smile at Slade's offers. "You're sweet, dear, but we're set. We hire most everything out these days. And I only do errands—outside of Saturday's mishap—when the caregiver comes. I won't make that mistake again."

Reed hated to hear Kurtis be hard on himself, and yet, he understood it.

Wasn't he doing the same internally with Lindsey? Wondering where he'd gone wrong...questioning what he could have done differently.

"You're doing a wonderful job, Mr. Swink." Slade's delivery was soft but firm. "Anyone can see that."

Kurtis blinked rapidly, emotion evident. "Thank you, my dear. I'm so glad you two stopped by. And that your brother was a Good Samaritan the other day."

"He has his good moments."

Kurtis laughed heartily at Slade's jab.

"We should get going," Reed said, checking with Slade and intercepting her nonverbal agreement. This obviously wasn't the time or the place to question Ruthie about the past. "We're glad to see you both are doing well."

"Yes." Slade stood and retrieved their tea mugs. "And we're just across the street if you need anything. I'll put our dishes in the kitchen if that's okay?"

Kurtis popped up, a joint audibly clicking along with his movement. "Let me." He swept them from her grip and hurried around the corner. A loud crash sounded. "All's well!" he called out. "Just a little glass."

"Can we help?" Slade called back.

He poked his head into the living room. "If you could just stay with Ruthie while I clean this up, I would greatly appreciate it." He winced. "I'm sorry to ask for one more thing."

"*I'm* sorry that our visit caused you more work," Reed responded, but Kurtis had already returned to the mess.

Ruthie attempted to push up from her seat on the couch,

and both Reed and Slade moved to help her. Once standing, she shuffled across the living room. They flanked her in case she needed assistance.

Ruthie reached an armoire, opened it and retrieved a thick mauve photo album with gold edging.

"Didn't you know my son, Peter?" She spoke to Reed and flipped to a page about halfway through the book. She pointed at a lanky dark-haired boy in a track uniform standing with a group of other teammates his age. "Were you in the same class?"

"I was closer in age to your grandson, actually."

"He was so good at track. Did you run track in high school too? Is that how you knew each other?" Ruthie must not have registered Reed's response.

"I did run track." *In a completely different time and place.* He took a page out of Slade's playbook and stuck to the simplest of answers since expounding would likely only cause confusion for Ruthie.

"I thought track would get him a college scholarship, but he got kicked off the team his senior year because of Vinny's influence." Ruthie's mouth pursed, and Slade's formed a small O. "Didn't you say you knew Vinny also?"

"No, I didn't know Vinny."

"Probably a good thing. Vinny seemed to taint whatever came near him. Still, he didn't deserve to die like that."

"Do you remember anything about that night, Mrs. Swink?"

Slade. How had Reed let her talk him into this awful plan? What did any of it matter now?

"I certainly do." Pops of pink broke out on Ruthie's cheeks. "I told the police everything, and they didn't listen."

Reed was relieved to hear the vacuum still operating. If Mr. Swink were to return to find them questioning his frail wife about Vincent Dunn, he might just throw them off a cliff.

"There were two vehicles." Ruthie raised shaking fingers. "One with headlights. One without. There was a terrible storm that night, and it had woken me. That's how I saw the truck and the car."

The album loosened in Ruthie's grip, and Slade rescued it before it crashed to the floor. She returned it to the shelf and closed the armoire door.

Ruthie reached out and touched Slade's hair. "You know, dear." Her gaze was somehow direct and vacant at the same time. "You were there." Mrs. Swink's hand fluttered to her chest. "I feel a little light-headed. Maybe I should sit down."

"Let's get you back to your seat." To Slade's credit, she didn't attempt to prod further. She took Ruthie's arm, and they moved slowly across the living room, returning her to her perch on the sofa.

Slade seated herself next to Ruthie like a bookend, and the woman sagged against her, her eyelids beginning to droop.

Apparently, the encounter with them had drained her. Reed hoped it wouldn't affect her adversely in other ways.

The vacuum turned off, and Mr. Swink joined them. "Sorry about that. I have to make sure to get every shard so that Ruthie doesn't step on one. Thank you both for helping me out. Here you go, dear." He shifted Ruthie upright so that Slade could vacate the spot as her placeholder.

"We're sorry we caused you more work." Slade gave Mr. Swink an impromptu hug, and the man's eyes brightened with emotion. "Thank you so much for the tea and cookies. And please let us know if we can do anything for either of you while we're in town."

Slade and Reed said goodbye and exited the house, neither speaking until they reached the street and pine trees blocked them from the Swinks' view.

"I was not expecting that."

"Did you have to push?"

"I'm sorry." Slade paused and faced him. "Once we got there

and I saw her condition, I wasn't planning to ask. But when she brought him up, I—"

"You couldn't resist." Reed's lungs formed a slow leak. "At least she didn't seem too upset." The last thing he wanted to do was leave the woman agitated.

"I doubt she'll even remember we had that conversation."

"Or she'll relay every detail to her husband, and he'll think we're evil."

Slade winced. "Oh, I hope not. They're so sweet." They began to cross the street slowly, no cars in sight. "Do you think she really talked to the police back then and they didn't listen?"

"No idea. Maybe they listened. Maybe the vehicles she supposedly saw had nothing to do with Vincent's death."

"I just wish we could understand what she was trying to relay."

"Everything she said could be a figment of her imagination or the result of warped memories. We can't know what she's thinking because *she* might not even know what she's thinking."

"But she seemed so confident. The way she talks about it— it's like she really does remember. I'm inclined to believe her."

Of course she was. "Now you turn trusting."

Slade released a short laugh. "Think about this street." She waved a hand over the empty asphalt. "How often do we see cars on it? Almost never. No one drives up here except for the few who live here. Two vehicles late at night—especially one without lights—does seem suspicious."

Reed conceded her point with an angled jaw.

"What did she mean when she said I was there? Who is she remembering? Does she think I'm *Mom*? Everyone says we look alike, even though I don't see it."

"Who knows what she was talking about with that." They could guess. They could leap to conclusions like Slade probably wanted to, but the truth was they didn't have any real understanding of Ruthie's ramblings. "Please tell me you're not going to bug Mom about this. She cannot handle one more thing."

"Mom hasn't wanted to discuss Vincent from the start. I'm certainly not going to bring it up now."

That, at least, was a relief.

They'd reached the house, and Reed held open the screen door. Slade's eyebrows elevated with humor as she passed him. "You do realize that little excursion backfired on you, right?"

His exhale slipped into the groan-annoyance-exasperation category. "Oh, trust me. I am well aware."

Chapter Twenty-Five

"Maybe we should go kayaking another time." Cyrus's comment broke Slade from her reverie.

"I thought we already were going kayaking." And yet… Slade glanced out the windows of Cyrus's truck. They were still parked in her grandparents' driveway. "How long have you been waiting for me to orbit back to earth?"

"Maybe five minutes." His concerned but patient gaze rested on her. "I asked you a question when we got in, but you were looking at your phone, and I don't think you've surfaced since. I was trying to give you time to deal with…" He nodded toward her phone, which had landed in her lap. "Whatever it is you're dealing with. You okay?"

She wasn't.

Not since receiving a second email from human resources around noon today. After the first landed in spam, Slade had saved the address to her trusted contacts. Today's news had come through just fine.

Though it had sent her stomach exiting through the bottoms of her feet like a runaway elevator crashing through the foundation of a building.

When she'd gotten into Cyrus's truck, Slade had stupidly decided to reread the HR email while he drove them to the lake, hoping upon hope that she would find something encouraging that she'd missed the first two times.

"If you're breaking up with me, I'd rather have you tell me outright than beat around the bush."

Beat around the bush sounded like something Grandad would say. "And I've stored the details of my breakup speech on my phone?"

"It's possible."

"How can I break up with you when we're not dating?"

"Good point." He gave a nod eerily reminiscent of his father, which she quickly filed into a manila folder labeled Not Going There. Slade was still weirded out by the idea of her mom with his dad, even if it had happened a lifetime ago.

"I've been wondering if maybe you think of me platonically." Since the first time they'd hung out, they'd spent every evening together. They were on fast forward, and while Cyrus was constantly texting or calling her, hugging her, holding her hand, invading her world, silently communicating that he was there for her, he also kept her at a distance in other ways. They'd never kissed. And while Slade didn't need Cyrus to make the first move, she also couldn't get a clear read on him.

"I don't—" His Adam's apple bobbed, and his hands gripped the steering wheel and released. "I do not feel platonically about you."

Slade studied his strong jaw line. He was obviously warring with something, because a small tick surfaced.

"You've been through a lot." His anguished expression shifted to her. "Is it so wrong to be careful with you?"

Slade had wondered if his restraint had something to do

with Jude. "He's already stolen enough from me. Don't add to the list." She tempered her admonishment with a faint smile.

"So, you're saying kissing is on the table but discussing anything about what happens with us after you leave Colorado isn't?"

"Right." If all went as planned, they would finish The Armpit tomorrow, then load the trailer the used furniture store planned to drop off, and she and Reed would be heading out of Colorado this weekend.

Slade had already reserved her ticket.

"So, if I were to lean your way right now..." His vision flitted to her lips, and he shifted slightly in her direction. "That's acceptable?"

Slade began to gravitate toward him but immediately wrenched herself back upright. "You can't talk about it first. That ruins the surprise."

He gave a nod that reached for serious but was tempered with suppressed laughter. "Got it. I'm going to need a notebook to keep track of all the rules." He reached across the seat of the truck and captured her hand. "So, back to what's on your mind."

She could tell him she didn't want to talk about it, and he would let her get away with that. He was too good to her. Too easy on her.

"The law firm notified me that they finished the investigation into Jude. And into me too, even though no one asked me for more details than I originally sent in."

He squeezed her hand. "And?"

"They found no wrongdoing on his part, and it seems he then agreed to drop any countercharges against me."

The minute the email had popped up on her phone, Slade had thought that they were finally reaching out for her side of the story.

She'd been nervous to detail what had happened again.

She'd never expected to find their verdict already decided. "That sounds like—"

"A threat," she filled in. "If I pursue this further, no doubt whatever he's made up about me will be brought up again. But if I leave it alone, he'll move on. It's a gauntlet. A warning. An incentive to drop my complaints. He's manipulating me. Still."

Cyrus released a low growl. "Feel like I need to visit Florida."

His defense of her was as comforting as Gran's cardigan that was tucked into her keep bag.

"I don't want him to win, but the battle just feels too big. I wonder if I'll ever forgive myself—"

"Don't give him that much power." He echoed her admonishment from earlier. "None of the blame for any of this should ever land on you."

"Part of me just wants to move on." There, she'd admitted it. The idea felt like failing, and yet, just considering it ignited relief. "I tried. I did my best. Right?"

When he didn't respond immediately, she spiraled. Was she the mess her mom—and much of the outside world—always considered her to be?

If Slade were to list her accomplishments in a column next to Jude's, he would come out the clear front-runner.

She'd never held a job for longer than a year or two.

Had been fired on more than one occasion.

Categorized life as an adventure versus a mountain to be conquered.

Slade missed her dad and her grandparents—the people who'd always considered her a rare wildflower instead of a roadside weed.

"Hey." Cyrus tucked her arm against his chest, the *thump-thump* of his heart strumming against it as he pressed his lips to her knuckles. "You absolutely did your best. You did the right thing, which is all you can do. This isn't on you to carry. Not alone like this."

Cyrus had encouraged her to reach out to other women at the firm, but Slade had resisted because she knew what their answers would be.

They couldn't afford to risk losing their jobs. If they'd desired to come forward, they would have done it when she did—when she left the firm.

Cyrus released her hand and turned the key one click, causing old-school, crooning country music to fill the cab of the truck. It had the crinkly, nostalgic quality of being played on vinyl.

Part of the reason Slade found herself attracted to him—beyond him being amazingly supportive and encouraging and somehow seeing the best in her—was that he didn't fit the mold either.

He had the habits of a fifty-year-old while in his twenties—he went to bed early and got up early. He worked tirelessly and was meticulous about the business he shared with his father. He lived in a house that definitely qualified as a cabin—a simple place with two bedrooms, one bathroom and not a stainless-steel appliance in sight, with a deck that butted up to open space being the largest part of it.

Slade had gone over last night, and they'd sat on the deck and watched a mama moose and her baby walk by like it was the most natural thing in the world to be fifteen yards away, quietly observing them.

Cyrus's walls were filled with photos of him fishing or hunting with friends. He had a record cabinet, circa 1970, and shelves of vinyl to play on it, only a handful of which Slade recognized.

It was the kind of eclectic place that crawled into your bones and burrowed there, whispering, "Don't leave. Maybe you could be happy here."

Slade hadn't had a response for that, so she'd ignored the whispering house-slash-cabin.

The song finished, and another filled its place, though the words and meaning were lost on Slade.

"Do you want me to go? You have a lot to process."

"It's hard to process something that's a dead end. And I definitely don't want you to go." Beyond her family, Cyrus was the good in her world right now. "I need the distraction."

"So now I'm a distraction?"

A rusty smile slid into place. "You've always been a distraction."

His eyes crinkled back at her, then shifted to the rearview mirror. "Looks like one of the bungies is loose. Hang on." He'd borrowed the two kayaks stashed in the bed of his truck from a friend.

Slade's fingers hovered over her phone, barely resisting the temptation to check the email one more time, to search for a redeeming detail one more time. Like a severance package or the promise of a glowing recommendation letter.

The passenger door opened, and Cyrus filled the space. "Now that I have a green light for this—" he leaned into the vehicle, his work-calloused hands gently sliding up to frame her cheeks "—I can't resist."

His lips met hers—first hanging on to those threads of cautiousness he'd been harboring with her since she'd told him about Jude, then switching to something more urgent, like he too felt the days remaining turning to hours, minutes, moments.

And just like that, her world crumpled and rebuilt and got hazy and confusing.

Slade hadn't imagined that the connection between them could amount to this. That it would feel like landing after a lifetime of turbulence.

Cyrus melted her. His endearing simplicity wound around her heart like his fingers were burrowing into her hair.

Slade had thought before that maybe she'd never met *the*

one because *the one* didn't exist. She'd assumed it was a choice and no one had ever tempted her to make that choice before.

But now she was starting to think it was a combination of those two things and probably a thousand more things.

The sound of an engine droned on the street behind them. It wasn't her family—Mom was out on a walk and Reed was out on a run—so Slade ignored it.

Cyrus's hands shifted to her legs, scooting her across the seat, closer, until they crashed into each other like she was a wave, and he was her personal seawall.

Slade faintly recognized that the engine had switched to an idle, and Cyrus must have noticed the same, because he gave a grumble of annoyance as he slowly, regretfully eased back from her.

"Expecting someone?" he asked, voice raspy, forehead tipping toward the street. "Whoever it is, they have terrible timing."

"I'm not."

He offered her a hand of assistance, and Slade slid from the passenger seat to the driveway. An airport shuttle van was parked on the street flanking the house.

"They must be heading to a neighbor's. Or have the wrong address."

The driver strode to the back of the van, opening the double doors. A carry-on appeared on the street, and another person stood with the driver for a few seconds—probably tipping—while blocked from their view.

The driver closed the doors and returned to his seat as Slade's sister-in-law wheeled the suitcase toward the driveway.

"Lindsey?" What was she doing here? Was Reed expecting her?

She wore wide-legged jeans, wedges and a flowered midriff shirt, her auburn hair shoulder-length. She was stunning, and yet, visibly shattered—her face drawn as tight as if she was currently enduring level-ten pain.

Lindsey rolled to a stop in front of them.

"Hi," she greeted Cyrus. "I'm Lindsey."

He introduced himself. "Good to meet you." Despite how much Slade had dumped on him regarding her brother's marital issues, Cyrus remained his good-natured self. "I'll give you two a minute to catch up." That tender you-okay? look of his swung to Slade. "Be on the deck if you need me." And then his teasing smile sprouted. "Gotta get some golden-hour shots for my Instagram anyway." He strode toward the deck, took the two steps in one long stride, and disappeared around the side of the house.

"Was he serious?" A wrinkle formed on the bridge of Lindsey's nose as her vision followed in his wake. "Is he some kind of influencer?"

Laughter bubbled up. "He's kidding."

"Oh." Lindsey's smile sprouted, creating soft lines that wilted just as quickly as they appeared. "I'm sure you're wondering why I'm here." She continued without waiting for Slade's confirmation. "I've been trying to get ahold of Reed for the last few days, but he won't answer. I know why but I—" Tears pooled, and she shook her head in lieu of continuing. "I know you're Team Reed, as you should be, but I have to talk to him." She swiped the moisture now slipping down her cheeks. "Please, don't turn me away. I know you probably blame me for all of this."

"I don't. Reed wouldn't let me."

Lindsey gave a small, emotional laugh. "I see he's still his perfect self."

Slade found a grin forming. "Have you ever known him to be anything else?"

Her eyes refilled. "Never."

Despite Reed's admonishment not to, it had felt natural for Slade to plant herself firmly on her brother's side. And yet, she loved this woman too. They were more than sisters-in-law.

They'd grown close over the years. Slade hadn't allowed herself to mourn that relationship because she was so focused on Reed.

She leaned into Cyrus's truck through the still-open passenger door to snag some tissues and handed a stack over to Lindsey, who used two in succession.

"He's on a run. The house is open. Help yourself to whatever's inside. We were just about to leave." Which they would still do in order to give Reed and Lindsey some privacy.

"I can sit outside if you—"

"Absolutely not." Reed would kill Slade if she banished Lindsey from waiting in the house for him. Plus... "You're family, Linds. No matter what happens between you two."

Her face crumpled with the kind of emotion that brought Slade back to her encounter with Jude.

"Thank you." Lindsey took a shuddering breath—no doubt an attempt at regaining control. "I know it's a lot to ask, but can you please, *please* not tell Reed I'm here? I'm petrified that he won't talk to me if he knows."

"Reed would never—"

"*Please.*" She gave a hiccup as a new rush of moisture sprang.

Slade's stomach pitched. Would Reed forgive her for allowing Lindsey to blindside him?

He wanted resolution between them, even if it wasn't the answer he hoped for, right?

Please don't make me regret this. Love him, Linds, like I believe you do.

"Okay. I'm sure he'll be back from his run shortly. Go easy on him. He—" *He adores you.* Slade slammed her teeth together. "Just go easy on him—that's my request."

Lindsey's head bobbed. "Thank you." She released a tortured exhale and embraced Slade, leaving a hint of her sweet, subtle perfume in the air before gripping her carry-on and rolling over to the house, up the stairs, through the unlocked door.

A few seconds after it clicked shut behind her, Cyrus came down the deck steps.

He rounded the truck to the passenger side where Slade still stood, and without a word, wrapped her up in the kind of embrace that could end civil wars and world hunger.

Slade burrowed into his mountain-fresh scent, into the kind of stability she'd never craved before him.

He pressed a kiss to her forehead. "You okay?"

"Sort of. Let's get out of here before Reed comes back and never forgives me."

"Done." Cyrus waited for Slade to climb into the passenger side and then closed the door behind her. He went around the vehicle and settled into the driver's seat. "I'm thinking we table kayaking for another time."

"Probably a good idea. I'm going to be worthless company tonight anyway." She would be wondering how Lindsey's surprise arrival was affecting Reed. She would be shoving down her despair over the HR email. And on the back burner was that encounter with Ruthie on Monday morning and the strange information she'd relayed that Slade still hadn't sorted into anything comprehensible. But she had become more convinced of one thing: Ruthie hadn't seemed confused. She'd seemed confident.

Certain.

Who had Ruthie been referring to when she'd said *you were here?*

Could it be Mom?

While working on The Armpit with Mom and Reed yesterday and today, Slade had considered asking her mother about what Ruthie had relayed.

But Mom's original reticence to discuss the article, plus Reed being present—Slade could only imagine how upset he'd be with her if she were to cause Mom stress after that near breakdown earlier this week—had kept her lips superglued shut.

If Mom had been in town at that time, why wouldn't she have just said that?

Hiding it made no sense.

And maybe holding on to this search and her ferocious curiosity no longer made sense either.

Poking into what happened to Vincent had started because Slade had been desperate for a distraction, and she was able to disengage from his death because it was so far in the past. It was like watching a true crime documentary and then turning off the television and walking away.

But Cyrus was a far better distraction than anything regarding Vincent was turning out to be.

When Slade had talked to Keely yesterday, her new friend had pulled the truth regarding her growing feelings for Cyrus out of her. "Stay! Move here!" Keely had crowed, and then proceeded to send Slade job openings.

A massage therapist position at a Keystone resort had caught her attention, and Slade had emailed them her resume...without mentioning that she'd already left her last employment. But the cost of living in Summit County was unreasonably high, and Slade would need more than that to survive. She hadn't said anything to Cyrus regarding the fact that she was entertaining the idea of staying in her grandparents' town, because it was a decision she had to make for herself.

Besides, the two of them were too new for it to have anything to do with him, despite Keely's teasing.

"On your worst day, you could never be worthless company." Cyrus put the truck in reverse. "I need to grab my dad's weed whacker. Mind if we buzz by there?"

"Sure. No problem."

"Thanks." He backed out of the drive and headed for his father's.

Evening sunshine poured through the open window and warmed her skin. "Why'd you wait so long to kiss me again?"

His low laughter answered her. "Why did *you* wait so long?"

"That's what you get for attempting to be noble."

"And I suppose there was a smattering of logic mixed in. Like, not kissing you would have somehow made it easier to let you go." He continued under his breath. "It wouldn't have." He beamed one of his magnetic, slightly mischievous grins her way. "I promise—no more attempts to be noble. And logic is clearly overrated."

Slade's mouth curved. Hadn't she been saying as much her whole life? "Clearly."

Cyrus parked in his dad's driveway and turned off the engine. "You coming in? I need to tell him what I'm here to steal—I mean borrow."

"You didn't text him you were stopping by?"

"Why would I do that when he's a handful of houses away? Not everyone is afraid of human contact and phone calls like you."

"Rude," she delivered with a laugh. "Sure. I'll come." Her wariness regarding Garrett had fizzled now that she understood what had first ignited it. And all the man had done since their arrival in Colorado was assist and save them.

Maybe it was time for Slade to set aside any remaining skepticism. Especially since this thing with his son didn't seem to be fading.

Cyrus knocked on the door and then opened it. "Dad?" His call went unanswered. "He's probably out on the deck. He's turned into an old man who watches the birds and the weather and the activity on the lake in the evenings."

"Sounds familiar." Hadn't they just sat on Cyrus's deck last night doing the same thing with a different view?

His cheeks creased at her quip. "True."

They walked through the living room, and sure enough, perfectly framed by the sliding glass door was Garrett, sitting on the deck, facing the lake.

And seated next to him was Slade's mom.

"Huh." Slade's feet faltered as she watched the third major surprise of her day unfold before her. Had her mom been disappearing over here in the evenings under the guise of her walk? Or was this a one-off situation?

Slade didn't need Reed present to know what his admonition would be: *obviously, they're friends. You don't need to jump to conclusions.*

But this clandestine encounter was circumspect to her. The alarm bells she'd *just* silenced began pulsing again.

What am I missing here?

It took Cyrus a moment to realize she'd stopped, at which point he followed her line of vision and digested the same scene as her.

"We don't know that it means anything," he supplied.

Slade was afraid it meant far more than she'd previously imagined.

Chapter Twenty-Six

Reed sensed someone the moment he stepped into the house.

He paused by the screen door, his vision adjusting to the lower lighting.

A figure sitting in the chair next to the fireplace stood. A figure that looked an awful lot like his wife. The one he'd just been thinking about on his run despite all of his attempts not to.

Had he conjured her himself? Was she real?

"Lindsey?"

"Hi." She remained stationary in front of the chair.

Reed crossed the space slowly, concerned that if he made any sudden movements, she'd poof into thin air.

"What are you doing here?"

"I had to talk to you." Her caramel eyes were lined with red crayon, the makeup below them smudged and faded. Reed knew the remnants of tears well. She'd—they'd—perfected them over the last handful of months.

Reed's attraction to Lindsey had never faltered, but encountering her now, after their absence from one another, was like being hit with a rogue wave that buckled his knees.

"You said that in your messages, but I thought—" He'd thought so many things.

"It wasn't the kind of news I could deliver over text or voice-mail."

Fear wrecked him. What if she was sick? She'd grown panicked after her mother's diagnosis. Worried that the same could happen to her. Reed had continually assured her she was young and healthy, but what if he was wrong?

Or maybe she'd met someone. Maybe she wanted to speed up the process of their divorce and had nobly decided to deliver that blow in person.

"I need to sit." If she was going to deliver news that had to be carted across the country and delivered in bodily form, he required the support of furniture beneath him. "How did you get here?"

She perched on the edge of Grandad's favorite mustard chair again, and Reed chose the sofa.

She explained the last-minute ticket, the shuttle. Exhaustion from the long day of travel radiated from her wilted posture.

"I ran into Slade in the driveway. I begged her not to warn you I was here, so please don't blame her for that."

"I won't." Though a heads-up would have been nice. "Are you okay? You're scaring me, Linds. What's going on?"

She studied her fingernails, pushing back dry cuticles—a nervous habit of hers. "On the flight, I went over what I would say when I got here." Wide, vulnerable eyes swept up to his. "And yet, here I am, speechless."

Reed's quick dinner from earlier threatened to make an appearance. Even with the worst stomach flu he'd ever encountered, he hadn't known his gut could twist or squeeze like this.

"Just say it. Whatever it is, we'll figure it out." It would kill

Reed to let her go if that's what had brought her here, but he would find a way through it. Somehow.

"I'm pregnant."

Reed's world spun off its axis. He hated himself for his next question, but how could he not ask?

"Whose—" His voice cracked and sputtered.

"Yours, of course. I haven't been with anyone else, Reed. We're still married."

"Separated."

"That doesn't count as a free pass to me." Shock and hurt created grooves across her forehead. "Does it to you?"

"Of course not. I haven't thought about another woman since the day I met you. I just— It's been so long. I didn't realize…"

"Me either. It took me a bit to figure out why I was feeling the way I was."

At the end, when they'd… Reed had thought they were reconciling, but he'd realized later that Lindsey had been saying goodbye.

"I found out the night you suggested we take a break from talking."

"And you've been trying to reach me ever since."

She confirmed with a nod. "It's been awful. My mind's been going nonstop. One second, I'm over the moon. I mean, how much did we want this? And the next, I'm panicking over what the future looks like. What we're going to do. How we're going to raise this baby."

"What do you mean, how we're going to raise the baby?"

The baby. Just like that, Reed had accepted that his estranged wife, the woman sitting a few feet from him, was carrying his child. He could doubt that, but that would be like doubting his whole existence, his whole marriage.

He wanted to drop to his knees by her chair and bury his head against her stomach so he could get close to her, to both of them.

"I mean joint custody or co-parenting or whatever we decide to do."

"Joint…" She was talking about raising the baby as separated parents. "You don't want to give us a second chance? You don't want to be together?" Reed couldn't imagine a better catalyst for trying again. A better reason to succeed.

"For the baby?"

"And us. I love you, Linds. I never wanted this separation."

"I know. It's all my fault, right? I'm the one keeping us apart, and you're the—"

"Stop!" Reed skyrocketed to a standing position.

Lindsey winced and sank against the back of the chair, her hands curving protectively around her still-flat abdomen.

Reed rounded the couch, putting distance between them. The idea that she'd just lurched away from his fury slayed him.

He squeezed the sofa cushions, neck bent. "I'm sorry. This is a lot to process. But that's not an excuse." He met her gaze head-on, attempting to communicate determination. To communicate that she could trust him. "It won't happen again." He would make sure of it. No more anger. No more fighting.

"I started that one. And the thousand that came before it."

"You don't get all the credit."

Her wobbly smile felt like a win.

Reed moved to the coffee table and perched on the edge, leaving only inches between them. "I can't believe we're having a baby." He reached for her hand, which she amazingly didn't tug back. Even that trivial touch leveled him. He covertly attempted to inhale a scent that was inherently her—a mix of the light perfume she wore, a faint hint of her shampoo, the mint from her lip gloss.

Her countenance brightened. "It's wild. I'm so happy, though."

"Me too." He couldn't wait to meet a little one that was a combination of the two of them. "This baby is going to be so loved."

"I keep crying about *everything*," she said with a small laugh, motioning to the new moisture pooling.

"I'm sure that's normal. Hormones, right?"

She nodded, and a few tears spilled. Reed snagged the tissue box from the other end of the coffee table and handed it to her.

"Whatever happens—whatever we decide—you are not alone in this, Linds. I'll be here every step of the way. I promise." He wrangled his tongue into submission and forced out the next declaration. "Whether we're together or not."

Her shoulders seemed to physically shed the weight they'd been holding, and she made a small sound of relief.

"Thank you."

Reed would guess that's what had propelled her across the country. Not for him—at least, not exactly—but for the peace of knowing she wasn't alone. Ever since her dad abandoned them that had always been a trigger for her.

The person he loved more than anyone in the world had been carrying this burden by herself, panicked about the future, all because he hadn't picked up the phone to answer her texts or calls.

"I'm sorry I didn't answer when you reached out. I wasn't sure what was going on. I thought—"

"That I was causing drama, trying to get attention from you? That does sound like something I would do. Especially lately."

"Neither of us have been acting like ourselves. You're not alone in that either."

Reed wanted to plead with her to give them another chance, to fight for the opportunity to raise their baby together—happily married.

But she hadn't come here for that. Despite that their absence from each other had made Reed even more determined to make their marriage work, apparently Lindsey had not experienced a similar epiphany.

If she needed more space, more time to process, there was nothing Reed could do but give it to her.

"Do you think we can figure out how to be the good versions of ourselves for this one?" She palmed her stomach, her vision following the movement, tenderness softening her features and hollowing out Reed's chest.

He wanted desperately to love her as both the mother of their child *and* his wife. He wasn't sure what he was missing or why he wasn't enough. Why he couldn't be the kind of man Grandad and Dad had been. If he was, surely this would be a different conversation. Instead of discussing how they were going to raise the baby separately together, they'd be discussing raising the baby *together* together.

"Of course." He dredged up a reassuring smile. "We're going to have to."

Chapter Twenty-Seven

Marin had not sought out Garrett on her walk. But just like the last two evenings, she'd approached his portion of the street to find him standing in his driveway, hands in the back pockets of his jeans, waiting for her.

She was beginning to wonder if he'd always been waiting for her.

He'd convinced her to sit on the deck with him each evening, but he hadn't had to do much convincing.

Being with Garrett was so easy that it almost felt circumspect. But then, he'd always been like a comfort sweater to her. One that slipped into the back of the closet but was there when needed. It might have a hole or two, but the softness was unmatched.

"Did you prefer the toddler years or the high school years better with your kids?"

"Toddler. Slade was a wild one in high school. It wasn't that she even broke that many rules. It was that she had to push on *everything*. What about you?"

"High school. I liked going to all of their sporting events. Liked when their friends came over. When Poppy took off, friends seemed to be the best medicine for the boys. I set up a man cave in the garage so they all had a place to hang out."

"That was nice of you."

"What can I say? I was a great dad."

Marin laughed. "You still are." She was the one who constantly struggled with feelings of inadequacy. "Slade and I still clash sometimes, and I'm not even sure why."

"You're both strong."

Marin liked to think so. "She's always had this attitude like I don't believe in her."

"Do you?"

"I do. But I don't always understand her, so I think it comes across like I don't."

"Parenting adult children is so confusing. More often than not, I think I get it wrong. Everything is more hands-off, but they still come running when they need something."

"Maybe it's strange to say this, but I hope they do." She thought about Reed and how he'd told her so little of what was going on with Lindsey. Of Slade and how she'd never explained what had happened with her work. "It's a compliment if they come to you." Where had Marin gone so wrong with her children?

"Suppose so."

The sound of the sliding glass door opening caused them both to turn in their seats.

"Mom?" Slade stepped onto the deck, followed by Cyrus. "What are you doing here?"

"I was out on a walk when I ran into Garrett." It was the truth, and yet Slade had never been one to be satisfied with a superficial answer, which her pinched brow confirmed.

"Join us if you want." Garrett motioned to the two chairs on the other side of the gas firepit.

"We're good, thanks." Cyrus and Slade rounded to face them. "Dad, I actually just stopped by to borrow your weed whacker."

Garrett sent Marin an amused glance, as if to say "and here's one looking for assistance right now."

"Not sure where it is, so I'll help you look." Garrett pushed out of his chair, releasing a noise-slash-breath that both of them probably made whenever exerting any physical effort. Sometimes, Marin was surprised by how many parts of her body could ache and complain just rolling out of bed in the morning. Getting old was both a blessing and a daily surprise in physical limitations.

The two men went inside, presumably headed for the garage, while Slade resembled a hummingbird in midair, unsure of her next move.

After a moment of contemplation, she flopped into the chair next to Marin that Garrett had just vacated.

"I did not think I could handle one more surprise today, but they just *keep on coming.*"

"What happened?" Marin had spent most of the day with her daughter. What had she missed?

"Lindsey just showed up at the house."

"At whose house?"

"Ours. Gran and Grandad's."

Marin digested that shocking information. "Did Reed know she was coming?"

"No. And she begged me not to warn him." Slade huffed. "And for some reason, I agreed." Vulnerability laced her tone. "Think Reed will forgive me for that?"

"I would imagine so. Did she say why she'd come? Is she okay?"

"She didn't say, and I have no idea."

"I certainly hope she's here with good news."

"Me too."

Marin studied her daughter's profile—that determined chin,

the pert nose, the ear with four holes in it that Marin had fought like a soldier about to face death and now found she couldn't care less about. So many things she had thought mattered so much, but as the years passed, she found herself thankful for the basics—family, friends, breath, sun, water, food.

"I also," Slade continued, "stumbled upon my mom getting cozy with the father of the guy I've been hanging out with, so that's awkward."

"There's nothing between Garrett and me." At least, nothing they'd discussed. "I know how much us dating in high school upset you, Love, and I wouldn't do that to you." Marin had already had the love of her life. She wouldn't stand in Slade's way...whatever that looked like. Slade was picky when it came to dating. Was she serious about Cyrus? The idea caused a hitch in Marin's gut. If they stayed together long-term, it would mean a continued roundabout connection between Marin and an off-limits Garrett.

It would mean continued vigilance regarding the past.

"Garrett was just massaging my hand because my joints have been stiff." At some point during their conversation this evening, Garrett had begun gently kneading Marin's aching wrist and fingers, and she'd melted at the relief from the pain she'd grown accustomed to over the years. Pain that she'd trained herself to ignore as much as was humanly possible.

Having it recognized by Garrett, having him somehow innately understand the right level of pressure to use, was better than a first kiss or the feel of sand beneath her toes. It was the sensation of being seen without demanding it.

Of course that would be the first thing Slade would notice.

"I wasn't talking about that, though, now that you bring it up, that's also suspect."

"Then, what did you see that has you all in a tizzy?" It wasn't like they'd been making out. And certainly not as if Marin had spent a full ten seconds analyzing Garrett's mouth tonight, wondering what it would be like to kiss someone again. Was it like riding a bike? Would she remember how?

Despite her assurance to Slade just now, Marin's brain had spent a copious amount of time roaming into Garrett territory this week. Into dissecting the current that spanned between them. Into wondering if it was possible or worth it to start over at her age.

All taboo topics.

"It was how he was looking at you."

Marin's stomach dropped to the lake bottom. "What do you mean?"

"He was looking at you the same way he was in the prom pictures Reed showed me."

Had he been? Marin had grown so comfortable with Garrett over the last couple weeks that she'd forgotten to keep her guard up. Forgotten why it all mattered so much in the first place.

But it did.

She still had people to protect.

"There's a lot of history between us, that's all."

"What does that mean, Mom? Are we talking high school... or are we talking in your twenties?"

"My twenties?" Marin's heart stampeded, and she prayed Slade wouldn't be able to witness or hear her thundering pulse.

"Della-Sue once told me that you and Garrett were close in your twenties, and I chalked it up to being a mistake."

"When was this?"

"When Keely and I went to breakfast."

How shocking that Slade hadn't demanded answers that very day.

"Della-Sue was in an awful motorcycle accident right after high school. Poor woman. She still suffers from the effects of that."

"She mentioned the accident." Slade tucked her knees into the chair and shifted so that her back was against the armrest.

Her arms wrapped around her shins, her attention homed in on Marin. "Were you close to Garrett in your twenties? Was Della-Sue right?"

She'd said she wouldn't tread anywhere close to lying to her kids again, so outside of getting up from her seat and literally fleeing the premises, Marin was left with only one choice.

"Garrett and I were close...for a very short time...in our twenties."

The hurt that splashed across Slade's expression was a sledge-hammer to Marin's chest.

"Did you cheat on Dad?"

"No." At least, not in the way Slade was asking. But Marin often wondered if her closeness to Garrett at that time could have been classified as an emotional affair. But since she and Ralph had never qualified it in those terms, she wasn't going to start now.

"You were in Dillon?"

"Yes."

"Why?"

Despite her pledge, Marin couldn't bring herself to state the full reason. "I was visiting Gran and Grandad."

"Wait—I'm not related to Cyrus, am I? Are we going to find out something terrible if we take one of those ancestry tests? Is Reed really my brother?"

"Lovetta Slade!" This girl! She went down the rabbit hole so quickly. "You and Reed are biological siblings, and you are *not* related to Cyrus. I told you there was no affair. This was before you two were even around."

Slade's pupils darkened and spilled wide like pools of ink. "How long before? Like thirty-four years ago? When she said I was here, she *was* talking about you."

"What? Who was?" Marin was lost, yet even so, a spiral of dread began to curve its way around her organs, up her wind-pipe, into her aching joints.

"Mrs. Swink. Reed and I popped over to check on her Monday morning while you were supposedly discussing house stuff with Garrett, and she started talking about the night Vincent Dunn died. She mentioned some vehicles and that she'd talked to the police, and then she looked right at me and said, 'You remember. You were here.'"

Old Ruthie Swink. Not a huge surprise that she was still gossiping about Vince's death all these years later, though Marin imagined her daughter had helped to bring that summer up in some form or fashion—despite Marin's original hopes that she would let that period lie.

At the time of Vince's passing, Ruthie was quite vocal about what she believed she'd witnessed. Marin had always been thankful her details hadn't led to any big revelations, because she'd worried they might incriminate Garrett or even shed suspicion on her.

Marin desperately wanted to abandon this treacherous conversation, but Slade would never allow it. Her daughter would simply follow and demand more answers. It was better to stay and direct the dialogue, in the hopes of keeping everything from unraveling.

"I wondered if she meant you," Slade continued. "But I couldn't imagine why you wouldn't have told us you were in town at that time when I found the article. You acted like you barely knew a thing about it. But that's when you were here, wasn't it? The timing when you were somehow close to Garrett while married but supposedly not having an affair."

Ouch. When she said it that way...

Marin didn't answer this time. Slade had already come to her own correct conclusion.

"Why didn't you tell me when I found the article? Why would you hide that?"

"Maybe she's not hiding anything. Maybe she just doesn't like to talk about that time. None of us do." Garrett's voice came from behind them, and he rounded to face the chairs they occupied. "Cyrus is putting the weed whacker in his truck." He focused on Marin as if silently checking whether she was okay.

She did her best to send back nonverbals that assured him she was...or that she was at least trying to be.

Slade's vision tracked between them. "What am I missing here?"

Neither of them spoke. Chickadees flitted above them, communicating back and forth. A distant hum of an airplane droned.

"I just don't understand why you're being so secretive about this. It doesn't make any sense."

"Garrett's right. None of us like to think about that summer. It was traumatic and hard on Gran and Grandad to know someone died below their house, even if they didn't have any involvement with him. Really, I think the better question is, why do you care so much? Have you been looking into this the whole time?"

"Because my boss came on to me in Florida." Slade's delivery wobbled. "I quit my job, and I needed a distraction when I got to Colorado. So yes, I have."

"Oh, Love." Marin's voice cracked with emotion. "Why didn't you tell me?" Marin couldn't have done anything to right the wrong Slade had experienced, but she could have helped her carry it. It was such a blow to know—finally—what Slade was going through and that she hadn't trusted Marin enough to share it with her.

Now her daughter's digging made so much more sense.

"I just... It's hard to talk about." Like mother, like daughter. "When I got to Colorado, I needed to focus on something other than my issues. And when I asked you about the body found below Gran and Grandad's property, and you were so elusive and dismissive, my curiosity went wild."

Marin's eyelids shuttered. She hadn't known what to do or

say when Slade had first found the article, and she was at even more of a loss now.

"Your curiosity went wild about what?" Cyrus joined them, rounding to stand shoulder to shoulder with his dad.

"Nothing." Slade waved a dismissive hand. "Just this guy who died on my grandparents' property forever ago. Which these two act so weird about you'd think they were involved in some kind of conspiracy or cover-up." She gave an amused snort and rose from her chair. "Ready to go?"

A line divided Cyrus's forehead. "You were asking them about Vince Dunn?"

Slade's body turned rigid. "I was."

"Why?"

"I was just curious about what happened to him and using the distraction as a Band-Aid for…" She gave a pained, miniscule shrug. "You know."

So, Slade had shared what was going on in her life with Cyrus. Marin was thankful for that, at least. Glad that she wasn't weathering the loss of her job and her boss's advances without any support.

"When you asked me about my dad, were you fishing for information about this?"

"I was just getting to know you. Why would I be—"

"Was that what this—" he motioned between them "—was about?"

"Cyrus." Garrett frowned, shooting him an undercurrent of warning.

"What? No." Slade's chin quirked to one side, her obvious bewilderment mounting.

Marin pressed fingertips against her rapidly twitching eye. It was time to abandon her plan to steer this conversation in a safe direction and make a run for it.

"We should go, Slade." Marin stood. "We should check on Reed and Lindsey."

"My dad was cleared." Cyrus's arms crossed, and he stepped slightly in front of his father like he'd taken on the role of a bodyguard.

"Cy, enough." Garrett's tone held a sharp, blunt edge.

"He's had to put up with people gossiping for decades, while I've spent my whole life dealing with whispers. I can't believe you of all people are looking into this."

Oh, Cyrus. What have you done? Marin's joints froze in protest, her rapid heartbeats causing her to feel the light-headedness she would have welcomed thirty seconds previous. Especially if it would have caused her to faint, thereby halting the recognition and understanding now sweeping her daughter's countenance.

Slade's shocked-bordering-on-apologetic gaze landed on Garrett. "*You* were the person of interest?"

Marin knew Garrett wouldn't lie, and she didn't fault him for that.

But when he gave his trademark head nod in answer, she mourned for the past she'd so carefully stitched together that had just been torn wide open.

Chapter Twenty-Eight

Her mom had been in town at the time of Vincent's death.

Her mom had been close to Garrett at that time yet supposedly not having an affair.

And Garrett was the person of interest in Vincent's case.

What would Slade find out next? That Vincent was her uncle?

Reed was right—Slade made a terrible detective.

Answers had been right under her nose like a stinky pile of laundry the whole time, and she'd been oblivious.

"I didn't know." Slade spoke to Garrett since he was the only understanding face at this impromptu deck party. At some point, the four of them had squared off with each other as if about to engage in a fight. One Slade hadn't signed up for. At least, not purposefully.

"So, if you were in Colorado too…" Her attention switched to her mom. "Does that mean you were investigated also?"

Mom visibly swallowed and gave a quick, stilted head shake. "No."

"And yet the two of you were close…" Slade felt as if she

was scratching the surface with dull fingernails when what she really required was a shovel.

"My dad doesn't like to talk about Vince. Maybe I should drive you home."

Cyrus was kicking her out? If Garrett had been wrongfully accused of something all those years ago, Slade could understand why Cyrus didn't want that resurrected. But what she didn't understand was how he could doubt her intentions or believe she'd been using him to find out info about his father.

Where was the guy who'd instantly seen the good in her?

A strangled, agitated noise came from her throat. "I don't need a ride." Slade turned to her mother. "I'll see you at home." *And then we'll hash this out.*

Mama-Mar had mentioned them leaving to check on Reed and Lindsey, but now it was obvious that was just another attempt to keep Slade in the dark, to get her out of here before Cyrus spilled everything.

At least Slade finally understood why her radar had been pinging regarding Garrett from the start. There had been something more there, something off, something to uncover.

Slade headed inside through the sliding glass door, but when she turned to shut it, Cyrus was on her heels.

He stepped inside after her and closed it, hemming them into the cool, quiet space.

"I didn't know any of that. You're the one who just revealed it all to me."

His chest heaved, but he didn't speak. His eyes were hooded in a way that she'd learned could mean he was about to kiss her until she forgot her name...or hate her for something she didn't even know she'd done.

"It was simple curiosity about Vincent. I just wanted to understand the circumstances surrounding what happened to him. And why he was on my grandparents' property. I don't think that's so terrible of me. I had no idea your father was involved."

"He wasn't involved," he bit out.

She hadn't meant it that way.

His arms crossed, stretching his T-shirt tight across his chest. "I just don't understand why you had to dig. Have you been talking to other people about this? Are the rumors going to start back up again?"

Cyrus sounded…vulnerable. So that's what his anger was masking.

"Only Keely, and I'm sure she hasn't mentioned it to anyone. We researched old articles at the library. And Ruthie Swink brought up a few things about Vincent. That's it. I didn't know this would mess with you or your dad's life in any way." Why in the world had Garrett been named a person of interest in the case? Slade was dying to understand the hornet's nest she'd smacked into. "I was just trying to distract myself from what happened with Jude."

At the mention of Jude, a flicker of recognition and empathy surfaced in Cyrus's expression, but it vanished as quickly as it had appeared.

"Still." His gaze floated over her head. "You should probably deal with your own stuff instead of digging into other people's."

Deal with her own *stuff*? How could he say that to her when he knew better than anyone what she'd been going through? How much she was struggling over next steps—when to give up and move on or whether to hunker down for a fight.

Slade must have winced or gave a pained breath or something, because again, a trace of the old Cyrus surfaced.

"I didn't mean…"

And yet he didn't finish the sentiment. So he did mean.

"What a mess." Marin should probably follow her daughter, but she also never wanted to go home and engage in the conversation Slade would surely initiate. "What do we do?"

"About what?" Garrett seemed to be observing her like

someone might a stray dog. A little wary but also wanting to help. A little concerned she might have rabies.

"About what just happened! How can you be so calm about this?"

"Why would I not be calm?"

Marin released a pent-up breath. "I'll talk to her. I'll make sure she hasn't brought this up with anyone else in town."

"What am I not understanding?" Garrett gripped her arms and gave a gentle shake. "I'm okay, so why aren't you?"

Marin teared up. "Because it's my fault." She had relived that altercation so many times, and the blame always landed on her.

When Marin had first run into Vince at the grocery store in town, she'd remembered him from high school, and they'd spoken for a few minutes.

That had been it.

But shortly after, he'd begun showing up at the same places as her. His dilapidated truck had slowly cruised by her parents' house on more than one occasion.

Marin had told Garrett about Vince's unwanted attention when she should have left him out of it.

And then, when Vince had put his hands on her in the café parking lot, Garrett had barreled out of the restaurant. Everyone in the café had witnessed his attempt to get Vince to leave. Everyone had witnessed when things got physical between the two men.

And then Vince's body had been found the next morning. So of course the police had gone knocking on Garrett's door.

"You would never have been questioned in his death if not for me."

"He was stalking you, Mar. I have no regrets over putting him in his place, even if it did raise suspicion. My only regret was that standing up to him provoked him to go to your parents' house that night. If anything had happened to you all... I don't know how I would have survived that."

The police had believed that Vince was trying to disable the alarm before he fell to his death. He'd obviously been out to cause some sort of harm that night, whether to Marin, the house or even her parents. The idea that he could have hurt them— or worse—if he'd gained access had haunted Marin ever since.

She shivered despite the beautiful evening temps, and Garrett enveloped her in a hug, his chin pressing comfortingly against the top of her head.

"It's all in the past, Mar."

But it wasn't. Not with Slade looking into it.

Seconds ticked by. Marin's heart sputtered like an old tractor, and slowly, as if it was the last thing he wanted to do, Garrett released her from the soothing embrace.

"Slade's not going to rest until she knows what happened." Which meant Marin had to ask the questions she'd never wanted answers to so that she could decide what to do with those responses.

"So, tell her."

"How can you say that?" She studied him. The lines that swept his mouth. The tanned skin of his neck. The peppered-gray hair. How could he be so cavalier about this?

"I don't understand what you're so worried about with Vince's death. It's not like you were ever under suspicion."

"No…but I could have been."

"What are you talking about?"

"I wasn't where I said I was that night…and neither were you."

His eyes narrowed. "What does that mean?"

"Why didn't you come over that night?" Marin had always wondered. And yet, she'd always been so thankful that he hadn't, because that would have placed him at the scene of Vince's death.

"I think you know the answer to that."

And just like that, thirty plus years disappeared, and Marin was twenty-six and heartbroken. Twenty-six and tempted to numb everything with Garrett's assistance.

His vision brushed over her lips and away, as if he too was reliving that time.

"Before you came out here, Slade asked if we'd had an affair in our twenties."

"What did you tell her?"

"That we didn't. By a narrow margin." Marin still imagined that their friendship could have been labeled an emotional affair. But then, Garrett had been helping her process about Ralph, so that wasn't quite right either. "I went looking for you that night."

The tendons in Garrett's neck visibly tightened. "You left the house? But your alibi—"

"I had perfected going in and out of that window with the disabled alarm during high school." As he well knew, because he'd been the one she'd been sneaking out to be with. "Mom and Dad never fixed it, even though I did let them know that it was broken. I didn't want my parents hearing me that night, so I snuck out the old-fashioned way."

"That's why the police thought you'd never left the house."

She borrowed one of his head nods. "And I let them continue thinking it, because it was my alibi. And I couldn't tell them where I really was because it would have nullified your alibi."

His brow creased with unspoken questions.

"I went to your apartment to find you. To figure out why you hadn't come over." In some ways, Marin had always known why Garrett hadn't shown up. To protect her from herself. To protect her from making a huge mistake with him. Because he'd known she loved Ralph. And she'd assumed Garrett had loved her enough to not let her break her own heart.

"When you didn't answer your door, I used the key from under the mat. I waited inside for over an hour, but you never came home."

Garrett's gaze swept from her to the lake as he digested her revelation. "You never said."

"How could I? We barely spoke after Vince was found. I knew I could never admit where I was that night, because it would have placed me outside of the house and made your alibi fraudulent. So, once the police deduced I'd never left the house because the alarm hadn't been turned off, I kept quiet."

"And all these years, you assumed what? That I'd killed Vince?"

Not exactly. Marin swallowed to combat the sudden dryness overtaking her mouth. "I wondered if you had come over that night and had stumbled upon Vince trying to break in. I thought maybe you'd...stopped him."

"With a well-placed shove?"

"Not on purpose. But I didn't know if things had escalated, and—"

"I didn't kill Vince. Accidental or otherwise. My only beef with him was in the café parking lot, right in front of everyone."

Marin inhaled shakily as she fought back tears. What would she have done if he'd answered differently? She knew in her soul that she would never have been capable of turning Garrett in if he'd been protecting her and her parents. And yet, living with that knowledge would have been torturous. Always wondering if some internet armchair sleuth was going to start digging. Always fearing that the past could come to light.

Fierce relief permeated Marin. She was *so* grateful not to carry that burden going forward. To be able to stop shoveling dirt over that part of that summer. Slade could have the whole truth without it implicating Garrett or Marin.

Most of it anyway.

"But then...where were you when I went to your apartment?"

"I was with Poppy."

"I didn't even know Poppy was in the picture at that time."

"We'd just started hanging out when you came back to town. I didn't tell you—"

"Because I was too busy talking about myself." Marin had been so selfish back then. Maybe she still was that selfish girl.

"Poppy was angry I was spending so much time with you, and she demanded I make a choice."

"Rightfully so." Marin hated hearing that she'd been a thorn for Poppy and Garrett. Especially after all the good he'd done for her.

"She lived in the condo complex next door, so I had walked over."

"Which is why your neighbors vouched that your truck never left the lot."

"Yes. And then I remembered my laundry on the way home and stopped to grab it from the dryer. If the woman who'd just moved in next door hadn't spotted me in the laundry room, I'm sure the police would have investigated me further."

"Why didn't you tell the police you were at Poppy's?"

He rubbed fingertips against his eyelids and heaved a sigh. "Because I wanted to leave Poppy out of it. She was so upset with you, so jealous of you. I didn't trust her not to do something stupid. I didn't trust her not to attempt to implicate you in some way. And yet, I still married the woman." He shook his head. "So many red flags."

"All these years, I thought that because I knew your alibi wasn't right, I was afraid—"

"You were afraid I'd helped him over that ledge." His eyebrows shifted up, the corners of his mouth joining his mirth. "Awfully *presumptuous* of you. Got that one out of the Marin dictionary. I can't believe—" he continued with equal parts amazement and amusement "—that you thought I'd kill someone for you. Even for us, that's a bit of a stretch."

Even for us. Those three words summed up so much about

them. Represented that they'd been something solid—an *us*—even if it had been such a long time ago.

"I'm glad you're finding all of this so funny. I didn't think you'd sought him out or anything. I just wondered if you'd shown up and things had snowballed in a dire direction."

"That would have been a *dire* direction." The contours of his face shifted from teasing to serious. "If I'd come across Vince attempting to break in that night and something had gone terribly wrong, I would have told the police. I'm not the kind of guy who can live with a murder under my belt for over thirty years, even if it had been in self-defense."

Of course he wasn't. Marin knew Garrett's character and yet she'd let herself fear the worst all these years.

Answers clicked into place like missing puzzle pieces, and relief swept through her like a storm rolling across the lake, leaving a smooth surface in its wake.

"So, if it wasn't either of us… Was anyone involved that night, or did Vince really just fall?"

"I long ago had to accept that I'll never know the details of that night. I think those answers died with Vince."

Marin could live with not knowing as long as her people—including Garrett—wouldn't come to harm because of the events of that summer.

The only question that remained was whether Slade could do the same.

Chapter Twenty-Nine

Reed hadn't imagined that anything could top the awkwardness of Lindsey showing up to announce she was pregnant—and that she wanted to stay and assist with the last leg of the house purge—all while being uncertain if she wanted to remain married to him.

And yet, in true Henderson style, his family had managed to up the discomfort levels to off the charts.

First, Slade had come home, obviously upset about something but not saying what.

Then Mom had followed shortly after.

Now the two of them were positioned across the kitchen from each other, leaving Reed and Lindsey—who'd been in the living room attempting to converse like well-adjusted adults instead of a wounded, separated married couple—caught in the crossfire.

"Are we going to finish the conversation we started?" Slade took a seat at the table, her arms folded defiantly. "Although, what's the point? You're only going to give me half-truths anyway."

"I can tell you what happened, Love," Mom said wearily. "Now that I know." She leaned back against the kitchen counter like it was assisting in keeping her upright. Dark smudges created half-moons under her eyes, and she kept pressing her fingertips to her right temple.

"Now that you know?" His sister's interest piqued at that, her body shifting forward.

"What went on between you two since I last saw you?" Reed questioned. Hadn't it only been an hour or so previous that everything had been calm?

"I think I'm going to go unpack." Lindsey rose from Grandad's chair.

"There's nothing you can't hear, Lindsey. You're family. You're welcome to stay." Upon her return to the house, Mom had greeted Lindsey with genuine excitement. As if her arrival boded well for Reed...and as if she had more than enough love for both of them. There'd been no hint of animosity. No withholding affection from Lindsey in an attempt to side with her son.

Mom had thrown her arms wide and held on to Lindsey like she was her own long-lost daughter.

Reed had never been more thankful for his mother than in that moment.

"I appreciate that, but I might rest for a minute. Long day."

"Of course."

Lindsey grabbed her suitcase from behind the love seat. Reed had already relayed that she could have the bedroom and he would sleep on the couch, which she thankfully hadn't fought, because it was a battle he wouldn't have conceded.

She needed sleep. Needed to take care of herself. Reed could see the toll their separation and the pregnancy had taken on Lindsey's body. She looked as if she'd dropped weight instead of gaining it. As if the elation over being pregnant was outweighed by the stress of fearing she might have to go it alone.

Yet another thing he could blame himself for.

"First door on the right upstairs." Reed nodded to the suitcase. "Want me to get that for you?"

"That's okay. It's light." She sent him a reassuring smile, as if to say *I'm not going to do anything to jeopardize this little life.* Her footsteps faded up the stairs.

"*What* is going on with you two?"

"What is Lindsey doing here?"

He and Slade spoke at the same time.

"She's pregnant," Reed offered up. "She just found out. So despite us not being together at this point, we're having a baby." He wasn't sure if Lindsey was okay with him relaying that information, but he shared it out of the desire for support. His mom and sister would rise to that challenge, no matter how the relationship between the two of them was defined.

Slade's eyes grew wide, wide, wider. "Congratulations?" Her delivery of that word pretty much summed up his every emotion.

Mom gave a small squeal, slapping a hand over her mouth. She bent slightly, like the news had physically impacted her, then crossed the room and enveloped him in a hug.

After an extralong squeeze, she eased back, her hands framing his cheeks. "This is fabulous news. You and Lindsey will be amazing parents." All of his anxieties and doubts must have been scrawled across his face because she held his gaze like a lifeline. "It will be okay."

How do you know?

"It will be okay," she reiterated. "You guys *will* figure it out. A baby is always a celebration. They bring out the joy in life." She beamed at him once more before inhaling and turning to face Slade. "Okay." Her voice held finality. "Let's have this out."

"Do I need to be here for this?" Reed would much rather check on Lindsey. See if she needed anything.

"Yes." Two clipped replies answered him.

Mom rounded the table and pulled out the chair across from Slade, her body pouring into it like liquid without a vase.

"What do you want to know, Love?"

Reed leaned against the back of the sofa, a distant and hopefully nonparticipating spectator.

"Why was Garrett the person of interest in Vincent's death? Why didn't you tell us you were in town when Vincent died when I first found that article? What was the point in hiding all of that?"

Reed reared back at the assault…and the revelations.

Garrett was the person of interest? No wonder Mom didn't want to talk about it.

And she was in town at that time?

Maybe sitting down wasn't such a bad idea.

He dropped into the chair next to Slade.

"I didn't tell you kids I was in town when Vince died for numerous reasons." Mom folded her hands primly on the table in front of her, ignoring the slight tremor that Reed witnessed. "When I was in Dillon thirty-four years ago, I ran into Vince at the grocery store, and we talked for a few minutes. I knew of him from high school, but I didn't know him well. Only that there were plenty of rumors going around about the kind of person he was. I attempted to be kind to him by asking what he'd been up to since high school, and that's all I remember. But shortly after, he began showing up wherever I did. I spotted him driving by the house, sometimes numerous times a day. He would call and hang up—at least that's who I think was doing that."

Slade sat forward in her chair. "He was stalking you."

"Basically." Mom's expression morphed to sympathy. "What you said about your work, Love—I understand it. Not exactly the same, but I am so very sorry that happened to you."

Wait. What? "What happened with your work?"

"Oh." Mom cringed. "I just assumed you'd talked to Reed about it. I'm sorry, I didn't mean to—"

"It's fine if he knows. I should have told you guys right away, but I just..." Slade's palms lifted and dropped back to her lap. "I was victim blaming myself, and I didn't want anyone else to jump on that bandwagon to assist me." She faced Reed. "One of the partners tried to sexually assault me, but I was able to get out of the situation. And I just found out today that human resources finished their investigation based on my complaint and didn't find him at fault for anything. So really, it's over before it even started."

"No!" Mom cried out. "How can that be?"

"I have a few theories. Like Jude being besties with the head of HR."

Reed's skin heated with anger at what Slade had experienced. "What kills me the most is that you've been going through this alone." He repeated what Slade had said to him when she'd learned about his marriage issues. It was just as true for him as it had been for her. "I should have been there for you."

"I'm sorry." Her eyes pooled with tears and remorse. "It was a me issue, not a you issue."

His sister was incredibly strong. To be demeaned like that would be heartbreaking for her. Reed understood why she would be hesitant to talk about it. Hadn't he done the same with his issues?

He hugged her, and her shoulders sagged under the load they'd been carrying.

When she pulled back, she forced a brighter expression. "Can we talk about my problems later? I want to hear what Mom has to say."

"Sure." He could give Slade space, but he did plan to be there for her. Reed would help in whatever way he could.

"Go on, Mom." Slade waved her hand in a continue-please motion.

"I was at a local café that's no longer in business, and when I left to walk to my car, Vince cornered me in the parking lot. He wanted me to go somewhere with him, and when I didn't agree, he grabbed me and tried to physically force me into his vehicle. That's when Garrett walked outside."

"Hold on." That was odd. "Garrett just happened to be there?"

"No." Mom's stoic demeanor faltered. "I was there with Garrett but left before him."

With Garrett...while she was married? People had friends while being married, certainly, but an ex-boyfriend?

"They were close in their twenties." Slade shot Reed an I-told-you-so look. "She admitted that Della-Sue had been right."

Huh. Interesting.

"Garrett was a good friend to me at that time."

That was a unique way to phrase that.

"Did Dad know about your 'friendship' with Garrett?" Slade used air quotes.

"He did."

His sister's answering squint broadcasted disbelief.

"Garrett and Vince got into an argument," Mom continued. "And when Vince wouldn't leave, things got physical. Everyone in the café saw the altercation through the windows. And the next morning was when Vince's body was found."

"Whoa." Slade shifted forward. "So, everyone assumed Garrett—"

"Exactly. And as for why I didn't explain that to you guys, it was because..." She swallowed. "I knew Garrett's alibi wasn't legitimate, and I didn't want anyone unearthing that. I certainly didn't want you two becoming complicit in obstructing justice. Because that's what I could have been accused of doing for decades. The less you knew, the better."

"How did you know Garrett's alibi wasn't legitimate?" Slade asked.

Mom paused as if choosing her words. "Because he was supposed to come over the night Vince died, and when he didn't show, I went to his apartment and waited for him. He always left a key under the mat, and I let myself in." Or maybe she'd been deciding whether to deliver that information at all. That was...wow. It definitely raised suspicion regarding their "friendship." "So, I knew he hadn't been home that night even though that had been part of his alibi."

"He was supposed to come over, and when he didn't, you went to his place?" Slade spoke each word slowly.

"Yes."

"But you're still claiming this wasn't an affair?"

"Yes."

"Mm-kay. I can't believe how much pressure you put on me to be perfect—"

"I didn't—"

"You did. *Find a group of friends who lifts you up instead of taking you down! Participate in extracurricular activities even though you hate and are terrible at every single one of them! Get better grades like your brother!*"

"I never... I may have said some of those things," Mom stated quietly. "But it was always for you. I was just trying to encourage you." Her hands twisted in agitation. "This is why you didn't tell me about the law firm, isn't it?"

Slade held Mom's gaze, hers defiant, and then gave an almost imperceptible nod.

Had it been the same with him? Had Slade believed that Reed wouldn't be on her side or would judge her in some way? Hadn't he always been there for her?

Tension seeped into the corners of the room, stealing the oxygen.

"Mom." Reed had questions of his own. "Why didn't the police look into you regarding Vincent's death? What was your alibi?"

"I had learned to skirt the alarm in high school, and since I didn't want to wake up my parents, I left that night without triggering it. The police concluded I'd never left the house, and in order to protect Garrett's alibi... I didn't correct them."

Slade let out a small squeak of surprise. "*You* snuck out in high school?"

Funny that in this onslaught of new information, that's what Slade focused on.

"I have long lived with the fear that someone could decide to reopen Vince's case. That Garrett's or my broken alibi could be uncovered. I also feared..." She hesitated before continuing. "That maybe Garrett had come over and happened upon Vince breaking in that night and things had escalated. That maybe in the midst of protecting me or my parents, he'd accidentally been involved in Vince's death. And that's why I didn't want anything from that time to come to light. Because if Garrett had been protecting us..." Mom squared her shoulders. "I wouldn't have gone to the authorities with that information. It was terrifying to think of what Vince might have done if he'd gotten into the house. If he would have harmed my parents... or worse." Mom shuddered and swiped under her lower lashes.

"According to the autopsy report, Vince had enough drugs and alcohol in his system to take down a much larger man. He certainly wasn't in his right mind. After you left Garrett's, Love, I asked him where he was that night, uncertain if I would be able to share his answer with you two or if I would need to find a way to keep it buried. But he explained that he'd been with Poppy—his ex-wife—the night Vince died. Her apartment had been across the street from his, so he'd walked. That's how neighbors had corroborated that his vehicle had never left the lot and how someone had spotted him in the laundry room on his way home. He confirmed that he wasn't anywhere near this house or Vince that night."

"And you believe him?" Slade interjected.

"I do."

"So, all of this time, you were protecting him."

"Yes. I was protecting everyone."

Silence reigned.

"But why didn't you just ask Garrett earlier if he'd been involved?"

"Now that I know the truth, of course asking him makes sense. But I didn't know what his answer would be. And if I'd inquired and his response had been different... I didn't want the added guilt or culpability of knowing he'd been involved in Vince's death and then not coming forward."

Slade raked fingers through her blond-white-silver hair, sending a number of loose strands floating. "So, you're saying that you still don't know what happened that night."

"I don't. Garrett doesn't. If someone does, it's not coming to light anytime soon. Not when it's been buried this long."

Obviously, Vincent had been up to no good, which the police had been aware of. They likely hadn't spent copious amounts of time on his death, or they would have found the holes in Mom and Garrett's alibis.

It was easy to wonder how much more they'd missed, and yet, Reed was still—as he'd always been—content to let the past lie.

There were too many things in his present he needed to sort through. But now he understood that it was Slade's present that had sent her digging into the past, searching for a place to bury her head while she waited for human resources to handle her complaint. While she waited for HR to disregard her complaint.

"So, what now?" Slade questioned.

"I suppose that's up to you. I have to finish this house, so I have enough on my plate. But if you need to keep looking, then—" Mom shrugged "—do what you need to do. But I have no idea what you're going to find. If anything." She stood, wobbling for a second before righting herself, her fingertips pressing into the worn wooden tabletop. "I hope you both can forgive me for not divulging the details of that time. I was just trying to protect you." She blinked rapidly. "And on that note, I'm going to take my cue from Lindsey and head to bed."

Chapter Thirty

A faint *creak-thump-creak* woke Reed.

He sat upright on the couch, the blanket pooling around his waist, and found Lindsey rummaging through the food cupboard, her movements painstakingly cautious.

"Morning." He spoke quietly in the hopes of not startling her, but she still whirled in his direction.

"Did I wake you?" She kept her voice low.

"No." He wasn't about to admit she had. "You all right?"

"Yes. I just have to keep something in my stomach, or I get nauseous. I meant to pack saltines, but I threw everything together so fast that I forgot."

Reed stretched and pushed off the blanket. He'd slept in sweats and a T-shirt he'd had since his college days. One Linds used to borrow to sleep in. It still carried hints of her sweet, addicting scent in the fibers.

"I think Slade had some crackers for soup at one point." He joined her at the cupboard. "Let me." He motioned for her to scoot aside and rummaged through the upper shelf, creating a crinkling-shuffling sound that ricocheted off the empty walls of the house. The photos and artwork that once filled the space had been placed in the garage for the used furniture store pickup or marked for one of them to keep. It was the emptiest Reed had ever seen his grandparents' home…and the most real selling it had ever felt.

"Here." He found some flaky round crackers in the far back corner and handed them to Lindsey. "Not saltines, but will they do? Otherwise, I can run to the store for you."

She shoved one in her mouth and chewed. "These will work." She inhaled another and then her shoulders relaxed, as if the food was already doing its job. "I think I'll be okay now. But thank you for offering."

"Sure. Let me know if you change your mind." He yawned. "Come sit. I'm not fully awake yet." He headed back to the couch, and Lindsey followed.

She sat on the other end and faced him, propping a pillow behind her back and stretching her legs across the cushions. Out of habit, Reed lifted her feet and redeposited them into his lap. He began to knead her soles, and she let out a whimper.

"That feels so good." She continued eating crackers.

A foot rub was her kryptonite. Reed couldn't count the number of hours he'd logged doing exactly this. Though he was a little surprised that she wasn't vetoing his touch.

"It's nice to be able to do something. I hate that you were having to figure this out on your own, without support."

Her analytical gaze trained on him. "You really are so perfect. You gave me your room and your bed. You rub my feet. You offer to go get me crackers."

"Those aren't big things."

"You forgive me for racking up thousands of dollars in debt."

He inclined his chin. That one had been a little harder.

"Do you remember what your response was when you found out?"

He remembered that he'd found the bill…that she hadn't told him about it before she'd been caught. Reed shook his head in order to gain her perspective.

"You said *we'll figure it out*. Like I hadn't just derailed everything. Our lifestyle. The nest egg for the house down payment. The savings in case we needed fertility treatments. All of it, out the window. It was like you were a parent disappointed in their kid's actions, but you still loved them and wanted to help."

That was exactly how he'd felt. Along with blindsided and hurt and a thousand other emotions he hadn't been able to name.

"I didn't understand how you could be so perfect about it. That you didn't lose your mind."

"I did a little."

"Not like you could have."

"Why do you keep using the word *perfect*?" Like it was a weapon, no less.

"Because sometimes you're *so* flawless that I feel like I can never be on the same level as you. I'm always going to have abandonment issues. I'm always going to make mistakes and bumble things, and you—"

"It's not like I don't mess up."

"But it's also not like you do. Tell me the last thing that you botched."

"I made a pretty massive mistake at work just before I headed to Colorado."

"Intentionally?"

"Of course not."

"What else have you got?"

"I made plenty of terrible choices in how I handled things with you. We argued so much, and I should have kept calm. We should have discussed things respectfully."

She gave a short, sardonic laugh. "You weren't the one who pushed our arguments toward mudslinging, Reed. That was me."

"There's no way you're the only one to blame."

"The truth is, sometimes I did know what I was doing. I wanted that kind of reaction out of you. Wanted you to stoop to my level, so I drove you to your limit."

He switched from the sole to the pad of her foot, his mind rewinding through the fights, scanning for proof of what she'd claimed.

Lindsey pushed at the cuticles on her left hand, her next words barely above a whisper. "I think I derailed because of Chad." She always referred to her father by his first name...or something worse. "I stumbled upon Bliss's Facebook page, and she had some things public." Wife number two had never even acknowledged Lindsey's existence. "I found out their daughter had a baby." She also never referred to the children from his second family—his only family, according to how he acted—by their first names. "It was suspiciously around the time I started racking up the credit card."

That would have been good information to have at the time. "Why didn't you tell me?"

"I was tired of myself, of the fact that even after so many years, he can affect me like that."

He squeezed her ankle in what he hoped was a comforting gesture, wishing he could tug her across the cushions and onto his lap. Wishing he could hold her and make her pain disappear.

"I thought I would handle it. But I handled it by destroying us."

"You didn't destroy us."

"No?" She released a pained, strangled sound. "Sure seems like it."

"Why are you telling me now?"

She twisted the top of the crackers closed and tossed them onto the coffee table. "Because of what you told me last night."

After the conversation with Mom and Slade, Reed had quietly knocked on Lindsey's door and cracked it open to check on her.

She'd motioned for him to come in. Reed had sat on the other half of the bed while she faced him, lying on her side, groggy and gorgeous.

"What happened?" she'd asked, and he'd filled her in.

It had taken a herculean effort not to slide into the space next to her after they'd talked. Especially since she probably would have let him, in her sleepy state.

But Reed hadn't been about to do anything that would derail the chance of them reconciling.

"I know Slade is angry with your mom and thinks she had an affair. And maybe she did. But even so, realizing that she messed up and that she and your dad came through that time, despite whatever happened between her and Garrett...it made me feel less alone. Less screwed up somehow."

"Does it give you hope that we can do the same?"

"A little. But all I can think is, what if we try and fail? What if we end up not being able to speak to each other without arguing? What if my mom is right? If we end things now while we're still on good terms...would that be better for the baby?"

Reed didn't know the answer to those questions. He only knew what was best for him—and that was the three of them together.

But he had no idea how to get Lindsey to arrive at that same conclusion.

"I met with Jessa a few times, and she gave me some insight into her experiences." Jessa was an older woman who Lindsey worked with. She'd mentored Lindsey through her broken family dynamics on more than one occasion. But Reed had noticed that Lindsey hadn't mentioned the other woman in months.

He felt a stirring of hope over them communicating again.

"Jessa suggested that I was self-sabotaging because of my abandonment issues. That I was trying to push you away out of the fear that otherwise you'd eventually tire of me, stop loving me, leave me." That made sense. Especially with the way she acted after the credit card debt had been revealed. Instead of being apologetic, she was angry. Almost as if challenging him to storm out, just like Jessa had alluded.

"I'm not—" Reed heard the bite in his tone and tempered it. "I'm not leaving you. Unless you refuse to let me stay."

The ball was in her court. It always had been.

Slade lugged a cardboard box from the top shelf, dropping it to the floor of The Armpit unceremoniously. "More papers. Not it!"

"You picked it, you sort it," Reed declared from the other end of the room, where he and Lindsey were dealing with boxes of old toys that, like most things they'd uncovered in this house, weren't worth anything outside the sentimental value they held.

Slade had been doing her best this morning to focus on The Armpit instead of the stilted dynamics between her brother and his estranged wife.

Were they back together? Or were they planning to co-parent as friends?

From what Slade could tell, *they* didn't know the answer to those questions.

They seemed to gravitate toward each other, then realize their close proximity and jump apart. It was like watching a YA movie where the main characters were besties who were afraid to confess their love for each other lest their relationship implode and they lose each other completely.

Super-duper fun to be trapped in the same room as them.

Reed must be tormented not knowing what the future held. Numerous times this morning Slade had been tempted to clap her hands together and announce, "Okay! Let's all sit down and figure this out." Like she was a modern Dr. Phil. But then, she couldn't solve her own issues—regarding Cyrus or Jude—so she wouldn't be forcing anyone else to dissect theirs.

"What's so terrible about a box of papers?" Lindsey reached up to tug a small bin from the top shelf, and Reed swooped in and retrieved it for her.

"She's not going to injure herself, or the baby, moving something the size of a shoebox, Re-Re."

Lindsey laughed. "Right? That's what I keep telling him too."

"You two do not need to be on the same team. At least not if it's the opposite of mine."

Slade and Lindsey exchanged matching grins.

"Finding papers in this house," Slade explained to her sister-in-law, "is equivalent to finding a box of dog poo."

"Slade!" Reed's reprimand was followed by a chuckle. "It's true, though."

Lindsey laughed. "That's a *terrible* visual!"

"I can hear everything you guys are saying from here," Mom called from her perch at the dining table, where she was sorting a similar box. "Just bring it to me. I'll do it."

Slade wasn't about to refuse Mom's offer, even if she did think Mama-Mar was in denial over having an affair with Garrett.

Was it wrong to consider sorting papers as Mom's penance for the choices she'd made that summer?

The woman who'd expected so much of Slade over the years had expected so little of herself.

How could Mom have done that to Dad?

After that conversation last night, Mom had gone to bed as if physically weary from the revelations. Slade had followed suit, exhausted by her anger at their mom and the fact that, all these years later, she'd been cozying up to the man she'd once cozied up to while married to their father.

It felt as if Mom were yanking Dad partway out of the grave to deliver one last blow.

And then Slade had woken this morning with a Cyrus-sized hole aching inside her chest cavity.

She'd never let anyone carve a space inside of her so quickly, so thoroughly, and she had no earthly clue how to fill that wound or dull the sting.

Everything between her and Cyrus had begun and ended so fast that, if not for the constant pain, Slade could almost believe that they'd never existed.

She dropped the box onto the dining table. "Did you find anything important in the last one?"

"Nope." Mom propped her readers on top of her head. "But how can we just toss it without checking?"

"I could. I mean, it's not like we're going to find a few extra bank accounts or anything."

"Though that would be nice. It is tempting to just toss it, but if I do, I'll always wonder if we missed something."

Isn't that exactly what you wanted us to do? Miss that whole portion of the past when you hurt Dad?

Before Slade began questioning her mother yet again about Garrett or Dad or any of it, she pivoted and returned to The Armpit.

They had plenty left to do and a limited amount of time to do it.

The used furniture store planned to drop off a trailer for them to begin loading this afternoon. Which they would then pick up on Friday afternoon. Pest control would begin on Friday after The Armpit was fully cleared out. And on Saturday, Mom would drop Slade, Reed and Lindsey at the airport.

Slade had heard from the Keystone resort, and they'd scheduled a short phone interview for around noon today. If the masseuse position panned out, Slade had decided that she was going to attempt to figure out a way to stay in Dillon. The owner of the yoga studio who'd hosted yoga in the park when she and Keely had attended had also contacted Slade this morning—

thanks to Keely's referral—and asked if she was interested in taking over a handful of classes on a permanent basis.

If Slade could come up with a schedule that allowed her to do both jobs, she just might be able to squeeze by with enough to afford living in Summit County.

Keely had even offered to let her sleep on her couch for a bit while she looked for a place of her own.

Things—regarding where she planned to live at least—were coming together.

But other things—like Cyrus and deciding if she wanted to pursue the Jude stuff with the workplace-harassment firm Reed had mentioned to her this morning—were still as unsolvable as the circumstances surrounding Vincent's death.

Slade placed the small step stool next to the shelving and climbed up in order to retrieve an extra large box that had been shoved to the back corner.

"Why do you guys call this room The Armpit?" Lindsey asked.

"Because Grandad called it The Pit when we were kids, but Reed mixed it up and said armpit." Slade wrenched the massive, weighted box in her direction and managed to lug it down without breaking it or herself.

"After that, the name just stuck. Eventually, Gran stopped pretending she was storing useful things in here and started calling it The Armpit too."

The box was heavy enough to contain more papers, and there was no way Slade could dump another load of those on Mom. She winced while flipping open the cardboard flaps... and found gold.

"More of Gran's journals!" Slade dropped to a seat on the floor and pulled out a stack. She didn't want to give any of these up, but she had no idea how to store all of them. Scanning them made sense, but that would be a full-time job.

She quickly sifted through them, on the hunt for the year of Vincent's death.

And lo and behold, there it was at the bottom of the pile.

As she flipped through the pages, her breathing stalled and sputtered, reminiscent of something her car would do. She jumped to the middle of the journal under the assumption that it would get her to the summer months.

"You planning to work today?" Reed tossed a balled-up piece of paper at her, and it bounced off the floor near her knee.

Slade ignored him, intent on her search, the aged pages crinkling under her fingertips. She reached the morning Vince's body had been found and scanned the day.

Gran had detailed what she'd eaten, as she often did. She mentioned a few police officers who'd been at the house and that she'd fed them apple crumble and coffee.

"That's it?"

"What are you finding over there?" Reed questioned.

"Absolutely nothing."

How could Gran not have written something about Vincent? Had she purposely kept information off the page?

The next day revealed just as little.

Slade tossed the journal on the floor in frustration. It landed open, and her mother's name leaped off the page.

She picked it back up.

"Seriously, Slove." Reed unceremoniously dumped a box of fake flowers into the trash bag. "Your work ethic today is sorely lacking."

She held up a finger. "Hang on."

Slade scanned the entry, dated almost four weeks before Vince's death. *Ralph affair. Pick up Marin from airport at 2:00.*

Ralph *affair*? What did that mean? She checked the following day.

Marin still asleep at noon. In between the notes about what

Gran ate or cooked or cleaned, the subsequent days held simi-lar snippets.

Marin won't eat. Marin only sleeps and cries. Garrett stopped by to visit Marin at my request. Barely spoken since her arrival.

Fear ignited in Slade's gut.

No communication from Ralph. Garrett stopped by again. Tried to get Marin to leave the house for lunch.

"Slade?"

She glanced up to find Reed and Lindsey staring at her. The tears streaming down her cheeks dripped onto the page of the journal, and her voice refused to function.

Slade pushed up from the floor, the notebook tight in her grip, and exited The Armpit.

She stopped at the end of the table. "Mom." Slade's world toppled and spun, and the room swayed with it.

Marin glanced up, her brow instantly furrowing. "Love? What is it? What's wrong?"

Slade pressed her palm against the table for support. "Why didn't you tell us?"

"I did tell you."

Slade lifted the journal. "You didn't tell us this."

Chapter Thirty-One

"What did you find?" Reed spoke from behind Slade. She hadn't realized he'd followed her out of The Armpit.

Slade flipped the journal back to the entry that had started it all and handed it to him. Lindsey leaned into Reed, scanning as he did.

"Love, what is going on?" Mom sat in the middle of the large table, surrounded by piles of paper, her expression utterly confused.

"It wasn't you." Slade could barely speak as the truth registered like aftershocks through her body. "You didn't have the affair. Dad did."

Mom's reaction was hard to categorize: a flash of fear, a hint of resignation, a dose of "how can I salvage this?"

"Gran wrote about it." Not in detail, but enough to imply what had really gone on that summer. *Ralph affair.* Slade could never unsee those two cryptic words.

"Mom?" Reed held up the journal, his body rigid, the ligaments in his arms and neck visibly strung tight. "Is this true?"

After a moment's hesitation, Mom gave a confirming nod.

Slade pressed both hands against the tabletop, her head sinking forward under the weight of this discovery. "That's why you were in Colorado."

"That's why Garrett was a *friend to you*," Reed filled in quietly.

"I've been blaming you for having an affair when you were just escaping Dad's, weren't you? Why did you let me do that? Why did you let us think it was you?"

Mom didn't answer. She got up from her chair and moved toward the sink, but on the way, her knees buckled. She caught the countertop, stopping herself from crashing.

Reed was next to Mom in an instant. He led her to the couch, and Lindsey filled a water glass and followed in their wake, handing it to their mom once she was seated.

Slade stayed immobile. She'd entered that quicksand she'd been so wary of as a kid, and it was suctioning her ankles, calves, thighs, pulling her down, down, down.

Dad? She tipped her chin up to keep her head above the sludge about to steal her ability to breathe. *I believed you were the best person on the planet...and you believed in me. You were my champion.*

If her dad was a fraud, what did that say about Slade? Had his encouragement—his faith in her—all been a lie too?

Throughout her feisty teenage years and beyond, Slade had always sided with her father—as if he'd been the better of her parents.

But the opposite was true.

Mom had forgiven *him*. And they'd built such a strong marriage afterward that Slade and Reed never realized the turmoil that had come before. They'd never once questioned if their parents might divorce. Not once! Slade had known how unusual that was, but she hadn't known the excruciating effort or choice that had gone into making that happen.

Mom had been the champion all along.

Lindsey seated herself on the sofa next to their mother.

Reed perched on the coffee table, facing Mom. "Why didn't you tell us? Why did you protect him?"

"I was protecting all of us. But especially you two."

"Who was it?" Slade slipped past the sofa and beyond the coffee table, pacing in front of the fireplace.

"You don't know her. After we reconciled, we moved to Arizona. We started over, and in some ways, we left the past in Dallas. I honestly don't know who that man was—who that version of your father was. He'd started a new investment job at the time, and he'd become obsessed with meeting the goals he'd set. He worked all the time, and I became needy. But the more I sought his attention, the less he came home." Mom drank from the water glass and placed it on the coffee table before continuing.

"By the time the affair happened, I was a shell of my former self. I couldn't make your father see me or hear me, so I ran away. I came home to my parents' house hoping that he would follow. That he would fight for me. But he didn't. At least, not right away. I understand how it looked with me and Garrett, and I'm not denying that we were bordering on an emotional affair ourselves. That I let myself get too close to him, too dependent on him. But in so many ways, he's the reason I'm here right now. His friendship is the reason I survived that time. But you are right, Love. I think things could have easily progressed beyond that. Especially if he had actually come over the night that Vince died. I'm certainly not innocent in all of this."

Mom might not be blameless, but she also wasn't the villain Slade had made her out to be.

"After Vince's body was found, when Dad realized that something terrible could have happened to me and that he could have lost me for good…it finally woke him from the trance he'd been in. It snapped him out of the affair. He apologized and begged me to start over, and we did. He knew that I'd spent time with Garrett. We were completely honest with each other, and we started over from scratch."

"I can't reconcile this picture of Dad with the man we knew." Slade couldn't reconcile that any of this had happened. "And that you both kept us in the dark our whole lives."

"Your dad was such a phenomenal husband—and eventually father—after we started over. He became the man I'd married again. When you were little, it made no sense to tell you. And then later, your dad was prepared to be honest with you both, but I wouldn't let him. I stopped him."

Slade paused in front of the fireplace opening. "Why?"

"Did you think we wouldn't be able to handle it?" Reed questioned.

Slade knew in her soul the answer to that was yes, at least when it came to her.

"I didn't want to taint your view of your father, based on a blip in the past. Neither of you had been born yet. I told myself that it had nothing to do with you. Only me." Mom's intake was pained. "You both adored your father, and he adored you. *That's* who he really was, and that summer faded so far into the past that it was as if it had never happened. And since I'd wished it had never happened, I buried it and buried it until it didn't exist anymore."

"Except it did exist." Reed pushed up from the coffee table in agitation, and Slade plopped onto the love seat. Reed took the spot by the fireplace Slade had vacated, his arms crossed, his stance shuttered. "It was his job to come clean. It says a lot about him that he didn't. That he let this remain hidden. He was the one always pounding honesty into us—"

"*I* was the one who couldn't handle it," Mom cried out. "I couldn't live through it a second time." Tears plunged down her cheeks in quick succession. "That period of not being chosen, of not being loved by the *one person* who I was supposed to be able to trust more than anyone else has never left me."

Silence followed her delivery.

Slade concentrated on one shaky inhale and one hissing exhale at a time.

Reed scrubbed his hands over his face.

More calmly, Mom continued. "No matter how well we rebuilt, there was always a spec, a scab, a remnant. It's been layered over a thousand times, and there was *so much good* in our marriage, but underneath, it was still there. I think Dad knew. I think that's why he let me get away with not telling you kids. It was another way he tried to love me well."

Lindsey massaged Mom's back in a comforting gesture, sympathy tears—for herself or Mom or both—surfacing. "You're right. No matter how much things improve, it's always there, buried deep. Always trying to rear its ugly head."

Mom wrapped an arm around Lindsey and pulled her into a hug.

Slade's vision crashed into her brother's, and she saw her own pain reflected back at her.

They'd always viewed a story like this as someone else's. Someone like poor Lindsey. Someone they'd gone to school with. A neighbor kid maybe.

But never them.

Slade had—and she imagined Reed probably had too—secretly reveled in the fact that they were untouchable.

They were special.

But all of that had been an illusion.

Turns out they'd just never known their own story.

Reed had been missing for close to two hours after the revelations of this morning.

Marin had understood his need for space when he'd stalked out of the house, but Lindsey's worry over him increased exponentially as time passed. The three of them continued purging The Armpit while he was gone in order to keep busy and because they were under a deadline with the used furniture store trailer arriving this afternoon. But eventually, Marin offered her definitely-not-in-need-of-additional-stress daughter-in-law a deal. She would go look for Reed if Lindsey rested for a bit.

Reed had left the house on foot, but Marin took the car. Who knew how far her running son had run.

She went down to the bottom of the hill and traversed the streets in the neighborhood, but twenty minutes into her search, she'd found no sign of him. Marin drove the loop at the top of the street and slowed as she passed Garrett's.

His garage was open, his truck parked inside.

Maybe he'd seen Reed.

Marin parked on the street and walked up the driveway. She stepped into the garage and scanned for him. He was at his workbench, concentrating on a project and unaware of her.

Marin gave herself one moment to relish the sight of him. Had it only been yesterday that she'd sat on the deck with him and let herself—despite promising Slade otherwise—imagine the possibility of a future between the two of them? So much had changed in mere hours. Including Marin letting all of those momentary, fanciful ideas slide right out of her brain until it was empty and void and lonely again.

"Garrett."

He slapped a hand against his chest and spun to face her. "If you had life insurance on me, I would accuse you of trying to cash it in by giving me a heart attack."

A smile formed. "Sorry. I thought you'd hear me walking in."

He stepped toward her, his concern evident. "How did things go at your house last night?"

She made a so-so motion. "It's been interesting, to say the least. I'm actually looking for Reed. You haven't seen him, have you?"

"Is he out for a run?"

"No. He left the house on foot about two hours ago. He— the kids learned about Ralph this morning, and that's when he took off."

Empathy carved deeply into his cheeks. "I'm sorry. Are you okay?"

"I think I will be. I just need my kids to be okay." She'd always needed her children to be okay. Had wanted to protect them from all of this.

"I haven't seen him. Do you want help looking?"

How very Garrett to offer to help. "Not at this point, but thank you. Lindsey was upset, so I told her I'd look for him." He didn't seem surprised by the mention of Lindsey being in town, so Cyrus had likely shared that information with him. "I'm sure he's fine." And angry and confused and hurt.

"You still planning to leave town this weekend?" Garrett's voice held all of the familiarity and peace and comfort she craved.

Marin swallowed to alleviate the wasteland occupying her mouth. "Yes."

"And here I thought that maybe instead of growing old separately, we'd grow old together." A portion of Marin's bruised and rebuilt heart plummeted to Garrett's garage floor. She imagined it down there against the cool cement, attempting to beat when one half was missing. "I got the impression you were thinking along those same lines," Garrett continued without waiting for an answer from her. Likely didn't expect one. "Figured we could drive each other to doctor's appointments." His slow, teasing grin ignited. "Help each other fill out Medicare forms. Compete to see who gets a grandkid first."

Marin had wanted those things too, for a split second. But it was a mirage. Life was too complicated for what Garrett was proposing.

"I'm…" Marin squelched the tears waiting in the wings. "I

have to focus on the kids right now. This has all been a lot. Plus, Slade and Cyrus—"

"Hit a rough patch, unfortunately. It's too bad. I thought they seemed good together."

"I imagine they'll find their way back to each other. Don't you?"

"Possibly."

"And if they do, I can't be the one to stand in their way. Slade was so disturbed by the idea that we'd ever dated. Attempting to be together while, or if, she's with Cyrus… I can't."

Marin understood Slade's upset on that front. Parents being romantically involved while their kids were also romantically involved was a strange concept.

Garrett took a few beats to respond and then delivered one of his acknowledging head nods, communicating both grief and acceptance and, somehow, no judgment.

"Funny, I didn't think we'd still have to put our kids first when they were adults."

Funny. Marin hadn't either.

Chapter Thirty-Two

Marin spotted Reed moments after leaving Garrett's house, seated on the neighborhood overlook bench, his back hunched as if hail was pelting him instead of bright, warm rays of sunshine.

He must have just reached the spot, because otherwise she would have seen him while driving by.

Her tires crunched into the gravel on the side of the road as she parked, but Reed didn't turn from the panoramic view of the lake or the gray peaks hemming in the water.

Marin joined him on the bench. "I would have given you more time to yourself, but Lindsey was worried about you."

He faced Marin, his expression pinched with worry. "Is she—"

"She's fine. I told her I'd look for you if she rested. I'll send Slade a text so that she can check if Lindsey's sleeping and let her know you're okay if she's not." Marin sent the message and then returned her attention to Reed. "I'm sorry, honey. Sorry for what you found out. For how you found out. Sorry that I wasn't strong enough to let Dad tell you both when he wanted to."

"It's really difficult to hear that he hurt you, Mom."

"I can understand that. It was terrible to be hurt like that."

Marin had wanted so badly to spare her children this pain, but now that it was all out in the open, she could only try to love them through it. No doubt the information they'd learned yesterday and today would have lasting implications on their lives. They would need time to process and grieve a loss of innocence regarding their father, regarding both of their parents.

"Why did you take him back?" Reed's vision clung to hers as if he could unearth answers in the space between them.

"I don't think there's an easy answer to that question, but ultimately, I still saw the person I'd married in him, and I wanted that version of him back. It was the hardest and best thing I've ever done."

He sat silently, processing, his gaze cast to the stunning views before them. "I don't know if Lindsey and I should try again or not. Maybe we should just cut our losses and raise the baby together without being together. In some ways, it does seem simpler."

"I wondered that same thing with your dad—was it better to let him go? To stop fighting for him? In a way, my escape to Colorado was exactly that. Leaving Dallas was my Hail Mary pass, and I didn't know at the time if it would work. It certainly didn't at first. Without the tragedy of Vince attempting to break into the house, I'm not sure anything would have changed. Not sure Dad would have ever been stunned back to reality."

Marin hoped that in a similar vein, the shock of Reed learning about his father's affair would somehow propel him and Lindsey toward each other instead of away from each other.

"Every choice has its own complications. One that feels simpler now might turn out to be the harder one down the road. Or the opposite can happen too. Sometimes, we just have to leap. Decide to go for it...or not." Though that last option broke Marin for her son and Lindsey. "I have found that staying stagnant is a recipe for disaster. Decide on a plan and move forward. Either way, you and Lindsey *will* heal with time."

"I always thought you and Dad were special. Different from other marriages. Like you could work anything out. I never once heard you raise your voices. Lindsey and I have done so much of that in the last few months, I can't imagine recovering from it. I'm torn in two directions over what we learned about Dad. One half of me is in shock. I can't believe he didn't tell us, although I understand why you didn't want to revisit that time. It feels like he was a different person. Like I didn't know him at all. And the other half of me thinks if you two overcame what you did, then can't Lindsey and I do the same?" He released an agitated exhale. "But just because you and Dad came through your issues unscathed doesn't mean we will."

Marin choked back a derisive snort. "Oh, Reed. We didn't come through anything unscathed. And neither will you. We went to counseling for years. We worked so hard on our marriage. We set rules and protections in place. We chose each other day after day from that point on, and there were both good and bad days. And now it's over thirty years later, and I can still hardly talk about it. I would not qualify that as unscathed. But even so, I'd do it all over again to have what we had. I'm sorry we didn't show you our struggles better. We did you kids a disservice by hiding all of that. That's my fault. Some wounds, no matter what you do to heal them, are always going to leave a scar, and we live in a world that tells us scars are imperfect. But really, they're a sign of battle. Something worth fighting for. You and Lindsey, if you get through this, will probably always have this scar. And if you try and it doesn't work, Reed, that's okay too. You will still have value. You will still be loved. And you have never—even in this— not for one minute of your life, been a failure."

Her beautiful son was crying. Crying because life had not gone according to his well-scripted plans. Because she and his father had been messy, broken people. And likely because he and Lindsey also fit that description.

Marin embraced him and let him weep for the loss of innocence and the unknown of the future.

Two things that she had painfully, by her own experience, come to understand were consistently present in life.

Despite her brother's accusations this morning regarding her work ethic, Slade was the only member of the Henderson family still doing exactly that.

When Slade checked on Lindsey earlier to relay Mom's message that she'd found Reed, she was awake. But after finding out that Reed was okay, she decided to nap.

Mom and Reed were still out doing who knew what. "Avoiding work, no doubt." How was it that Slade was handling the revelations of this morning better than her brother? She would have expected the stalking out of the house to be her mode of operation and the silent processing to be his.

But they'd gone *Freaky Friday* and switched roles.

Not that Slade felt peace or understanding about anything she'd learned. On the contrary, the news that the man she'd considered near perfect had cheated on their mother was beyond her comprehension.

Everything she'd believed to be true in her life was evidently false. And processing that was going to take time. At the moment, she felt a buzzing, shocked numbness in her limbs. Slade may not have been around when the turmoil went down between her parents, but it still felt a little like Dad's choices had happened *to* her.

No wonder Mom hadn't wanted his actions to come to light.

Some hurts ran so deep it was almost as if a person's psyche played bodyguard and refused to let them surface.

All Slade's life she'd thought she and her mom were opposites and that their struggles had originated from being so different. Now she wondered if they were more alike than she'd ever realized.

Slade propped fisted hands on her hips as she surveyed the empty, enclosed trailer that had just been delivered.

After Reed had stalked out of the house this morning, she, Mom and Lindsey continued working on The Armpit. And after Mom had left to find Reed, and Lindsey had been coerced into resting, Slade managed to get through the last handful of boxes on her own.

The house was empty except for basic furniture that would stay during showings—beds, couches, dining table and chairs, coffee table. Either those items would be included in the sale or cleared out once it was under contract.

Although, now that Slade had finished interviewing for and accepting the masseuse position in Keystone, she planned to ask her mom if she could keep Gran and Grandad's bedroom set to use once she moved to Dillon.

That way she could sell her things in Florida and not have to worry about driving them across the country. And she'd have one more thing to remember her grandparents by.

Slade would fill her family in on her updated plans of moving to Dillon when they returned to the house. *If* they ever did.

She opened the wooden double garage door and surveyed the right place to start in the maze of furniture and artwork and accessories that needed to fit in the trailer.

Her grandparents' lives, all packed up.

They'd reached the end, and yet Slade felt undone. A small portion of that was because they'd never figured out what had happened to Vincent. A bigger portion was the Cyrus-sized hole. And the biggest part yet was the ending of an era.

This house had been her haven for so many summers.

The idea that it would be in someone else's hands very soon was wildly hard to comprehend.

But knowing she would be returning to Dillon shortly was lessening the sting.

Sure, she still had things to sort through—like subletting her apartment—but she would figure it out.

She always did.

Slade carried a nightstand up the metal loading ramp and into the trailer, her footsteps echoing in the empty cavity. She was terrible at puzzles. Reed was going to come home and take one look at how she'd packed this thing and either howl with laughter or try to redo it. At which point, Slade would likely slap him.

She couldn't move the big furniture by herself, even though that's what should get loaded first. And she didn't want to be doing this until midnight tonight or all day tomorrow, so she was going to start with the boxes and the smaller furniture she could carry.

And if any of her family members had an issue with that, they could—

"Cyrus." At the sight of him standing in the driveway, Slade paused two steps down the metal loading ramp, her heart a ragged old T-shirt that wouldn't survive another wash.

"Hi." His stance was comfortable—his feet about a foot apart, his hands tucked into his pockets—but his face had aged in the hours since she'd last seen him.

"I'm guessing you didn't sleep much last night either." Slade pressed her lips together too late to stem the could-be-offensive comment.

He released an amused breath. "Is it that obvious?"

"Only because it was the same for me." She continued the rest of the way down the ramp until they were facing each other.

"I was just driving by and saw the trailer. Wondered if you needed help."

"Really?" That was quite a coincidence.

"No. I came to see you and used the trailer as an excuse."

Well. That was more interesting. "The drive-by sounds like a better fit for your true crime documentary."

His take-her-out-at-the-knees grin sprouted. "I'll be sure to make a note of that for the producers. Hey, remember yesterday when I basically accused you of trying to take down my father? And of using me to do it?" Sincerity spilled from the honey-brown pools of his eyes.

She did, in fact, remember that.

"I'm sorry for what I said. It was...vicious." His gaze cast down to his work boots, and the dust on his jeans and Stoneridge Construction T-shirt made Slade think he'd come from a job. "Mommy issues are the worst." He glanced up, humor and sadness battling for control of his mouth. "I'm a bit overprotective of my dad because he saved us—me and Byron. He wouldn't let us fall through the cracks, no matter how many times we tried to kick him to the curb."

Tears pricked and stung. Her dad had done that for her too. He could still be her champion—just a human one who'd made mistakes and followed up with better choices.

"I can understand that."

"Do you think you can forgive me?"

Hadn't she already? Even though it had hurt, Slade understood where Cyrus was coming from last night.

"Yes. But can you tell me...?" She wasn't sure how to ask this, but she had to know. "Is that how you really feel about me? That I would do that on purpose? That I would use you—"

"No." He stemmed the bleeding coming from her. "Not for one second. The moment I met you, it was like walking into a wall." He winced. "That didn't come out right."

Slade laughed.

"From the moment I met you, you stopped me in my tracks, Slade of the Slades. Somehow, you're the lightning and the storm and the sunshine that comes after. Cynical." He raised an amused eyebrow. "And funny and kind and so concerned about others that even in the worst of times, you're thinking of them and not yourself."

Well. Slade swiped under her lashes, her body humming with the affection Cyrus so easily bestowed in her direction. How could he know her so well, so quickly? How could he see into her and take the messy along with the good, like they were both equal, wanted parts of her?

"I'm really sorry I dredged up terrible stuff for you." She tugged on his sleeve, the desire to touch him nearly overwhelming her. "I promise I didn't mean to."

"I know. I knew. Unfortunately, I just had to throw a hissy fit about it."

Understanding and humor surfaced. "We all need a good hissy once in a while." She had so much to tell him. About her dad. About his dad. She wasn't sure Cyrus knew that Garrett had saved her mom once upon a time. That he'd protected her even from herself. Slade could understand that now. Could see that Mom hadn't been looking for love that summer. She'd just been trying to keep her head above water, and Garrett deserved the credit for helping her do that. Slade no longer felt the same tension or suspicion regarding him, now that she knew all the details.

Cyrus surveyed the trailer. "I take it you're almost out of here."

She nodded in affirmation. Though not for long. Another thing she had to tell him. "The trailer gets picked up tomorrow afternoon by the used furniture store that delivered it, so we need to get it loaded before then. And then Mom's dropping Reed, Lindsey and me at the airport on Saturday. After that, she's going to swing back up here and fill her car with the things we've set aside as keepsakes, then head to Arizona."

Though Slade's could stay in Dillon, she now realized. She could probably store them in the garage until the house sold.

And hopefully by then, she'd have a place—or at least a room—of her own.

"How would you feel about me visiting you in Florida?"

A warmth started in Slade's toes, climbing up, up, up until her face surely displayed it. "I could use someone to road trip with me." A cross-country drive sounded better with a partner. Someone to choose every other playlist and partake in traveling snacks. And that way, if her car conked out along an interstate somewhere, she wouldn't have to solve that scenario alone.

"You're driving back to Florida? I thought you just said you were flying."

"I'm flying to Florida on Saturday. And then after I get everything packed and settled there, I'm driving here with my things."

Understanding dawned. "You're moving here?"

"Yes. I love this town. Always have. It's not because of you, so don't feel any press—"

Suddenly, Slade was airborne. Her feet dangled above the ground, and Cyrus's face burrowed into her neck. She subtly inhaled his scent and not so subtly melted into him.

"Your move might not be about me." His words vibrated against her skin, causing a rush of goose bumps. "But I'm planning to take full advantage."

He slowly slid her back to planet Earth, Slade's flip-flop feet finding the ground to be less stable than it had been only moments before.

The fact that Cyrus was kissing her like she'd been missing for a decade might have something to do with that.

Slade realized as his mouth captured hers that she'd been holding out for perfection all these years without even recognizing it. Someone like her dad.

But now she knew just how flawed her dad had been.

She was okay with a real relationship...although she'd love to avoid the pain her mother had suffered through.

Which was exactly what Mom had been trying to prevent for her children all their lives.

Cyrus pressed a kiss to her forehead, her eyelids, her cheekbones, before edging back slightly.

"Lovetta." Another thing to tell him.

She earned a confused expression and an angled jaw that reminded her of Reed. And then she earned a massive, bright-as-that-sunshine-he'd-just-mentioned grin.

"I made the cut?"

"You made the cut. But I need you to know what you're getting into."

His arms, which were still around her, tightened in answer.

"My brother mentioned a firm that deals with workplace harassment this morning, and I'm going to call them." The decision cemented as she spoke it out loud, and a peaceful, this-is-the-right-step-for-me confirmation filled her. "Things could get messy. It's not about money. It's about—"

"The women you worked with," he filled in. "And anyone who has ever had to deal with something like this."

He definitely understood her well, despite the amount of time they'd known each other.

He tucked her hair back, his gaze tender, direct, supportive. "I'm here for you whatever comes."

Slade believed him, and better yet, for the first time in maybe forever, she believed in herself. Slade had realized after the revelations about her dad this morning that she'd been using her mom as a crutch her whole life. Letting what she perceived as her mom's lack of confidence in her dictate her own. She'd blamed her insecurities on her mother not believing in her, but it had been—at least in part—an internal issue all along.

"So, if we get this trailer loaded, are you done?"

"Yes, but it's so much—"

"You have no idea how fast I can work if time with you is the reward."

Laughter bubbled. "So, we're just going to be okay again? Shouldn't we need a longer conversation to right the wrongs between us? This feels too easy."

"Why does it have to be difficult?"

Indeed, why? Maybe some things in life were just easy. If so, Slade planned to take this and him and the future and run... because there were plenty of things in life that weren't.

Chapter Thirty-Three

"I don't know the last time I ate that much." Lindsey cradled her stomach. "I hope the baby doesn't decide to send their order back."

They were sitting on one of the benches at the park that overlooked Lake Dillon, the sounds of children on the playground equipment behind them creating a faint—and sometimes not so faint—backdrop. They'd grabbed take-out street tacos from a local place on the way, and Reed considered the pops of color that had returned to Lindsey's cheeks a win.

"I thought you said keeping food in your stomach helped?"

"It does. But I just haven't had much of an appetite lately, so I've been eating little bits here and there."

Because of him. Because of their issues. Reed was determined to change that.

"Do you care if I conk out on this bench?"

In answer, Reed scooted to the end and motioned for her to do exactly that. She used his lap as a pillow, stretching her legs across the seat.

"We could go back to the house. I'm sure this isn't very comf—"

"Absolutely not. It's so gorgeous here." Her hand encompassed the lake, which was dotted with paddleboarders, rental boats and numerous sailboats congregating on the west side near the dam. "I get why you loved it here so much as a kid." Lindsey peered up at him and then closed her eyes, either in an attempt to shield her from the brightness of the remaining sunlight or seeking relaxation. "I can't believe how fast we loaded that trailer this afternoon. Not that you let me do much of anything to help."

"You carried a few boxes." Some light ones.

"You're going to be annoyingly overprotective during this pregnancy, aren't you?"

"Probably," he conceded, earning a laugh from her. "Cyrus was definitely a man on a mission."

When Reed and Mom had returned to the house, Cyrus and Slade had just begun loading the trailer. Reed had jumped in, and he, Cyrus and Slade had moved the big pieces. Lindsey had come down shortly after, and she and Mom had been relegated to smaller items for obvious reasons.

"And he and Slade were out of there just as soon as the last item slid into place."

"He's good for her, I think." Reed didn't know Cyrus well yet, but he imagined he would soon, because he saw that click happening between Cyrus and his sister. The one he'd felt when he started dating Lindsey.

"I think so too. I like them together. Slade seems softer with him."

Reed liked him and Lindsey together too. He hoped this wasn't the kind of situation where there could only be one happy ending, because he wanted that for both of them.

"Are you going to tell me about your escape this morning?"

Reed ran a hand along her auburn hair. If she was going to

use him as a pillow, he was allowed to touch, right? "Sorry I deserted you to deal with The Armpit and my mom and sister."

"I understood. That was a lot to take in." Her cocoa eyes observed him. Waiting.

"I want us to try again, Linds." Reed didn't see the point in mincing words. After that conversation with his mom this morning, he'd decided that failing—for him—meant not trying.

The only question was whether Lindsey would feel the same.

If they didn't attempt to reconcile, Reed wouldn't be able to move forward. But if they tried and failed, he would know he'd given everything. And he was prepared now to shift in one direction or the other. No more hanging in the balance. Mom was right—staying in limbo wasn't helping anything.

"I get what you meant by the perfection thing now. I had grown so angry at myself over the last few months. I'd been holding myself to this unattainable standard that I'd believed the men in my family had upheld before me. But the more I strived for that, the more I failed. I didn't know my dad had fought through things and come out on the other side. I always thought he'd just been amazing from the start. So, I understand what you were trying to explain...and I promise just to be my terrible failure of a self from now on."

Lindsey released a quiet, tender laugh. "Not exactly what I meant, Straight A's."

His mouth curved to mimic hers. "Every time we tried to move forward in the last couple months, I asked you for assurance, for an unbreakable promise." For more perfection—or at least what he'd perceived that to be. "I wanted you to be determined to fight for us and certain of our success. Because reconciling without both of us being firmly committed and confident was terrifying to me. But now... I just want you to give us a chance." Lindsey's hand sought his, and she entwined their fingers as Reed forged on. "I've always loved you, Linds. I just did a horrible job of showing it."

"I've never doubted your love for me." Her hand snaked behind his neck, her fingertips creating a comforting pressure against his hair. "I was the one wallowing in my abandonment issues instead of reaching out for help. I'm probably going to have days where I try to push you away again. But I'm also going to do everything I can to learn how not to do that."

"That's good enough for me." He kissed the inside of her wrist that was resting against his cheek, as a promise, a pledge.

"Are you sure? I know you, Reed. I don't think—"

"I am. It will be." He would make it true.

"Then, it's enough for me too." She grew teary. "Reed, I'm really, *really* sorry for everything I put us through, including the debt."

It was the first time she'd apologized for the credit card without broadcasting anger at him. Maybe the first time she'd meant it.

"I'm sorry for what we put each other through. No more blame on one of us, okay?"

She gave a small laugh that ended in a pained exhale. "I'll do my best with that."

She was right. They would both have follow-up things to work through. They'd done a number on their marriage. It would take time to unravel it all. But as long as Reed knew there was a chance, he wasn't planning to give up.

Maybe he'd found himself in Colorado after all.

Slade had never been able to name what it was about her grandparents' home that made it feel like her safe place, her haven. The people, of course, but what else? The views, the furniture, the style, the smell?

Whatever it was, Cyrus's house-slash-cabin had it too.

This time, when it whispered to her that she should stay, Slade silently assured it she was going to do exactly that.

She and Cyrus sat on his living room floor, stacks of Gran's journals on the coffee table in front of them. As they'd packed the trailer this afternoon and Slade had set aside things in the garage for her move to Dillon—news which her mom and brother had not only taken in stride but been supportive about—she'd realized that she hadn't wanted to leave the journals there during the house showings.

It wasn't like anyone would snoop, but the details of Gran's days felt intimate and priceless, and so she'd asked Cyrus if she could store them in the shed on his property. He'd agreed quickly, as easily as if she'd asked to borrow a dime.

"I don't want to put you out," Slade had said. "Are you sure?"

"Of course I'm sure. If there's something I can do for you, then I'm going to do it. Don't you know how this works? Haven't you ever had someone be Team Slade?"

In a romantic relationship, apparently not.

Her eyes had betrayed her by filling, and his had crinkled with tenderness. "Lovetta Slade Henderson." He'd framed her cheeks with those slightly rough palms that upped her attraction to him because of the hard work they represented, and then he'd kissed her somehow softly and firmly at the same time. As if to say, *I'm here. I'm not going anywhere.* "This is how relationships work. Get used to it."

Slade would have to adjust her expectations, because he was right—she was as new to this as she was to getting vegetables into her system daily.

She'd confiscated a stack of empty plastic totes from the house purge that would protect the notebooks from elements or animals, and now Cyrus was helping her arrange the journals by year and label the bins, because evidently, he had the same organizational skills as her mother and brother.

Weirdos.

He leaned against the chair behind him, stretching his legs out. "I think I figured out at least part of the reason that I had such an overexaggerated reaction last night to you looking into Vince."

Slade set the journal in her hand on the coffee table, giving him her full attention.

"It's my parents' anniversary tomorrow. Or what would have been their anniversary, I guess. Sometimes, even all these years later, it hits me hard. Probably because it's the only day I remember my dad being even the remotest bit irritable. It was like he only allowed himself one day a year to grieve what might have been, and that was it."

In the past, Slade might have shown sympathy but not fully understood what something like that meant to someone else because it had always been so good between her parents. But now? Her empathy had grown by leaps and bounds.

"I get that. My parents' anniversary is in August, and I'm already dreading it. I hate seeing my mom alone." And yet Slade had been so appalled by the idea of her mom being involved with Cyrus's dad that she'd denied her the chance to change that circumstance with the person who had consistently been a supportive friend to her in the past and in the present. Slade wasn't 100 percent certain that her mom would welcome a romantic relationship with Garrett, but her instincts said those odds were in the high nineties.

No matter how much Mom tried to downplay it, it was obvious she cared for Garrett…and even more obvious that he cared deeply for her.

Slade swallowed around the lump of guilt that had formed in her throat. "My parents never missed celebrating an anniversary. And now I understand why that was so important to them." On the drive over, she had filled Cyrus in on everything she'd learned. He hadn't been surprised in the least to hear how his dad had assisted her mother when she'd fled to Colorado in the wake of the affair.

Cyrus went back to work, and Slade followed suit, giving him space. She had a feeling she was going to need a lot of it in the upcoming weeks and months as she processed all she'd learned about her mom and dad.

Something about what Cyrus had said pricked at the back of Slade's mind, like a light bulb that needed a final twist to be fully engaged.

"The anniversary." Her fingers gripped the journal in her hand, the metal binding creating creases in her palm. "I only checked the year Vincent died, not the anniversary of his death."

"It's worth a try." Now that Cyrus understood Slade's curiosity regarding Vincent had nothing to do with his father, he was no longer upset.

They searched and found a handful of the years following Vincent's death, and then Cyrus let her scan them while he continued sorting.

Slade flipped to the first anniversary, her world screeching to a halt at the glaringly strange entry smack-dab in the middle of the page.

Just like those four squares on Sesame Street, one of these things just didn't belong.

Chapter Thirty-Four

Marin opened the screen door for Garrett, and a cool rush of evening air entered with him. "Fair warning—I have no idea what she found." Ever since Slade had called, speaking in rambling run-ons and demanding everyone gather at the house so she could reveal something she'd uncovered about Vince, Marin had been trying to get her to spill.

But Slade refused to share information until everyone involved was together, so that they could all make a joint decision.

Marin didn't understand, but then, that wasn't new territory for the two of them.

Garrett leaned close, eyes sparking with mirth, volume low. "At least you're not worried it's going to implicate me this time."

Marin's skin ignited at his murmur, almost as if his lips had whispered across her neck instead of his breath.

Good thing she planned to drive back to Arizona on Sunday after dropping the kids at the airport on Saturday and then returning to load her car with keepsakes. Marin wasn't sure she could resist the draw of Garrett without the reminder of *why* she was resisting him being present with her in Colorado.

"Touché."

Garrett made a handwriting motion, as if he were noting the word she'd used for his Marin dictionary.

"Okay, we're all here!" Slade exclaimed. "Sit, sit."

Garrett and Marin sat next to each other, adjacent to Cyrus and across the table from Reed and Lindsey. Even Lovetta was present, her face expectantly filling the screen of Marin's phone, which was propped against the salt-and-pepper shakers in the middle of the table.

"All right, Love. What's this about?"

Slade paced the lane between their chairs and the back of the couch. "Cyrus and I were packing up Gran's journals to be stored at his house when I realized that I'd never checked any of the anniversary dates of Vince's passing."

"And?" Marin prompted, her pulse fluttering and sputtering with interest. Had Slade actually found something valid? Or was all this fanfare over some sparse, so-called clue?

"I opened to the first anniversary and in the middle of the page was this totally random line." She read from the journal. *Found Della-Sue standing in the street in front of our house.* Slade glanced up triumphantly. "Can you believe it?"

"Maybe she stopped by because she was mourning." Garrett's palms lifted and returned to the table. "Della-Sue and Vince dated for quite some time."

"Through high school and after," Marin added. If this was all Slade had to go on, calling a meeting definitely ranked as overkill.

"Information I had to find out from this note tucked in Gran's journal." Slade's hand skyrocketed victoriously into the air, a piece of folded lined paper in her grip. She sent an accusatory look Marin's way. "You sure never mentioned a connection between them."

"Of course not. Because I was keeping anything related to Vince under wraps. And then once you learned everything, I never thought of Della-Sue's connection to him as being pertinent."

"Apparently, it was. I found her letter to Gran on the third anniversary of his death."

"What is it?" Reed asked. "A signed confession?"

Slade's eyebrows rose in triumph. "Close." She unfolded the note and began to read.

"Dear Thelma,
Thank you for saving me, one cup of coffee and dessert at a time.
Thank you for not letting me turn myself in for Vince's death."

A wave of shock echoed around the table. Undoubtedly sensing everyone's questions and interest, Slade continued reading.

"When I followed Vince to your house that night, it was because I was angry that he was paying attention to Marin. She was married. Anyone who knew her knew she loved her husband, despite whatever had brought her back to town."

Marin teared up at the vindication in those simple words delivered as a gift all these years later. Even Della-Sue had been able to see that her heart had never wavered from her husband.

"But Vince had been enthralled with her in high school, and the moment she returned to Dillon, he became obsessed with her. I had given Vince everything—literally every part of me—and yet he was so quick to toss me aside for a prettier penny.

Marin had felt guilty that summer over Vince's infatuation with her. As if she'd done something to incur it. But the only thing she could be accused of was showing him a morsel of kindness when she'd run into him at the grocery store. Marin loathed that Vince's fixation with her had caused Della-Sue pain. As Garrett had reminded her the night she'd had dinner at his house, it was Vince who'd made that choice. But both she and Della-Sue had suffered because of it.

When I confronted him at your house and he attacked me, I was simply trying to survive his anger. And when he lunged at me and lost his footing, I thought his descent over the cliff was my fault.

That I should have saved him somehow.

When I took the risk of shining a light down there and witnessed his broken body—neck, back, everything out of order like a pile of pick-up sticks—I knew it was too late, and so I ran. I was afraid that I would be blamed.

I was afraid no one would believe me.

But you did.

Thank you for encouraging me time and time again that, despite how he'd treated me, I would have helped him had it been possible. And that if I had managed to grab hold of him, his momentum would likely have pulled me down also, and they would have found two bodies on the rocks below.

You stopped the endless cycle of guilt that I had grown so weary of living with.

I used to think it wouldn't have mattered if I'd died that night too. That no one would have even noticed I was gone.

But you changed all of that. Just one person really seeing me is enough for me.

Thank you for helping me recognize that Vince had been abusing me from the start. And for helping me to admit that my injuries had come from his hand—not a motorcycle accident as I'd made up."

"Oh wow." Lovetta sniffed through the phone. "Poor thing,

to live with something like that and never say what had really happened."

"I can't believe it was Vince who caused her injuries," Slade echoed somberly. "When I met her at The Buffalo Café, she was still telling that tale."

"Her story has been consistent all these years." Garrett's sorrow over the abuse Della-Sue had endured was obvious in the way he had to swallow twice before speaking. "And here I'd thought we'd done a good job as a town of supporting her. I can see now that we completely missed the boat."

"I don't think you did, actually." Slade leaned against the back of the couch. "The one thing I noticed at The Buffalo Café was how well-known she was. Everyone talked to her. It almost felt as if everyone was protective of her."

"And she certainly couldn't have gone around telling people that her injuries had, in fact, come from Vince and not an accident," Marin supplied. "It would have caused suspicion regarding his death to shine on her. She had to keep silent, even if Gran had helped her to admit that to herself."

"Exactly." Slade lifted the letter and read again.

"I know it was your own pain that taught you how to stand up to an abuser. I love watching you with Stu and thinking, maybe someday I'll find my second chance."

Slade paused, her vision bouncing to Marin and then Lovetta on the screen. "Did you two know Gran had been through something like that?"

Their heads shook in unison, and Marin's eyes formed a new sheen of moisture. "She always helped at the women's shelter. And at church, she would beeline for the single mom or the woman who appeared frazzled or lost. We never knew why she was so passionate about that. Just that she was."

Gran. So shocking to realize all she'd known about Della-

Sue. And that there were pieces of her own past they'd never been privy to.

"There's more." Slade resumed reading.

"Thank you for showing me how to spot the good and the bad in people. For preventing me from entering into another relationship like the one with Vince. You taught me that I'd rather be alone than abused, and it is the greatest gift that anyone has ever given me.
You've forever changed my life.

DS"

Aftershocks at all that had just been revealed rolled along Marin's spine.

"I can't believe Gran kept a secret like that for decades." Reed's tone held undertones of awe. "Do you think she told Grandad?"

Shrugs answered him. They would likely never know the answer to that unless something else popped up in one of her journals.

Lindsey's arm wrapped through Reed's, and she leaned against his shoulder. "The only certainty seems to be that your grandmother saved Della-Sue in more ways than one." Ever since Lindsey and Reed had returned from their outing, there'd been a sense of hope and peace radiating from them that had been previously missing.

It appeared they'd decided to fight for each other instead of with each other.

Marin would have supported them both, no matter what, but when they'd walked in the door holding hands after Slade had contacted them and demanded they return home for this meeting, she'd experienced a massive surge of relief. Marin had silently cheered them on for taking such a scary, brave step forward.

Even after all these years, she remembered exactly what that precipice felt like.

"When Ruthie alleged that I was here at the time of Vincent's death, I thought she was talking about you, Mom. But now I realize she was more than likely thinking that I was Della-Sue. When I met her, Della-Sue told me that she's always had a whitish streak in her hair, even at a young age. Just like this." Slade pointed to her own. "Ruthie must have seen more out the window that night than anyone realized."

"No wonder she was so upset no one listened," Marin said. Especially when she'd been so vocal at the time.

"So, what do we do now?" Slade took the open seat next to Cyrus, and his arm crested her chair, his hand resting against her neck. It had been obvious when they'd been loading the trailer this afternoon that the two of them had also figured out their issues.

And now that Marin knew Garrett hadn't been involved in Vince's death, she only felt joy over Slade being with Cyrus. It would be so wonderful not to have to be on alert regarding the past anymore.

Seeing both of her children being well loved by their significant others—and vice versa—was a gift Marin had prayed for all their lives.

Reed spoke first. "Sounds to me like Vincent sent himself over that cliff."

"I agree," Cyrus added. "I don't see a reason to bring up any of this now."

"Besides, that note isn't even signed with a full name." Reed motioned to the letter lying in front of his sister. "Just initials. We're just guessing that it's Della-Sue."

"Wait," Slade squeaked. "It's obvi—"

"And if we don't know for certain that she was on the property that night, then there's nothing to discuss with law enforcement."

"Ah." Slade cracked a smile. "Good point, brother."

"Vince caused enough harm." Garrett spoke quietly. "I say we keep this between us. If the police had wanted to investigate more, they would have done it then. It's obvious she didn't cause his death and, despite her remorse, couldn't have saved him."

Agreement and head nods came from the table unanimously.

"Sounds like it's chilly there and maybe y'all should have a fire tonight," Lovetta chimed in. "Be sure to find some kindling to get it started. Old paper should do the trick." She sang a line from Johnny Cash's "Ring of Fire."

Despite the circumstances, Marin chuckled. Only Lovetta could sing at a moment like this.

Marin agreed with the others—there was no point in disrupting Della-Sue's life over something that everyone at this table believed wasn't her fault. Vince had attacked her and lost his footing. She hadn't shoved him. He'd fallen to his own demise, just like the investigation had concluded.

Obviously, her mother had thought the same, or she wouldn't have convinced Della-Sue not to go to the police.

How wild to think that her mom had a past that Marin didn't know about. She'd never mentioned an abusive relationship, but she had taught Marin and Lovetta to be strong. She'd pointed out red flags and trained them well. No doubt she deserved the credit for Marin finding and loving two good men in her life. And it was no doubt why Lovetta was so comfortable and confident being single.

Two different paths, one phenomenal set of parents who'd guided them there.

They might be selling the house, but the gift of their family would always be with them.

A fiery ball of emotion lodged in Marin's lungs. She pushed up from her seat. "I'm going to take a minute." She forced open the cantankerous glass door and stepped onto the deck, closing it behind her.

Cool, refreshing air swept across her skin. The water below shimmered and lapped gently at the shore in the fading light. Marin braced against the deck railing and breathed deeply of a scent so uniquely Colorado Rocky Mountains that it caused a pang to resonate in her chest.

She would miss this—this house, this spot, even this town. She would miss Garrett. And she would miss her children. This period with them, though filled with turmoil at times, wasn't something she regretted.

She had about five minutes to herself before the door behind her creaked and complained about doing its job. She didn't turn when it closed or when she heard Garrett's footsteps.

"You were in that exact spot when I came by that summer. Your mom was so worried about you." His strong forearms settled against the deck railing next to her.

"I know she asked you to reach out to me." Her smile flitted to him. "Your charity case."

"Aw, Mar. We both know you were never that to me. You okay?" He motioned toward the house. "That was—"

"A lot," she filled in.

"Yep." A burst of laughter fought its way out to them. "The kids are discussing getting ice cream. Apparently Lindsey's appetite has returned with a vengeance, and she has a craving."

A pang of desire sliced through Marin like a freshly sharpened knife. She could picture a future with the people inside the house and the one next to her outside the house. Add in Byron and his wife. Add in future grandkids.

The longing almost caused her knees to buckle.

"Your daughter just pulled me aside and apologized to me." "For what?"

"For accidentally digging into me…and for keeping us apart. She said she didn't want to be the reason you were alone."

Her jaw slowly unhinged. "Wow."

"She also mentioned something about always wanting to be

a hippie, and that us being together while our children are also together would definitely qualify all of us as that. Or something along those lines."

That sounded exactly like Slade. Marin laughed, incredulous, shocked.

"So, what now?" Garrett asked, and then he waited.

Waited as if he'd been practicing for decades.

Suddenly, Marin was a toddler with a limited vocabulary. She tried to form words, but they fled her brain.

What would Ralph think about her loving her high school sweetheart? Marin's allegiance to her husband had never wavered while they were married. Even when Garrett was a friend to her that summer, she'd always wanted to reconcile with Ralph. Would never have ended up in the predicament she'd been in if not for his choices… But then, he'd known that.

He'd apologized for being the domino that started their downfall more times than Marin could count.

"So?" Apparently Garrett's patience had a limit.

Marin's mouth sprouted a curve at that. "So?"

"Are you playing hard to get, Marin Slade Henderson?"

She laughed. "I don't know how to play anything."

"I say we spend summers in Colorado and winters in Arizona."

Her eardrums whooshed like she was running a load of laundry in them. "This morning when Reed and I were discussing how scary it can be to love someone, I realized that I was doing that with you. I didn't want to torment Slade by being in a relationship with you, but it was also—"

"A way to protect yourself."

"Yes. How did you know?"

"You've had a lot of grief to bear these last few years. It only makes sense to form a barrier around the part of you that's had to carry that pain."

Marin blinked at the instantly forming moisture. "And you gave me the space to figure it out…"

"Because you needed it. And Slade did too."

"So, this weekend wasn't going to be goodbye?"

"Not for me. Not if you were willing to let me wait the two of you out."

Tears slipped and slid down her cheeks.

"I'm okay if you need time," he continued. "Just tell me you'll think about it."

"No."

The skin around his eyes tightened with questions. "I was teasing about the logistics."

"The logistics sound perfect to me. But I don't need time to think about it. And I don't need any convincing. It seems you have undeniably found your way into my heart over these last few weeks, yet again. It just took me a minute to admit it."

"Undeniably, huh?" Amusement creased his features, and he cradled her face, his thumbs sweeping away the remnants of her tears. "I'm thinking I should wait to kiss you until our kids aren't a few feet away behind a glass door. You have an opinion on that?"

She laughed. "We could close the drapes." Something about Garrett brought out the besotted teenager in her who her kids would be surprised even existed.

His hooded look sent anticipation skipping along her skin. "I'm sure they wouldn't notice that at all." And yet his grin held hints of temptation.

"Garrett…what if this turns out to be complicated?" Even with Slade's concession, it would still be hard for her children to see her with someone besides their father.

"Whatever it turns out to be…" His arm pressed comfortingly against hers as they both faced the water, the now-charcoal night creating a cocoon around them, giving the illusion of privacy even though snippets of conversation and laughter could be heard through the faulty glass door. "We'll figure it out."

And suddenly, Marin was as confident of that as she'd been

of Ralph when she'd first met him…and when she'd taken him back.

Just like she was confident that, despite all that her children had learned and would have to process over the next weeks, months, years, they would be okay.

Maybe even better than okay.

They would likely continue to experience bouts of upset with her regarding what she and Ralph had kept from them, and she would continue to apologize for that. But they would wade through those dark moments together. Just like together, they would all pretend Della-Sue's letter didn't exist. Much like that summer Marin had tried to forget.

But at least this time, everyone agreed that forgetting was the right thing to do.

★ ★ ★ ★ ★

Acknowledgments

This book would not exist without so many people. When I told my husband I wanted to try writing something different from what I'd done before, he immediately replied, "do it!" I'm so grateful to him for always seeing the best in my work and encouraging me to take risks. Thank you for celebrating each milestone like it's the greatest of victories and for listening to my many plot ideas. And thank you to my children for putting up with my writer's brain. My son claims I have a lag time in responding to things he says, and I blame the book ideas filling my head. Thank you to my daughter for being the first reader of this story and giving it your stamp of approval. I love our family. You all are my greatest joy.

I cannot imagine navigating bringing a book into the world without dear author friends. Jessica Patch saved me from making *so* many mistakes as I navigated adding a mystery element to my writing for the first time. Any errors are all mine. And Jill Kemerer is the queen of encouragement. My fellow Love

Inspired authors are the best cheerleaders for each other, and I'm honored to be part of such a fantastic group.

Thank you to my agent, Rachelle Gardner, for accompanying me on the long journey to make this particular book happen, for reminding me it *would* happen, and for encouraging me to keep going. And to the women who walk through life with me, who keep me grounded, who pray for my children, who listen to my writing ramblings and rejoice over book news as if it's your own, you are gifts to my soul. I love you, dear friends.

The crew at Harlequin Love Inspired Trade is phenomenal, from the editors to the cover designers and everything in between. Thank you for taking a chance on this book. Shana Asaro, my editor, thank you for being a champion of my work and for guiding it and me to this place. You have the gift of encouragement and somehow always know just what to do to make a book better. I'm so grateful to work with you.

To the amazing authors who endorsed this book, thank you, thank you, thank you. I cannot express how much your words and the gift of your time mean to me.

To my mom, my biggest fan, the one who buys numerous books during release week, who sells my books to the stranger standing in the book aisle with her, my best marketer even though she's not on social media, thank you for always believing in me. And Dad, thank you for teaching us about hard work and God's grace. I am beyond grateful to have such a wise father. As with everything I write, all glory goes to God. To my aunts, cousins, family, friends and readers who have been on the lookout for my next book, thank you for giving me the time to craft this story. I am so thankful to you for reading because it means I get to keep writing. I truly would not be here without you.

When I decided to set this book in Dillon, Colorado, I knew the cliffs above Lake Dillon were the perfect setting. I took some fictional liberties with the ages, styles and locations of homes in the neighborhood. The Buffalo Café in the book is loosely based on the Mountain Lyon Cafe in Silverthorne. I also took fictional liberties with the library newspaper search scene, as some newspapers within that time period are available as online PDFs. Since I began writing this book, hard copies of the newspaper are no longer available at the library because all editions are in the process of being digitized. Thank you Summit County, Colorado, for lending me the best setting for this book. I am a fan of your water, your trails and your people.

Get 3 FREE REWARDS!

We'll send you 2 FREE Books <u>plus</u> a FREE Mystery Gift.

Essential Inspirational novels reflect traditional Christian values. Enjoy a mix of contemporary, Amish, historical, and suspenseful romantic stories.

FREE
Value Over
$40

YES! Please send me 2 FREE Essential Inspirational novels and my FREE mystery gift (gift is worth about $10 retail). After receiving them, if I don't wish to receive any more books, I can return the shipping statement marked "cancel." If I don't cancel, I will receive 2 brand-new novels every month and be billed just $24.98 in the U.S., or $30.48 each in Canada. That's a savings of at least 26% off the cover price. It's quite a bargain! Shipping and handling is just $1.00 per book in the U.S. and $1.50 per book in Canada.* I understand that accepting the 2 free books and gift places me under no obligation to buy anything. I can always return a shipment and cancel at any time. The free books and gift are mine to keep no matter what I decide.

Essential Inspirational (157/357 BPA G2DG)

Name (please print)

Address   Apt. #

City   State/Province   Zip/Postal Code

Email: Please check this box ☐ if you would like to receive newsletters and promotional emails from Harlequin Enterprises ULC and its affiliates. You can unsubscribe anytime.

Mail to the **Harlequin Reader Service:**
IN U.S.A.: P.O. Box 1341, Buffalo, NY 14240-8531
IN CANADA: P.O. Box 603, Fort Erie, Ontario L2A 5X3

Want to try 2 free books from another series? Call 1-800-873-8635 or visit www.ReaderService.com.
